Circling Byzantium

By the same author:

Count a Lonely Cadence
The Entombed Man of Thule
Such Waltzing Was Not Easy
Give Him a Stone
Getting Serious

Circling Byzantium

Gordon Weaver

Louisiana State University Press Baton Rouge and London 1980

Design: Patricia Douglas Crowder
Typeface: VIP Bembo
Composition: G&S Typesetters, Inc.
Printing: Thomson Shore, Inc.
Binding: John Dekker & Sons, Inc.

LIBRARY OF CONGRESS CATALOGING IN PUBLICATION DATA

Weaver, Gordon.
  Circling Byzantium.

  I. Title.
PZ4.W3628Ci [PS3573.E17] 813'.54 80-13628
ISBN 0-8071-0694-1

Always,
  for Judy, Kristina, Anna, and Jessica
  and for Walter Everett, Jesse McCartney, and Gary Stringer

O chestnut tree, great rooted blossomer,
Are you the leaf, the blossom or the bole?
O body swayed to music, O brightening glance,
How can we know the dancer from the dance?

Yeats, "Among School Children"

World Full of Yahoos

I am distressed for thee, my brother Jonathan: very pleasant hast thou been unto me: thy love to me was wonderful, passing the love of women.

II Samuel 1:26

THE sun gets so hot in the late afternoons, even as early as May. Something happens to my eyes. My mind seems to skip away from what I'm at, where I am, taking my daily around the lake. It's the heat, the sun coming right through the sorry excuse for a hat I wear for walking, my age (sixty-three, if it's anyone's business but my own). One minute I'm walking as fine as you please. Then it hits me. And then I might as well be in another world.

I might have guessed, I said to him. *Would you mind telling me what's this hoo-ha about a quarter to dock my boat?*

Not then, taking my daily around the lake, but later, I fear it must mean my death. Strokes. A series of small strokes, such as took my mother, like the bites of a drowsy mouse nibbling my grey matter whenever it wakes enough to feel hungry. A series of set-ups for a massive sledgehammer of a stroke to leave me stiff as a vegetable in a hospital ward God-knows-where.

I think about this, lying awake in bed with the porch shutters up to hear the night wind in the pine-tops, and I shake under the quilt like a man freezing to death, the mildest of May nights.

"To hell with it!" I cry out. "Go ahead, do it. Go ahead!" And it works well enough to allow me to sleep, even though I haven't the foggiest who or what I'm shouting out to.

It's the sun. I refuse to wear dark glasses, and once I'm out of the tunnels of deep shade on the old lake road, out on the county road's blistering pavement past Ward Booth's, I have to squint to see my way clear of taking a header into the drainage ditch beside the road. I need a pair of dark glasses. Maybe I just plain need glasses. Squinting into the light gives me a pulse I can feel behind my eyes.

It grows until it pinches like a loaf of yeast bread inside the pan of my skull, looking for room to set, and it's all I'm worth to keep from giving in and cutting through the resort road at Prader's pavilion.

I might have guessed. Would you mind telling me.

I'm on the last lap, the home stretch, past Prader's pavilion, around the bend in the state highway (the old high road to Oshkosh), and I couldn't even see the ice house if I dared stop to turn around and look for it, out of sight now. What keeps me going, laying one foot down in front of the other on the dry sand shoulder of the highway, is faith in the clumps of oaks that overlay the road with a sweep of shade dark and deep as a tank of cool water, just in front of the Silvercryst property. I mark that shade, stake it out in my mind, try to feel an easing of the sizzling going on behind my eyes.

My face is screwed up against the sun like a prune left out-doors to rot and my eyes burn with perspiration rolling down from my hatband, crawling into the corners of my eyes. I can feel what rags of hair I have left plastered to my scalp under the sorry hat, my shirt stuck to my back, a sweat and heat rising in my crotch like I'm straddling a bonfire. My toes and the soles of my feet smoulder inside my shoes.

I begin to wonder, sometimes, if I'm mad instead of the last sane and sober person in this world.

My eyes. If I try, squeeze my eyes together even tighter, lift my head up, the full weight of the sun on the back of my neck like a hot iron bar, all I get are the heat waves dancing on the concrete slabs of state highway stretching out ahead of me, promising that dark tank of shade if I can last to the Silvercryst property around the next bend. That, and maybe tips of pine boughs somewhere up at the outer reaches of my vision, like black, skeletal fingers paling at the edges of the white, blinding light of the sun.

Now I'm blind. It's only uncertain, scratchy footing I find in the sand and gravel shoulder of the road that keeps me from blacking out on the road to be killed like a mosquito, smashed flat, squashed by some Yahoo vacationer. Or his Yahoo kids, out trying to set speed records and/or kill themselves and anyone else in the bargain stupid enough to go anywhere on foot in a three-county region.

Taking my daily, I always managed to make the shade at Silvercryst. God looks out for fools and children. It was like being doused with a bucket of ice-cold water, taking my breath away. I'd get myself over against the trunk of an oak or an elm, heaving and blowing like a beached walrus. When I settled down I had vantage to watch the cars full of Yahoos and summer-long people, and behind me, the cars running in and out of the Silvercryst parking lot. Even with that snot Wilson kid keeping his doors and windows sealed off with weather-stripping to cut his utility bill for the air conditioning, I could hear the damned jukebox, and once in a great while the piano playing. Some Yahoo's wife with no doubt a half-dozen lessons under her belt, and all of them three-quarters inebriated, unable to wait for the limp-wrist piano-bar entertainer Wilson brings in every night from Oshkosh to play while his customers drink themselves into a stupor and what-they-surely-call-sing-along to the words flashed on a screen with a slide projector.

I would sooner suffer cardiac arrest as have gone inside to rest up before heading on for my place. Besides which, a daily is no daily unless you work at it, which is no doubt an idea contrary to the current logic of anyone I've met in the past two decades.

Sometimes, leaning against the tree, the roughness against my back was all that kept me awake. I could have dozed like a baby there, and maybe that's what helped cause the lapses, the breaks. When I seemed, for all the world, to lose my hold on when and where I was. That, and plunging back out into the heat of the day again, like stepping into a boiler room.

What I had to put up with in the way of sights was no help either. I'm the kind of a man can give himself a migraine just thinking an unpleasant thought. Back out in the sun again, and it's easier to see for a while at least. If there were anything to see, that is.

One rental cottage after another on the lake side. Try to get a glimpse of the water, sparkling like diamond chips, dotted with fishermen, cut across with waterskiers, and the Yahoos are there, cheek by jowl, to hit you in the eye.

I said to him: *I might have guessed. I might have guessed. Would you mind telling me.*

Some Yahoo sprawled in a canvas chair about to give up in the seams under his backside, a head like a rosy cabbage, wearing opaque sunglasses under what the five-and-dimes are selling for trout-fishing hats this year, dry flies stuck in the brim, an aloha shirt gaudy enough to blanch anyone short of the Jew-bohunk at Prader's pavilion (*I said to him*), draped over a gorilla's stomach convenient for setting down the beer can peeping out of a red pig's trotter of a fist, dangling a pair of pipe-cleaner legs that would make even mine look good. Feet like shoeboxes shod in crepe soles guaranteed not to slip on the deck of a yacht. A tool-drawer of a mouth jars open, belches like as not, speaking the Yahoo-language at the apparition I must look, passing before his glazed marble eyes behind those reflecting sunglasses.

"What say there! Hot for walking, I'd say!" And maybe, if this is one with super-super-Yahoo animation, the pig-foot of a fist releases the beer can to sit on the gorilla gut under the tarpaulin aloha shirt, and pink fingers open like a fat tropical spider to stir the gnats that just naturally gather about something like that.

What I'd like to say in return goes inward to provoke the hornet's buzz behind my pinched eyes, and I keep focus on the edge of the road, one foot in front of the other, knowing there's escape coming up in the next lot line. Forty feet of lake frontage: dimensions of the Yahoo's idea of two weeks in paradise. Except there's sure as God made little green apples another one waiting for me at the next cottage.

Ah! Here's one with what passes for imagination in this

6

world. No more, doubtless, than the twinge of his in-born initiative toward more for less! Rent a salt-box of a cinder-block and beaver-board cabin that leaks in the rain, swelters in the sun, sucks up every low-lying draft of cold air the lake gives off; pack it full to the gills with women who know no better than to parade in broad daylight with a head full of steel or plastic curlers, behinds the size of medicine balls straining their short-shorts, jerseys striped like a chain-gang convict's, skin the hue of a three-day-dead perch's belly; set this wonder of the times we live in off with nails, finger and toe, daubed with goo the color of animal blood; add offspring too many and obnoxious to count, whose chief delights seem to be screaming, crying, and thrashing the sawgrass and cattails for frogs to kill, or maybe breaking the back of a garter snake, if they chance on one, before dragging it over a red ant hill; then call as many people as name's you know in your neighboring Chicago or Milwaukee tenement to invite them to divide the cost of all this chaos with you.

Surprising what a forty-by-one-hundred-foot lake lot can hold. Sometimes war-surplus tents, flaps thrown back to air out the night stink and let in the mosquitoes. A camper or two, true modern wonder, sheet steel and aluminum cells bolted to the back of overpowered pickup trucks, enabling your Yahoo to carry his Chicago or Milwaukee tenement life with him all the way to the shores of Silver Lake, Wisconsin. And the truly dexterous: air mattresses and horse blankets in the back of a station wagon with its tailgate down. It's like passing the main cage at the monkeyhouse, except apes are generally endowed with the curiosity to look up from picking lice from one another.

Is it any wonder I sometimes suspect I'm mad, or have been transported by someone mad to the center of a madhouse that is the wonder of all this world, complete with trees and sand, for the inmates to root in? And a lake besides to catch their spills?

It begins with the perfectly sensible resolve to take a daily constitutional for my health, and ends a mess of automobiles

7

whipping past my ears, blowing horns at me as if I've no right to walk the shoulder of the high road to Oshkosh, the sand shifting under my shoes, threatening to toss me head-first into the drainage ditch for a spectacle at the feet of hordes of Yahoos crammed into forty-foot-wide lots on the lip of Silver Lake. Like some quick-spreading fungus borne north on the air from the cities. The sun like God's curse on me for not crawling deep inside my own place and closing the hole after me.

I might well have gone mad, any number of times this past year. But everything, even in this world, comes to an end. Pfaff's Moose Inn always broke through the glare and the shimmering heat waves over the high road, and I always turned in there, short of my place just off the highway on the lake road. I think it saved me.

Not that anything but fear for my own sanity or health could force me to face what I knew I'd find there. You have to be cracked to go against this world from one minute to the next. But what else was I to do, I ask?

It's worth a man's life to cross Highway 21 to the Moose Inn. When it was the high road to Oshkosh, unpaved, you could hear a wagon or a rare truck or Ford flivver coming from over a mile away in either direction. When the Moose Inn was Pfaff's, before. I stop dead in my tracks to get my wind, wipe the sweat out of my eyes with a handkerchief already a soggy ball from riding on my hip. Gather my wits.

One last terrible clearing of open sun and heat, the concrete giving off waves of heat like a dry pancake griddle over a coal fire. It nearly takes my breath away, and I can feel the heat of the cement through the rubber soles of my sneakers. The seam of tar, boiled soft by the sun, glistening in my eyesight like an obsidian snake, catches at my heel, near trips me up flat on my stomach. A man could lie there in the middle of the road to be squashed like a June bug or cooked to a turn by the sun, whichever came first. And I come close to falling again when I hit the sandy smear that does for a parking space—or would, if Walter Weller had any trade to speak of. It's like stepping off into a bog.

I must make a fine picture for any passing Yahoo to see: Leland Spaulding, Jr., cutting a caper somewhere between a dipsomaniac staggering in for his first of the day, and maybe the village idiot stricken with St. Vitus dance, out without his keeper in the late afternoon. All the while flapping my arms like a plucked bird attempting a takeoff from a short run.

Now wouldn't that be a moment for a man to meet his death? Come to your end out in public in this day and age, like as not I'd get carted off to the Waushara County dump in lieu of burial. Knock on wood.

A thin lip of shade under the eaves of the Moose Inn. But no relief. I huff and choke like a strangling cat before I get around to clearing my eyes again. Stand a minute to put together the will to go inside. The streak of parking area, the highway like a white-hot glowing bed of coals just waiting for a fakir, the ragged tops of pines, a smudge of green broken with white cubes of cottages built to separate a Yahoo from his money during his annual two weeks free of the chains they use to keep them at their machines in Chicago and Milwaukee factories. And in my ears, either the sputtering of my own overheated blood, or else it's the cicadas setting up in the sawgrass in the drainage ditches. And now and again the hysterics of Yahoo children discovering how to do the cannonball off the end of a pier into four feet of lake water.

When my pulse approaches what can pass for normal, and I've about decided I can bear all this for another day in the hope I'll wake tomorrow morning to find a miracle (the whole shooting match swept away by the hand of a merciful God), Walter Weller's window air conditioner bangs on just around the corner of the building. Like the belch of a mechanical monster. If I cock an ear, I can hear the regular drip of condensation falling into a puddle—this beneath the shudder of the machine in the window and the hoarse whisper of the fan.

There wouldn't be much point in not going in now.

The screened-in porch used to be there for a purpose. Walter Weller uses it as an airy catch-all for tables too scuffed up and cigarette burned to pass muster even under his poor light-

9

ing, for the rusted chrome-plate and ripped vinyl chairs spilling the guts of stuffing. Old bar stools he's not shrewd enough to sell to some other failing barkeep, nor energetic enough to cart off to the county dump. No doubt it's fine for spiders. The screen door crashes shut behind me, which I'd object to if I thought it could be heard inside. The element of surprise is about all I have left.

The door giving away to the bar would be a challenge for a man both younger and heavier than I. Complicated by a knob that turns and catches correctly maybe one in four or five times. I have to lean into it like a sailor walking upwind on deck during a high sea. When I care enough to make the special effort, I can force my way into the bar without grunting like a warthog.

"Ho! Thereheisthereheisthereheis! Old Man Mose! The Old Man of the Hills! The Marathoner! Ghost Who Walks! Hello, hello! Greetings and salutations, condolences and felicitations! Look what the cat dragged in out of a hot day!"

Walter Weller: it's what passes for friendly banter somewhere in the gin-muddled interior of the alcohol-sponge he uses for a brain.

"Front and center! You're late and you're out of shape! You missed piss call, and the chow line's closed! Don't fight the problem, and don't harass the troops! Your ass is grass, and I am a lawnmower!" The Alleged Major. I vow again to write a discreet letter to the adjutant general at the Pentagon, settle his blow-hard hash once and for all. My guess would be they drummed him out for chronic dipsomania, with perhaps a partial disability pension (out of sheer mercy) for moral stupidity.

"Christ sake," said Walter Weller, "you look half-dead. Sit down before you keel over, old-timer!"

"His trouble is he's out of shape," says the Alleged Major. "Fall out in five minutes, full field pack, weapon, steel pot. We'll march at a route step." Oh, they are a pair of rare finds to come upon!

"So what's the word from the outside world, Pops?" says

Walter Weller. He should be good for at least two or three more sallies of this quality.

"The poop from group, the thing from wing . . . " The Alleged Major can be counted on to run dry rather quickly, a function of years of alcohol blurring the synaptic lapses.

"I'll sit when I'm ready," I said. In a minute my pupils have dilated enough to begin to make out the room, the bar, the remarkable sideshow of a pair huddled up on stools directly across from me. Hunched over the bar like two slightly bloated turkey vultures. The greetings, at least, are over. They mutter into their half-empty glasses. Small favors merit appreciation in silence.

But the Moose Inn can't even boast a little quiet. The window air conditioner thrums like the first stages of an earthquake. By the time my eyes are letting in enough light to discern the strip of ribbon tied to the grate, quivering straight out into the air for all its three inches or so, the cold has got me to the bone. My shirt and slacks are glued to my skin like icepacks, my feet numb and hard in my sneakers, my molars aching, ears plugged, fingertips tingling. The noise of the machine gets inside my head, as if I throb in time with the machine, walls, floor. It imparts a metallic stink to the air in the barroom, not unlike the burning of electrical insulation.

Things start hitting me in the eye.

The bar shaped like a diseased kidney with just enough light coming through at the edges of the drawn window shades to show exactly where Walter Weller has given it a lick and a promise with a dirty cloth. Dappled here and there with rings from tumblers, an occasional scattering of cigarette ash. Colors. A clock with a red plastic face lit from behind. The advertising of Schlitz, Blatz, and Atlas Prager. The frozen-blue cast of indirect fluorescent bulbs along the joint of ceiling and wall. Something sickly orange in cellophane bags on a wire rack, rods of cordovan sausages the length and thickness of a five-cent pencil, a jar of obscenely green olives, pimento eyes (Weller has survived for years on these, I contend). The pastels of what was once (when they drew a few clothes on them) called a Petty Girl calendar, the chrome-plate register showing *No Sale*. A muddy silver of sinks and work space behind the bar, the walls something, unwashed.

Placards, unevenly sprayed gilt on dark blue, that say *Time Wounds All Heels* and *We Aim To Please: You Aim Too Please* and *We Are Neither Slow Nor Fast, We Are Half-Fast* and *What, Me Worry?* under an idiot's face, and *What Do You Mean I've Had Enough?* below the doctored photograph of some freak with messy hair and two pairs of eyes.

"I think he's turned to stone," said Walter Weller. "You look like one of those wooden cigar-store Indians, for Christ sake!"

"I saw a cigar-store Indian once. An actual one, in a museum," said the Alleged Major.

"If I sat you'd feel compelled to get up to serve me," I said. "Or have you given that up? You wouldn't have to leave your drink at all if you went self-service. Have you thought of that?" I said. More muttering in their cups. I suspect they rehearse ripostes.

"This I needed," is what Weller comes up with. But what gets Walter Weller off his stool is the Alleged Major rattling the ice in his tumbler. He lurches like Pavlov's dog at that.

"Can I prevail on you as long as you're servicing your partner?"

"Don't tell me," Walter Weller says, groping for ice in the bin. "A bottle of Atlas Prager."

"The last of the big spenders," is the Alleged Major's contribution to the glee.

"Martinis haven't yet gotten your memory," I said. Muttering.

"You're a whole barrel of yucks, you know that? Every time I feel down in the dumps I can count on you to roll through that door, and it really cheers me up, you know?"

"High point of the day," the Alleged Major tosses off over the rim of his tumbler. If Walter Weller doesn't get a fresh vodka-and-sour to him quickly he's liable to take a bite out of the glass.

"It must be the first of the month," I said, "or is it the fifteenth? I can't recall at the moment just what day it is the Veteran's Administration sends out the checks." Muttering. Walter Weller finds a bottle of Atlas Prager after knocking over maybe a half dozen others in his cooler. "Am I presuming too much if I ask for a tumbler and a napkin?"

"Your 'umble pardon your lordship," Weller said. "Seriously . . . " getting my napkin (three of them stuck together by his wet fingers), "are you sure your old man wasn't some royalty from Europe or something?"

"My father was a banker," I said, very clearly and calmly, *"and, later in life, a commissioned officer in the military service of his country! I have documents to substantiate that!"* I call across to the Alleged Major. He is too much taken with his new drink to notice or respond to innuendo.

"So you've said," said Weller, and left it at that. His cheeks full of olives, like a squirrel carrying acorns off to his tree, a martini the size of a milk-shake held like a sacramental chalice with both hands to guard against spilling, he makes his way to the stool next to his fellow dipsomaniac.

Several minutes of what would be silence without the grinding of the air conditioner, I contemplate the threads of cigarette smoke being sucked away from the tip of the Alleged Major's cigarette. It requires something less than a certified public accountant to locate the causes of Walter Weller's continued and accelerating business failure. I am hardly gregarious, but was taught by my parents that it is impolite not to speak to whoever confronts you.

"It's a very hot day."

"Now tell me some news."

"I thought you'd like to know. I can't imagine either of you having occasion to venture out of doors." The Alleged Major seems struck by something profound. Or is it, perhaps, the pinch of an ulcer, the lining of his stomach at long last protesting his diet? He removes one hand from his tumbler to dig furiously at the scalp beneath his dull brown hair, contorts his face into a network of seams, even closes the muddy eyes that I have never observed to blink.

"So how's my competition coming along?" said Walter Weller.

"What competition? You have none. To have competition one must first compete, and that is rather more than I can conceive you doing in the foreseeable future." I was quite startled by his laugh. The Alleged Major even managed something that might have been only an effort to clear his nasal passages. "I fail to see the humor—" I began.

"You old fart, get off it!" Walter Weller said. I should have left that instant, without paying for my beer. "The Polack," he said, stopping to gulp at his gin. "Don't tell me you didn't stop by the resort and give the Polack your two-bits worth, Spaulding! I know better than that."

"What's the Polack have to say for himself today?" the Alleged Major said. "He still got Batterman running like the general's dog-robber for him?"

"You don't know me at all so well as you think you do. You don't know me at all," I said. And for some reason known but to the good Lord, that seemed to catch their attention.

Walter Weller pulled his martini away from his face, set it on the bar with care, wiped his lips with both hands, forced his sodden eyes on me. The Alleged Major lifted his head up from where it drooped, chin all but on the bar, between his narrow shoulders. Oh, the two of them are quite an attraction!

"Ho ho!" said Walter Weller. "I detect a certain note of something there!"

"You don't like our friendly Polack?" was the best the Alleged Major could do.

"The two of you make me sick!" I should have left.

"What have you got against progress, Spaulding?"

"I never liked Polacks, not a one of them. But *you*! I thought sure you were the type to like our friendly Polack, Papa-san."

14

"I've yet to meet the man could define the word *progress* to my satisfaction," I said. Have you ever had a conversation with a Mongoloid idiot? Ever tried to explain something to a deaf-mute? Never argued with a badly spoiled child? It was madness to remain there with them! I wonder if I am mad, if I have always been mad, if that day was the moment I became mad.

"You don't know the half of it," Weller said. "He's got plans, that sonofabitch, believe you me, and the bastard must have the scrotum-hold on half the banks in Milwaukee the way he's pouring it on out there! That bastard's an operator, old-timer. You don't recognize a big time operator when you see one, Spaulding."

"You know what the world's greatest invention was?" said the Alleged Major. He never thought to wait for an answer. "The wheelbarrow. It taught Polacks how to walk on their hind legs!" I thought at first he was having a spasm of some sort, then saw, when he raised his face again from the bar, his lips drawn back from his long, dirty teeth, that he was laughing.

I should have gone, run out, back to my place, locked the door behind me, closed up the shutters. I must have been mad. "You're so stupid you can't see your own doom in it," I said. "Do you care if you lose your business? What chance have you got when he opens up that circus he's making of Prader's?"

"What chance have I got, period," Walter Weller said.

"Guess where a Polack hides his money," the Alleged Major was saying to no one at all.

"You won't recognize it when he gets done, I promise you," I said. "Yet here you sit, all of you, you, that snot Wilson at Silvercryst, the entire township of Wautoma, you all sit and do nothing!" Walter Weller had finished his martini, sat swirling the melting ice in the tumbler, as if trying to generate the momentum to get off his stool to make himself another.

"You're a goddamn gem, Spaulding, you know that?" he said, so softly I could barely hear him, though now the air conditioner had quit, completed its cycle with a slamming noise. "Come in here like death-warmed-over, sit there like a goddamn hanging judge. You really cheer a guy up, Pops, you know that? What the hell you suggest we do, get the Silver Lake Association to hire somebody to shoot the Polack son-ofabitch? Get off my back, Spaulding, okay?"

"You persist in being stupid," I said.

"Lawrence of Poland!" the Alleged Major was saying, "Lawrence of Poland, see!" collapsing into this laughter again.

"In my father's day, for one—" I said.

"For Christ sake, let's not get into that! You mind? I really don't give a crap about how everybody drove horses and all, okay? Like there were only five cottages or what-all on the whole damn lake, but who gives a damn, okay?" I thought he was falling off his stool, but he recovered, tumbler in hand, shuffled to the gin and ice behind the bar.

"What do Mr. and Mrs. Flamingo have on their front lawn?" said the Alleged Major.

"In my father's day," I said loudly, "it was only necessary to say a discreet word to persons in authority. A discreet word to the proper persons, at the right time. Things were not permitted to advance to a state, you ignoramus!" I shouted. Walter Weller stopped what he was doing, gin bottle poised over the tumbler, other hand delving among the olives. The Alleged Major was lost somewhere in the middle of excruciating laughter and coughing to death on cigarette smoke.

"Watch out you don't give yourself a heart attack, old man," Walter Weller said.

"It's your fault!" I said. "You, Wilson, Batterman. You could have gone together, talked to people in Wautoma. Don't you pay taxes, or is business so bad you can't even claim that distinction any longer? A discreet word! You could have prevented Batterman selling!" They were both laughing.

They were laughing at me.

The Major-Who-Was-No-Major was not laughing at his own asinine jokes, he was leaning forward, belly across the bar, holding his forehead with one hand, pointing one dirty finger of the other at me, a laugh like an asthmatic hyena would have. Walter Weller had to steady himself against the end of the bar, the gin in the bottle he held jiggling as he shook with laughter, laughing at me. His eyes filmed with tears of exertion.

My face flamed, and I gripped the edge of the bar with both hands to keep from quivering, my mouth dry, throat hot with anger, no words coming to me to strike them with. *Would you mind telling me what's this hoo-ha about a quarter to dock my boat on the beach? I might have guessed. I might have guessed, I said.*

"You're insane," I said when they had run down to hiccoughing and gargling their tongues. "You're both insane, and you don't know it, and there isn't the glimmer of a hope for any of you left in the world," I said. This set the Alleged Major off laughing again.

"You silly old fart!" Weller said. "Where the hell have you been keeping yourself? You dumb fart! Wise up to the world, will you? Batterman's on his knees with thanks every night for getting out from under that white elephant, you old jerk! Wilson figures to ride it out, and there wouldn't a miracle save me now or a year ago. You silly old cock!"

"You're insane, you must be insane," I kept saying, but I doubt they heard me. The Alleged Major was trying to smother his laughing, both hands over his mouth.

"The Wautoma Township Council figures the Polack is the greatest thing since sliced bread, you old ninny! Where the hell have you been keeping yourself, for Christ sake!"

I don't remember what else they said to me. I don't remember if I finished my bottle of Atlas Prager or not. I must have paid, taken a soggy dollar from my wallet, laid it on the bar or handed it to Walter Weller. They kept laughing, saying things, insulting me. I must have gotten off my stool, walked to the door, fooled with the broken knob mechanism until it caught, pushed out onto the porch, through the flapping screen door. I must have done all this without knowing where I was.

I was outside, standing under the dilapidated stuffed moose's head that was once Otto Pfaff's pride, and it was dusk. I could not have been inside with those two that long, so I must have been standing under the stuffed moose's head for a

17

long time, a spectacle for Yahoos passing on the Oshkosh high road. I don't know how long I stood there. And I don't care to know.

I don't remember if the light above the moose's head was on yet, don't recall if there was sufficient light to look up and see the cracked putty stuffed in the large, round nostrils, rapidly being washed away by winters and springs, the black empty eye socket that at dusk makes it seem the moose head winks obscenely, the rack of antlers, white as bleached bones when seen in the moonlight before Walter Weller remembers to flip the switch that turns on the light above the mounted head, drawing the gnats and mosquitoes that feed the spiders web-bing the shallow dishes of the rack of antlers, like metallic lace in the electric light. The hair is weathering off the neck of Otto Pfaff's once-fine specimen, the exposed hide (is it hide or fab-ric?) like canvas. When Walter Weller remembers to flip the switch that lights the stuffed moose's head and his forever-empty parking lot, everyone sees (I see!) the trophy head is battered, useless, an eyesore, a thing to laugh at, fugitive from every cartoon of follies stored in attics and basements and deep closets. It is a thing to rip down, cart off to a public dump, burn or bury. Otto Pfaff's prize, the last moose bagged in the state of Wisconsin (south of a line running below Rhinelander, below Eau Claire, running just above the northern border of Door County, where all the cherries grow), the most magnifi-cent trophy of all the trophies that decorate Otto Pfaff's mar-velous inn on the high road to Oshkosh. Once before.

It is late, night, dusk-becoming-dark.

In the falling dusk, the time when there is neither day nor night, I sense the moment so fleetingly that it is gone before I can look again to see it as I sense it, the quick blending of day into night. The moose head, Otto Pfaff's trophy, last moose taken by a hunter in the state of Wisconsin south of a line running . . . . The moose head seems to be alive. I think the stuffed head is still alive, and often dream of it, fall asleep

18

thrilled that I will dream of it, *know* I will dream the living moose head staring out at me with glass ball eyes from the wall of Otto Pfaff's inn, just above the porch door, where it looks out at the high road to Oshkosh.

I know that in a moment I will sleep, and I will dream Otto Pfaff's moose is alive, looking at me, I sense all this, listening to my mother and father, still talking softly in the cottage parlor.

First, sunset.

Sunset: we have our supper on the cottage porch, overlooking the lake, in order not to miss the sunset. Sweet corn and tomatoes from our own vegetable garden, the bread father will drive three miles in the trap to buy from the farmer's wife, Mrs. Schleuter, whose bachelor son raises melons to sell in Milwaukee. Tea. The tea steeps under a cozy that was Mother's mother's in Ireland.

"Will you pour or will I?" Mother says.

"Ah," says Father, "the Irish will have their cup of *tay*, now won't they!" He pours tea for us all, then takes the leather case from his pocket, removes a cigar, cuts, pierces the end, sends me to the kitchen for what old Mr. Heddermann-the-ice-man calls a Lofoco match.

Father sucks the flame into the end of the black cigar, Mother holds her saucer in the palm of her hand. The tomato plate glistens, slicked with pinkish water in the wavering light of the table candles, the ragged cobs of corn heaped like peeled logs, yellow-white in the light of sunset and candles. I do not stir the milk and sugar into my English tea for fear of losing the sucking sound of Father's black cigar if I hit the cup with my spoon.

"There's a picture for you," Father says.

"I should say," Mother says, and, "Red sky at night, sailor's delight."

"Look at the lake," I say, and know they are looking at me even if they do not speak.

At sunset, the sky over the lake streams color, streaking the long, thin clouds in washes of orange, rose, red, outlined in darker blue shadows against the paler blue of just-darkening sky. The tints on the thick pines crowding up against the strip of sandy beach across the lake, visible only in spots through our own pine trees hovering outside the cottage, are only there as long as the silence lasts between us, while no one speaks, and Mother does not drink her tea, Father does not smoke the black cigar smouldering between two fingers, scenting the air on the porch. And I do not touch my spoon to stir. I make the silence last while the tints go to black on the horizon across Silver Lake.

It does not last. It does not last more than a minute, perhaps two, but seems, while it lasts, that it will never, never end. I am so happy in this, sitting on the cottage porch with Father and Mother, watching the warm orange ball of the setting sun merge with the almost-black horizon of pine trees across the lake, turning the underside of the few rags of clouds in the sky through the spectrum of color, conscious of Mother, her tea-cup held above the saucer on her palm, as if it floated, sus-pended in the darkening air of the porch, the sense of my father's bulk, his shape in the fanbacked wicker chair dominat-ing the supper table, Mother, myself, the porch, the lake, the setting sun across the water, the scent of his cigar wrapping us, it, all together, away from everything, *with* everything!

How could I believe, even hope it might last?

The breeze. The wind came up, fresh, with the setting of the sun. I feel it, suddenly, against my cheek, along my bare arm. There is barely perceptible movement among the long, heavy boughs of the white, Norway, and jack pines that throng our property, stand like pickets around the cottage and the horse barn out at the entrance to the lake road. Then they are heaving, the straight trunks waving near the tops of the trees, and the wind soughs among the pines, ruffles the white napkins on the table—everything, everyone, is moving now.

"My stars, the tea will be stone cold!" Mother says, putting down her cup to settle the knitted cozy all the way over the teapot. Father holds his cigar in his teeth, grimacing against the smoke rising in his nose and eyes. He stands (the wicker chair

20

creaks loudly), removes it, coughs, clears his throat, puts the cigar back in his mouth while he buttons his vest, reaches for his coat, puts it on, removes his watch from its slit pocket in his vest, opens it, removing the glowing cigar from his mouth to cough again as he squints to read the time. Mother finishes her tea. "A cup of tea is nothing if it's not absolutely piping hot!" she says. Father laughs. I want to laugh too, but am still held, for only an instant more, knowing it would not have lasted even this long if I had dared touch it.

"Now," says Father, "if I could find the right man for the responsibility, I might take my stick and invite one and all for a short stroll across the way."

"Let me clear these things," Mother is saying. Father buttons his collar, his coat, and I am already leaving the porch.

"I'll get! I'll get it!" I cry; they laugh. Into the darker parlor, to the umbrella stand, where my hands find the smooth, glossy knob of my father's walking stick.

"What," he would say, when I asked why he needs this to walk to Mr. Pfaff's inn, "would I do if a black bear were to cross our path?"

Mother says, "Don't say such things to him, Leland! There are no bears in these woods, and if there were any, they're as frightened of us as we would be of them." I draw it out, stretching up on tiptoes to clear its sharp, metal-sheathed tip of the edge of the umbrella stand. Like drawing a giant's sword from its scabbard.

"Come along now you two or it'll be too dark to see your hand before your face," Father says. Mother blows out the last lamp, Father closes the cottage door behind us, and we step off the concrete slab porch at the rear of the cottage, step out into the rapidly deepening dusk, step out towards the huge, looming darkness that is our horse and trap barn on the lake road, toward the rounded, hard-packed high road to Oshkosh that we will cross in the last afterlight of dusk to reach Mr. Otto Pfaff's inn, back in among a stand of tall pines, just across the high road to Oshkosh.

"The air in these pines is better than any sachet I've ever

smelled," Mother says, lifting her head to breathe deeply, trusting Father's arm to hold her if she stumbles, eyes closed to smell the air.

"I've got to get a sickle after these ferns," Father says. He cuts with his stick at the ferns growing over the edges of the path around the barn. The tip of his cigar flares in the air like a firefly as he draws on it, jumps as he takes it from his mouth. As we pass the barn I hear Phil, our trap horse, stomp, the sound muffled by the straw on the floor of his stall, hear the faint click of his halter as he pulls against the rope anchored at his manger.

"Remind me, both of you," Father says, "to grain Phil and see he's bedded down for the night when we come back." We know, Mother and I, that we will forget to remind him, but that he will never forget to do it, going out to the barn with a lantern in the total dark while I get ready for bed.

"I don't think we'll have rain tomorrow either," says Mother.

"We could use a spit of rain," Father says. We walk the short stretch of lake road, emerge from the pall of darkness cast by the pines on both sides of the narrow sandy-dirt road, stand on the open road to Oshkosh, as if listening for the sound of a truck or wagon in the distance, the last faint light of dusk still in the air.

On the other side of the high road, winking as I move my head, are the lights from the windows of Mr. Pfaff's inn, there among a very thick stand of pines. I can discern the heads of horses, ground-tethered, the outlines of traps and wagons, and hear the voices, sometimes the clear strains of Mrs. Pfaff's accordion, even singing. I must have thought aloud.

"What?" says Mother. "What did you say, Lee?"

"The moose," I said. They laugh.

"Take Papa's hand while we go across," Mother says, always, so that I will learn the habit of crossing roads and streets carefully, for living in Chicago, winters. I slip my hand into my father's and we cross the high road, enter the line of pine

22

trees. And I steel myself to look directly up into the wide-open eyes of Mr. Otto Pfaff's stuffed moose head.

Oh, this is a thing to grace this world in the very last cast of dusk-light, a thing to half-frighten, half-delight a boy, to send his imagination spinning, to make his mind's eye leap to the shape of the last great-great-grandfather of a moose lifting its magnificently antlered head from the dank pool of some remote, dark marsh, his long jaws chewing the roots of a lilly-pad to froth, its brown-rich hair sleeked with water, its bulging eyes flickering. The roar of an enormous shotgun, longer than the boy is tall, in his nostrils the faint-sharp odor of gunpowder hanging in the wet air of the marsh, the moose bellowing, pitching over on its side into the algae-covered water, sending out waves like some sinking ship, thrashing to pink suds the swamp water now mixing with its blood. Hooks and chains, a plowhorse to pull the carcass up on dry land, a sled-like stone-boat to drag it out of the green woods as night falls, bitter cold. Mr. Otto Pfaff hanging the gutted moose outside the Wautoma Post Office for all to see, a newspaper story, the head severed by a butcher, shipped by train to a Chicago taxidermist. My father releases my hand to hold open the porch door for Mother to enter ahead of us, an instant in which I look up, still as a stuffed boy, into the glass eyes of Mr. Otto Pfaff's trophy moose head.

"Lee?" says Father. "Come on, son, I'm holding the door for you."

"I'm coming, Papa." I pass under the arch of his coat sleeve, and between them, enter Mr. Otto Pfaff's inn.

Dark, the walls finished with peeled, stained and varnished pine half-logs, the caulked seams between the logs, the big knots in the logs a dark red-black, the walls glistening as if they had been sprayed with oil. The light from candles and kerosene lamps bounces, slides on the glistening walls. Pine posts dot the central room, supporting the roof. I tip back my head to look up into the darkness, shot with fits of flickering light, that recedes to the pitch darkness of the peaked roof. The poles are alive with the artistry of the Chicago taxidermist whose name I know (*know!*) I have heard, but will never remember. A grey squirrel climbs the post just to my right ("Good to see you, folks! How is the small mister—come to drink beer with Papa by Otto, huh?"), the red fox squirrel is over in the corner, as if watching, afraid, the lynx that stands on the spirit cabinet behind the bar. One paw raised in mid-step, ears forward, white cat's fangs bared, pale red tongue drawn back in a throat-deep growl, eyes dancing yellow-gold slits in the shifting light of candles and lamps ("I get the electric here sooner than you think, folks!"). And the fish, stretched out on varnished plaques, spines arched. Pike, pickerel, bass, trout from streams near Redgranite and Wild Rose that Otto will not tell even Father how to find.

"Going to stick your fist in the muskie's mouth tonight, huh, mister?" Otto says to me. I nod. He leads me to the mounted muskellunge, nearly five feet long, its mouth open in a hoop bigger than my head. Otto stands behind me, takes hold of me under the arms, lifts (the scent of schnapps, his hair pomade, a sweetness cut by alcohol!). I stroke the fish's wide flank, expecting it to be slick, cool, like the skin of the bull snake Father caught under our boathouse, held for me to touch, but it is rough, pitted, warm with the air of the inn's central room, the mid-summer evening.

"Make believe you're gonna reach right inside him and yank his insides out once," Otto Pfaff says. Mother and Father watch, smiling gently. I reach out my hand (small, white—*my hand*), fingers spread and extended, slow, steady. I touch the needle-sharp tips, row on row of teeth, all sizes, gingerly at first, then almost bold.

"Bite 'em off!" shouts Otto Pfaff in my ear, and though I knew he would, my hand leaps out of the muskellunge's yawning hoop of a mouth like a darting bird. Father and Mother laugh, Otto laughs.

I laugh, and he swings me up, over his head, upside down. The room spins, halts precariously upside down as he holds me directly overhead, his sweet-schnapps breath in my nose, my

y in shop or cottage or out in a boat, fishing on Silver Lake.
eat and drink, hoping to hear Mrs. Pfaff play her black-and-
ory accordion, sometimes even to sing, move their feet un-
r the clean tables in time to polka music.

"You see, how busy, folks!" says Otto Pfaff.

"Please, Otto," my mother says, "just for a moment. You
rely would enjoy a few minutes' rest off your feet!" Otto
aff gestures at the crowded tables where people sit, the men
ith their collars on and buttoned, women with gloves laid
atly across the corners of the tables, handbags under their
airs, hands folded in their laps except when reaching up to
ke their glasses to drink. He rolls his pale blue, only faintly
atery eyes behind the lenses that catch and hold highlights
om candles and kerosene lamps, twitches his nose (the horns
f his waxed moustache jump in concert!).

"For you, folks, okay." He brings the bottles to mix his
rink at our table, an *abergut*, brandy with just a sweetening
ollop of peppermint schnapps dropped on its shimmering sur-
ce. "So!" he says.

He lifts it as a gem cutter must lift a diamond to examine
or faults under his magnifying glass, stops just beneath his
ed, red lips. "Good times, folks," he says. Father tips his glass
Otto's direction, Mother's eyelids flutter as she sips at her tall
lass of beer as if it were hot English tea.

He winks, one split second's wickedness shared with me,
pens his red, moist lips under the iron-grey horns of his
axed moustache, then snaps his thick wrist. For an instant I
ink he has swallowed brandy, peppermint schnapps (*aber-
t!*), tumbler and all. No, suddenly the empty tumbler, as
lear and bright as if it had just come, washed clean, from the
ink, is held up in front of his eyes, held delicately in the tips of
is thumb and four fingers. He turns it, it sparkles in the light
f the candles and lamps, he examines it, as a gem cutter
ppraises a finished stone. Father takes a long, slow drink from
is glass of beer, eyes half-closed, throat moving above his
uttoned collar, Mother sips at her beer, brings her lips hesi-

26

wide, terrified-delighted eyes inches from his. Otto
blue, faintly watering barkeep's eyes behind the refl
lenses of his gold-rimmed spectacles, the spike-hor
waxed moustache all but touching, stabbing my ch
feel of his blunt fingers, like iron bolts in my ribs, f
tanned, hairy black, starched white cuffs rolled back

"Should I let him fall?" he asks my parents. The
sways, rolls as he rocks me back and forth, my brea
coming in gasps. Mother, Father, smiling upside do
room, the snarling lynx, all pitching like a ship in a
loop of the enormous fish's open mouth like a pit w
me to be thrown into the blackness of its depths.

"We'll save him, he's a keeper," says Otto Pfaff.
flop of the room, the ceiling beams replaced by the
planks of the floor, Mother, Father, Otto, lynx, mu:
all in place again, the aroma of sweet-schnapps brea
pomade and moustache wax fading in my nostrils, a
ing, my ribs aching pleasantly as I heave for breath t
with them. We are all laughing.

"Let's sit you down, folks," Otto says. He holds
for my mother, gives the rough cloth a nervous swi
edge of his hand to catch a last crumb, leaves us to re
a great foaming pitcher of beer, a metal pitcher store
in it to chill it against our coming. I plant my finger
its silver side, feel them quickly numbing.

"Join us, Otto, please," Father says.

"Oh, so busy!" Otto says, lifting an arm to swee
of crowded tables, people from Wautoma, Redgranit
koro, Mount Morris, as far away as Wild Rose. The
eat the dinners cooked on a wood stove in the steami
in the back by Mrs. Pfaff. Hocks and cabbage, *Kalbsl
schnitzel*, blood sausage and sauerkraut, brown and b
bread, *Brodkartoffeln*, and the beer delivered by train i
all the way from Chicago. They came to eat Mrs. Ot
dinners, to hear the evening breezes in the tops of the
that all but hide us from view on the high road to Os
feel the fresh lake breeze that rises with sunset after a

2

tantly to the rim of the glass, like a wary bird drinking in a puddle after a cloudburst.

Slowly, with perfect control, Mr. Otto Pfaff winks at me once again, his right eye, behind the reflecting lens of his gold-framed spectacles. His cheeks twitch, his moist lips pucker as he swishes the *abergut* in his mouth with his tongue. As his right eye closes fully, he swallows it, only the shadow of movement showing in his throat.

"Ah!" he says. *"Das ist aber gut!"* We laugh, we all laugh. And while they talk, while the people in long dresses and buttoned collars talk and drink beer, some of them still eating late dinners of hocks and cabbage or *Kalbsbraten* or *Wiener-schnitzel*, or slices of cold ham with dark bread and pickles, I sit on the hardness of the cane-bottomed chair, my feet dangling in space over the wide pine planks of the floor, my chin barely clearing the tablecloth, my own image reflected back to me in the glass mantle of the kerosene lamp in the middle of the table, my hands squeezed together in my lap. I watch, every-thing, and I listen.

"Folks, tell me," Otto says, "you think we'll have this war now?"

"I doubt it, Otto, I seriously do. We have no reason to want to go to war. Wilson himself doesn't want war, if I read him correctly," says my father. He looks across the glowing lamp at Otto as he speaks. I see his hands busy in front of his vest, clipping, piercing the end of another black cigar from Cuba.

"Let's hope we don't get into the war," Mother says.

"I for sure hope not, folks. Me, so I'm an old *Deutscher* from way back. Most of these folks are." His hand, his eyes behind the spectacles, sweeping the room full of people, talk-ing, eating, drinking. Mrs. Pfaff, three heavy mugs of beer in each hand, hurrying to a long, crowded table from the bar. "We don't want us having a war with Germany. We all got people back there, folks, so how would we all feel if we go and get ourselves in this mess they're having. I got letters, folks, the Mrs., she gets letters from her people back home. I tell you folks, it's getting terrible there, folks are starving, some of them."

"I don't honestly think we'll have ourselves a war, Otto," says Father. Cigar smoke falls out of his nostrils as he speaks, rises in the air, fades into the darkness of the beamed ceiling. "It would be bad for all concerned. Business would be hurt by a war, for instance." I do not know what wars are. I do not know what Germany is, do not know who Wilson is. I know where I am, that I watch and listen.

"I for sure hope so, folks. Hey, did you hear all this talk! Some big resort they say Prader's got in mind to build down by the Neshkoro road, where it comes out from town, folks?"

"I think that's all just talk, most of it, Otto."

"Mr. Prader from Wautoma?" Mother asks.

"Sure, Mrs.," Otto says. "I don't know. For sure he's got the money to do it, I think. I hate to see that, that could hurt my business some here, maybe, huh?"

"Oh, Otto!"

"I doubt that, Otto," my father said. "Look around you." They look at the crowded tables. I look with them. I do not know Mr. Prader from Wautoma. "There's such a thing as loyalty, still, in this world, you'll have to admit. I wouldn't worry." My father holds the cigar out at arm's length, gazes on it, pretending to watch the smoke spiral out of the ash. "I feel fairly confident that nothing like that is going to take place, whatever the current gossip may be." He gazes at the thick streams of smoke fluttering out of his cigar. Mother sips at her beer.

"I for sure hope so," Otto says. "Hey, I got to do some work or the Mrs. will hit me with the bungstarter quick!" We laugh. We ask him to have another drink with us; he promises, getting up, to ask his wife to play her accordion especially for us. We do not stay long.

It seems to last a long time. Mr. Otto Pfaff steps behind the bar, rolls his stiff-starched cuffs and sleeves back another turn, seizes one of the tall Pilsner glasses, or one of the thick glass

28

mugs, one of the personalized steins that sit on a special high shelf (decorated with pictures in bright colors, the Rhinepfalz, the vineyards along the Main River, the cellars of a monastery where monks taste their vats of beer, drinking mottoes in German that I will never learn to read), holds it beneath the tap, pulls the handle to him, cuts it off as foam oozes over, falls into the copper-lined sink below. He trims away the excess with a wooden paddle like a doctor's tongue-depressor, wipes the base of the glass or mug or stein with a cloth kept tucked in his belt. He sets it on the wooden tray, ready for Mrs. Pfaff to carry it to a table.

It seems to last a very long time. Otto Pfaff draws beer, mixes highballs in a silver shaker, pours drams of brandy and schnapps and whiskey with a chemist's precision. Mrs. Pfaff hurries among the crowded cloth-covered tables until, finally, someone calls out to ask her to give us some music before it is time to leave.

"Ah, play something, just a couple songs!" her husband shouts from the bar. "You play and I give you all a treat, I sing right along." There is applause. I clap, clap, *clap* my hands until they sting, send shocks of electric aching up my arms to my elbows. Mother must reach over to put her hand on my shoulder, insist it is enough, Mrs. Pfaff will play.

Mrs. Otto Pfaff unhooks the silver clasps that hold the accordion shut. She stands in the middle of the room, slips her arms into the straps, quick, light and exact in movement, the way my mother slips her arm into the sleeves of the coat my father holds for her. Mrs. Pfaff seems to test the instrument, produce a raucous, uncertain squeal and growl from it. Then throws back her head, smiling broadly, arching her body backward, resting the heaving instrument against the point of her hip as, suddenly, song comes from it, her fingers dancing over the keys and buttons. She plays, and sometimes, yes, Otto sings, we all sing. It seems to last a very long time.

The men sit back in their cane chairs, coats and vests unbuttoned, legs crossed, foot bobbing in space in time to the accordion music. The women turn sideways, jackets and shawls

29

wrapped around their shoulders now against the cooler air of the deepening night. Men light cigars, drops ashes on the edges of empty plates and saucers. Women absently hold their cups and glasses, move the toe of one shoe in time to the music of the accordion—it seems to last.

I begin to hear the music as something inside me. Swaying my body on the hard cane bottom of the chair, I begin to feel the music's time inside me. The room begins to pulse, as if walls and floor and dark timbered ceiling expand and recede, breathe with the time of the music. The snarling lynx, the red and grey squirrels, trout, bass, pike, the giant muskellunge on its varnished plaque on the wall, all are wrapped in the dense, rolling of music from Mrs. Pfaff's accordion. I close my eyes to make myself more perfectly of and in the music's time, but do not notice, mark in any way that I have closed my eyes. It begins to seem total, forever, myself, always there and then, in this music that has no beginning or end.

"I suspect young Master Spaulding is about ready for a night's rest," says Father.

"We really must take him home, Leland," Mother says.

The music has stopped. My eyes are open, vaguely sore with fatigue, my bottom sore from the sharp webbing of the chair seat. The guttering candles and sucking wicks of the kerosene lamps throw a harsher, broken light.

The music has stopped. I look just in time to see Mrs. Pfaff snap the clasps of her instrument to, carry it out of the room. Men grate the legs of their chairs against the wide pine planks of the floor, pulling back from the tables, standing, stomping feet to force feeling back into legs, stretching. Women stand, gather handbags, readjust shawls, button jackets, look away to stifle impolite yawns behind small, clenched fists. Father buttons his coat, reaches up to pull at his closed, abrasive collar, stubs out his half-smoked cigar on a saucer. Mother lifts me off my chair, holds me while my legs quiver, then assert a shaky balance. Otto Pfaff has left the bar, gone to the porch to say goodbye to his departing customers. He holds the porch door open for the ladies, shakes hands with the men.

30

"Goodnight, folks!" he calls out to the rattling pony traps and wagons. "Goodnight now, folks!" he shouts over the sputtering and barking of automobile engines. Lanterns are being lit, hung on wagons. Horses snort, grind their shod hooves on the gravel-spread sand, clatter onto the hard-packed dirt surface of the high road to Oshkosh. They turn toward Wautoma, toward Omro and Redgranite, a few going as far away as Berlin (the next county seat), toward Mount Morris and Waupaca, as far as Wild Rose. "Goodnight, folks, be careful, there's not all so much moon tonight, you know!" he yells through his cupped hands.

"Will you be cold now, Lee?" Mother says, nudging me gently toward the door, steering me away from collisions with chairs, tables, the peeled and varnished pine poles supporting the roof of the inn.

"I can just as easily carry him on my shoulder if we have to," Father says.

"Goodnight now! Goodnight, folks! You come again! Goodnight!"

I had thought it would not end. I never thought of beginning or end. I did not think.

"Otto, you must come across and see us one morning soon," Mother says as we reach the porch.

"Otto, I've enjoyed myself," Father says.

"Ah, you see how busy I am, I hardly have time for a little fishing all summer!" There is a moment of confusion, bumping against my parents, a glimpse of Otto holding the door open for us, his hand grasping my father's. My brain whirls with a sudden rush of things, names: Wilson, Mr. Prader, a war, Germany, letters to Mrs. Pfaff. I see the darkness out beneath the pines, a black stretch of sky dotted with silver-white pinpoints of light, a wash of pale moonlight splashing the crown of the Oshkosh high road, a welter of noise, voices, horses' shod hooves on sand, gravel, hard-packed dirt, the dark-splitting racket of Ford automobiles accelerating, the beams of headlamps cutting swaths into the woods across the high road, the faintly throbbing auras of light from lanterns hung on traps and wagons. "Someday soon, Mrs., I'll come by with the Mrs., we'll drink a coffee, huh?"

I had not thought it would end, that music and talk and all would jerk abruptly to this. "Goodnight, Otto," I hear myself say.

"Ya!" he says, and bends to look me full in the face, his rosy, moist lips back, revealing flashes of gold inlay between his large teeth, the horns of iron-grey waxed moustache, his pale blue eyes, watering faintly behind the gold-framed spectacles, lenses catching shards of white-silver fire from candles, lamps, lanterns. "You, boy, you going to come fishing with me someday soon, huh? Huh? Maybe we'll take a gun, go back in the marsh and see can we find that moose's uncle, huh? Huh?"

"I believe this boy is all but asleep on his feet," Father says.

"He's so tired, Otto. We really have stayed too late," Mother is saying.

"Okay," Otto says. "Goodnight now, folks! Goodnight. Ya, goodnight! You want to take a light?" No, the moon will light us home, the walk is so short. No, we will not take a light. We walk out to the high road, my hands held by Father and Mother, pass through the patch of moonlight, enter the mouth of pine woods on the lake road, our path, my father's stick slashing at overhanging ferns that brush my legs. He releases my hand.

We can hear the frogs in the sawgrass and cattails down at the beach, croaking (goodnight!). We can hear Phil, our trap horse, pawing at the straw in his stall as Father opens the door to our barn (*goodnight, goodnight*). We can hear cicadas in the thickly growing ferns that choke the woods (goodnight), hear the wind, dying for the night, diminishing in the tops of the pine trees, invisible now in total dark (goodbye).

"Papa?"

"Go on now, help your mother find her way. We can't have her tumbling into the cistern, can we."

"Papa?"

"What is it, Lee?" He stops fumbling with the clasp on the

32

barn door, bends down to me. It is so dark I cannot see his eyes. Phil yanks, again and again, on his halter rope, anticipating the oats.

"Who is Mr. Prader?" Father laughs. My mother laughs with him.

"Will you listen to him?" he says to Mother. "Little pitchers," he says.

"Papa, who is he? Mr. Prader from Wautoma?"

"Would you know if I told you?"

"I don't know. Who is he, Papa?"

"Another Dutchman like Otto, only he's one who'd like to see a war because he thinks it would make him rich. Know any more now?" He straightens up to open the barn door.

"I don't know. Papa?" They laugh. Father and Mother. Mother tugs on my hand, leads me toward the cottage. My mother opens the kitchen door, leaves me to wait just on the step as she gropes for matches to light the lamp. I look back at the trap barn. There is a light there now, the shafts of the pine trunks casting shadows on the ground. Father has lit the lantern in the barn. Do I hear him singing, whistling to Phil as he pours a tin measure of oats into the manger? Stepping out from under the cottage eaves, I look up to find the sky directly above is not black, but a cold, deep, dark blue, bright with the glow of the large moon that shines like a comet through shredded remains of clouds. The stars do not twinkle. Goodnight folks, I am thinking. Goodnight, goodnight.

"Lee, come in now, son." Mother stands in the middle of the kitchen, the kerosene lamp at arm's length to keep it from blinding her. "What are you looking at, Lee?"

"Nothing, Mama."

"Come in and get ready for bed. Papa will be in time to kiss you goodnight."

"Goodnight."

"What? Honestly, you're half-asleep this minute, Lee. Come along, now."

She guides me, the flat of her hand gently pressing the small of my back. The lantern wick hisses as it burns, a tiny jet of air

33

escaping up the mantle, throwing a bobbing arc of soft light that contracts, expands, as we cross the cottage parlor, enter the doorway to the sleeping porch where my bed awaits me, already turned down. I shudder in anticipation of standing, undressed, at the foot of my bed while Mother searches the dresser drawers for a warm pair of sleepers.

"Can you undress yourself, or shall I help you?"

"I can do it."

"We'll brush teeth in the morning, it's late now."

"Will Papa come before I go to sleep?"

"I should think so. Kneel down and say your prayers now, Lee." I kneel on the hard pine floor of the sleeping porch, pray with my mother, ask God to make me good and love all people, to give His blessing to me, Mama, Papa. My mother listens as I ask God to bless Mr. and Mrs. Otto Pfaff, to bless Mr. Gust Steuerwald the farmer who sells us vegetables, to bless Mr. Heddermann the iceman, to bless Phil our horse, to bless all my grandparents in Heaven. *I bless everyone, everything.*

In bed, I let my hands lie on the tufted squares of the quilt. Mother folds the edge of the sheet down over the quilt. I think: *I will stay awake to talk to Father when he comes in from graining Phil.* But my mother asks if I want to use the thundermug before I sleep, and I say no, and she says she will take it out of the washstand cabinet, sets it on the small oval hooked rug beside my bed. I must say thank you, Mama, and I have forgotten my promise to stay awake to talk to Father, and she is gone from the sleeping porch, carrying the light away, and my eyes close themselves, and I hear only the last shush of wind dying in the high tops of the pines, and I sleep.

The last thing, waking, or the first of sleep (I can't know which) is the stuffed head of the moose over Otto Pfaff's door, its dark glass eyes looking into mine.

How do you know when you're going mad? Does a madman know, can he know, when he's over the edge for good and all? They say if you think you're cracked then you can't possibly be. In which case I'm sane and the rest of the people in this world are the cracked eggs. In which case, then, I'm sound as new money.

On the other hand, how does a man of my years, sound (supposedly) of mind and body—forgetting the constant minor assaults of sun and over-exertion—come to find himself, at God only knows what hour of the night, dressed for a day on the lake, standing smack dab astraddle the center line of State Highway 21 waiting (I presume) for a drunken farm boy out for the night in the family pickup, or better, a Chicago or Milwaukee Yahoo making a mad dash north to escape his own breed of madness in the city—either/or—to knock him (this supposedly sound of mind and body citizen of my years) broadside into a drainage ditch (and the next world, for good measure)?

Answer me that, as my late father used to say, and I'll ask you another.

Leland Spaulding, Jr., smack dab astraddle the center line of Wisconsin State Highway 21, approximately three and seven-tenths miles southwest of the town of Wautoma, county seat of Waushara County, waiting (what else?) for a Chicago-Milwaukee Yahoo with his wife and kids packed into the station wagon like so many biscuits in a tin, maybe a canoe or a pair of waterskis strapped to the roof, to knock him painlessly on to his just (God help me) reward.

Is it any wonder I wonder?

As luck-or-whatever would have it, not a vehicle in sight. I took hold of myself slowly, the way a man wakes, I suspect, from sleep after a hard night's drinking, the way a man comes to himself in a hospital surgery's recovery room, first to a sense of himself, his body, that he has legs, arms, fingers, toes. Then eyes and ears, and the smell of hospital surgery in his nose. Which is when I knew where I was, and at which point I had the good sense, or what remained of it, to get myself off the road before I became an anecdote for some Chicago-Milwaukee Yahoo to amuse his friends with over the following winter months.

I walked over as far as the shoulder of the lake road,

35

stopped to get my bearings. Dead of night, too dark to read the face of my wristwatch. The ache in my bones would have it well past the proper time for me to retire. Not the ghost of any traffic on the highway. Is that one car or two in the shadows on the driveway alongside Walter Weller's Moose Inn? One would be Weller's, the second, if I can trust my eyes in the dark, the rattletrap driven by the dipsomaniac who claims to have retired in grade a major from the United States Army.

Walter Weller's neon sign faltered, buzzed, doing all the good a thimble would me if I were to try to drain Silver Lake with it. A Yahoo, out on the lake on the mistaken notion that panfish bite better at night, pulled, pulled, pulled again on his outboard's starter cord, then quit, no doubt, to row to shore. What time could it be? There was no faintest wisp of wind against the finger I stick in my mouth to wet, hold up to the night sky.

So there I was, just at the edge of the lake road, gawking out at the pale stretch of concrete highway leading to Oshkosh, at the haunted-house of a roadside tavern Walter Weller calls the Moose Inn, straining my ears to hear the sound of an engine on the highway, the sputtering of Weller's defective neon sign, straining for the sound of some Yahoo's oars in the locks, the oar blades cutting the surface of Silver Lake.

So what else was there to do but put one foot in front of the other, walk the few hundred yards to my place, turn in for the night?

The moon ducked in and out of the uneven clouds, throwing a jagged pattern of shadows on the asphalt surface of the lake road as it shone through the pines the Yahoos and real estate shysters have been gracious enough to leave standing. I can remember when a hike around Silver Lake was as good as a trip through a darkened tunnel, what with all the pine trees, oaks, and maples as well. Talk like that to your average real estate gyp-artist, he's likely to ask to have you certified.

No chance of a man's losing his way, in any case. The string of rural mailboxes would guide a man home as well as a signal beacon. The joy of the nighttime is I can't see the arts-

and-crafts productions they think of to bolt the boxes to: milk cans filled with cement, chains with links welded together, and what is doubtless the Yahoo masterpiece of this era, a mailman in silhouette, his uniform painted a shade of blue no federal employee has been seen in since the last encampment of the Grand Army of the Republic.

Nor am I forced to see what must cost a pretty penny through a variety of mail order houses. Or maybe constitutes what the male Yahoos of the world call *hobby* work. Sign-boards of all descriptions, wired, nailed, tied to pine trunks at a level calculated to strike you hardest in the eye as you pass. *Piney Slope*, burned into what was once a good piece of wood. *Our Place*, painted in Chinese red on a field of canary. *Lakeside Lodge*, this done with some care, letters formed by a long length of marine rope, tacked to a board decorated with decals (ship's wheel, anchor, raised sails)—praise the Lord for nights following days, if for nothing else.

Rubbernecks never know what to make of my property. I've stood at the corner of the old barn, quite concealed, to watch them make the tour of the lake road. They're closed up in their station wagons, of course, with the air conditioning on, naturally, but the whole litter is plastered, nose and mouth, up against the windows. The sire of it all navigates with one hand, leaning across his wife to take it in. The wife—now and again I'll catch one with her hair-wave completed instead of in mid-process—doubtless with pad and pencil just out of sight to make notes on all this charm they're passing too fast.

All those cunning ways of putting up a rural mailbox, those original and artistic signboards. Then my place. What a real estate sharper like Carl Crowder in Wautoma would call *un-developed*, but what it is, for the passing Yahoo and his brood, is a rupture. What are all those big trees doing there? What is all that brush? (Sumac, most of it, since the ferns began dying out several years back, from God-only-knows what disease brought north by the very ones wouldn't recognize them out-side of a window planter!) What is that big red building? (A barn, you idiot spawn of idiot spawn! the same thing you see

37

in story books and magazine advertisements for milk!) Where's the cottage? (Behind all the trees and brush, idiot-child!) Who lives there? (*I do!* and I call for my mail at a rented post office box in the town of Wautoma, because I expect to be here a third or more of each calendar year, and if you'd lived long enough here to know *where* you lived—*that* you lived!—you'd know my name without arts-and-crafts-hobby-work signs nailed to pines older than your grandparents!)

There's an outdoor light up on the corner of the old barn, and, times I leave the cottage late enough of an afternoon, I flip the switch in the kitchen so it's on to light me in if I get back after dark. Which is not often. I could walk the path blind-folded in from the lake road without so much as brushing a leaf, a blade of grass. I thread my way between the pines, skirt the raised concrete cap of the septic tank, pick up my foot at just the right instant to avoid taking a dangerous header on the kitchen slab-porch. Reach out my hand, close my fingers on the cold ceramic doorknob (try to find those outside an antique dealer's or a country hardware in this day and age!). Fumble for the key mixed with coins, penknife, and the few smooth water-worn stones from the beach I'm in the habit of carrying as pocket pieces.

The door scrapes the sill, I enter. I expect something, antic-ipate, always, and always, entering, no matter how few min-utes I've been out, always I'm disappointed. Is it a wonder I doubt my sanity?

I didn't bother to turn the kitchen light on. There was only a little moonlight at the windows, that reduced by the curtains, but still, there seemed plenty of light to see my way through the kitchen. I'm not sure what I expected. I was tempted to step back out the kitchen door, check the yard, the barn—was it something outside? I stood in the kitchen for several minutes, not moving, not closing the door, the night air filling the room with the very fragile scent of the pines, as if I were afraid of disturbing someone if I entered the cottage noisily. Disturbing who, what?

"You better get a grip on yourself, Spaulding," I said aloud

38

in the dark kitchen, and I thought, as I said it, that I would reach out and flick the light switch, blow light into the room, perhaps to go to the refrigerator for something to eat before going to bed, get a drink of water, sit in the parlor, read a magazine to settle myself for sleep. I didn't.

I continued to stand there, listening to the echo of my own words in the cottage, listening, as if there would be an answer from someone somewhere in the other end of the cottage. I stood there, as if trying to catch voices, isolated words or phrases, and then I was suddenly afraid. Maybe I suspected there was a prowler, some hobo out of the woods broken in to sleep or steal. I shook a little, and felt very weak, and had to speak again to get my courage up.

"You're a peach of a spectacle for the world to see, Spaulding," I said, and I forced myself to laugh. Then I could walk out of the kitchen into the parlor.

There was more light there. The windows are larger, the lace curtains tacked back with swags. I walked to the corner shelf, reached up, took down the framed pictures, held them up to the light to see them. My parents, their wedding picture, Mother seated, her head tilted to one side, expression very softly pensive, as if taking this opportunity to consider all that had been before the photographer pressed his bulb, exposed the plate, and she had to stand, give back the flowers she held, and begin all that was to come. My father is smiling in their wedding picture, his smile shaded finely rakish by the pencil-moustache he wore as a very young man. It's difficult to say if he looks down at his bride with just a touch of condescension in his tone, or if he looks, obliquely, out at the photographer as well, as if saying to them both with this mild rake's smile: *Yes, certainly, this picture, and it is important, supremely important to me, but there is more, more to come, which only I am given to know. Nor dare I tell you any of what I know is to come, but there is more to come that I alone know, and so, you see, forgive me if you can, I cannot refrain from smiling, just so, as you see.*

I stood close to the window to get all of the uncertain moonlight, my shoulder touching the plume-shaped tieback. I

39

held my parents' wedding picture at different distances, to see if there was anything more to see, but that was all. The wedding portrait of Mr. and Mrs. Leland Spaulding, Chicago, Illinois, June, 1904. They will honeymoon at Mr. Spaulding's newly purchased summer vacation home near Wautoma, Wisconsin, returning to the city in three weeks' time, where Mr. Spaulding is prominently associated with the Corn Exchange Bank, La Salle Street. I set it carefully on the top shelf of the corner knick-knack, took down an enlarged snapshot taken with a box camera, the three of us, taken on the beach. Just at the foot of the steep, pine-covered slope, the beach.

Who took this picture? My father is just back from a swim, his daily exercise, out to the raft floated on old oil drums, touching the raft, submerging to reverse his course, the churning, methodical crawl, straight as a rifle shot to the beach. He stands, in the enlarged snapshot, hair plastered in a fraying fringe on his brow, trunks and jersey stuck fast with water, clinging to his body. His right hand on his hip, his left rests lightly on my bare, sun-browned shoulder. My mother seated, just to my left, in a canvas beach chair. She sits up straight in the chair to be photographed. The wide brim of her gardening hat protects her eyes from the sharp glare of sun on sand and water. Still, I see her eyes clearly in the photo, the same large, brown, girl's eyes that were so quiet with reflection in her wedding portrait.

Who took this picture?

I stand, between my father and mother, one hand up to shade my eyes from the sun's glare to see whoever it was hunched over the Brownie box. His truncated shoulder-shadow juts into the picture just at my feet. In my other hand I hold a tiny (even for the six or seven-year-old boy) sand shovel. The pail (was there a pail to go with it?) is not in the picture. Do I shudder at the wet touch of my father's hand laid on my dry shoulder? Am I really trying to smile for whoever holds the camera, or is it only a sneer against the harsh light? My face—the boy's face—is lost in the shadow of my hand.

So much is lost. I held the framed picture close to the

40

moonlit window in the cottage parlor, tilted it from side to side, as if I were trying to signal, like an Indian with a piece of broken mirror. What is that in my mother's lap? Magazines? Stationery, letters from Chicago friends she means to answer in an afternoon on the beach? What is my father thinking? Does he ponder the politics of Woodrow Wilson on this afternoon down on the beach below our cottage? Does he consider what steps he'll take to prevent John Prader from securing a permit to build a large resort at the far end of Silver Lake? Does he calculate the possibilities of war with the Central Powers?

What is the small boy thinking of this afternoon? The sun, water, sand, the next meal to be eaten. Will we build a fire in a circle of stones on the fine sand of the beach, picnic there, wait for the sunset, wrapping outselves in thick blankets to escape the gnats and humming mosquitoes? Lost.

I put the picture back on its shelf in the knick-knack. I could have stayed there till God knows what wee hour, could have reached blindly for more framed photographs. Father in his captain's Expeditionary Force uniform (to be major shortly after he reached France, when he assumed command of his machine-gun battalion, before Château Thierry). My graduation portraits (Winnetka Common School, Northwestern University). A studio portrait taken on Mother's birthday (1941, the last year before the gasoline rationing that would have made summers in Wisconsin impossible for us if I hadn't found a man with black market connections who remembered my father). What good would that have done me?

"Face up to it, Spaulding," I said aloud, or imagined I spoke out loud in the dark and empty parlor. I would have made a fine spectacle for a peeping Tom, wouldn't I? Muttering to myself in the gloom by the window, as if working up to an all-out bay at the moon skitting in and out of clouds beyond the tops of the oldest, highest pine trees on my property.

I went quickly, then, to the sleeping porch, undressed without hanging up my clothes, slipped quickly into the bed, drew the quilt up to my chin, around my ears, shut my eyes tightly, prayed, for an easy sleep.

I tried. I tried to blank you my mind, see it as the dead-white screen of an empty, abandoned motion picture theater. My mother, late in life, always wore a sleeping mask, but it was not my eyes, not what I might have seen of where and when I was that kept me awake until I made a decision. Nor did I fear my dreams. I can dream of hell and enjoy the show, dream anything and know it is only a dream as I dream it, enjoying it all the more because it is only a dream. I let myself listen for the sounds that often bring me sleep.

I listened for the hoot owl that has, for the past several years, chosen a tree limb of the corner of my property to roost in nights while it shrieks to the moon across the water. Some Yahoo will, doubtless, shoot it for an eagle one day soon, and be disappointed it's not good eating too. But the owl was elsewhere, off hunting or asleep on its limb. I listened for wind in the branches of the pines, but the wind had died for the night, would not blow up again until sunrise. There was no getting away from it.

The bar was packed to the gills with them, Yahoos, cheek by jowl, women, men, children belonging at home, and noise, music, what they call music coming out of the walls at you like a plague of roaring locusts, from jukeboxes in the room, in all the other rooms, a Muzak for madmen, and light, no cool darkness, but light every-where, and people cheek by jowl, ice rattling in glasses, tops being pried off bottles, cash registers ringing in chorus with the madmen's Muzak. But I went in, and I thought they would all get up and come at me, because everyone looked, and I was afraid, I admit to it, afraid, but I pretended to look for the Jew-Hunky-Yahoo himself, and I found him, not even really looking, only a pretense, but there he was, as large and ugly as life (I didn't think he had seemed so large a man when I'd seen before, at a distance) and I had to do something, because they were all looking at me as if I were an asylum escapee or the man from the booby-hatch come to fetch them all with a net in one fell swoop and the Jew-Hunky-Yahoo himself seemed to be looking at me, so I shouted, I cried out with the strength of all the hate in me I could find, I said, "I'm looking for the owner!"

I knew there would be no sleep for me until I decided. I

42

could walk the lake road ten times around in a single day, could beard Walter Weller in his ramshackle den of a Moose Inn till the cows came home, and there would be no rest, no peace until I did something. No matter what I knew, or felt, the Yahoos, this one or the next, or the next after that would, for all I had done to stop them, would have the whole of Waushara County paved with asphalt, fill in Silver Lake to build row housing on—God-knows-what-all!

I had to *do* something! I decided to *do* something, and then, wonder of wonders (will this world never fail to astonish me?), I went to sleep as easily as if I were a boy, tired from a day in the sun on the beach. A sleep so deep, so complete. For all I know I may have dreamed of Otto Pfaff's stuffed moose, jaws open, red tongue curled back in its black mouth, ready to swallow me whole.

I know better, of course, than to ask to wake refreshed. That's a horse of another color. I've gotten through a number of bad days in this world in my time, but it's not made me so arrogant as to expect improvement in the next one up.

Morning. Morning around here is about enough to make it all worth it. I have the habit of simply finding myself awake. No dreams oozing over into here and now, no fire siren in my dream translating to a ringing telephone—who would be calling me, in the first place? I simply wake up.

There's an instant there when I feel up to kicking off the quilt, bouncing out, challenging the International Grand Champion Yahoo of This World and The Next to ten rounds, no quarter asked or given.

In this corner, dividing his time between Silver Lake, Waushara County, Wisconsin, and the city of Chicago (winters only), Illinois, Leland Spaulding, Jr!

It's the light, as much as anything. The bright, clean light of morning is everywhere! Crowding the windows of the sleeping porch, splashing the walls and floors. I sit up in my bed, prop the pillow in the small of my back, draw my knees up, the quilt tenting on me, just to examine the grain of the wood where the sun tears back the shadowy corners to expose it to the eye. Light. It makes the patchwork colors of the quilt jump out into the air, turns my hands and arms golden, whangs me smack in the eyes like a photographer's flash-gun going off near the end of my nose! And warms.

Warm. This cottage has always seemed to take the cold in, clutch at it, soak it up, hold it, let it go only at the last. I remember, one spring, when we made the trip up from Chicago for the season, met by a man with an open touring car, no side curtains. It drizzled a cold rain all the way from the Wautoma depot, afghans wrapped around Mother and me in the rear seat, my father braving it up front with a cigar between his teeth, conversing with the driver (appointed by registered letter, confirmed by telegram or night letter to meet us at the depot with a vehicle). "I'm freezing!" I said to my mother.

"This is what makes the lilacs bloom so beautifully, Lee," she would say. I was already seeing the opening of the cottage for the season, Father, Mother, the man hired to meet us with the vehicle, busy building twig and pinecone fires in all the fireplaces. Opening the heavy shutters on the windows, unbolting the doors, like opening the doors of a meat locker, the stored cold of the long winter rolling out over us like a wall of sea water. Stepping inside to the dark, damp cold that had set deep in the bones of the cottage, set free to seep out and chill me to my core. They built snapping fires of pinecones, twigs, the hired man bringing armloads of kindling from last year's pile, bits of ice, spots of snow still stuck to the pale bark of the birch logs.

I stood and watched, feeling the warmth run from the leaping flame, pouring into my clothes, filling the bloused trouser legs of my knickers. We would thaw the cottage with the very air of spring that brought lilacs into blossom, dry the roof and walls with fires in fireplaces (I had them plugged when my mother feared they were no longer safe to use), one in the iron stove so hot it made the black metal glow red-orange, drove me from the kitchen with parched skin.

I can recall even in August, when we lit a small fire in the parlor hearth in the early mornings, just to blunt the edge of what was left of a windy, rainy night. I stood next to my father, both of us wearing robes over our clothes, feet still in lined slippers, hands clasped behind our backs, swaying at the knees as we let the small fire cheer us while Mother prepared a farmer's breakfast in the kitchen.

"This will get our blood circulating," my father would say. I would shudder, only listen, absorb the words, the delightful heat at our backs.

This light of morning warmed the cottage, and still there were intermittent gusts of wind rocking the big old pines on my property. I could, for a moment, have charged out of my sleeping porch bed like the wrath of hell itself to take on the World's Champion Yahoo. The full-length mirror, put there by my mother when I was a small boy to help me learn to dress myself, stopped me cold.

I would have done a deal better to sleep in pajamas, as I did as a boy. An undershirt and a pair of boxer shorts take the heart right out of you when you reach my years.

The Challenger: Leland Spaulding, Jr. Five feet nine, maybe ten inches if he had it left in him to stand straight. Chest depressed, Talmudic hump between his shoulders, pot belly (my father called it an *alderman*; he once spoke of Otto Pfaff's *alderman*) about of a size with his head—scarecrow's arms and legs, sticks with knots, knobs for shoulders, elbows, wrists, knees, ankles. What became of that skin, bronzed with the morning sunlight, seen against the colored quilt swatches?

The skin of a cadaver before the undertaker's cosmetician gets to work on it. A skin fish turn belly-up when they die, rise to the surface from the cold, green deeps to bloat in the sun among the sawgrass and cattails. The skin of chickens I've watched my mother singe over an open fire before she went after the pinfeathers with a tweezers. A skin so dead-white, so near-translucent you can barely resist poking a fingernail through it. A skin with all the tautness of wet kleenex—oh God have mercy on me!

It makes me dizzy, my dressing mirror, but there's nothing for it in the clean new light of morning pouring through the

45

porch windows but to start there and take it like a man. Hang on, Spaulding! I reach a hand out to the washstand to steady myself.

No action but what comes from principle, and no principles but what come from knowledge, no knowledge but what begins with yourself (I don't try to remember where I read that; it's the sort of thing my father would have copied out of the source). I step one step closer to my dressing mirror.

Skin. Dead-white, rising to peaks of a mucous-tint highlight over the knobs of wrists, elbows, shoulders, lightly wrinkled, soft, as if pus gathered to a head beneath it. Shading to dirty grey around the eyes, the folds of the neck, the corners of my mouth. Oh Lord, the hand that reaches out to test the mirror's surface! Gnarled, gone yellow from the faded wrist where my cuffs end, liver-spotted, the veins purple bas-relief, not like the glossy, marbled blue in my feet, legs, hams! *Oh God!*

What happend to all my hair? Would my father have gone bald, had he lived? I remember his hair, light, like mine, but so thick he was forced to lard it with brilliantine and Pinaud's Lilac Vegetal to make it lie in place. Mother complained of the stained, ruined pillowslips, kept doilies on the backs of easy chairs, sofas, in our Chicago home to spare the upholstery. Whose wisps, whose tatters on the fringes of my scalp are these? Twisted, snarled from sleep, I rake it with my fingers, raise it up in airy puffs, watch it collapse back again, dig at it with my knuckles where it thickens into disgusting little waves and curls around my dishlike ears, at the base of my turkey's neck. God have mercy!

Do I really dare pull down the skin beneath my eyes, lean close to the mirror (nose all but touching the glass!), look to the bottom of myself? Oh Lord. What are those marbles, those dabs of jellied mush passing themselves off for my eyes? (Mother always said, "Lee's got the most beautiful eyes. He comes by them honestly enough; his father had beautiful eyes.")

I blink: now they are hard as agates, cold as stones in

moonlight on the bottom of a free-running trout stream. Blink again, they are hot, moist as syrup, rheumy.

This . . . this is all there is to throw in the breach to stop that Jew-Hunky dead in his tracks! Bag of bones, I'd rattle in my hide like pebbles in a paper sack in the first wind—crooked, slouched, bent, slumped, stiff, sore, withered, weather-worn. The challenger, Leland Spaulding, Jr.

I close my eyes, teetering with fright, there on my sleeping porch, bare feet on the bare pine planks. *Tomorrow*, I think. I'll do something tomorrow. I'll write a few carefully worded letters to a few well chosen individuals. There are people still alive and kicking in this world who remember my father's name with respect! Tomorrow, I alibi, I'll drive into Wautoma, see that dumb Dutchman Schaeffer, see the members of the township council, hire myself a lawyer, wrap the Jew-Bohunk up in a tangle of court and law he'll be two lifetimes cutting free. I can feel my breathing come back to normal, hear the beating of my blood in my ears fade out to silence, feel the sense of balance reassert itself in my pipestem legs. I open my eyes.

I looked at myself, stepped far enough away to get all of it in the dressing mirror, come back again to verify at close range, head, hair. Pull back the dull, dry lips: long in the tooth, as my mother used to say of elderly women who would not admit to their age.

It's me, all right. And I thought: tomorrow, the next day, the Jew-Bohunk will be there. He doesn't hesitate, he doesn't ponder—he carries nothing more than his wallet and his contracts. Two weeks, a week, it'll be too late—*now!*

I'd be a liar if I said I stopped being afraid. I was always afraid. But I could turn my back on the mirror without supposing the image of my backside was sneering to me.

I was born afraid, but sometimes it makes me so damned angry I start to acting as if it weren't so. That kept me to my purpose through breakfast. After that there was nothing for it but to get on with it.

When I go to go down the slope to the lake (windows all

47

latched, doors locked tight—your near neighbor is free to rob you blind while you're away when neither he nor you know one another's last name, and give two hoots less for the fact!) it makes me think I'm about to step right out off the edge of the world.

I can recall being a child no more than three or four, when we'd go for a row on the lake. My father had been a competitive sculler (Yale, '01) in college, and I remember the impression of his varsity rowing jersey, its smell, the bright colors, the rough texture between my fingers as I plucked at it to get a fold of it in my grasp as he carried me down to our pier, Mother coming behind us, seen over his shoulder.

He wore that jersey whenever we went out for a row on the lake, the three of us. I rode in his arms, looking over his shoulder at my mother, who always carried a parasol for the sun. When we neared the crest of the steep slope, Father would cry, "Here we go!" and there was only an instant for me to turn in his arms as he broke into a trot, my fingers forgetting the feel of his rower's jersey, clutching now for a safe grip on his neck, in his hair.

Here we go! he cried, breaking into a trot, a lope, a full run. I twisted in his arms even as I grabbed for a more secure hold on him, thrilled and terrified. I turned and saw the dip of the slope's crest rushing at us, the blur of green foliage all around us, the whipping boughs of the tall pines on both sides. Above us, the crest of the slope was like the last horizon of all. Beyond it, below and leading away forever, as far as my eye might ever see, the sun-spangled surface of Silver Lake, glittering, snapping with white-hot highlights, suffused with pale blues, melting into the stretch of lighter, then darker blue of clear midsummer sky, broken only by pure white balls of clouds, the dark green opposite shore of the lake, almost a mile away, effaced by the glare of the sun.

Here we go! Reaching the crest, he leaped into the air to clear the edge, as if he meant to throw us (Mother lost behind on the path from the cottage) out into the blazing blue of lake and sky. I felt as if we might fall, fall almost forever, then

48

plunge into the cold or heat of that blue, fall again forever in its bottomless depths. I screamed, half-delight, half-terror.

My body jarred, jaw snapped shut as Father landed on the third-from-the-top-step, the steps dug out of the side of the slope by hired labor from Wautoma, erosion held back by creosoted railroad ties staked in place (I can still smell them in the heat of a dog-day!). Then aloft again, skipping a step, sometimes two, we pounded, soared, thundered down the slope—Mother is far behind—to the pale gold sand beach, our pier.

The boathouse, rushing down the slope, like a small chalet on a mountainside, is only a spot of clean white paint, red trim, as we fly past in mid-leap, to the beach where we collapse on the clean sand to wait, heaving for breath, for my mother to catch up with us, her parasol in hand, broad-brimmed gardening hat tied firmly under her chin against the wind that blows on the open water of the lake.

My father steadies the boat with one foot, helps Mother into her seat in the stern, lifts me onto his lap, then climbs the steps to the boathouse for his oars.

It was like stepping off the edge of this world. I wished, stopping at the old boathouse to get my Sears Waterwitch outboard engine off its stand, down to the beach (at my time in life I had no business doing work of this sort!) that there were something for a man to fall into. The trouble was, I had touched bottom, and there was nothing for it but rise or stay there.

Rack and ruin! I thought, dragging the Waterwitch out of the boathouse. My father had a saying: *Ichabod! Ichabod!* he would say with a teasing smile when Mother complained of something. The glory hath departed us. If my father had survived their war he would have understood. My mother never did. He kept her sheltered all their married life. What could she know?

Try, in this day and age to find man or boy willing to do a day's work with a shovel, a hammer, or a paintbrush for less than three days' wages! They laugh in my face, in Wautoma,

49

when I ask for the names of two or three young fellows with strong backs and weak minds who wouldn't mind earning an honest dollar or two for a little medium-heavy day labor. Unions are the source of it. My father understood pretty well where labor unions would take us all.

The paint has weathered off the boathouse, looks even worse than the cottage, if that's possible. If it weren't that the arches of my feet won't bear the pressure of ladder rungs, I'd take a crack at it myself, despite my age. The flooring inside has warped, shows the sloping ground through the seams. I don't stick around in there any longer than it takes to wrestle the Waterwitch outside. The wasps nesting in the exposed rafters might take it upon themselves to defend the place. Up in the loft, where my father kept a pair of canoes for a time, I hear a rodent, chipmunk, rat, God-knows-what scurrying for cover in the dark.

An easy trip down, dragging the engine alongside the steps, then another trip up for the gasoline can. Just enough fuel left in the bottom to slosh when I shake the red can, which means, no doubt, I'll run out somewhere midway home, but I haven't the energy left in me to tote the oars down from the boathouse as well.

I came within a hair of dropping myself in the drink, getting the Waterwitch on the stern of my boat. It's the damn, cheap pier! We used to put out a pier each year, a pier that stood up and said *solid* to you!

I remember my father, along with a couple of hired men, setting the pier in spring. They dragged the posts out from under the boathouse, the planks from inside (stored up with the canoes), put on their bathing clothes, waded out into the water with sledgehammers to drive the posts three feet into the sand bottom, nail the cross pieces on with two-penny spikes. Father used to clown for us (we came down to the beach to watch, Mother and I), screeching and shuddering at how cold the water was, in autumn, when they pulled out the pier and stored it away again, to keep it from being bashed, broken to

50

bits by the winter ice on the lake. I remember the hired men laughed right along with us.

That was what it might be proper to call a pier. Pine posts driven three feet into the sand bottom of the lake—*solid*. Pine planks twelve inches wide, nailed into the cross pieces with two-penny spikes. Four feet wide, twenty-six feet out into the water, with a tee-cross at the end, and two benches, where Mother sat while I fished for panfish with a cane pole and worms off the end. "Don't stand so close to the edge, please, Lee," she'd say. I wanted to be able to see the cork go under when the sunfish or bluegill or rock bass took my worms. That was what could be called a pier.

This is jerry-built, a system of iron pipes like a piece of child's playground equipment. Everyone uses them now, too lazy or busy to go out in the woods and cut pines. No pine to speak of left to cut if they weren't. This trembles and lurches under me, so narrow I have to look before I set down my foot, for fear of taking a dip with my clothes on. This pulls up with ease out of the sand it's anchored in, collapses, folds right up, can go right through the boathouse door. I'd wager against odds it can't last half a dozen seasons.

The sun was up full, and I had to sit a few minutes, resting, in the stern of my boat. I get giddy so easily, even with a hat on, when I exert myself out under the sun. And I knew what to expect, starting the Waterwitch. If I were not more or less sworn against the public utterance of profanity—parental influence, doubtless—I might have rendered the air a little bluer that day!

Have you ever snapped your starter rope in two, tied it back together again and tried to coil it with the knot in it? The starting mechanism is the one serious flaw in the design concept of the Waterwitch outboard motor. Needless to say the brand is long since discontinued. I'll feel that the day I need a part.

But I got it started, sat again to compose myself, my chest heaving, sweat standing out on my face, glossing my bare arms, let it idle to blow out the carbon deposits, before I started for Camp Waushara. Out on the open water like that, even shielding my eyes with one hand, all I could see, looking out on Silver Lake, was the fractured shimmer of the sun glancing off the surface, like standing at the entrance to a brightly lit fun-house hall of mirrors.

"You aren't backing off now, Spaulding," I said, and dropped the outboard into drive. And off I went to see what might be done, trusting in the Almighty to provide special Providence for fools and the near-mad.

What you can't see of Yahoo life on a walk around the lake road you can observe out on the water. What you can see from the lake road is only a hint of what's festering away unconstrained on the beaches. No way of avoiding it, but I know better, at least, than to plow out into the middle of the lake, even if that's the shortest route to Prader's resort. That would be asking some Yahoo to swamp me in his wake.

I recall when there was nothing much larger than my Waterwitch on Silver Lake, nothing bigger than outboard motors sufficient for trolling fishermen. And a *real* fisherman, like my father or Otto Pfaff, for instance, would never have considered it sporting to troll with a motor. It's a Yahoo speedway now.

They haul their boats up from Chicago and Milwaukee (where they sit fifty weeks of the year in garages or under tarpaulins in backyards to keep the flyash out of factory flues from spoiling the marine paint). The trailers are a menace, even on the new four-lane highways north out of Milwaukee.

Bad enough the ones renting cottages on Silver Lake. Lymancrafts shaped like artillery shells, flags flying. Find a Yahoo with a speedboat who's failed to provide himself with a yachting cap! Cutting a wake around you just to see you hang on to your gunwales while you rock near to swamping.

Your father-Yahoo at the wheel up front, playing with the gearshift lever, grinning like a deathmask at the spray hitting him in the face, yachting cap jammed down over his ears to keep from losing it in the slipstream. His wife and Yahoo-

52

offspring packed (they overload those boats to the point of criminal negligence!) in the second seat, all bundled up in orange life jackets in the event father-Yahoo dumps them all in the water for the joy of feeling the bumps against the hull as he circles to cut across his own wake. About half the time they're pulling a pair of water-skiers, who are, naturally, seeing how many silly postures they can assume before they spill headfirst into the drink, skis flying through the air like shrapnel. And then there are the cabin cruiser Yahoos, the Chris-craft class of Yahoo.

This one chugs past you at slower speed, true, but makes up for it by gathering at the rail to stare like you were a relic of some benighted age in history. They are very prone to wearing opaque sunglasses, this class of Yahoo, and to drinking highballs as they cruise the shoreline of the lake, rubbernecking. There is doubtless a law about alcohol in a boat, but I've more sense than to suppose it was written to be enforced with respect to people with vacation money in their pockets.

Just a cut below these are the pontoon houseboat Yahoos, paddling about the lake on what might have served as a rather elaborate raft with a shanty on it a generation or two ago. I have (and I swear to it!) seen them grilling meat over a charcoal fire in the middle of the lake on one of those monstrosities. Yes, and dump the hot ashes and coals over the side when they finished!

Need it be said that fishing in Silver Lake is no longer possible for anyone who takes that pleasure seriously?

It used to be fine fishing in Silver Lake. A few muskie (like Otto Pfaff's), mostly back in the still water behind Foxtail Point, pike and pickerel in the shallower, weedy waters near the culvert that connects with Fish Lake under the Oshkosh highway, bass all along the shoreline, and panfish (crappies, bluegills, sunfish) anywhere you cared to drop your line. My father was one of the men with property on the Lake who laid fish nests to ensure their breeding, crossed beams sunk on the bottom with stones to make a refuge for spawning females, safe from larger fish.

We would go out, the three of us, along the wild shoreline, Father in his college rowing jersey, a cigar between his teeth. Mother held me on her lap, and we watched the sunset while my father would cast for bass, close in to the cattails and sawgrass the Yahoos have cut, burned, bulldozed out to make beach frontage for more Yahoos to litter.

I get my eye full as I putt along, thirty or forty feet out from shore, following the contour of the lake to Prader's resort.

One unbroken strip of sand ringing the entire lake, like a long bleached bone, the green hide peeled back, drying in the sun. A man couldn't sleep, nights or days, when they were putting in their strips of beach, linking up one with another for a solid line over three or four years' time. Bulldozers and graders bellowing their noise out over the water during the day, pumps at work all night, sucking sand up off the lake bottom, spitting it out to make sunbathing and swimming beaches for Yahoos come North to rent two weeks in Paradise each. Now look at them.

A snakepit. Every Yahoo female between fourteen and sixty stretched out on their bellies on the sand, backs oiled, like half-done lobsters waiting for the butter and the forks. If the wind is right you can get a nose-full of the smell, coconut oil, burn cream, perfumed gunk sweet enough to all but make me retch over the side of my boat.

The Yahoo is never satisfied with a patch of sand, clear sun, and a faint lake breeze. Oh no! There's got to be blankets in combinations of colors in violation of the spectrum, and here and there the dome of a beach umbrella in blue, yellow, hot pink, Chinese red, circus-tent stripes. And what would all this be without transistor radios blaring Yahoo music loud enough for half Waushara County to hear? And the obligatory styrofoam coolers jammed with ice and beer in cans that will wash up on my frontage before the week is out?

They look like the dead, victims of some rare plague that left them on their stomachs, greased with muck that smells like lavatory disinfectant, were it not that now and again one of them will move. Here comes the male of the species, waddling down from the rented crackerbox of a cottage, complete in his knee socks, Bermuda shorts, aloha shirt, carrying a portable charcoal grill (dinner *al fresco* tonight!) the way a fat lady carries a washbasket. There, maybe a mosquito has the temerity to land on a woman's shoulder blade, and damned if a sick-white hand doesn't raise up from the plaid beach blanket to brush at the grease-slicked, sunburned back.

Or maybe it's the stutter of my Waterwitch coming through the general roar of speedboats out on the lake, through the electrified tin-can-clatter of the transistor (made in Japan). The female of the species lifts her hand to see what it could be. It's me, dammit, *Leland Spaulding, Jr.*! No law yet against my using the lake, is there?

It's as good as an obstacle course, what with the rafts they've set out. Edge to edge with the same interchangeable bodies, the same gleam of suntan lotion, the smell, the same occasional head lifting up with eyes behind dark glasses, the faces as rosy as the shoulders. See them on the streets of Wautoma, it's like an infestation of humanoid raccoons, dead-white masks around the eyes. I give the rafts a wide berth, never respond to waves or shouted greetings. Which is still not good enough to guarantee a clear path through the water. Floating air mattresses (hot pink is this year's color, replacing the pastels that sold last year), the same white-turning-pink skin looking lacquered under the sun.

Scan the open water, eyes shaded with the flat of my hand. Safe from waterskiers for the moment. Then head out on the diagonal for Prader's, visible at the far end of Silver Lake, the deeper-than-usual beach. No turning back.

It used to be a fine sight to approach Prader's at night on the water. Sign away your life if you cast offshore after dark now. It's a choice of being cut in two by a Yahoo speedboat without running lights, or may decapitating some Yahoo female swimming in the buff under cover of darkness. But it was a pleasure to see once.

If there was a moon, the moon laid a line of broken silver

on the water that seemed to lead you toward Prader's, no matter where you looked from, no matter the direction from which you approached. It was a fine sight, all the summer darkness broken only by the shimmering moonlight on the water, and on the far shores of the lake, the rare dock and boathouse lights that winked on and off as our boat cut through the water. Ahead of us (Mother seated in the middle seat, myself with my hand on the steering lever of the new Waterwitch), the pulsing bank of light from Prader's pavilion, his long double piers lit by strings of paper-shaded lanterns, deep orange against the black backdrop of pine trees, themselves black against the lighter blackness of the summer night sky. As we drew closer we could make out other boats (never more than three or four!) docking at Prader's, some families rowing half the length of the lake for only a short visit. We could make out the tunes being played, coming faintly but clearly across the water to us, through the slapping-sound of the water against our prow, and the even buzzing of the Waterwitch's motor on the stern.

Try to so much as think one thought rationally connected with another in this present day! Yahoos to left and right, bearing down on collision courses, Lymancrafts done up in stark red and green marine paint, chrome fixtures jabbing the sun smack in my eyes, nonsense pennants flapping on the decks, your ears cringing from the roar of fifty, sixty horsepower Evinrude and Mercury outboard engines, veering off at the last possible instant to leave me helpless, rocking like a chip in a windstorm in their crossing wakes! Even Batterman's beach looks like a safe harbor after a trip across Silver Lake in the Age of the Yahoo!

I'd thought to go directly to the pier to dock my boat, but turned aside and went on down to the end of Batterman's frontage when I saw the people working on the pier. Painting it mud-ugly-something, about what you'd get feeding a horse a raw bran diet for a fortnight.

For all the activity the Jew-Bohunk was supposed to be generating there wasn't much effort visible. The pier was being painted (crew made up of township boys from their look—three days' wages for maybe a day's honest labor—let the Bohunk fork out like that for too long!). The beach appeared to have been given a lick and a promise with a sand rake. I was in close enough to make out the natural stone walls the Bohunk-Jew seemed to be throwing up all over the property like it was a rat's maze he intended. But he was a long way from home-free if he intended his opening day for the very near future. The waterslide was still up on the beach where Batterman had it dragged each autumn to keep it out of the ice for the winter, like an abandoned oil derrick, canted slightly to one side.

My mother liked nothing so much, of a late, hot afternoon (in her last years, when activity of any sort was difficult for her) as to have a chair under the pine trees just above the beach, to sit there, enjoying the light breeze off the lake, watching the township boys who as good as lived through the summer on Prader's beach. Going down that giant of a waterslide, with all their crazy antics. Batterman himself would have been one of those kids, bent on breaking a neck to show off for people. Batterman was the one used to do the crazy things with adhesive tape, his suntan. Old Prader himself used to be good enough to assist me with one of the new, heavy chairs he had made to order for the pavilion. It was Batterman and his loony cronies who took to cutting their names in the wood with penknives.

Nobody noticed me. I ran my boat straight in at the end of Batterman's beach, as far away from the pier as I could get, cutting the Waterwitch and heaving it up when I heard my boat scrape bottom. My father used to jump out of a boat in the shallows, shoes and all, then march through the water as if it were dry land, pulling the boat up on the sand behind him. It's all I can manage on a good day to lift up the prow of my boat and drag it up far enough to keep it from drifting away on the open lake.

I walked up through the raked sand of the beach, up the slight grassy slope, and came out just at the merry-go-round

57

and jungle-gym Batterman had put in for the smaller children when he took over from Prader. Up away from the moist scent that always hangs in the air over the lake (when dead fish or rotting weeds don't drown *that* out!). I got myself a noseful of asphalt-stink from the Bohunk's new-laid pavement. The dirt and gravel road cutting through the resort from the Oshkosh highway to the county's road is by no means good enough for him.

I'll admit he had plenty of activity underway. I stepped among the pines lining the edge of the slope to keep myself out of sight. Oh, he had himself a regular rat's nest of activity messing up the place!

There were three of the township boys pretending to paint the pier, squatting on their haunches in the sun with their shirts off, bandanas tied around their heads, as if they meant to work up a sweat, dabbing their brushes in the cans of deck paint from time to time while they held a regular social hour, gabbing like a covey of old ladies in a tearoom, slapping casually at the pier's floorboards with their brushes just often enough to keep flies from settling on them. At what they likely asked per hour for all this the Bohunk must not have cared any more for how his money went than he did how he got his hands on it in the first place.

Green, dark green, is the only color to paint a pier. It sets it off to let you know it is a pier, and it doesn't splash itself against the backdrop of pines and grass. The average Yahoo tends to favor, naturally, deep yellows and approximations of fire-engine red.

The racket was worse than out on the lake, the three township boys out on the pier gibbering like darkies plotting against the whites, and just beyond them the men working on the maze of low natural stone walls and cookout pits, slopping mortar into the seams with their trowels, chipping the edges off lumps of granite and sandstone to fit. Masons who can do a job of work like that don't come cheap.

Two more men, local people by the look, were unloading lumber right alongside the pavilion. I shaded my eyes to try to

58

see the weathervane on the pavilion cupola, but the sun was too bright on the sheet metal for me to see anything. The big old elms behind the pavilion were well leafed out now, concealing all but the shade-silhouette of Batterman's house, the house Prader had built for himself, in 1927, after the first big boom of vacationers hit us, after all the soft money that got so easy to get your hands on, after their first war.

Two men unloaded something heavy, boxed, half-walked, half-trotted it into the barroom, a Wautoma woman I recognized stepping outside on the porch to hold the screen door open for them. A television set being delivered all the way from Oshkosh, going by the sign on the side of the van (do the locals really believe he'll do his shopping in Wautoma?). No counting the number of shapes moving around under the roof in the pavilion, like waterbugs skating on the surface under an overhanging willow, close to shore, the movement more than the shapes themselves in your eye.

At the other end of the Bohunk-Jew's stinking new asphalt connecting road, a farmer drove in on an old belching John Deere tractor, dragging a log chain of some sort behind him, like an old-style gasoline truck with a spark-safety chain. Racket, jumble, chaos.

That's when I spotted Batterman, down at the other end with the farmer and his tractor. And then I got what was my first good in-the-flesh look at the Bohunk himself. As big as Batterman, if not a hair taller, maybe a few pounds heavier. He was all I'd expected him to be. You can predict, in a good many cases, I've found. Name me a type. I can come pretty close without bothering to leave my armchair.

Pick a name, a type—I can predict it. Carl Crowder, the real estate shark (about the last of his line in these parts; they've sold all but the last few parcels and lots, all but the crumbs and one or two more family places like mine—sold, resold, subdivided, sold, resold again) in Wautoma. Alcoholic of course. Soft money coming easily in postwar land booms does that. But not so it can be noticed at a distance. No, at a distance of fifteen, maybe ten feet, he'll look pretty dapper, shoes shined,

59

trousers creased, tie pulled up to his collar and clipped down to his shirt, shirt pressed, hat clean and blocked. At ten feet you can see the dipsomaniac in his too-florid cheeks, the tiny ruptured veins in the end of his nose. But it's the scent gives away a Carl Crowder type, neat as a sandwich sign on his chest. Too much hair oil, too much and too sweet shaving lotion, and then at six feet away you notice he's always sucking a scented lozenge of some sort, tucked away in the pouch of his cheek or under his tongue. It doesn't take a certified genius to understand it's all to smother the odor of whiskey on his breath. A man that neat is that neat because there's so much dirt in the way he comes by his living, and he's not too stupid to know it himself. You see, quickly enough, how a Carl Crowder type has trouble keeping his hand steady enough to use a fountain pen, how he continually smokes cigarettes that make him cough like a consumptive. I *know* the Carl Crowder type!

The Bohunk-Jew is not quite that easy. The trouble is he's not the sort I'd bother much about seeing. Why would anyone—in his right mind, that is? Why should I have noticed the type before?

But if you bothered to look at all, they've always been around. Imagine a man, just an ordinary, plain sort of man. Then blow him up with air-or-whatever, until his body thickens, bloats, and you can't tell where his waist is, nor where his swollen head joins his shoulders, because the neck is somehow lost, so at a distance it's only the distended suggestion of a man you're seeing. His fingers are lost in thick mitten-hands, and there's a potato of a nose in the middle of the head, but eyes and mouth are lost. It's a crude something you see at a distance when you look at the Bohunk-Jew, and that's where you always see him, because two and three generations back you never saw him except out in a field between the spread handles of a horsedrawn plow, breaking topsoil, because that's what he was suitably constructed to do, with hands that might as well have been mittenclamps to fit plow handles, and blocks of feet inside heavy boots well suited for balance and traction in deep furrows. One generation back you still saw him only at a

60

distance (without eyes or mouth or fingers), if a bit closer, because he was still armpit-deep in a ditch with his mitten-hands clamped on the business end of an idiotstick, or up high in the cab of a teamster's van, or hunched like a surly trained bear at a bench or a lathe in a machine shop, or if still turning over topsoil in his field, it was at his proper distance, when you didn't worry that he didn't look a proper, ordinary, plain man, because he was perched high on his tractor seat, too busy to look up or speak, and you didn't need to notice him at all in the first place.

I didn't see him truly close at hand until the day of his opening. (*I might have guessed. Would you mind telling me what's this hoo-ha about a quarter?*) I didn't see him close at hand the first time I went over to Prader's resort in my boat. Close at hand, the roughness, the crudity, the gross consensus simply bangs in your eye! But I didn't see him closely then. I might have gone on down his stinking-to-high-heaven new asphalt connecting road for a better look. I might have stepped out from the shadows of the pine trees, but Batterman saw me, coming away from the Jew-Bohunk and the farmer with his noisy John Deere down at the other end of the road, down by the beached water slide. Young Batterman saw me.

I saw him coming before he waved. I did not wave back, for fear someone else would see me, think I was waving to them as well. I stepped back beneath the pine trees, out of sight. Batterman stuck his hands in his hip pockets like some county farmboy in to prowl the streets of Wautoma of a Friday night when all the stores on the main drag stay open late, and the pickup trucks are parked front-end into the high curb, fender to fender, farmer families crammed together in the cabs to watch the boys and girls walk the sidewalks, jostling one another in what must be a rude country courtship.

"Mr. Spaulding?" he said, stopping in the middle of the new asphalt, cocking his head like a robin not sure if I was a stick or a nightcrawler.

"I'd as soon you didn't announce it to the entire county," I said. Batterman is a soft-spoken man, but will come out with a

61

voice fit for a fishmarket if it's a question or a flat denial he's uttering. He dug his hands a little deeper in his pockets and came on into the shade with me.

"I thought it was you I recognized."

"Your eyes are better than mine. They should be, you're decidedly a younger man than I am," I said. He smiled. He reminds me of Phil, the trap horse my father kept until he left to join the Expeditionary Force. A good horse, but nothing special, what the English call a hack, what farmers used to call a plug. Just a horse, good natured and willing, but good only for ordinary work, without the spirit that makes one horse better than another. "Cat that ate the canary," I said.

"What? Oh." He smiles again, the way our old trap horse Phil used to pull back his lips when the bit in his mouth was bothering him. He looked down at his feet like he was discovering them on the end of his legs for the first time, scraped the toe of his shoe in the sand.

"Cat got your tongue as well in the bargain," I said.

"How's that?" Batterman said, looking up at me, shying his glance away out at the township boys pretending to paint the pier. Smiling again like our old trap horse Phil. He could afford to grin now, it wasn't him meeting the payroll at the end of the month. Not until he'd had time to get himself in over his ears in that tavern over in Redgranite he was buying into now, that is.

"Your eyes may be good, but your hearing's fading fast for a young fellow your age," I said.

"You're about the last person in the world I expected to see shining around here, Mr. Spaulding," he said when there was nowhere left to look at instead of answering me.

"You would be one to know that," I said, "but I'd suppose you were far too busy packing your bags for the getaway to care about such matters." That horse-faced smile again! "And tickled pink to see the last of us all, by your looks," I said.

"You must of heard wrong, Mr. Spaulding."

"In what respect?"

"I'm moving my family over to Redgranite and all here in a

62

few days, but I'm staying on here. For the summer is all," he said. And looked down at his shoes again.

"Why not?" I said loudly. Too loud. The boys on the pier looked over in our direction for a moment before they got back to subjects that held their interest. "Why in God's half-acre not?" I said, too loudly.

"What do you—" Batterman tried to speak.

"Of course you'll stay on here to work for that damned Yahoo! Of course! You'll stay on two seasons, three if he'll ask you, won't you? He'll need you to show him the ropes, break him in with the township people who matter, the council. Of a certainty you'll stay on here to grease the skids for him any way you can!" I said.

Then I had gotten all of that sort of thing out of me that was going to come out this day. It was pointless to shout at Batterman. He stood there, as big as a horse, staring down at the toes of his shoes, his hands crammed into his hip pockets, like a schoolboy in the principal's office. Like our old horse Phil, standing in the trap's traces, his head drooping down in the heat while he waited for us all to climb in the trap, for Father to flip the reins on his back, start him walking again.

"Mr. Spaulding," he said, lifting his head, dropping it, sighing, a little like the sound a horse makes trying to blow a fly out of his nostril.

"Forget I said it," I said. "Dismiss it from your mind. It does nothing and nobody any good."

"I only came over to speak to you because I figured it was me you were looking for," Batterman said.

"It most assuredly would not be him, would it."

"I'd say not." He pulled his hands out of his pockets like they weighed twenty pounds each, folded his arms across his chest. "I've got to get after some work here," he said.

"No doubt. Do forget the way I spoke to you. I must say it galls me to see you, of all people, running his dirty errands for him." He looked at me, the way a slightly stupid and lazy animal, a horse standing in the traces, will look back to see where the driver went, the way a dog will look up without

63

lifting its head from its paws on the rug when its master walks through the room, and then smiled. Batterman smiled at me like I was the village idiot.

"I don't understand you at all, Mr. Spaulding," he said. "This is my job. I'm a family man, Mr. Spaulding. I sold out my interest in this to Lewinski, and the deal is I stay with him this summer."

"Forget it," I said. "Put it out of your mind. Talking does no good at all."

He looked at me some more, like I was Chinaman dug his way through the center of the earth, popped out of hole at his feet, gabbing at him in Chinese. I knew how I'd wasted it all, the sleeplessness, risking life and limb with my boat to cross the lake to this place. I might as profitably have expressed myself to a tree, the heap of stones the mason worked with at the other end of the road. "You'd better get on with your work," I said.

"Yeah. Take it easy, Mr. Spaulding."

"Take it easy yourself. You're the one contracted himself out to a master, not I. You'd better tell him to hurry if he wants to get open to the public. He doesn't even have the slide in the water, or is that what the tractor's for?" I said.

He whipped himself around to squint through the sun at the racket they were making at the far end of the road. The tractor was chained to the water slide now, pulling the chain taut, the tower rocking at the top like a tree about to fall, the massive raft itself making a grating sound we could hear all the way down at our end of the road, even with the roaring of the farmer's old tractor, as it moved on the sand and gravel.

"They're hauling it off, not in," Batterman said.

"What?" I had to speak loudly to be heard through the noise. "Say that again," I said.

"They're not dragging it out in the water. He's having it hauled up where they can tear it up for scrap without fouling the beach. We're not putting the slide out, Mr. Spaulding," he said. "Lewinski's junking it."

"You don't make any sense, Batterman. What in God's

64

name are you talking about?" He stepped close to me before he spoke, as if he thought my hearing was bad.

"The Polack's scrapping it because he thinks the liability insurance on it will break him or something. I don't know," Batterman said. "He's scrapping it," he said. "When they get it hauled up off the beach they'll knock it apart to salvage what lumber they can," he said, and midway through it, his face close to mine, speaking loudly to get through to what he thought was my old man's hearing, they must have hit some sort of snag down there with the water slide, because the racket stopped, and Batterman finished up shouting at me like I was stone deaf. He spun around to see if he'd been overheard by the boys on the pier, the workers on the pavilion porch. "What the damn hell," he said.

"I heard you," was all I found to say.

"Look, Mr. Spaulding."

"Don't bother," I said. And then I said, "Boy, I knew old John Prader himself before you were ever born. I saw John Prader build this resort while my own father was off dying in their war. I watched John Prader have that slide built, right here in the ground we're standing on. I watched them drag it out and float it on the water. I saw John Prader go down it on the seat of his britches to test it out. He was wearing a cut-off pair of old farmer's denim britches, and a sleeveless undershirt. He was bald as Job's turkey even in those days."

He was looking at me like it was him that was deaf now, the way old farmers sitting on the benches out in front of the Co-op in Wautoma look at passing Yahoo women with their hair in plastic rollers, the way a stupid traphorse will look at you when you take his bridle in your hand and push on him to make him back up into the cart's traces.

"Mr. Spaulding—" he tried to say.

"Save your breath. You'll need it to talk to your Jew. Don't waste it on a senile old galoot who should have kicked off years ago to save his sanity."

"I've got work to do," he said shrugging, unfolding his arms, jamming his hands back into his hip pockets.

65

"No doubt," I said. He started to go. "You," I said, and he stopped, turned back to me. "I knew you, Batterman, when you were a snot kid spent all your waking time out here at John Prader's beach. I used to sit over there under the trees, my mother and I, and watch you cavort out there in the water like a ring-tailed monkey. You used to stick that adhesive tape on your skin for the whole summer. I knew." I tried to go on speaking, because for a moment he seemed to be listening to me, but there wasn't anything that was worth the words for all the good it might do.

"Mr. Spaulding?" Batterman said.

"What?"

"So what's the point?" he said.

"Exactly," I said. "You'd best get on with your work. They'll be looking for you in a minute." They were revving up the John Deere tractor again. "That's it exactly," I said, and, "Get on about your business. I have nothing more to say to you. Or anyone else." And he walked away from me, down the middle of the stinking new asphalt road, to where they were pulling the slide up the slope, onto a stretch of level, open ground, where they could knock it to pieces for scrap salvage without messing up the beach. I followed him with my eyes until the sun was too much for me. I had to look away, close my eyes, shake my head to clear it.

During the war, their second war, we'd drive over to Prader's shortly after lunch. Highway 21 was always good for a cluster of hitchhikers in those days, groups of three and four kids crowding the shoulder of the road so that you had to straddle the center line to avoid clobbering one of them, wanting a ride to Prader's, or into Wautoma. They weren't so old they could afford the dignity to snub bicycles, and I saw no reason I should risk my vehicle or my life by offering a lift to some crazy kid. In any case, I wouldn't have invited a stranger to share the auto with my mother.

It was the high point of her day. After her strokes, even the first mild one, there was so little she could enjoy. Then, while

66

their war was still on, she was still able to take care of herself, dress, bathe, eat, but she was without the stamina for walking or boating or digging a bit in the rock garden she had kept on the slope above the beach for so many summers. I felt it incumbent upon me to take her about and around in our automobile as much as I could. It was fortunate we were able to circumvent gasoline rationing.

Summer, and the sun is hot, the air motionless in mid-afternoon. I could roll the windows all the way down, crack the wings in front and back to catch the car's airstream if it weren't for Mother. I open the scoop in the hood (I keep my automobile clean, so no rush of dust and grit flies up in our faces as we pull out onto 21 from the lake road). I remember with regret for their passing the windshields of bygone autos, in two pieces, that could be opened, canted to let the fresh air flow in and over us (the three of us!) in the front seat.

It is summer, hot, the air motionless, and the clusters of hitchhikers up ahead before the first big curve in the highway seem to be standing next to a shimmering puddle of water that is always there in the distance, evaporating, reappearing farther on as we approach the three or four boys standing in a slouch on the shoulder of the road, arms extended into the path of my automobile, thumbs up. Sometimes they motion vaguely, as if weary with the heat, as if the heat of the day were a viscous-but-colorless-fluid in which they are suspended. As I pass I half-expect them to rock slowly in response to the fluid waves of motion set up by the force of my passing automobile.

"Oh, Lee, why not stop and give them a ride," Mother says.

"That would be fine," I say, "but suppose they wanted my wallet instead of a ride?"

"How silly," she says, looking away from me to watch the pine trees, the glimpses of cranberry marsh visible where there are short gaps in the wall of trees.

"It could be against Wisconsin state law, for all we know," I say, "and it's just as likely they're looking for someone going all the way to town." Mother dabs at her throat and forehead

67

with the handkerchief, wadded in a ball, in her hand, does not answer me.

The short drive seems longer than it should be (there is the sensible but unenforced wartime speed limit on all roads). The heat and harsh sunlight reflecting off bits of mica and quartz in the concrete makes our short trip seem longer and slower, broken only by the near-motionless clusters of hitchhikers. As if we, Mother and I, our automobile, are suspended in this sameness of no-motion and quiet. I feel a trickle of sweat course down over my ribs from my armpit. The tires make a sound, half-flapping, half-licking, on the pavement. There is a radio in the automobile, but we do not want, either of us, to hear about their war.

All changes when we reach Prader's. I brake the auto early and often, just in case someone has come up close behind me without my noticing in the rearview mirror. I roll my window down now, put out my arm to signal. Mother puts her handkerchief away in her purse, gently touches the back of her head to be sure her hair is in place (she can still brush, comb, set her own hair, until after the first severe stroke, which will come during the winter, in 1947, during the great snow that paralyzes Chicago for four days). The warm air suddenly blowing in on my face is a blessing after the still, muggy interior of the closed auto.

The blistering brightness of the open strip of state highway, the green of pines and wild shrubs and pasture grass that is dull, almost hazy under the sun's pulsing, are behind us. Ahead is the cool dimness of shade, the pavilion of Prader's resort under the overhanging canopy of thick-leafed branches, Prader's giant elms. Slowing the auto to a near-stop, I turn in, the tires' lick-slap turns to loud, satisfying crunches and crackling on the gravel and sand of Prader's resort road. Now we see people entering and leaving the restaurant and bar, the young people dancing and lounging under the pavilion roof. As we coast into the shady tunnel of the elms, searching for a good place to park, we see the flash of water like the glint of scraps

68

of foil turning in the lake breeze. We hear, as I slow the auto to park in the darkness of the shade, the chugging of the hand-pump that wets the long sheetmetal chute of the water slide, and we hear, as I turn off the ignition, the shooshing noise of one of the young boys going down the slide, the light smack of his body hitting the water, skimming across it.

"Well, let's don't sit here forever on my account, Lee," Mother says.

"I'll have Prader help me with a chair for you," I say.

"I wish you wouldn't bother. I can sit up on the porch like anyone else."

"It's no bother. You know you'd rather be under the trees here where you can see the beach and all."

"I hate to make a fuss," she calls after me as I go to find old John Prader. He will be behind the bar in the restaurant, talking with customers, or out on the pavilion porch, getting the breeze off the lake, available to take care of it if one of the young people loses money in the juke box.

He never alludes to my father's opposition to his building this resort, always asks after my mother's health, always quick, cheerful, taking one side of the huge wooden chair, more than carrying his share of the weight as we carry the chair across the dirt-and-gravel road to a nice spot under the pine trees.

"And how's yourself?" John Prader will ask politely when the chair is in place and we have gotten our breath.

"I can't complain." I am friendly, correct, but do not encourage familiarity in him. My own father, after all, strongly opposed the building of the resort, would surely have prevented it had their war not taken him away. I can admit to myself, when I choose to think on it, that I do not like questions about my health. Older and less vigorous looking men have not been so fortunate in obtaining selective service deferments (I truly believe their war, the second one, brought on the decline in my mother's health—her fear that I, too, would be taken from her).

"Well," John Prader says, "take care now."

"We shall." And I go to the parked automobile to help Mother to her chair. After that there is very little until we go.

It is surprising how little I recall, specifically, of their wars. The first one was important to me because there were letters from my father, passages of which he intended Mother to read aloud to me, all through the days of that 1917–1918 winter, which ended with spring and the news of my father's death in action in France. I read the newspaper dispatches, and, like so many boys, kept a map of France with colored pins to mark the front. Like the other boys at my school I tried to believe I hated the kaiser. I remember all that, the speeches of Woodrow Wilson, the Liberty Bond drives, so much of it, and so little of their second war.

"Would you like a nice cold gin collins?" I ask Mother, standing beside her chair.

"Not just now, Lee. Perhaps later. You go if you like, I'm fine here just as I am."

"I can wait until you're ready." I remain at her side, watching the beach, the swimmers, the boys' antics on the water slide.

For me, there is very little of their war. Oh yes, of course, gasoline rationing, the books of stamps for meat, shoes. The little things my mother insisted on, flattening tin cans and saving bacon grease to turn in to the butcher, and yes, the constant talk of it on the radio, newspapers, and buying war bonds because Mother thought we should. But I did not *care* that we won the naval engagement at Midway, nor that we had landed in Sicily or Normandy, did not bother to look at maps, and later, was not moved at the death of this Roosevelt (my parents very much admired the first one). I did not wonder what sort of man the little haberdasher from Independence would prove to be, was not astounded by the atomic bomb, did not ask myself if I believed Adolph Hilter dead in Berlin or alive and on the way to Argentina in a submarine.

What should I have *cared* for?

"Are you positive I can't fetch you something to drink? A soft drink?" I ask my mother.

"No, Lee. Not just now. Later, I think. I'm fine here, really."

I can *see* their war from where I stand directly beside my mother's chair. Three furloughed sailors stand just inside the pavilion, just under the edge of the roof, arms folded, legs crossed. They slouch, watching the pairs of young girls who jitterbug to the strident music of the pavilion jukebox. The sailors seem posed, as if seeking attitudes of irritated disdain to conceal their reluctance to approach the pairs of dancing township high school girls. As if they guard against approaching the girls for fear the authority of their white starched uniforms will fall away if they are awkward or unsuccessful, as if they fear their little white hats (suddenly I recall a dark blue child's sailor suit, mine when I was no more than six or seven!) will fall off the backs of their arrogant, lean heads, were they to move toward the dancing girls.

I stand beside my mother's chair, under the pine trees shading the crest of the gentle slope above the noisy, crowded beach, and I see cocky sailors make rituals of cigarettes, slow-nursing bottles of beer. I watch them watch the girls dance jitterbug steps to the strident music of John Prader's jukebox, the soles of their saddle-shoes making a rhythmic scuffing sound on the pavilion floor. I stand beside my mother's chair, see the gasoline rationing stickers on the windows of the parked automobiles clustered in the umbrellas of shade, see the autos belching naptha (cheap, noxious gasoline substitute) as they lurch into the resort road from the state highway. Men of my father's generation fumble at hand rolling cigarettes, little bags of Bull Durham held in their teeth as they stand, backs to the wind, to shield the troughs of paper, nudge the flakes of loose tobacco into place with unsure fingers (because they lack my patience to stand in the long lines at grocery stores when cigarettes go on sale). This is all of their war I care to know, or to remember.

Were it not that I want to be able to discuss things intelligently with my mother, I would read no daily *Tribune*, would

71

not fool each evening with the dials of our cottage radio to coax in the broadcasts from WGN in Chicago.

I watch the young people on the beach, swimming, cavorting on the water slide. There are always children on the beach, most of them from Wautoma. They walk the two and one-half miles from town, barefoot, towels and swimsuits rolled, clutched under their arms. They seem to alternate between spurts of energy, wrestling, throwing sand, burrowing in the sand like turtles come ashore to lay eggs.

Simply running, running for the sheer need to run. Into the water to swim a few strokes, splash at one another, gang up on a victim to give him or her a merciless dunking. Out of the water again, seeming to rise in the shallows like exhausted amphibians, blowing like seals, skins deep brown with day after day of this full summer sun, gleaming under a second skin of clear lake water as they march in to the beach to flop, roll over once or twice (coating themselves with sand the way a doughnut is coated with sugar crystals). Then they lie breathing heavily until some internal alarm sets them off again tussling, running.

"I think I could do with that cold drink now, Lee."

"What shall I get? A collins? You decide. I'll have whatever you have."

There are always one or two—no more—who do nothing but swim. Usually it is a solitary young man, who will clip his nostrils shut with a professional swimmer's device that is secured on a black cord around his neck. I watch him walk to the end of John Prader's pier, adjusting the clip on his nose, as fussy as an old woman with her pince-nez, stopping before he reaches the end of the pier to carefully insert rubber plugs in his ears. He walks to the end of the pier, stops with his feet together, toes over the edge. He breathes deeply several times, his arms moving sympathetically at his sides, then is motionless only a split-second before executing a perfect dive. He does not surface until the last of his momentum is spent.

Then he swims. He does nothing but swim, steady athlete's laps defined by the end of the pier and the water slide raft.

72

Persistent and methodical, the movement of his wiry body as fluid as the water he moves through, his face a pale flash seen only in the intervals when he must turn his head up to breathe, his mouth a small, perfect circle.

"Let's have a collins then," Mother says.

"It won't take a minute."

"Ask Mr. Prader to go lightly on the gin if you will. The two of you will have to carry me home in this chair if you don't watch out."

"Don't be silly," I say. "I'll see to it it's a mild one." And, "I'll be right back. Do you want anything from the automobile?"

"Go on, Lee. I'm fine just as I am."

And I do take my time getting our drinks from John Prader's bar. I pause before leaving, to look out once again at the beach, the lake. I measure the slow demise of this deep summer afternoon (1943? 1944? 1945?) by the change in texture and hue of the surface of Silver Lake.

In mid-afternoon it is the brilliant glint of shivering foil in the wind, looking sharp, jagged enough to shred the hide of man or beast foolish enough to embrace it. Later, it is light and soft in the sun, dark and firmer, in the shadows of weeping willows and pines on the shore. Later still, when we prepare to leave, it is blue, deepening ever more quickly toward black even as I look for a last moment before leaving with my mother.

The afternoon, the early evening of this deep summer day pass. Time passes, but if I watch carefully, pay attention, it will pass more slowly, seem, in a given instant, as if it does not really pass away at all, as if there is no such thing as time.

I nod, as I make my way to the restaurant-bar, to people who know me, people who have kept summer homes on Silver Lake for ten, fifteen, some of them twenty years. I nod to the occasional permanent resident. Wautoma businessman taking an afternoon away from his store to enjoy the sun and the lake, retired couple from Milwaukee or Chicago, come to live out their retirement here, on the lake or in Wautoma. I nod,

73

they nod, we wave, occasionally speak, though seldom beyond a greeting.

"Two gin collins, if you will," I say to John Prader, who leans against his bar, watching the young people's antics on the distant water slide. Their shouts and screaming are muted here, muffled by the stand of pines half-concealing them, muted by the heavy shade of the large elms towering above the pavilion building. The screened interior of the restaurant-bar somehow strikes me as a timeless place. I think, suddenly, of time, as I watch John Prader make our drinks, as I take money from my wallet, lean against the bar.

"Can I request two of those cherries for my mother? She's very fond of them."

"Certainly," John Prader says, unscrewing the lid of the jar of maraschino cherries again, stabbing carefully with his long fork. "No trouble at all."

I am thinking how suddenly very old and infirm John Prader looks to me. His hair is only a vestige, the gloss of his scalp shining through beneath the combed strands. His skin is very pale, the lines in his face, horizontal pleats in his forehead, twin troughs moving from each side of his nose down to the sagging corners of his mouth. His light brown eyes are watery, a vacant cast in them, as if he is not thinking of the business at hand, but of some time and place long past. John Prader is getting old, I suddenly think.

"There you go," he says. "And I thank you," as he counts change into my waiting palm. I try to note aging in his voice, to hear some catch or crack in his speech, some rasp or rattle in his throat, an awkwardness or thickness in his tongue that will serve as corroboration. But it is an impression only, from within me, some mood of my own.

"I'll bring your glassware back," I say, trying to account for why it is I continue to stand at the bar, a special, tall, frosted collins glass in each hand, beads already forming on the glasses, looking stupidly at John Prader.

He waves his hand. I need not concern myself for his glassware. The collins drinks seem very heavy, and the restaurant-

74

bar interior seems very, very warm and close, and I feel weak, fear I am dizzy. Only deliberate effort enables me to make my way to the screen door, nudge it open with my shoulder. I almost believe it will be dark when I step outdoors onto the pavilion porch, that everyone will be gone. As if a long, long period of time has passed since I went inside, everything changed.

No! I step out onto the porch, and it is as if no time at all has passed!

The furloughed sailors in their spanking white blouses and bellbottoms, the small, sparkling white seaman's caps stuck jauntily on the backs of their heads, still hold their stiff poses at the edge of the dance floor, still breaking pose only for a ritual lighting of cigarettes or to unwrap sticks of chewing gum. The pairs of jitterbugging township girls, skirts hitting above their knees, feet in saddle-shoes and thick, woolly ankle socks, flying to the strident music of the jukebox, making the same scuffing noise, punctuated by the thumping of their heels.

It is still late afternoon. The water has only gone green in my absence. 1943? 1944? 1945? I cross the dirt-and-gravel resort road, the ice in our collins drinks tinkling, and there is my mother in her chair under the pines.

"Two cherries! You're much too good to me, sir."

"You have to be a special friend of the barkeep to rate that," I say.

The surface of Silver Lake has turned green in my absence, flowing from light, almost pastel hues in the distance under the still-bright sun to darker shades in close, under the overhanging branches of weeping willows, within the reach of the shadows cast by the taller pines we sit under.

I stand close beside my mother's chair. We drink our delicious icy-cold gin collins drinks slowly, watch the young people swimming. It is as if I had not left her side to get our drinks, as if no time at all has passed.

"That certainly hits the spot," she says.

"It does indeed!"

I know some of the young people by name. The Booth

75

cousins, crazy boys both, grandnephews of old Ward Booth, who, when he retired from cucumber and melon farming—the only viable cash crops possible in the sandy soil of Waushara County—built a ramshackle filling station and grocery directly across the lake from our place, on the county road. The filling station and grocery as seedy as old Ward himself. Their war cut off the supply of migrant Mexican stoop labor necessary to harvest melons and cucumbers, and one needs more friends in state politics than old Ward Booth had to procure the German prisoners of war some farmers used to bring in their crops.

The Booth boys are crazy boys, muscular as orangutans, shouting back and forth across the water to one another like frenzied apes in separate cages. The Batterman boy is no less crazy, taller, leaner, more intelligent looking than the run of country boys I watch fooling on the water slide these late afternoons in deep summer.

There is something fine, near-perfect, in watching the Batterman boy fool about the water slide. He is well over six feet, wearing only faded boxer-style swim trunks, the seat in them worn with sliding down the sheet-metal chute of the giant water slide. He looks like an Indian at this distance, his skin tanned dark brown by day after clear day of this swimming in the hot sun, his hair worn a bit longer than even that of the boys who do not affect the fashion of the Heinie haircuts, brought on by their war.

Young Batterman's hair is very dark, crow's-wing black when wet. When he comes up for air, rises, breaks the surface of the water, he seems, for a moment, as if he will shoot all the way up and out of the lake, perhaps soar as high, higher than the top of the water slide tower, there pause, perhaps execute a flawless jackknife, plummet back down into the water, clean as a bullet, disappear into a froth. He rises, continues to rise until he is near half out of the water. In the midst of this, at the peak of his thrust above the surface of the lake, this young Batterman fellow whips his head in a three-quarter circle, spraying water from his head, neck, shoulders, his thick shock of glossy-black-wet hair flying back out of his eyes, plastering itself back against the top of his head. And then he slips back up to his chin in the water, stretches out, strokes powerfully, smoothly, back to the water slide raft. He seems to no more than touch the edge of the raft with his fingers, catapults out of the water, twists, turns, sits on the raft with his feet in the water, his shoulders rising, falling with deep, relaxed breathing. Or squats like an Indian on his haunches, staring out at something or nothing in the far distance of Silver Lake, gone green now in the late afternoon that teeters on the brink of becoming early evening.

"Oh, Lee, look what he's done on his back! There, that boy, the one at the pump now!"

"His name is Batterman, I think," I tell her. "He's from Wautoma. I gather he's something of a football star or hero or whatever. That's plain adhesive tape, Mother. When he takes it off, it wears away or whatever, the letters stand out against his tan as good as if they were branded on him."

The Batterman boy stands at the slide's water pump, working the handle back and forth rapidly with both hands, lubricating the sheet-metal slide chute with water for his friends, the crazy, simian-like Booth boys. They scramble up the tower ladder like monkeys ascending the trunk of a coconut palm. He looks a tall, slender Indian at this distance, and I know, even as I register the impression of his near-perfect physical proportions, that he weighs more than he appears to. He is the same physical type my father was, what used to be called rangy, wiry.

Young Batterman mans the water slide pump with both arms, his stance set, one foot well in front of the other, to give himself maximum leverage. Squinting against the bright sun, shading my eyes with my free hand (collins drink in the other), I discern the rippling flow of tensed muscles in his arms, shoulders, tanned, broad back.

On his back (foolery, the sort of thing his peers will admire) he has taped letters, common adhesive tape, his nickname: HORSE. The adhesive tape block letters are stark, dead white against his deeply tanned skin. At summer's end he will

77

remove the tape, the nickname HORSE then a pale flesh color against the full tan of his summer's swimming, something to amuse his friends (the Booth boys, others) with as they dress in the Wautoma Township High School locker room for football games. The Batterman boy is some sort of local star, hero of the game. Township merchants boast he will go to the state university at Madison, become famous, if only this war ends in time.

"It's a wonder they don't break their necks."

"What? Excuse me, Mother. I wasn't listening. Oh no. I think you're exaggerating."

"Knock on wood," she says, rapping the arm of her chair lightly.

Nothing will happen to the young people, no matter what antics they dream up for the water slide. They come down on their stomachs, backwards, lying on their backs, in tandem. They highdive off the back of the slide tower, jackknife and doubletwist, cannonballs from a height of forty feet, sending up a mushroom of water. Nothing will happen.

It is late afternoon, the sun still well up in the sky, the beach alive with small children, the girls and sailors in the pavilion, people driving in off the state highway for food and drink. The dedicated swimmer has finished his methodical training laps, sits now on the end of the pier, exhausted, shaking his head to get the drops of water out of his ears, but young Batterman and his friends are still fooling on the slide.

John Prader will still be behind his bar, or out on the pavilion porch to get the lake breeze. My mother tips her collins glass, reaches in with two fingers to get the maraschino cherries she so enjoys. I stand close to her chair, watching, watching it all. Only the hue of the surface of Silver Lake has changed, a darker green, running to near black in the shadows along the bank. If it were not for this, it would be difficult to say with certainty that any time at all had passed.

Yet, it does pass. Batterman and his friends are sliding and diving less, the chug of the slide's pump is heard only now and again, and the dedicated swimmer gets to his feet, walks up the

78

pier, past us, nodding shyly to us, is gone. The small children on the beach now kneel in the sand to roll their towels up, stand, brush at the sand on their legs, tuck towels under arms, walk off in the direction of Wautoma.

"I'm sorry to be such a bother, Lee, but I really am feeling chilly."

"I'll get your wrap from the auto."

"You'd better take Mr. Prader's glasses to him, hadn't you?"

"Of course. I won't be a minute. Shall I get your wrap first?"

"Take the glasses back. I'll be fine. It's just getting on a little late in the day for me is all."

I hurry across the resort road, gravel scraping under my shoes, reach the pavilion porch before I'm aware that the jukebox is no longer playing the strident jitterbug music. Where have the posing, furloughed sailors, the pairs of dancing girls gone?

From the porch I survey the resort area, but can find no one, nothing except the dim shape of my mother in her chair under the pine trees. She is dimming, dimmer, even as I strain my eyes to make her out there under the trees, her shape melting into the shape of the chair as the first dull edges of dusk seep into the stand of pines. I hurry into the restaurant-bar. I will speak, make small talk with John Prader, say something, anything. I will speak to John Prader, catch some hand-hold on this late afternoon becoming early evening.

But the restaurant-bar is empty. I set the glassware on the bar. They make a hollow rapping sound as I set them on the bar, look into the darkened corners of the room. I am alone.

"Mr. Prader? Mr. Prader?" My voice sounds weak to me, as if I were a tired old man, croaking for someone to come to help me. "Mr. Prader? Anyone?"

No one. It is very, very dark in the room, the screens blocking the little light of dusk that remains. I hurry outside, just as someone (Mr. Prader, back at the light switch in his kitchen) turns on the pavilion lights.

79

The lights leap on, a long row of the gaudy yellow bulbs strung on the edge of the pavilion roof, designed (they say) to repel mosquitoes (they do not work). The sand-gravel resort road is washed with the pale light from the yellow bulbs, looks now as empty, as lonely as if it were the cold cast of moonlight, as if it were gone suddenly full, deep night in the few moments I have been inside.

Mother? I look across the road to where I left her sitting. For an instant she is gone, her shape in the large wooden chair blended fully into the thickening darkness that is the stand of pine trees. *Mother?* I nearly shout, then see her, make out the even darker mass in the darkness of the pines that is my mother, her chair. I step off the pavilion porch, cross the road, walking quickly, as if hurrying will somehow arrest the hour where it is.

"Mother?"

"Where ever have you been, Lee? You must have gotten talking with Mr. Prader all this time."

"I'm sorry. No. I mean, Mr. Prader was in the back turning on the lights for the pavilion. Somewhere. I left the glasses on the bar."

"I'd begun to think you'd fallen in a hole."

"Don't be silly. Shall I get your wrap?"

"Good heavens, no! If you'll help me up out of this chair, I'd just as soon be going home if you don't mind."

"So early?" I say, taking her arm, lifting. On her feet, she stands still for a moment to get her balance. She looks at me as if I have said something indelicate.

"Early? Lee, in three-quarters of an hour you won't be able to see your hand in front of your face. You know how quickly evening comes here this time of year."

"So it does," I say, taking her right arm in my left, reaching around behind her as though I were her partner at the grand march of a formal ball, taking her left elbow gently but firmly in my left hand. "You're perfectly right. It's time for us to leave."

And I see, now that I am walking with her, supporting her,

80

slowly toward our parked automobile (a large black shape in the blackness under one of John Prader's giant elm trees, its branches blacking out the fading afterglow of dusk in the open sky) that the beach, the swimming area, the water slide are deserted. All the children have gone from the beach, all the boats tied at the pier, gone. The Batterman boy, Ward Booth's loony grandnephews, all gone. The slide tower seems a starker white against the falling dark of the sky over Silver Lake (the lake's surface now black, the breeze having died with the setting sun to leave it glassy, unruffled, like a liquid once hot, now cooling to harden like the surface of a polished, black mirror).

"They've all left," I say without meaning to.

"What?"

"I said, everyone has left, Mother."

"Of course they have. It's near dinner time, Lee."

"Yes. Here we are now. Just lean on me if you like while I get the door open for you." The automobile door, the chrome handle, are surprisingly cool to the touch. I help my mother in, see that her wrap is snug around her shoulders. She yawns politely, her eyelids flutter. I know she is very tired, that she will doze on the ride back to our cottage. I get in behind the steering wheel, close my door carefully so as not to shock her out of her repose with the noise. Through the windshield, the light is almost gone. I must turn on the headlights for safety's sake.

"I think I'm too tired to eat," she says just before I turn the key in the ignition.

"Nonsense," I say. "I'll fix us something light. We can get to bed early, get a good night's rest, feel brand new in the morning," I go on to say, knowing she is dozing already, not hearing me.

I back the automobile out into the resort road, shift into low gear, careful not to grind the gears, disturb her. There is not a solitary soul to wave goodbye to us, to even see us leave the resort.

There are still a few parked autos under the big elm trees,

81

but the owners are perhaps out fishing on the lake, or off across the county highway in one of John Prader's jerry-built rental cabins, his latest project to turn the resort from a steady income to something tapping the booming economy of their war. There is not a solitary soul about to wave or call goodbye to us.

I slowly, carefully release the clutch, hear the tires (wartime recaps) crackle over the sand-gravel (it is a *cold* sound now, as if with the fall of dusk the temperature had dropped many, many degrees, as if winter is coming, has come, and a bitter cold, dark night waits, a drive all the way to Chicago, there to wait through the winter on the hope of the next summer to come).

My headlights sweep up into the deep dusk of the sky as I brake at the crest of the rise, the access to the state highway. It is darker still, the headlights lost, diffused in the empty dusk of the sky, only the glow of the dashlights, fuel, battery, speedometer, light the interior of the auto now.

The highway is clear of traffic to left and right, safe to enter the highway now, right, toward Oshkosh, but I do not proceed. I hold my foot on the brake (my mother's head has fallen back on the seat, her mouth open in sleep), look back through the rear window at the resort. The red tail-lights of the auto cast a rosy aura on the dirt road directly behind us. The road fades into darkness, disappears for a moment before being splashed by the yellow bug-repelling lights of the pavilion. The bulk of the pavilion, Prader's fine, large house, merge with, are lost in the mass of elm trees. The lake is lost behind the mass of pines above the beach, the water slide's tower lost behind the pine trees.

If we could wait, stay through the supper hour, there would be people, sailors and dancing pairs of girls, and township boys, young Batterman, the Booths, come to join the furloughed sailors and soldiers, compete with them for the attention of the pairs of girls who dance, oblivious of them all. And there will be couples, come to sit in John Prader's restaurant-bar, drink, enjoy the cool, fresh air that blows off the lake,

82

through the pines above the beach. But we cannot wait, cannot stay.

I pull out into the state highway, accelerate slowly, very smoothly to avoid disturbing my sleeping mother. *Goodbye, I am thinking, goodnight, folks! Goodnight.*

I remember in a rush: the waxed moustache of Mr. Otto Pfaff, the music of his wife, the glass-eyed stare of a stuffed moose head, my father disappearing into our barn to grain Phil, our trap horse.

If it were not that I am (Leland Spaulding, Jr.) who I am, what I am, that I feel my responsibilities to my mother, the memory of my father (taken from me in their war!), if it were not for all this, and holding the steering wheel so tightly my wrists and knuckles hurt, if it were not for all this, my mother resting peacefully beside me (her rest is infrequent, uncertain in her old age), if it were not for this, I can conceive, can imagine myself weeping like an exhausted child, all the way home through the deepening dark of the summer night.

"What ever became of the Booth boys?" I say aloud. Nobody is near enough to hear me. The sun, the racket of the water slide tower and raft being torn to pieces too small for anything but kindling, the John Deere tractor bellowing exhaust in spurts as the farmer drags away another support, a crew of locals with sledges, axes, crowbars hacking, picking at the heap of lumber, the remains of the tower, twisted sheets of metal that were the slide. Nobody can hear me, nobody listens.

Batterman and the Jew-Bohunk stand off to one side, sidewalk supervisors, hands in pockets, squinting into the wood dust that comes up from the shredded hulk of the tower, the air above them a cloud of brown dust and blue tractor exhaust.

What ever did become of the Booth boys?

I think I set off down the slope to the beach with finding the answer to that in mind. The local boys painting the dock had taken a break, gone off somewhere at any rate, their brushes left lying across the tops of the paint cans to get tacky

83

in the sun. My shirt was plastered to my skin, perspiration beading out on my face, gathering in the folds of my neck.

I feared I would be dizzy, lacking the strength to lift my boat off the lip of the shore, that I might take a header into the drink when I went to hop on the bow, but I shoved off, climbed aboard, and somebody or something was still on my side, because the Waterwitch caught on the third pull with the mended starter rope.

I could find out what happened to the Booth boys. The Waterwitch runs like a Swiss clock, and the lake is, for the moment at least, clear of Yahoo fishermen and swimmers and speedboat racers crossing their own wakes just to feel the bounce lift their butt-ends off the cushions for an instant.

I could make a bee-line past Chicago Point (named for the Chicago millionaire who originally owned all that frontage; my father knew him well—the frontage broken now into Yahoo-size lots packed with Yahoo cabins), dock at Booth's store. Old Ward Booth. To what end?

Spaulding? he might likely say. *Leland Spaulding? You went off to be an officer in the first war in France.* Or, as likely, *Spaulding? Spaulding? I never heard of any man with the name Spaulding.*

To what end confront Ward Booth? The old man barely able to see anything more distinct than the shapes of passing autos on the county road, half-deaf so that I would have to shout in his ear like some Yahoo wife calling her children in from the beach to eat lunch. His mind, memory frayed to the point he cannot make the jump from one thread to another, and so once he catches hold of a fragment of the past (it can be 1910, 1925, 1940, the day before yesterday) he sits tight there, talks as if the world is that world (1910, 1925, 1940). You can shout your throat sore for all the good it will do toward getting the old man any closer in time and place to where you happen to be.

To what end stand out in the blistering sun, waste my time and energy on old Ward Booth, unshaven, lost behind his thick spectacles, his frail hands in his lap, the veins in his hands, throat, at his temples a blue-black, pulsing like his heart means

84

to last forever. The old man has a tick, a way of nodding (some disease of dotage?) always, as if saying yes, yes, certainly, of course, yes, to everything, to autos passing on County DD, to me when I stand in the heat of open sun, shouting until my throat is raw, to all things and places and times (today, 1940, 1925, 1910). Nodding, yes, yes, to even the weak push of his own heart that seems unlikely ever to want to quit.

No. Not this day. My old Waterwitch outboard ran like a fine clock, and I stayed on a course for my cottage, hugging the shoreline, past all the swimming rafts floated on oil drums, empty now of Yahoos, past the continuous strip of beach deserted now of Yahoos, like sandy ruins after a great fire, their charcoal pits still smoking a little where they left them untended (they'll burn these woods one day!) to flee the mosquitoes that come with late afternoon.

I went home, ate an early supper, went early to bed, fell easily and deeply asleep, but toward morning woke from a dream about Ward Booth.

I dreamed Ward Booth was speaking to me, telling me the whole story of his ninety years of life, and I stood somewhere in hot sun spotted with the broken shade of very tall pine trees, listening to it all. There was little coherence in the dream, or if there was, I do not recall it coherently. I seemed to think I was standing a goodly distance away from the old man, but his voice was loud, clear (his half-swallowed, gravel-scratched voice in life turned up in volume), as if he spoke directly in my ear, as if his voice were coming from inside my ear.

I cannot remember the dream beginning. It simply was there, old Ward Booth was telling me the story of ninety years of life, but I could not follow it.

I caught moments, snatches. He remembered all the boys and men who went away to the world wars, the circumstances of his comfortable retirement from cucumber and melon farming (he described the excellent drainage of the sandy soils of Waushara County), how he remembered me as a small boy at my father's side, that he could recite the full names of the first

85

dozen people to purchase property, build summer homes on Silver Lake. Now and again he would break his narrative to say things, such as the fact that his vision was excellent despite his ninety years, that only fools took his thick spectacles for a sign of failing eyesight, that he had the strongest heart of any man in the states of Wisconsin, Illinois, and Minnesota, that his ninety years proved this, and that he intended to live much, much longer than his mother had.

I could not follow it. This is gathered from what I could hold onto after I woke, very frightened by this dream, early the next morning. I remember that I wanted to hear his story, wished he would speak more slowly, that he might begin again at the beginning, and I remember waiting to interrupt him (I could *not* speak in this dream!), to say: *what about your grand-nephews?*

Is it any wonder I was thinking I was sure to go mad? It never occurred to me to simply ask Batterman, the next time I went to Prader's resort. I had other things on my mind when I went back there.

The fact of the matter was, I still had to do something. It wasn't enough to just talk to people. It wasn't anything, just talking, remembering. I was too old to hike the lake road anymore, and it was no good trading insults with that pair of dipsomaniacs at Otto Pfaff's Moose Inn, no use shouting myself hoarse at Old Ward Booth (I kept recalling snatches of my frightening dream of Ward Booth's story of his life!), no point bothering Batterman to aggravation. No good.

I would have made the trip to Wautoma, talked to the people who run things, the sheriff, township council, if it would have helped. But the world has changed too much from the day when a man like my father could initiate action with a few well-placed words. That's no good anymore, because this world is not the same world. And I am not the man my father was. No good.

I could not sit in my cottage, hiding from the heat and the sun. I tried that, but that was no use, no good any longer either. It was cool in the cottage, the humidity no problem if I stayed still, sat in one of the wicker porch chairs or rested on the daybed in the parlor, my hands folded on my stomach.

It was pleasantly dark and cool with the shades pulled, and except for meals and going to the lavatory (installed when it became impossible for my mother to walk out to the outhouse with a lantern—that was 1941? 1942?). I could sit or lie the day and night through. I had no difficulty sleeping soundly nights either. I recall no dreams, no dreams of anything after the frightening dream of old Ward Booth.

I had thought to enjoy this. When I returned from the resort, dreamed my dream of Ward Booth's ninety years, I had thought (knowing I could no longer hike the lake road, would not waste talk on Weller or Batterman, not waste talk on people in Wautoma) to enjoy myself. I had thought to lie quietly in my cottage, and except for meals and the lavatory, do nothing but think, think and remember. But it turned out I could not.

I sat in one of the old wicker porch chairs, the bamboo fall curtains lowered behind the screens to keep out the sun, enough space left open near the sills to let in lake breezes. I folded my hands in my lap, closed my eyes, told my legs, arms, body to relax, tried. I sat, waiting for whatever thought, memory, might care to come. When nothing came I urged it a little.

It is a new morning, I make myself think. Father and I are seated on the porch to enjoy the warmth and light of the new morning's sun. Mother is in the kitchen. We can hear her taking plates from the high cupboards, hear the sharp smacking noise of the ice-box door closing, latching, as she prepares our breakfast. Father has taken out a cigar, but will not smoke until breakfast is over. I watch, I am watching all this, wondering if we shall go into the parlor for breakfast, or if Mother will serve us out here, on the porch.

I urged this, to see and hear it, but it was not possible anymore. I heard the wickerwork creak with me as I stirred in my chair. I caught myself tapping the back of one hand with the forefinger of the other (my mother developed this habit in her last year, a nervous tic that exasperated me!). I opened my eyes.

The sunlight flared at the edges of the fall curtain, shot highlights between the strips of bamboo. The fall curtain moved slightly with the wind. The wind rustled the boughs of the tall old pines outside the cottage, the sense of dappled, shifting shadows present with me on the porch. A bluejay twanged very close to the porch.

I got up and went into the parlor, lay down on the daybed.

It was much cooler in the parlor, the night's chill still held in the walls, the shades pulled, room dark. I am usually comfortable on the parlor daybed, but the fabric felt cold and damp through the back of my shirt, the old mattress uneven, the fringed pillow hard. I stared at the ceiling, but streaks of light and shadow played there, and I was counting the laths in the ceiling, following the dark seams between them with my eyes. I closed my eyes, waited to see something.

Nothing. Blackness, darkness, and then a series of spots in pale colors that floated, closer and closer, in clusters, paled to translucence, merged, faded to blackness. I opened my eyes. The parlor, dim, streaks of light and shadow on walls and ceiling, the pedestal table, piano that I cannot play (my mother's musical ability not inherited), chairs, framed prints, artificial flowers (made in Japan, *before* their second war) in a hobnail glass vase on an endtable-magazine rack (*Reader's Digest*, *National Geographic*, old, old issues of my mother's Butterick pattern books). The cottage parlor, myself on the daybed.

It was awkward, uncomfortable, to raise my head off the pillow enough to look directly at the pictures of my parents. Their wedding portrait, my father in his A.E.F. officer's uniform, my mother in her last formal sitting, little less than a year before she died—I can tell that her expression is not right, vacant, distracted—myself as a boy, at college—Northwestern, class of 1929, just as the world fell to pieces at my feet once

88

again, their Depression, my degree in banking never tested, my father's estate in trusts that would last, that still suffice.

I raised my head from the fringed pillow, chin almost touching my chest to see the pictures clearly. My neck twinged immediately, and I knew it would give me a headache. Still, I squinted through the dim, diffused light of the parlor, focused on the pictures in their ornamental frames. Nothing.

Black and white portrait photographs, dated in style and tone, framed in ornamental frames of a kind no longer widely available, set in careful arrangement on a shelf above an old out-of-tune piano I never learned, lacked the ability, to play. A young couple, Chicago society, who invested their energies in a summer home rather than join the social whirl of Chicago lakefront society that was to come to an end with a war that destroyed the young man of good family and modest fortune and remarkable ability and aptitude for banking. A young man, still in his early thirties, the sort who felt compelled to fight in a war he could not have approved of, the considerable mark he would have made in this world a thing of imagination and regret and bitter recrimination because the man died in a war only fools could have cared about. A beautiful woman in the prime of her years, growing older so slowly. So slowly it did not seem as if the time were passing, it did not seem that time passed, and when it had there was only the old, tired, ill woman, not senile, but hesitating, slipping, balking at the brink of senility she understood waited if time lasted long enough for her. A boy less interesting, less appealing, probably, than most ordinary boys. A boy caught up and held by the sight, sound, smell, touch, taste of anything and everything in this world, so that there never was any time, could be no time, nothing measured against time. All his boyhood-manhood-old age on him now. Craning his scrawny Job's turkey of a neck in a dim parlor to gawk (like a Yahoo at an automobile show) at framed photographs above an old piano (he cannot play). All bound together in his sense of himself, his boyhood-manhood, father (dead more than half a century!) and mother (seeming not to age, suddenly aged and infirm of body and mind), and the fact at last to be faced (in a dim, cool cottage parlor on an uncomfortable daybed, because no other thoughts will come to the old man with an aching neck and pounding forehead!) that he never had any of it.

What is peculiar—makes me suspect I was (am) completely dotty—is how much like a dream it was. Or, more exactly, how I was able to think about all the things, times, people that seemed to have left me forever. Right up to the moment in the middle of the afternoon when I cranked up my Waterwitch and started across the lake to the resort. To *do* something, put in my appearance at the opening day stupidity.

It was like going back a couple of generations in time. Nothing to hear but a bluejay off somewhere among the pines, twanging as if it would do something about the heat. Going down the slope to my beach, only the shifting blotches of shade and hot sunlight I could feel against my cheek.

The surface of Silver Lake—empty as a desert under the almost cloudless sky. No Yahoo fisherman dropping his beer cans over the side, no speedboats cutting wakes in the smooth surface, no waterskiers performing pratfalls for the general public, no swarms of Yahoo offspring clustered like barnacles on the swimming rafts anchored along the shoreline in both directions, no slabs of pink Yahoo-woman flesh slowly reddening to an oiled burn under the sun on the lip of sandy beach running away on both sides of me to meet directly across at Ward Booth's pier, circling the lake.

Somewhere back up the slope, off in a high old pine that creaked now and again in a faint gust of wind that could not be felt against the skin, a bluejay complained about the hot stillness of the day. Just at my feet, the water made a warm, lapping noise as it touched the beach where I stood a moment before unmooring my boat and cranking the outboard.

Is it any wonder, as I chugged off toward Prader's resort, my mind half-fretting the Waterwitch would choose this day and hour to die, and the day would end in a hot, humiliating, hand-blistered row, that I searched the far reaches of the lake shallows for a boat with a man casting for bass, a woman with a wide-brimmed garden hat seated in the stern, a small boy?

I chugged on my way across the lake to Prader's, searching for the boat in the far reaches of the shallows (if I was-am mad, then sobeit!). It was too bright, too hot to turn in the seat, look back across at the other side of the lake toward Booth's pier. Ward Booth might as well still be a farmer in the prime of his adult life, still gathering the parcels of sandy soil here and there that would go to make him the most successful grower of melons and cucumbers in all Waushara County. Searching the shallows for the boat (the man, woman, indistinct small boy hunched, watching and listening, on the rower's seat, the oars in the locks, hanging at rest in the still water). I did not worry if I was or would be mad.

The reflecting swords of sunlight off the water blurred my vision to a tight, sweating grimace, and I could not even make out, after a time, the cleared beach edging the lake, the salt-box cottages jammed cheek-by-jowl together like a gaudy belt behind the beach. It might as well have been two, three generations before, everything since then consumed in the hot waves reflected off the water, burning my old man's eyes no differently than they did when I was a small boy, down at the water with my father for a swim, my mother seated in a beach chair in the available shade, a book in her hand, to watch us.

It was not long before I began to hear the Yahoo music being played at the resort. Sound carries a long way over the water.

Then it was not long before the sputtering of the Water-witch was all but lost in the music racket gushing out across the water from the resort. It was nothing but what I had expected. Yahoo music, rhythms fit for Negroes, louder, amplified, crazy. I figured out it was more than one group playing at the same time, more than one piece being played, as if it were a competition to see who went deaf first. Then I could not even hear my outboard motor above the racket.

It was enough to turn a man of ordinary purpose away. It was all drums, a throbbing bombardment pulsing in the clear, hot air, making the air seem to leap and subside in rhythm with it as I slowed my boat to find a mooring. It was all guitars, electrified, shrill, metallic, screeching and screaming in time with the dancing of the heat shimmer on the horizon, jabbing, stabbing at my ears in unison with the sunlight splinters coming at my eyes off the surface of the lake. It was all horns, saxophones with cracked reeds, breaking through the drums and guitars in long, hoarse, aching wails that echoed behind my forehead.

Yahoo music for a Yahoo-world gone mad in Yahoo-ism, the insane noise that must live like a caged idiot inside each Yahoo-soul, set free now by this Jew-Hunkie-King-of-Yahoos to celebrate the world they have made in their own image!

I sat, stunned, drowning in their music, eyes squeezed shut against sound and sun, numb with the banshee-yelping of it, brittle old man's bones in my arms and legs ready to vibrate, shake to dry bits and pieces from the concussion. Somehow I remembered to cut the motor, drifted in toward the fresh-painted pier, opened my eyes to the assault while I searched for an open spot to moor my boat.

Not a chance. The Yahoo is an early riser, can be counted on to fill parking lots at sports stadiums with his automobiles, will form up in long four-abreast lines to purchase any refreshment vended to the public, will reserve ahead all the motel beds on any given interstate highway, will jam camping grounds in national parks with his trailers and vans, will swarm like locusts over any patch of grass not denied him by fences, locked gates, or security watch. The Yahoos had taken every available mooring at the resort's new-painted pier, every foot of beach frontage where I might have pulled up my boat.

All grades and degrees of Yahoo vessel—big Lymancrafts complete with windshields, red running lights fore and aft, flags mounted on the varnished decks, bulbous Evinrude and Mercury engines (60, 75, 90, 120 horsepower!), imitation cowhide upholstery, pastel life-preserver cushions, radios mounted in the front dash, steering wheels and three-speed-forward-with-reverse gearshift levers, all the way down, through all

92

permutations and combinations, to the hideous silver-and-green rowboats (registration number decals on their prows) rented by the day or week from Wilson's Silvercryst resort. All of them bobbing in the gentle waves, bumping against each other, against the pier, like a motion picture without sound, because the end of all Yahoo music is a noise so full on the ear as to equal a silence nothing gets through.

I took an oar out of the lock and poled myself in closer to the beach, trying to spot an opening to pull up my boat.

"Park your boat?"

He said it again before I could turn on the seat (nearly lost my oar in the water, slopped drips of water all over my shoes and the legs of my trousers getting turned to look at him). "Park your boat for you?"

"What?" I squinted him out of the sun, a boy, sixteen, seventeen, eighteen (they all look the same age), standing on the Yahoo's fresh-painted pier, hands on his hips, slouch-shouldered, jaws worrying a wad of chewing gum, hair long enough to be a young girl's in my day, looking back at me like I was something floated up on the beach smelling bad enough to ruin his digestion.

"Park your boat," he said again, as if they had hung a tape recording on the chain he wore around his neck.

"Park my *what*? What does it appear to you I'm attempting at the moment? Show me a free stretch of beach where I can pull up and I'll be forever in your debt."

"Full up," he said, shifting his gum to the other side of his head.

"So I see. Do they pay you to communicate the obvious, boy?" I started to put my oar back in the water.

"I'm just paid to park the boats is all," he said. I poled closer to him, reached out to keep from bumping Lymancraft chrome, flag drooping limply on the varnished deck.

"Do tell. Then he's paying you for nothing, since I can't seem to find room for any more. Unless your eyes are better than mine." Service of the new management. I thought: special attraction for opening day—your Yahoo will appreciate that.

93

He likes to be called *sir*, delights in free matchbooks and dishes of salted peanuts *gratis* with his cocktail, will return again and again, like a plague, to the man or place that welcomes him with a bit of folderol.

"I'll just tie you up out on the bouy," the boy said. He dislodged one hand from its perch on his hip, leaned a little toward me, pointed out over my head, over the water. I craned my neck to follow him, saw the orange float bobbing on the water about where Prader's slide had been.

"Do I walk on the water to get to shore?"

"Nosir. I'll take it out." He peeled his tee-shirt up over his head (*Skin-a-rabbit* my mother used to say, undressing me for bed!), dropped it on the pier at his feet, unzipped his jeans, stepped delicately out of them, like a lady preparing to enter her bath, a pair of faded red trunks on underneath (my father's swim trunks were blue, *blue*, I remember!).

"That's extremely white of you, I must say. He thinks of everything, I guess. Nothing too good for his guests. At least the first day out, is that right?" He stood at the edge of the pier, knelt and reached over the bow of the Yahoo-craft to steady my boat while I stepped up on the pier (a perfect print of my crepe sole on the high sheen of the Yahoo-craft's front deck!). Still squating, holding my boat with one hand, the other out to me palm up, like a begging Hindu out of the pages of *National Geographic*.

"You can pay me now and I'll take her on out," he said.

"What's that?"

"Two-bits," he said, wiggling the fingers of his extended hand slightly.

"Repeat that for me," I said.

"Quarter," he said. "It costs a quarter. Twenty-five cents. For parking your boat here."

"Move aside. Move, I can get into my own boat without your help. I was handling small boats a good quarter-century before you were ever dreamed of. I said to move out of my way. I'm neither too old nor too dignified to save myself the fourth part of a dollar."

"I'm supposed to collect for docking your boat here," he said. Now he hunkered over to one side, still keeping my boat steady in case I wanted to leap back across the deck of the Yahoo-craft without taking a header into the drink.

"So you said. I'll thank you to stand aside."

"You can dock someplace else if you want, but if you want to here it's a quarter charge."

"Am I hearing correctly?"

"It's a charge," he said. "Don't blame me, mister. I'm just working for Mr. Lewinski is all."

"Mr. Who?" Now he got hold of the anchor line in the bow of my boat, stood up to face me. His knees cracked as he straightened. "You're saying there's a charge to dock a man's boat when he comes here meaning to spend his money. Is that it?"

"Yessir." We stood there on the new-painted pier, him holding my anchor line in the bow of my boat.

"You're saying there's a charge to dock a man's boat when he comes here meaning to spend his money."

"Yessir." We stood there on the new-painted pier, him looking at me like I was senile as well as half-deaf, his free hand having found its ledge on his left hip. Me, Leland Spaulding, Jr., squinting against the sun coming off the water all around us, lost, stunned by the sheer gall of the Jew-Bohunk, charging his customers money to become his customers, selling space on the beach, mooring slots at the pier, moorings out on a bouy anchored in the water where Prader's water slide used to float.

"I mean, you don't have to pay it if you don't want to. I mean, you don't have to dock here. You can dock someplace else, I guess. If you want to keep from paying the quarter, I mean," he said.

"Do tell." I felt with my fingers for change in my trouser pocket, studying his face as best I could, what with the sun trying to blind me. "That's mighty white of your Mr. Ski, I must say." I found a quarter, gave it to him. He dropped it on the heap of his clothes on the pier, tossed my anchor line back

95

into my boat, shoved it free of the pier with his bare foot, then stepped lightly up on the deck of the moored Yahoo-craft (his bare footprint, next to my crepe sole, printed on the high varnish!), stood waiting a moment to let my boat clear a space on the surface for his dive. I can tell a good swimmer. He crept to the outside edge of the Yahoo-craft's deck (the boat tipped steeply), curled his long toes over the edge for purchase to get some loft into his dive.

My coin caught the sun, flared like a tiny fire in the middle of the boy's heap of tee-shirt and trousers at my feet on the pier. I stayed to watch him dive after my free drifting boat.

He was nowhere as large a boy as young Batterman had been, not as muscled and lean, his skin shades lighter even with a good early summer tan, but it was like seeing young Batterman out there on the dock, and I even checked to be sure there were no letters stuck up in the middle of his back.

Then he dove, got a good lift with his legs off the deck of the Yahoo speedboat, cut the surface of the water like a warm knife going through whipped butter, did not come up again until he reached my boat. He lunged up out of the water, blowing, whipping his long hair out of his eyes, reached over the side of my boat to take the anchor line. He struck out, holding the line in one fist, for the mooring bouy, hardly slowed by the pull of the boat behind him.

I was seeing the swimmer, the dedicated swimmer that always seemed to be there at Prader's beach, the swimmer my mother and I would watch as we sat under the stand of pines above the beach, sipping the cold collins drinks in tall, frosted glasses, waiting for the time to pass until dinner, when the time seemed never to pass.

He was still stroking for the mooring bouy when I turned on my heel and walked up the pier to the pavilion grounds, walked away from Prader's slide and young Batterman and the dedicated swimmer, into the racket of the Yahoo bands that seemed to be playing everywhere all at once.

I could feel sandy grit under the crepe soles of my canvas shoes already at work to wear the fresh paint off the Jew-

Bohunk's pier. Where a man was asked to lay out the fourth part of a dollar to dock his boat!

Then there was no hearing anything against the racket coming at me from all sides. There was one cluster of them playing their racket from the walled off area the Bohunk had cut out of what had been a fine stand of old pine trees, elevated on some sort of platform, surrounded by young people dressed as if for a donnybrook, half-dressed, some of them scarcely dressed at all, young girls in skimpy shorts, shoulders, backs uncovered, clustering around the Yahoo band the way flies gather in clots on tacky paper, beer bottles and cigarettes in their hands, jiggling to the racket of Yahoo music as if it passed through them like electric currents, standing, sitting, arms draped on, around each other, all without the least sense that a public existed to register all this in the broad light of day!

The public, parents, senior generations of Yahoos, observing it all (or not seeing it!) as nice as pie, ringing the cheap picnic tables there for the purpose. A Yahoo feast underway, styrofoam coolers packed with ice to keep the beer cold, sacks of food, jars, cases of soft drinks for Yahoo toddlers, seated backside to backside on the narrow benches built right on to the tables to prevent carrying them away when the hordes leave. Your Yahoo is a hardened thief, believing, no doubt, that anything left lying in a public place is subject to a Yahoo law much like the one governing salvage at sea.

And all of them, racket-makers, twitching youth, gorging adults, smeary children, enveloped in a fog of charcoal smoke oozing up out of the new cookout pits anchored in cement in tiny clearings dotted here and there by a benevolent Yahoo-deity. My eyes smarted in the smudge cloud I passed through, the smoke fixed fast there until dark would bring a breeze off the lake to break it up, push it away.

Oh, he was having a success!

I had to turn sideways, crab-walk between the double row of automobiles parked on the edge of the new asphalt resort road, reeking tar-stink in the heat. Worth a first-degree burn of a man's skin to touch up against the baking chrome trim of a

97

Yahoo-mobile, smell of super-heated vinyl interiors blistering in the sun, and once through the double line of parked automobiles, my crepe soles catch in the sun-softened asphalt, the black strip of road printed forever with the tracks of Yahoos, Yahoo-mobiles.

And the pavilion, walled off from the road now, the center of the beehive, ant-heap, rat's nest of Yahoo-people, the bulk of the pavilion like the *Titanic* before she keeled over belly-up to sink, swarming with crazed survivors clinging for dear life above the killing-cold water. Yahoos of all ages pouring in and out, Yahoos jamming the pavilion porch, the crowd spilling over the edge of the porch, flowing into the stinking new asphalt road, merging, mixing with the hordes at the charcoal pits. Opaque sunglasses, Hawaiian shirts garrish enough to take out a man's eye, bare feet in sandals and tennis shoes, cameras on straps around sunburned necks, yachting caps, gold-brown legs in short-shorts, hairy, muscular legs a piano mover could take pride in, swollen white thighs quivering like suet-jell, hanging paunches, humped backs, pink, tan, fish-belly-white arms, hands wearing wristwatches and rings, the clear-cut outlines of brassieres and undershirts.

I skirt the edge of the pavilion porch, thread my way between the untouchable masses of Yahoos (a glimpse of a sweated, haggard face—young Batterman's fine features smeared with a lightning lapse of years!) toward the rhythmic slap-slap-again of the new aluminum screen door giving way to the restaurant barroom. As the music-racket above the beach recedes, the space is taken by the second gang of racket-makers inside the pavilion roof so as not to miss the distant, random ear of any fool seeking the peace of an instant's quiet between himself and the world at large.

It is akin to dog-paddling through a huge school of fish, gaudy, shrieking-hued tropical fish, empty, pale dishes for eyes, obscene mouths gasping for the air that comes in bubbles fluttering in the noxious haze of heat, asphalt-stink, acrid charcoal smoke, hands moving like fins in gestures that mean nothing, swimming slower and slower against the flow, and I am drowning slowly in the wash of Negro-Yahoo-racket-music that pours over everything from every direction, my eyes smarting, watering, nose and throat choked, skin slimed with perspiration.

I fear I will faint, fall, be kicked aside by the heavy feet clumping on the boards of the pavilion porch, out onto the sun-soft asphalt, be stomped into the black surface, frozen there when it cools and hardens with dusk and night, a fossil the Yahoos would gladly pay one more twenty-five-cent piece to view. One-fourth part of a dollar to see the old man (Leland Spaulding, Jr!) locked fast in place, expression of stark madness on his face!

The new aluminum screen door (no end to the efforts to make this world efficient, complete!), dull silver, flaps, slaps open and closed, the silver tooth of a black mouth that swallows an unbroken stream of Yahoo-fish-flesh, spits them out renewed, new light in their pale dish-eyes, new color in their pink-tan-white skin. Heat and shove and stink outside, the sea of racket-noise flooding my ears, the aluminum tooth snaps open and shut, glimpses of a blackness that looks cooler, smaller, and the strains of yet another fountain of their music spurting out to pack itself with all the rest in my ears.

I start to enter, am struck in the chest by the door, almost thrown back into the flow that swirls behind me. I falter, recover my balance, push back, feel myself sucked inside. For an instant I am blind, like a man stumbling out of a sun-lit blizzard, into the dark closeness of a heated refuge. My eyes slowly dilate, allow me to see what I have put my foot in. For time to think, see, I take the screen door with both hands, slam it hard behind me, step in far enough to be free of its swinging path.

A mistake. The Yahoos (thick at the tables, the long bar, deep in their drinks, food, the recorded music that, in here, overpowers the bands outside) somehow catch the crack of the door smacking its frame. The assembled Yahoo celebrants, mouths feeling for the rims of glasses and bottles, fingers busy with forks and cigarettes, are arrested in motion. They seem to freeze into a painted tableau for me, turn slowly on their chairs, stools, look at me.

An inner council of Yahoo-dom, select of the select, above the common variety's charcoal cooking, beer-spilling, matured beyond the rowdy pleasures of Yahoo young—Yahoo elite, sitting, suddenly arrested in motion by the slammed screen door, sitting, as if in judgment, on me, Leland Spaulding, Jr. They turn, slowly, on stools, chairs, turn their pale, blank eyes on me in judgment, suspend the glasses, bottles, cigarettes in mid-course toward their gasping mouths.

If I do not speak out, assert myself, I will fall in terror!

"I'm looking for the owner," I said. I start at the volume of my own voice, full of certain anger (no old man's feeble quaver!), as clear and solid as the ring of a steel hammer striking some true metal. The assembled elite of Yahooism now fix their dead eyes on me. What, they must wonder, is this?

And behind the long bar (Prader's bar is gone, the room changed beyond recognition), a tic at one corner of his mouth, a squint around the eyes, a slight furrowing of the glistening, broad forehead, he wipes his enormous hands on a rag that seems to float to the end of the bar. A barrel-shaped torso on casters comes out to confront me. I set my feet, clench my fingers into puny fists.

He did not look so large, standing behind the long bar, did not seem so particularly large a man, seen at a distance the day they demolished Prader's water slide.

"Where the hell is the proprietor?" I said. I could not make myself look directly at him. I could sense him, feel him very close to me, even think I heard his dirty breath above the racket. He seems so large, standing close, a wall of odor, breath, a hulk of something contaminated that seems to lean toward me, close, threatening to topple over and crush me.

"I'm the owner," the hulk says. "It's me you want." The voice is also contaminated, a voice that echoes out of the distance, like the music-noise, a voice moist and cold in my old man's ear, dark against my failing eyes. I must look at him!

"I might have guessed," I said. He is a large man, the

100

largest Yahoo in the world; Batterman was never so large (my own father was not so large!). He tips even closer to me to hear my words in the mess of noise we are immersed in. He is perhaps Batterman's age, but his hair, like mine, has begun to go. He slicks it back from his high forehead, hair a dismal grey-blonde, greased with something that smells like cheap toilet water.

His skin is pink-gold, glistens with perspiration (like mine!), pocked with scars on the points of his chin, on his throat just beneath the line of his jaw. I see the chain he wears around his neck (some Yahoo-sacred medallion). He leans closer still, his shirt damp through, perspiration glossing his massive arms, beads glistening on the thick, curly blond hair of his arms. His mouth is open, moving silently, gasping for words, his teeth a dingy yellow-white, the glint of saliva, his red tongue, heavy breath stinking in my nostrils. He seems on the verge of a collapse that will take my brittle old man's bones along with it, press out the scraps of air I hoard in my lungs, squeeze me dry of the last trickle of chilled blood in my hardened veins.

I believe that if I can muster the correct words, if I can find a formula to shout in his leering, peasant's face, I can break him, destroy this Yahoo-King in his Yahoo-shrine, here among the elite of his Yahoo-world.

"Would you mind telling me what's this hoo-ha about a quarter to dock my boat on the beach?" I said.

It would have been as well, better, to say nothing. It was just something I happened to say. I could only look at him, at the crowded room, wait for the opportunity to leave.

"It's a charge," he said.

"Clearly, but what's the charge for? Can you explain that to me?"

"For docking on my beach."

"You mean to stand there and have the gall to tell me I can't dock my boat to come up here for a beer without paying you a quarter?" It did not matter what I said. I did not care what I said, but the Yahoos jamming the room seemed to think it important. The Yahoos in the room seemed to close in on us to hear his answer. They lean precariously on their barstools, scrape their chairs on the varnished pine floor to see without straining their necks, suspend the motion of their nervous hands, cigarettes, forks, glasses, closing on us, mouths gaping silent, like fish drawn to the glass wall of an aquarium, their pale eyes glowing now with expectation, waiting to hear the answer of the King-Yahoo.

"It's my pier and my beach. If you object, don't park your boat there no more." The words of the Jew-Bohunk King of Yahoos. The wisdom of the Yahoo, in so many words. It seems to satisfy, delight listeners. It is as if the racket of Negro music had ceased, allowed his words to be heard, as if the moist, warm air of the room lifted for an instant to allow the answer to be delivered. And they are satisfied, smug, delighted.

The noise of bands, jukeboxes floods back into the damp, thick air, the cigarette smoke drifts toward the slow fans set in the ceiling.

I must say something! I cannot allow them to have it all, give them all, lose all of it without so much as a word. Some men, men like Walter Weller, Batterman, Wilson, can let it happen, all slip away, without protest. I *will not!* It does not matter what I say, so long as something is said.

I said: "I guess I hadn't heard the Jews had taken over here yet." The particular words do not (did not) matter.

Nobody seemed to hear. The racket still crams my ears, the stuffy room is dim with tobacco smoke, the Yahoos frantic with food, drink, the pulsing of their mouths (words drowned in racket). The King of Yahoos before me seems made of some spongy, sodden mass that neither sees nor hears. I cannot be sure he still breathes his sour breath. No one has heard, and I can only leave, having lost (but *not* given!) everything to them.

So I left them all where they sat, stood, banged the screen door behind me.

The sun was ferocious out on the pavilion porch, the crowd large, nudging, jostling, bumping me out onto the soft asphalt

102

of the resort road. The music-racket was louder, sharper in the air, the smudge of burning charcoal from the picnic area darker, more acrid. But I walked through all this, through the swaying pine trees above the beach, down on to the new-painted pier where the local boy sat, dangling his feet in the water, boats rising, falling gently about him at their moorings.

"You leaving already?"

"You're decidedly perceptive for so young a man. Do I swim for it myself?"

"Nossir." He got up, stretched, as if he had been sleeping long and deeply, head back, mouth open wide, then trotted to the end of the pier, dove across the bow of a moored boat, stroked out to where my boat was tied to the float, right where Prader's slide had been, once.

I watched him closely, as best I could in the piercing heat and light, when he returned with my boat in tow, as he drew it close for me, his skin, hair, wet from his swim.

"I thank you," I said. "And can I assume I don't owe you something more for retrieving?"

"There's just the one charge," he said, twitching his shoulders, as if he were numb with cold. He was just a local boy with a summer job. He bore not the slightest resemblance to young Batterman.

Batterman. I had not seen Batterman on my way out. No matter. The old Waterwitch surprised me, surprised the watching local boy, no doubt, by starting on only the third pull of the mended starter rope. I would have been just as content to row home, blisters and all.

I wipe all that from my mind. Put it all out of mind, memory. After that there is nothing left to do, nothing to do but wait. For the season to end.

Time is very strange. It can seem to whip you along like an express train, and events, all you care about, are like the ties between the tracks as you look back at the landscape running away from you, or like telephone poles spaced evenly at eye level. They all look alike, blur into a ribbon that dizzies you if you try to pick one out from another. Time can be like that.

I cannot even tell the exact number of days since I returned from Prader's resort, hauled the Waterwitch up the slope to the boathouse, drained its fuel and oil, stored it back away under an old, half-rotted canvas. Was it the same day, or the next (or the next after that?) that I dragged my boat up on my beach, flipped it over to keep the rain and snow from filling it?

How many days has all this been? No matter. I clear my mind of all that.

Time is very strange. It can seem to slow, to stick, stop dead, like a moving picture film that catches, slows, stops on a single frame, changes somehow from moving pictures to the single three-dimensional picture in a stereoptican viewer (somewhere, in some drawer or chest of this house is a rickety wooden viewer, a box of the double-image photographs printed on thick slabs of cardboard, warped in two generations of winter dampness and freeze, spring thaws, summer dryness. Time can be like that.

I wait for the season, summer, to pass, and time has slowed to a sickly, hot crawl. The days ahead (July, August) stretch out, the end of it like a mountain in the clouded distance, like the line of the horizon, retreating, ever further away for each painful, stifling movement toward it.

I cleanse my mind of all this, the present. I live in a great empty silence.

I will not leave the cottage except for quick trips by automobile to Wautoma for food, for mail. There is no place to go, nothing I want to see.

I wait for the end of the season. There will be work then, the shutters to close and seal, the boathouse on the slope, the barn, checks to be written, electricity to be canceled, natural gas to shut off, arrangements made to have leaves raked and burned to avoid a fire hazard. I wait for this, for the end.

Time does pass. This I believe. I have only to consult myself in the full-length mirror in the cottage's bedroom wing.

There is day, night, morning. The nights are remarkably chilly. The mornings are most pleasantly cool. The days are very warm, unbearably hot by late afternoon. Sitting in a corner chair behind drawn shades, I feel my skin dampen, my clothes feel heavy, sticky. There is real relief as dusk and evening bring breezes off Silver Lake. The pines set up a loud rustling above the roof of the cottage. Time does pass.

It seems to have stopped, ended, but it goes on. This I know. The summer will end, the season, and I will close up my cottage for the year. I wait, wait for this (there is nothing else left), and it seems as if it will not come. I know it will.

After? I will return to Chicago, and winter will come, quick and fierce and long. What I wonder is, what shall I wait for then?

I have stripped my mind of this world, here and now, and the past is so far, so very far behind me, back behind so many horizons, where I can fetch no real memories of it. If there was a future, I could know what to wait for, through the long bitter Chicago winter (winters are blank gaps in my life, empty landscapes covered with gray snow, without even horizons to distinguish them).

I wait for the end of summer and season, for the endless winter of the city of Chicago. And I hope, with what's left of me for hoping, there will be at least the memories of memories to hold to through winter.

That is a poor thing, I say to myself, for an old man to wait for, to see him through a winter so long and cold it seems never to end.

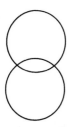

At the Center of Time

In the giving up and the letting go,
in the quiet earth's eternity,
unprovided and afraid I come
to what I would and what I would not know.

Pauline Hanson, *Across Countries of Anywhere*

Batterman stands on the very point of time. And thinks nothing of it. Nor will he likely ever.

Batterman stands. In the reaches of the cosmos, darkness extends forever. Invisible stars flicker in and out of their lives of unseen light (a few thousand years, a few thousand thousand years, then gone). Gases swirl, gather, dissipate. The universe spins, a few planets, paradigm of a single electron, somewhere along a certain path toward its cold finish. Spacetrash, obsolete litter, pocks the dead surface of earth's moon. Far above Batterman, just beneath the ceiling of the summer night's sky that roofs his head, passes a motley procession of satellites. Some still blink, transmitting in codes. Most are already silent hulks describing arcs long since pointless to even those who cast them.

Occasionally, rarely, an aircraft will cross below the broken clouds, red lights like the points of a distant constellation whose shape will not yield to any curious eye. But aircraft over the northern skies of Wisconsin are rare, quickly gone (the red running lights dim, seem to stutter, falter, soon disappear), and Batterman, roofed by the sturdy ceiling of the Redgranite Bowl-A-Go-Go, will not be among the curious one or two or few (if any) who raise their eyes to the warm night above Waushara County. He only stands.

He barely hears the blaring saxophones (from out the largest, if not the finest, Seeburg juke available through a midwestern distributor), barely hears the shrill screeching twang of electric guitars, hardly feels the thump or throb of the drums.

They are like the sound of his own breath, the coursing of his own blood, things a man scarce hears or feels, seldom has cause to wonder at. He stands.

Batterman stands, arms folded easily, loosely, across his large chest. He has a goodly, ample paunch, artlessly concealed beneath a loose—not gaudy—aloha shirt. Ample enough to rest the weight of his forearms as neatly as if a comfortable ledge had been prepared there in advance of this moment. The bared forearms are large, traced with steely sinews even when at rest. The skin looks burnished under the off-white, indirect florescents shaded by a valance above the back-bar. The skin of Batterman's arms looks very clean, as if it would be cool and dry to the touch. Batterman's skin is naturally tan, the even shade of tan that so few are born with, that but few more achieve with great care and patience under infrared lamps.

Batterman looks like a man long accustomed to resorts, the solariums of exclusive spas, some man of assured wealth and much travel who, at ease in his pampered, exquisitely tanned skin, can now afford to relax in delicate shadows. While lesser men strive for all that he has. Such is Batterman, standing behind the bar of his bowling alley and go-go joint, on the very point of time, in Redgranite, Wisconsin.

And all above him, and all about him, the not-Batterman turns and trembles, sweeps and spins. It is of the essence of Batterman, that which *is* Batterman, that the universe, as perceived by Batterman, is registered, understood, in a fashion akin to his awareness of himself. They are, in fact (the Batterman and the not-Batterman), inextricably entwined, one-in-the-same. At least insofar as Batterman is concerned. If he were to be concerned.

He stands, Batterman, at the center, *as* center, of the universe. Behind the bar in his go-go-joint and bowling alley, his arms folded, and all is like the sound of his breathing, the pulsing of his own blood, things he little notices, almost never has cause to wonder at.

He *is* comfortable! He is a tall man (seeming taller even

than he is), tall enough to half-stand-half-lean behind the bar, his large, symmetrical buttocks propped on the seat of a high barstool, the stool hidden beneath and behind the bulk of his shoulders and hips. His feet, lost in the dark space beneath the bar, are lightly crossed, just at the ankles. And for all his real and seeming comfort, for all his lack of interest in all that presses upon his lazy senses, very little will ever surprise him.

Summer help, a Redgranite kid home from the campus of the state college at Oshkosh, handles the orders the two waitresses bring from the booths on the opposite side of the barroom, and from the small round tables radiating out in uneven rows from the go-go cage at the back of the room. The Redgranite kid is busy. The waitresses (local women, both, oddly, service wives come back to live in with parents while their husbands pull a tour in Vietnam) are under orders to push the customers a little for refills while the cage is going.

The waitresses are thin, efficient women. They are old enough, traveled enough to know when to crack their blank expressions into sterile grins at something a customer says, and to know when not to break the indifferent freeze on their mouths. The service wives are a couple of goddamn gems, for Batterman's sort of place, and he knows it, runs it through his mind now and again as he watches them work, giving orders over the bar to the Redgranite kid, carrying loaded trays out between the crowded tables with nary a spill or a slop.

Batterman registers the kid, who will do (he is no-better-no-worse than three dozen like him he has employed through the years at Prader's) for the summer, and he watches the two come and go, knowing they are goddamn gems to find on his doorstep, satisfied that he is wise and fair to pay them better than he has ever paid female help before.

Batterman is never off-guard, no matter his appearance behind the bar. If the orders come hot and heavy (the orders *do* come hot and heavy when the babe takes her break from the cage), Batterman senses the kid's panic before he starts to flake at the rattle of orders the waitresses shout at him across the bar.

The kid never gets the chance to shout back at them to slow down so he can write a note of it. A stunned look starts over the kid's face, and Batterman steps in.

His legs unwind, his arms unfold, he launches out from the barstool in the corner. One large, dry, cool hand is laid gently on the Redgranite kid's shoulder, the heel of the other braced against the back edge of the bar as he leans forward in front of the kid to face the waitresses, who are just beginning to leak traces of irritation into their voices as they run over the orders for the kid.

"Let's have that all one more time so I can give him a hand," Batterman says to his gems on the other side of the bar. "You take every other one and I'll get the rest, Mickey," he says to his bartender without ceasing to look at the waitresses.

There is a kind of beauty in it. Mickey, the Redgranite kid home from the state university branch at Oshkosh for the summer, responds to the touch of the cool, dry, tanned hand covering his shoulder. Mickey seems to settle inside his clothes, as if the weight of Batterman's large hand were a refreshing draft of this summer's night air washing through the smokey barroom. Mickey looks alert, reaches for glasses, ice, the correct bottles off the backbar shelves.

The service-wife waitresses drop the frown lines out of their foreheads, release the corners of their mouths, tightened to turn the cracks customers will make to waitresses wearing spike heel patent-leather shoes, black net stockings to the hip, clinched waists, sateen blouses cut in front to show a little of the goods. Like Mickey, they are calmed. Batterman looks them straight in the eye—*He's got the most absolute bedroom eyes I ever seen*, Velma Ledbetter once said to Marge Doerflinger. *I see what you mean*, Marge said. *It's not my idea of it exactly, but I can see what you mean.*

Batterman holds them with his eyes, and though he speaks without raising his voice, they seem to hear him as clearly as if they were all in church. It is a little mysterious. The girl has left the cage, but the Seeburg is still going full blast. Pulling the plug on the Seeburg would be disaster, girl or no girl in the cage. And the crowd does its talking while the girl is on her break from the cage. They order up, look around, hit the lavatory, move from table to booth to bar to shake hands with somebody they know, call for change for the cigarette machine. Still, Velma and Marge hear what Batterman says.

"If that clock doesn't move any damn faster I'm killing myself," Velma says.

"I can name a certain creep at a certain table's getting his wrist broke the next time he touches my leg," Marge says.

"Two seven and seven, two plain soda, two straight up with chasers, four Bud, a Schlitz, a People's, right?" Batterman says in a voice they hear clearly through the Seeburg, all the yak, the clatter of glasses and ice from Mickey on the other side of the bar.

Batterman never misses a trick.

He knows (standing, arms folded, legs lightly crossed at the ankles) as well as the girls themselves that two ten-minute stints in the go-go cage, every hour on the hour, with the lights off, the cage empty for twenty minutes of the hour is no picnic. Yet Batterman is perhaps the only male inside Redgranite Bowl *not* watching the go-go cage when one of the girls is doing her stint.

It is difficult to say what Batterman watches, standing there behind his bar. Everything and nothing. Yet he never fails to check the broad face of his wristwatch, never fails to give the girl in the cage the nod when time for the shift or the twenty-minute break falls. He never wonders how it is he never misses the time. He checks the watchface without breaking his position against the stool. He has only to tip his square chin downward, to slant his wrist. The luminous hands and numerals can be read in the dim glare of backbar phosphorescents, the bleed from the colored glow of the spots focused on the cage. It is time.

Batterman pivots his buttocks a bit on the upholstered seat of the stool, turns his head to watch the cage until he catches the girl's eye. The rush is off the bar. Mickey has time to wipe up in front of customers seated at the bar, take the orders they mumble out of the corners of their mouths, empty ashtrays, straighten his till. Batterman, waiting to catch the girl's eye when the record changes on the Seeburg, does not appear to be checking the house at the same time.

But he sees the focus of the eyes of his customers, to a man locked on the girl in the cage, their features indistinct in the darkness, tails of smoke rising from cigarettes and cigars idle between their fingers, free hands holding glasses and beer bottles, waiting, many of them, for the break so they can turn away to call a waitress for refill. Marge Doerflinger is circulating slowly, a measured route between the crowded tables, trying to keep from snagging her stockings on somebody's heel. Velma is off in the far right corner, near the door. She tries to look like she's looking for someone who wants a waitress (they will raise a hand, an empty glass, into the smokey haze above their heads from time to time), but is really resting her fanny against the paneled wall, taking advantage of the slack-off to ease her aching feet.

Between them, they push—not hustle—the customers for drinks, and it keeps the orders up enough so that Batterman loses no money on them, even at the good wages the women get, nor on Mickey, behind the bar, either. For the first time in his life, Batterman is making money. Coining it. He does not question that. He knows his new solvency for a fact, sees it at each end-of-month accounting, can and does speak of it on occasion, but feels no awe, no special delight beyond a deepening of the comfort and security he has always known, wherever, wherever in time he has been.

The trick is to catch the girl's eye in the cage just at the precise moment of stasis between records. While the music is blaring out of the Seeburg (volume up all but on peak) the girl dancing has her eyes tightly closed. To naïve customers, the go-go girl in the cage appears rapt with ecstasy. Batterman knows better.

Marilyn VanDamm who comes from up at Kaukauna, where every second person you meet is old-country Dutch to look at (and twice-so between the ears), closes her eyes against the colored lights. It could be worse, dancing in the cage, if Batterman could see his way clear to get the strobes he has been advised are the thing for his sort of set-up. Strobes popping in her face would surely make Marilyn VanDamm sick to her stomach if she danced with her eyes open. As it is, the color wheels turning slowly in front of the bank of spots hung from the ceiling make her feel dizzy if she leaves her eyes open.

So much the better. An old fart, sitting at the bar, a man in his fifties, never seen before or since by Batterman, once said to him as Marilyn did her stint in the cage, "Where the hell do you find them, fella?"

"Beg your pardon?" Batterman broke his stance to say.

"They must be weird, women like that, like they're doing it or something all alone up there," the anonymous old fart said. Batterman had nothing to say to that. The old fart was back looking at Marilyn VanDamm, from Kaukauna, who had to keep her eyes closed while she danced if she wanted to avoid dizziness. If customers thought she was having some kind of experience out of it, up there alone in the cage, so much the better, Batterman thinks.

Dutch-between-the-ears Marilyn VanDamm from up at Kaukauna, with all the rest of the Dutchmen. She is a fair-to-middling dancer, if the dancing matters at all, that is. Marilyn's face is plain (she reminds Batterman, just the faintest, of his wife, of his wife's face) in the face, but has good long legs and arms, which make up for a plain face with a dancer. If the dancing itself matters to anyone. Marilyn is lean enough to look good in the spangled bikini. She has pretty fair goods up top. Fair enough.

If that matters. Nothing very particular matters, Batterman understands. Nobody looks at the cage girl's legs or face or goods. What holds them like a vise, Batterman knows without bothering to think he knows, is the whole thing. The dark, smoky room, the Seeburg up to all but peak volume, colored lights, shadows in stripes on the girl's (if you call it dancing) body, the spangled bikini (Marilyn's is red with silver spangles, Bobi's blue with gold)—the whole of it is what holds them. Whatever goes on inside their heads.

Marilyn's extra is her long brown hair. She hangs it down in front of her shoulders, where it can swing, bounce as she moves to the Seeburg music. Marilyn's two fine swatches of brown hair flip with the beat of the music, cut across the shadow lines cast by the bars of the cage on her skin, accentuate the hammer and plunge of her long white arms, the cock and snap of her good legs.

Put it all together with her closed eyes, Batterman understands, you get imaginations working. Good dancer, bad dancer, is not the point. Marilyn is good enough, all considered together, the way she comes off in the cage. Good enough to pack them in, hold them like she had them in a vise, hold them there waiting for her to come back up to the cage for her next stint.

"Lord God-a-mighty!" they shout at Marilyn on a good night.

"Oh, do it, do it, do it!" they often scream from out of the dark under the haze of cigarette and cigar smoke.

"Sweet Jeeee-zuzz!" they yell at Marilyn.

Batterman knows the summer regulars who like to do the yelling. He knows the general type (age, clothes, what they order to drink) that will mouth off at Marilyn in the cage. He does not give any sign of noticing them. He never comes from behind the bar to quiet anyone, though his waitresses are confident he could, and would, if anyone got far enough out of line. Nobody has, so far.

They shout, some of them, scream like banshees from time to time on a good night, but they also get a look at Batterman, standing, arms folded over the tent-like aloha shirt, tendons rippled in his tan forearms, the way he seems not to be noticing. Nobody seems ever to drink enough to want to get *too* far out of line.

Batterman genuinely likes Marilyn VanDamm. She is nothing so special as his waitresses (he does not know if he

116

would trust her to handle money), but she also turned up on his doorstep, sort of, just when he needed her. He got a line on Marilyn through a shirt-tail relative right here in Redgranite. Marilyn was boarding over in Neshkoro, where she had gone to have her illegitimate child. She was supposed to have resort experience, summers in Door County. He drove over to see her, and she ended up working the go-go cage for him, pulling shifts with Bobi Peplinski. That Marilyn can dance a little is so much coincidence to the good.

Batterman keeps a couple of secrets for Marilyn VanDamm. He is absolutely trustworthy with other people's secrets. Marilyn's parents did not, originally, care where she went to have some Kaukauna Dutchman's kid. Now they would like to know where she lives since she packed up with the kid and left Neshkoro. They will not find out from Batterman, nor from the Redgranite shirt-tail relative. Batterman has seen to that. There is a new trailer park in Omro, down the road toward Oshkosh, and Marilyn uses a different name there. Her neighbors think she works at the Chicago Pickle Company in Redgranite. They will learn no differently from Batterman.

She trusts him. "I suppose that shit-ass is having a hemorrhage for me to get up there," Bobi Peplinski said to her once just as Marilyn came out the back door at the end of her stint.

"So where do you get off calling names?" Marilyn said.

"Okay! Don't bite a person's head off, huh?"

"Keep it to yourself if you want to call people names," Marilyn said.

"A person don't even hardly dare say nothing to some persons, hey," Bobi said, getting up to go in. She slipped the poplin jacket off her bare shoulders—it is an old jacket of Batterman's, loaned to the cage girls to keep any evening chill away—and tossed it to Marilyn as she went in for her stint in the cage.

Batterman positively would *not* trust Bobi Peplinski with money. He does not trust her at all. The trouble with Bobi Peplinski is there are secrets Batterman does not know. Batterman knows the man who knows Bobi's secrets. And trusts that

117

man, in business matters, beyond any other. So hired Bobi Peplinski on another's word.

"I'm not getting my foot in something I'll want to wipe off with a rag someday, am I, Romy?" Batterman said to the man he trusts—in business—beyond any other.

"What is it with you?" Romy Lewinski said. "You got nose trouble, you have to be sticking in your face where it don't need nothing?"

"No. I just get the impression there's some rough stuff, maybe, about her I should get straight before I commit myself." Romy Lewinski went through a tic he had, a business of turning aside his face, pretending to stare at something far away, as if he had suddenly remembered an important appointment. This business of Romy Lewinski's was to show how stupid he thought Batterman was being. Batterman understands how much a piece of business this thing of Romy's is, but, still, it always makes him feel as foolish as Romy is telling him he is.

"Leave it alone, but, okay?" Romy said when he finished his little tic, had turned back to face him.

"I will if you say so. I didn't mean I needed anything more than your word, Romy. You know that. I'm just concerned."

"The hell with concerned," Romy said. "She's had her lumps, I'll grant you. It don't concern no skin off your butt. Come on, now. Take her on, she'll do good enough what you need her for, you'll thank me for it soon enough. Okay?"

"I don't for a minute doubt it," Batterman said. He never has. In business, Romy knows.

If dancing *did* matter, Bobi would be out on her ear before the next record came on the super-amplified Seeburg. Bobi's dancing is absolute nil. Which is part of what makes him think there is far more than meets the eye when it comes to Bobi Peplinski.

Bobi is hard as nails. Small, plenty lean enough to look all right for the cage in the blue-gold-spangled bikini, but too much muscle to look really good, thinks Batterman, when he

118

bothers to look or think. Even under the colored spots her skin is too pale, like something under a rock or a bandage too long. Or, maybe, for instance, in prison where they do not get much in the way of fresh air or sunshine. Someday, Batterman thinks, he is going to drop a reference or two to Tacheedah Women's Prison in earshot of Bobi Peplinski. Just to see what happens. Direct questions get him no place.

"Looks like somebody had a longish night," he said one late afternoon when she came in.

"Says who?"

"Close your eyes, you'll bleed to death."

"Oh bullshit!" Bobi Peplinski said, going past him. What was he supposed to say to that?

One guess is good as another for the original color of her hair. Stark platinum now, glinting under the cage spots like a burnished chrome helmet. Hard. And sharp, all angles. The planes of her face jump out at the customers, heightened by the lights, the shadow stripes thrown over her by the cage bars. If she has experience, Batterman figures, then it was carnival kootch shows, stag smokers, cathouses, likely as not, he figures. The Seeburg music always sounds dirtier when Bobi Peplinski is in the cage.

Cannot dance to save her soul from Hell. Never lifts a foot off the floor of the cage. Bobi Peplinski is a hip-thrower, a pelvic jerker, bumper, grinder, undulator. All Batterman hears is the drums when Bobi does her stints. She might as well not have legs. Never more than a light trembling at the knees in time with the music, and those thighs, stringy, pale as white-meat chicken, show not a quiver in a carload.

Batterman doubts anything could make her sick. He has wondered at her past—was it Tacheedah, a cathouse in Plymouth or on Milwaukee's south side (where else would Romy Lewinski get a line on her?), dope, what? Whatever, she is a hard one, a survivor. She does her time in the cage, eyes wide open. Nary a blink. She might have decent eyes if it were not for the blue-black gunk she has the idea she has to wear.

"I don't know where you got the notion," Batterman said to her, "but it's not Cleopatra you're playing up there every night."

"So what's that supposed to mean?" she said.

"Can you go a little easier on the make-up? I don't care what you do on your mouth—it needs something dark just to show up decent, I realize. But you could stand about half that on your eyes."

"First I heard any bitching," Bobi Peplinski said. Is that her real name? Batterman has wondered.

Much beyond that, he does not often wonder. He will never trust Bobi Peplinski. So long as she keeps her hours on time, he will keep her on. He will be glad when the season is over. Come Labor Day, he can let her go back to wherever she came from, or wherever Romy Lewinski may have lined up for her to go. Batterman does not worry it.

Labor Day will come, like everything else always has. He will cut back, wrap up, clean up for the long winter. Get ready for the long slow time, the few locals who will come by to drink a little beer and look at the empty cage at the back of the barroom. Broken by the small crowds during deer season, a few ice fishermen (Romy will have the lion's share of that trade, over at Silver Lake).

It will be a long, easy winter. It will be comfortable, warm inside the Redgranite Bowl-A-Go-Go. There will even be a little play (with small side bets) on the single duck-pin alley that nobody looks twice at all summer. Batterman will stand behind his bar, work it without help during the winter. Gross will fall off drastically, but so will overhead. Winter, like everything else, all though his life, will come. Batterman will get by.

He does not trouble himself with anticipation. Then is then. Now is now.

"She's got nice boobs, but she moves like a damn mannequin," says a man sitting at the bar. Batterman smiles, does not alter his posture.

"You may have something there at that."

120

"Deadest-ass looking broad I ever saw," says the man at the bar.

"You pays your money and you takes your choice," Batterman tells him. The man goes back to his drink, back to watching Bobi in the cage, fades back into the smoke-filled darkness, blends with the glow of the colored spotlights. Now is now.

Bobi Peplinski chooses to live (she says) all the way over at Oshkosh. Let her. Why should he worry? He never has, really, not even over the worst times, disappointments, failure, real trouble. Batterman stands.

It is a good night at the Redgranite Bowl-A-Go-Go. Mickey is hard put to keep up, even while the cage is going. Batterman will step in to help if and when. His two gems, the service-wife waitresses, are moving, pushing-not-hustling the crowd for refills, grabbing half a minute when they can against the wall to take the load off. The Seeburg is blaring at all but peak, full to the gills with quarters and halves (there will be a full morning's music left in it when he pulls the plug at closing time tonight).

Now: Bobi Peplinski does her stint in the cage, all planes and angles, sharp slices of shadow from the wooden bars of the cage, skin a sick-white, cast over with rolling reds, green, orange, blue, gunked-up eyes staring like a dummy's out at the crowd, hands doubled up in small fists, arms bent rigid, legs set firm, feet flat on the floor of the cage, pelvis going every which way but loose. She holds the crowd, which is what Batterman pays her for.

It is a good night. No point in closing the register drawer between sales. Out on the back stairs, Marilyn VanDamm sits out her break, Batterman's old poplin jacket over her to keep off any chill in the late night air. The front door opens and closes all night, new customers, bunching up at the entrance, peering into the smoke and noise for a place to sit, a free stretch of wall to lean against. Batterman is coining it. The getting is *good*! Not to worry.

Outside, the Redgranite main drag is empty of people. They roll up the street at night in Redgranite, even during the heart of the summer season. There are only two other taverns in Redgranite. Emil Bender's draws a few old farmers from this end of Waushara County. The other has a new name (El Gato) to let the Mexican pickle pickers know where to go for a drink if they are not up to driving all the way over to Wautoma. There is a Tasti-Freeze for the teenagers at the Oshkosh-Omro end of town, and a trucker's restaurant just inside the township line, heading toward Wautoma. There is one cluster of overnight cabins that has not yet learned to call itself a motel. Its lights are so few, so weak, that few travelers see it against the line of pine trees behind it.

All stores, even the druggist, close at six. In front of El Gato, a few Mexicans will loiter, sit on the fenders and lowered tailgates of their pickups. By nine, those who have no money to spend will have given it up, gone back to their camps for a good night's rest to take into the cucumber fields in the early morning. Those with a little money will have held off as long as they could stand it, gone inside to join those with money, make a night of it. Out on the sidewalk in front of El Gato, the ballads of Jorge Negrete, mariachi instrumentals, compete with the sound of Batterman's Seeburg down the block.

Cars, nose in to the curb, fill all available parking space. There is the noise, the neons from Batterman's, the lesser noise and light from El Gato, the glow behind the curtains at Emil Bender's, where a few old farmers, a few bachelor sons, linger over beer and schnapps, talk indifferently or bitterly of this season's going prices for cucumbers, melons, truck produce.

A few hundred yards off the main drag, just outside the township line at the Oshkosh-Omro end of the town, hard against the railroad siding, the Chicago Pickle Company is still going strong. Workers on the loading docks, out tending the brine vats, can hear the throb of the music on the wind. Some bite their lips in envy, spit in disgust into the vats of curing cucumbers. The graveyard shift will not come on for an hour, and there is overtime for anyone willing to double up. The season is short, cash hard to come by.

Without the Chicago Pickle Company, the town would die,

as it all but died when the granite quarry shut down, when paving bricks gave way to macadam and asphalt in upstate Wisconsin and Minnesota. Boys swim in the quarry pit now. A couple have drowned in it over the years. At the quarry, now, on a clear summer night, the music of El Gato and the Red-granite Bowl-A-Go-Go cannot be heard. The quarry is too far back, nearly a mile on what is left of the access road from the main drag. The landscape at the quarry, the stretches of stark, dark red granite, the basin of black water, is as dead seeming as the moon that illuminates it.

Batterman stands, relaxed, easy, behind his bar. It is a *very* good night. If he were to check his wristwatch (there is no need) he would see it is nearly midnight—a day, a date, hangs on the verge of ending, a new day, date, to emerge, become. He feels no curiosity, no need, no faintest urge with respect to time.

Not a table, not a stool, not a man-size space against any wall unfilled. Velma and Marge are getting all they can handle. The orders are nearly as heavy while the cage is going as they are during the break. Mickey's hair has begun to flop over his forehead, into his eyes. No time to brush it back carefully, Mickey swipes at it with the back of his hand. Batterman will step in to give him a hand in a minute, spell him, send him out back for five minutes of fresh air. Bobi Peplinski dances no better than ever, but Marilyn is dancing better, it seems, and this sort of crowd appreciates it.

He stands, comfortable. He is, for the first time in his life, turning the big dollar. Twice as sweet because unexpected. Batterman is not one to anticipate. His wife and children have turned off the TV (it takes a tower antenna to bring in the channels from Green Bay, Oshkosh), gone to bed. They sleep, comfortable and secure, in the new ranch-brick, central air and heat, which will not take twenty years to clear if nights, seasons like this keep up.

Everything happens anyway. Just happens. Why argue with it? There is Batterman, and there is not-Batterman, but the difference between the two (to Batterman, if he were disposed to ponder it—which he is not) is more trouble than it is likely to be worth.

A man takes a stand, the way he figures it. Makes his move. Puts up a bid. Something always happens, no matter what. Take it as it comes, Batterman would say. Let what is coming look out for itself. *I'll still be here no matter what, right?* Batterman might well say.

At the center of it, everything, he lifts his arms, spreads his fingers, rises to the balls of his feet, his toes, as if he meant to dive rather than slide. For an instant he almost believes he will dive, could dive, leap out far enough to clear even the tip of the slide's chute. Pick his spot like a precision bomber (this must be how it looks to a bombardier, sighting through his Norden), there, between the end of the dock, the slide chute, the shallows where little kids are farting around (little as minnows to the eyes of Horse, alone, atop, at the center of all on top the slide tower). He can imagine himself doing it, all but feel himself leaning forward in his stretch toward the sky, sun, alone.

"So, go! What are you waiting for, eggs in your beer?" Horse's arms collapse to his sides. He drops to the flat of his feet, steps to the edge of the platform, leans out, over, looks down at the upturned face of Georgie Booth, forty feet below. Georgie's face is screwed into a sour squint, sun over Horse's shoulder flooding his eyes, his straw-colored hair plastered wet down over his forehead, cowlick perfectly defined in scalp-white.

"So pump," Horse shouts. "I'll go. Pump it, will you?"

"What am I supposed to been doing, Jerk?" Georgie says. "What are you waiting on?"

"Pump it. I'll go!" Horse says, steps back away from the edge of the platform. He drops to sit at the chute, heels resting on the hot metal. The chute is dry, his hair has dried in the sun and breeze on top the slide tower. How long has he been up here? Horse wonders. What has he been thinking about? Georgie Booth must have pumped his arm sore, waiting for him to take his turn. He hears the very distant voices of Georgie and his cousin, Bud, hears the racking, busted sound of the pump going again, feels the vibrations up through the superstructure, the platform boards, into his hams. He waits for the lake water (it will feel cold now that he has let himself dry) to reach the top of the tower, spill out the hole just beneath the platform, wet the chute for him.

A moment to look around, scan. At the center. The hand-pump sends its shudders up through the tower, little kids are splashing around in shallow water between the slide and the beach, somebody kneeling on the end of the dock, reaching down in the water with one hand (testing for a swim?), a couple of rowboats pulled up on the beach, pine trees on the crest of the bank (somebody, people in there, sitting on chairs under the pines, hidden in shadow), the swell of the pavilion roof across the road behind the trees, the jutting gables of the top floor of Prader's house set in the middle of the big oaks, unpainted sheet-metal roof (paint that, Horse thinks idly, or it'll rust sure as God made green apples).

The pump thuds and cracks, as if the mechanism were made of wood. Horse waits for the cold water to gush, wet the slide.

He turns his head slowly. Silver Lake slides out of the corner of his eye, behind his back, sandy lips of beach every so often, the deeper green of pine forest, chunks broken out for summer cottages. Twisting his trunk, the body of the lake flows fully into his vision, narrows, as he frowns, to less than a bright mist at the far end, where it turns left in a curl around Foxtail Point. The sun off the water dizzies him for an instant. Horse blinks, shakes his head to make out a few fishermen, boats at rest dotting the surface that sweeps away from him even as he strains, frowns, to catch and hold it.

"Go! Damn, go! Horse!" Georgie Booth screams from below. Horse turns back to the slide. His legs, feet, are awash in icy cold lake water, the pump going so hard it makes a booming sound in the superstructure of the tower.

"You waiting on Christmas!" Bud Booth is yelling to him

from the end of Prader's pier. Horse did not see him swim over from the slide raft. He will go on his belly, steer for Bud Booth at the end of the pier.

Horse pulls up his feet, takes sure hold of the wooden edges bolted to either side of the chute. The water strokes his belly. He eases himself forward until only his insteps touch the rough edge of the platform. Cold water (not as cold now) gathers along his ribs, shoulders.

"Showboat!" Bud Booth shouts through cupped hands.

Horse is like a bullet, pointed to blaze out the muzzle of the chute. Bud will look for him to go for distance, try to make the shallows where the little kids are. He will aim for Bud Booth on the end of Prader's dock. Horse's back is baked hot, dry by the sun (back hot, dry; stomach, ribs cold, fluid). He releases the edges of the chute, humps, thrusts forward, feels his toes rasp the edge of the platform. A millisecond. Horse's body does not seem to realize it is free to obey gravity. He seems (to Bud Booth on the pier, the kids watching from the shallows, the seated watchers hidden in shadow by the pines on the crest of the bank) to be hung in the silver chute, a slash of lean brown muscle, splayed, thick shock of raven's black hair. Then slides. *Slides.*

As if propelled, catapulted. Horse streaks down the slide chute, a fine spray of silver water spouting in front of his locked hands. He hits the water, planing its surface, the spray before his hands erupting now into twin wakes of clear water like panes of glass. His body, a brown torpedo, cuts a clean path that curves perfectly to the right, straightens as he twists his trunk back to the left, homes in on the end of the long pier, where Bud Booth squats, leans forward, attempting to shout something at Horse, shooting through the water toward him.

Horse steers by feel, his eyes shut instinctively against the surge of water in his face. Feels the moment of sudden lift when he leaves the chute, the slap of the surface against his chest, hard belly, legs, *feels* the instant to lean, twist right, then roll back left. Feels the force of the slide sag, ebb away, the sinking of his body beneath the surface, where he kicks, lunges

126

for the light he sees now through the surface above him, eyes open again. The watchers see only the churn of his wake dissipating, the boil on the surface where he sank from view.

"Showboat!" But Booth is screaming in a breaking voice at the opaque, scrambled waters of the lake just below the end of the pier. "Showboat! Hey!"

Horse breaks free of the surface, explodes up into the clear summer air, rising as high as Bud's waist, twisting as he rises (the way a porpoise in an aquarium leaps free of its tank, hangs in mid-air to snatch fish from its keeper's hand), flips, flings his head to one side to clear his eyes of the thick, raven's-black hair. "Showboat!" Bud Booth is still shouting, hoarse, face red, neck bulging.

Horse seems to hang at the zenith of his upward thrust, then collapses, like a bronze balloon deflating slowly, gracefully, without losing the essence of its bright shape. Flows back into the water, just beneath the surface (Bud Booth sees the shock of hair fan out at the surface like seaweed rising, torn loose from the bottom of the lake).

"Come on, Showboat!" Bud yells, voice failing.

Horse rises again, shoulder-high, spits into Bud's enraged face the mouthful of cold lake water he has secured on his descent. A straight stream, thick as a cow's pissing on a rock, full upon Bud's face. "Bastard!" Bud screeches, wipes at his face, leaps for Horse in the water, a high, round cannonball of a jump. Too late.

Horse, submerged quickly and easily as a mud turtle, has turned, strokes now, just visible, cutting the water like a shark, already halfway back to the slide raft, where Georgie Booth dances like an idiot, waiting for someone to pump for him while he climbs the tower to take his turn down the slide.

"*Waaagh!*" Horse shouts, blowing away the water that clings to his mouth, slipping up onto the edge of the raft. His broad, tan shoulders raise, lower, as he bellows air in and out of his lungs, wipes hair back from his forehead. He kicks at the water, splashing at Bud Booth, who only now reaches the raft.

"Clean your damn clock, son," Bud says from the water.

127

"Fool if you try, coward if you don't," Horse says, standing up.

"Am I getting pumped for or am I doing this for my health or something?" Horse shields his eyes from the overhead sun, makes out the fuzzy black silhouette of Georgie, halfway up the tower ladder.

"Don't look at me, I took my turn," Bud says, hauling up out of the water, coming to his knees on the wet pine planks of the slide raft. Horse laughs. At them, himself. For all of it. Joy.

"I'll pump, shag your dumb hinder up. My granny climbs faster than you," Horse says.

"What?" Georgie calls down, then starts up, fast, agile as a monkey up a palm trunk (the way Japs can climb trees to take a sniper's post, thinks Horse; in a movie, somewhere, he has heard they can grip with their big toe like it was a normal person's thumb).

"You should talk!" Bud says, voice weak, still heaving for breath, on his knees.

"You're out of shape," Horse says, not meaning it. Bud drops his head, still blowing for air, does not answer. Horse steps to the pump (the water oozes up between the pine planks of the raft, slicking them, cool, glossed, against the soles of his feet). He lays one hand lightly on a beam of the superstructure (needs paint, he thinks; paint's peeling; paint it or the water or the sun, one or the other, will get it sure; rot). Takes the pump handle with his right arm, braces his feet, left hand on the beam, pushes hard, slow and even, precise, to get the suction started.

Slow. It gives slowly to the increasing force of his arm. He snaps it back (the mechanism cracks, as if it would break). Again, slowly forward, but more easily. A whimpering of suction sets up in the pipes. Snaps it back, forward, less resistance, back, forward again, this time with comparative ease. The crashing return of the handle alternates with the shuddering suck, throb of water moving up the pipes to wet the chute for Georgie Booth. Back and forth, with ease now. Rhythm.

128

"What's he waiting on!" Bud says. "I've got a turn coming up next, you know."

"Keep your shirt on."

Why hurry? Still, here below on the raft, pumping, Horse feels himself at the center of it. No rush. What's to rush? *You think I got all day?* people say. For certain. Horse Batterman does. Better believe it. He pumps for Georgie, his arm, motion fluid, natural as the incessant lap of water that oozes up through the seams in the floor of the raft, cools his toes, feet, pleasantly.

Time. Here and now. Horse loses himself in the rhythm of pumping. Feels again his feet go *cold-warm-cold-warm* with the rocking of the lake. He finds his eyes examining the layers of white marine paint peeling along the grain of the superstructure beams. Water or snow (winter). Rot it sure, thinks Horse. His hand, fingernails curled under, heel braced hard against the wood, is dark brown against the fading white paint.

He thinks suddenly, sees, the slide in winter. Drawn up on the beach at the far end, next to the ice house, the tower leaning dangerously because Prader is careless, drags it too far, one corner of the raft lifted against the bank. The bare planks of the raft are under the white crust of winter-long snow and ice, swept smooth, merged with the angle of the bank above the beach by the winter-long Canadian wind that whips the tall, black trunks of the pine trees, the open fallow fields, pastures where a few cattle huddle up against windbreaks and sheds to escape it.

Horse Batterman shudders in the imagined cold (everything is white, the sweep of snow and ice crust stretching out across the dormant lake, broken by black dots that are the tents and windbreaks of a few ice fishermen, the large square of black, oily looking water where they have cut ice, dragged it off the lake on sleds to store for the coming summer).

Horse cringes involuntarily, feels as though he has opened his eyes after a short, light nap. Sees his brown, broad hand against the paint wearing with the grain of the beam, hears the crack and thud of the pump, his right arm back and forth, effortless, tireless. His thrust causes a popping in his ears as his skin quivers to gooseflesh. The breeze has all but dried him. He feels his hair thickening, setting in place as it dries, hardening in the sun and wind. He shudders again, as if he were suddenly very cold.

"What's he doing, for crying out loud?" he says to Bud. Bud Booth gets up off his knees, passes him (Horse continues to pump, like a machine), grasps a beam, leans out over the water to grimace up at the top of the tower, into the sun.

"What you waiting for?" he yells up at his cousin. Horse examines Bud Booth. Skin pink, reddened by the daily sun at Prader's, hair the same pale straw as his cousin's, smeared to his scalp by the water in strips (the same exaggerated cowlick twisted into his crown), lips gone red-blue from swimming. Horse lowers his eyes to the skin of his arm, burned dark as any Mexican pickle picker by the days out at Prader's.

He is not sure what he is thinking. He shakes his head, as if there were water in his inner ear from swimming. *How do you like a taste of your own medicine, Horse?* he hears the distant voice of Georgie Booth say.

"That jerk's playing games," Bud says, swinging back in, under the tower. Horse laughs, keeps pumping, laughs harder.

"Let him," says Horse. "I can pump till hell freezes over."

Continues to pump. But has left the center of it. Does not hear the shouting back and forth of the cousins, Bud demanding his turn on the slide, Georgie insisting they deserve it, a taste of his own medicine for Horse Batterman. Horse has left the center of it, stares dumbly at his brown hand against the white paint. He shivers with gooseflesh, sees winter. In winter the slide sits awkwardly, at an angle against the face of the bank rising from the beach. He cannot see the beach. Everything is hidden beneath the snow, swept clear, black-white and hard (glistening like points of mica and quartz in concrete when there is some winter sun) by the bitter, howling wind that blows from Canada.

There is little sun. The sky dulls to the paleness of dingy

snow-cover, feels lower, just above his head. The only water lies in black rectangles where they have cut ice for the next summer's season at the resort. Days are short, not full light until he is in the school building, trying to keep his eyes open against the numbing hiss of the radiators, the thick, too-dry heat, the maddening voices of his teachers. Days are short, even on wartime. Sometimes his teachers talk about the war, even read the tiny V-mails from boys who graduated, enlisted, went away, or who left, quit the way Georgie and Bud say they will, because they cannot wait through one more autumn, spring, June, to get to the war. They say they think the war will not last for them, will not wait. Horse does not know.

Georgie, Bud, his teachers, parents, the *Argus*, the Madison and Milwaukee papers, all talk about the war. Horse does not understand clearly, is not interested, can barely stay awake through the schoolroom heat, voices, knowing how short these days are.

Short days, but winter lasts too long. There is not enough in it. No football, no Prader's. The short days of winter drag for Horse Batterman because there is only time, and nothing, so little to do, and he has no choice but to wait it out, wait on it. Until, somehow (though the short days seem forever), time does pass. And the center seems to come back into things again.

It comes spring again. It always does. And Horse Batterman can forget about time, because there is no rush, and he is at the very center of it all.

"Hey, Horse!" Bud Booth says from the ladder, on his way up the tower for his turn. "Wake up and die right!"

"What?"

"*What* Hell! You heard me! Unless you feel like pumping right on for me too."

"What?" Horse sees his powerful right arm, pumping, the pipes thudding with the flow of water up to the chute, the crash of the pump handle and piston rod against the cylinder collar. His arm flows like the piston, greased now with his sweat. He continues to pump, looks away from Bud, sees

131

Georgie Booth side-stroking for the raft, the last of his slide wake rippling into the dock.

"Let him take his damn turn like everybody else," Bud says.

"Go on if you're going," Horse tells him. Bud Booth goes up the ladder, blends, vanishes into the sun as Horse's eyes follow him up.

"Serves you right, sit up there all day on your hinder while I'm pumping my guts out for you," Georgie says, rolling out of the water, onto the raft.

"Blow it out your other end," Horse says. "Nobody's asking you to pump." He feels nicely warmed up, right, the way he is after calisthenics, wind sprints, several slow, comfortable laps around the track. Football practice (one more season coming to Horse, but he does not anticipate; it will come). His right arm, shoulder, the long muscles of his back are hot. Good. He feels the faint lake breeze cool the sweat on his face. *Good.* Now.

It is not winter. The days have no span, beginning or end. Are. *Good.* Horse pumps. Bud Booth has decided to stall at the top of the tower. Well and good. Who's in a hurry? Horse thinks.

"So who are you showing off for now? All the little twats went home, ninny," Georgie says, lying out straight on the raft. Like a man fallen asleep on the sand for a tan. Dead-white, touched with pink by the daily sun at Prader's on the points of his shoulder, the freckled bridge of his nose. He looks like a man asleep or dead. Horse, pumping, looks toward the beach. Empty.

Almost empty. Nobody on the dock, the children gone (cleared out of the water, rolled their towels, gone toward Wautoma, thumbing rides), gone. Only the vague figures of the couple (woman seated, man standing next to her chair) all but hidden watching from the deepening shade under the stand of pine trees at the crest of the bank.

"You made your point!" Georgie stands to shout up at his cousin. "Come on, before showboat here breaks his arm off all for nothing!" Bud shouts something back (Horse half hears, cannot make it out) from the top of the tower.

Where did they all go? He continues to pump.

The lake breeze is just a hair cooler against his sweated skin, enough to make him stiffen to resist a shudder. He twists his trunk (still pumping) to sweep the expanse of water. One, two fishing boats at anchor, no more. The sun far enough toward the horizon now that he can focus without squinting, make out the two seated fishermen in each boat. *Where does the time go?*

"Look out below!" Bud Booth cries out from the chute just before he leaves it, hits the water, throws his feet up to allow for a longer skim over the surface on the seat of his trunks. Horse releases the pump handle, surprised to find his fingers stiff, numbed from the effort of his grip. Flexes them, turns his hand, left, right, examines the whitened knuckles, tips, nails, skin of his palm shriveled from half a day in water.

"Pansy," Georgie says. "He always holds his nose. You'll never catch him high-diving. He always has to hold his dumb nose."

"Pump for me. A quick one," Horse says, starts for the base of the ladder.

"Gimme a break!" Georgie says.

"It's your turn, right?"

"Come on! We got to head in. The old man'll have our asses otherwise."

"Just one," Horse says, foot on the first step of the ladder. He sees the longer, thicker shadows cast on the water by the slide tower. Beyond Georgie he sees the emptied beach, dock, no parked cars visible along Prader's access road. A few boats ride the easy ripple of the lake, moored on the other side of Prader's pier. He sees Bud Booth stroking for the pier. "One more time," he says to Georgie.

"Come on, Horse, I told you. We got to get our fannies in gear home."

Leaning against the ladder, Horse feels a faint suspicion of fatigue slip through his innards. He leans until his forehead rests against a step, senses his fingers would not grip if he

133

willed it. His legs want to shake. The breeze off the lake is cooler, cold. Horse's mind pivots—only for an instant—as if seeking a center, to know the directions open to him. What the hell time would it be now?

"What time is it?" he asks Bud, eyes closed, forehead resting against the warm wooden step.

"Search me. You think I wear a watch in swimming? Come on, Horse."

He feels himself getting sick to his stomach. Like a warm autumn day, when he has eaten too much or too little, given too much or not enough in the football drills. He tips back his head, opens his eyes to the clear, darker blue of the sky. "Race you to the dock," he says to Georgie.

"Forget it."

"Spot you ten yards and still wax your ass," Horse says.

"Hey! You should see your face! You got white crap all over your face from the ladder!" Georgie Booth laughs an idiot laugh. "You look like a damn Indian!" he squals. Horse tears loose from the ladder, crouches like a bear, like a rushing tackle.

"Make you eat that one, son!" he says, charges Georgie, who turns, dives from the dock, Horse whooping after him, dives into Georgie's wake, is lost in the dark cold of the water. He will catch Georgie before they are halfway to Prader's dock, will duck him a good one, release him. Lost in the water that shocks, icy cold in the instant of his plunge, then swirls, warming, fresh, warm, all about him as he kicks to add force to his momentum, strokes hard, gropes, feels the flicker of Georgie's ankle at his fingertips, closes, pulls him under for a ducking to remember.

Lost in the water, eyes shut, hands, arms, filled with the struggling Georgie as he pulls him under the water, a presence, noise and pressure in his ears, mixed, blending with the mock-horror shouts of Georgie Booth as Horse pulls him below the surface for a rough ducking.

Horse, lost, finds the center of it all, himself, at perfect ease. He ducks him just enough. Nobody ever gets hurt or angry.

They are able to swim in to Prader's dock, fast friends, taking their time to get Bud's goat. Bud waits, huddling against the cooling air, impatient. "Fool around all you want, see who it is gets it in the neck same as anybody else," he says to his cousin.

"Don't blow a tit," says Georgie.

"We can hitch a ride," Horse says. "You worry too much." And, "Come on, let's get changed if you're in such a rush to get moving." They walk up the pier, hop and skip from one patch of sparse summer grass to another to avoid sandy feet. Horse checks: the watching man and woman have left their post beneath the pines, the chair she sat in gone. Is it somebody brings one of those fancy folding racetrack chairs? They walk slowly across the hard oil-dirt crust of the access road to soak up the warmth that still radiates from it, like the top of a bake oven (when Horse's mother makes bread) in winter, after a day fooling on the frozen ice or tobogganing somebody's hill in the teeth of the wind.

"Dead as a doornail around this dumb place," Georgie says.

"You want egg in your beer?" Horse says.

"Foam on the bottom," Bud says, punches his cousin in the deep muscle of his arm, knuckle jutting from his fist for best effect.

"That can earn you a fat lip."

"Nothing but fear and common sense holding you back," Bud says, putting up his hands, open, for a slap-fight.

"Come on," says Horse. "Remember what a shit you're in to get home?"

Dusk is falling fast, but it is still too early for Prader to turn on the new yellow lights, set along the edge of the pavilion roof to keep bugs away from the dance floor (dance tonight! thinks Horse). There are cars, two of them, parked parallel on the other side of the road, just at the end of the bar and grill. He makes out the shapes of people, Prader, his customers, inside, behind the screens. The pavilion, as they pass, is vacant and dark as a hay barn. Prader will not move the jukebox out from the barroom until after dinner time. The jukebox will go for maybe an hour, while he sells tickets for the dance, then be unplugged, slid back inside the bar and grill when the dance band gets set up (high school kids from Oshkosh; Horse knows them, every Saturday night from mid-June to Labor Day, all summer long).

Horse can all but hear the songs they will punch on the jukebox (Georgia Gibbs, Jo Stafford, Sinatra, Connie Haines, all his favorites—he likes them *all!*). All but hears the shuffle of the dancers, the soles of their shoes rasping on the sand grits left by swimmers who go up from the beach in the afternoons to get out of the worst of the sun, drink a bottle of pop.

"Shag buns, Horse," Bud calls to him from the double outhouse where they change.

"If you're coming with us. You should hardly bother ever going home at all. Why don't you move in? Maybe Prader'd let you sleep in the crapper," Georgie says, disappearing in the outhouse doorway. Horse hears them laughing together inside. He hurries, feels the warmth of the dirt road give way to the damp grass under his feet. The outhouse stink (Prader has not replaced the door some jerk tore off two Halloweens ago) rolls out over him as he turns to enter.

Why not? he thinks to say to George, to make some wise-crack of it. But does not. They would not get it. Would not be funny.

"Shag buns, Horse."

"Keep your shirt on."

"When you giving up and taking off that tape? You're black as a nigger now," Bud Booth says.

"I'll let you know when the spirit moves me," Horse says. Bud and Georgie are busy, lacing their sneakers, checking their pockets to see nothing has fallen out (they stashed their clothes, sneaks rolled inside jeans and t-shirts, up in the exposed over-head rafters of the crapper roof), tucking t-shirts inside their jeans, rolling the short sleeves up above their shoulders to

136

expose their biceps. Horse stands up to lace and tie his ragged sneaks, foot up on the wooden seat of the one-holer. Pivoting, he places his back squarely in the middle of the mirror on the opposite wall (silvering flaked, evaporating—a challenge to comb your hair in it), then turns his head once, quickly, to see his back and shoulders in the mirror, the dirty tape letters square in the middle of his back. Horse. Block letters. Rough, square-cut, three inches high. HORSE. Quickly turns back, stares hard at the laces of his shoes, his fingers pulling them up tight, tying.

HORSE. He cut the letters out, standing over the wastebasket in the kitchen at home, the roll of adhesive from the bathroom medicine chest, his mother's sewing scissors. "Why don't you get my pinking shears and do it up brown if you want to make a spectacle of yourself," she said—late in April, before it was warm enough to go swimming, go without a shirt. "You're not waltzing around here without your shirt on until it gets decently warm. I don't care how cute you think you are," his mother said.

Let him have his fun, his father had said. "He's so silly," his mother said. My God, his father said, the war's getting him soon enough, what's the difference what he does if it pleases him. "You're not to go without your shirt until it's warm," she said.

"I need to get used to it," Horse told her. "It'll probably itch like crazy at first if it's like taping your ankles for football. Help me, Mom. If I do this myself I'll futz it all up." She went into the bathroom with him, placed the strips of adhesive in the middle of his back as he directed her, watching it all with his mother's vanity mirror in his hand, catching the reflection of the medicine chest mirror over the sink, letters reversed to normal in the second mirror. HORSE.

"You're getting a swelled head," she said.

"I'm not either. That's not it. It's just for the heck of it."

True, and not true. By mid-May it would be warm enough to skin off his shirt on the softball diamond behind the consolidated school, while he worked the yard and his mother's flower beds and the Victory garden. He would tan quickly, easily, without burning rosy-red first, blistering, like the Booth cousins. By June, with Prader's open, he would be swimming every day, never wearing a shirt before sunset, and his tan would deepen, go dark brown, darker brown. He did not set a date for taking off the tape. From time to time it loosened; his mother replaced it for him with the new letters he cut from the adhesive roll. He would wait until it *felt* right. Then remove it. HORSE. HORSE. Pale, ghost-white letters, like a brand in the middle of his back.

"You should sell advertising space on your hide," his mother said. "The cannery might like to buy some of that space."

"Will you let him alone about that?" his father said to her. She was not really irritated with him. She believed, also, that the war would get him. She hugged him when she finished patching the water-loosened letters, hugged him hard and kissed him on the arm, all the higher her head came. Horse took his bulk, musculature, from his father's side, but nobody in the family's memory had been so tall.

"I wish I knew her name," she said, watching from the bathroom doorway as he put the tape back in the chest above the sink.

"Whose name?"

"The girl you're setting that bait for."

"Mom," he said. He did not know why he did it. Or he did.

"Will you shag buns?" Georgie Booth said.

"I got to comb my mop," Horse said, bending at the knees to get the top of his head centered in Prader's crapper mirror. "Prader should invest in a new mirror. I can't tell if it's my part or a cracked spot," he said.

"Oh sure. So Showboat can comb his dumb hair."

"We get back late, I'm like as not grounded for tonight," Georgie said.

"You and me both."

"What's the diff in the first place," Horse said. He broke

138

sharply at the knees to view the part in his hair a last time, patted the top of his head gently with the flat of his hand, leered at himself in the cracked mirror a last time, shook his comb, slipped it into the hip pocket of his jeans. "What's so hot tonight you got to get out for anyway?" he said.

"The damn dance is all," Georgie said.

"The which?" Horse said. "Tonight? Here? That's right. I forgot all about it," he said.

"Wake up and die right for a change," Bud Booth said.

Horse stood, blocking the empty doorframe of Prader's outhouse. He looked up at the exposed rafters, as if there were a notice to read posted there, or as if he had put something more up there, tucked behind a beam to keep it safe until he was ready to pick it up. "I completely forgot it's the dance here tonight," he said.

"I give up," Georgie said.

"Are we supposed to walk through you or over you, or are you planning maybe moving your big fat ass outside?" Bud said. Horse laughed, braced himself in the doorway, let them strain and grunt for half a minute, trying to budge him, then let go, and they fell, stumbling after him, out into the first true edge of dusk in the air. In a moment they were on the shoulder of the highways leading into town, thumbs out for passing cars.

Horse Batterman straggles on the walk toward town. He drags his feet, scuffs the soles of his ragged sneakers in the sand and gravel of the road's low shoulder. The Booth cousins do not bother to gripe at him for poking. They get a dozen yards ahead of him, walk side by side, hands jammed in their pockets, muttering about being late, what their fathers will say, do. Their rolled trunks and towels protrude from hip pockets. When they hear a car coming behind them, they pivot, continue walking backward, put up their thumbs. When the car passes without slowing they pivot with it, retract their thumbs, extend middle fingers, curse the driver into the slipstream that drowns their words even as they utter them.

Dark falls rapidly now, the sky about the pines on either

side of the road darkening faster, yet so subtle in its falling as to escape the register of Horse's inattentive eye. Horse hears the approaching cars before they do, turns before they do to stretch out his thumb. He does not turn around to continue walking toward town until after he is sure the Booth boys have turned first, are assaulting the car receding toward Wautoma with their middle fingers, shouting uselessly, their backs to him when at last he pivots around again. He does not want them to see his face.

Horse is smiling. At himself, at everything. At what, he is not sure. He all but laughs. If they could see his face, they would be after him. He will not let them see him. He does not know why he is smiling, what it is threatens to break up into his thought in stupid laughter. What is it?

Something to do with forgetting the dance tonight in Prader's pavilion. A mix of things, a mish-mash. Everything. And nothing. The dance. There is a dance twice a week, and he always goes. He will go tonight, no more than get home, alibi to his parents for being so late, eat, run. Bum a ride with somebody, stand and hitch a ride in the A&W parking lot at the edge of town if need be. Walk it in the full dark, and back, if need be. He always goes. He will go with the Booths (he does not believe their fathers will ground them).

Something to do with the dance at Prader's, that he could have forgotten it. As if he had never been to one before (as if he had not gone to every one, every summer that he thinks he can remember), as if there had never before (ever) been a dance each Friday and Saturday night through full summer at old man Prader's Silver Lake Pavilion. Every Friday and Saturday night each week of summer, through the Fourth, right up to Labor Day. What's so funny about that? Horse asks himself, but clenches his teeth, grabs at his throat to strangle the laughter boiling into his mouth. He has no answer.

Everything. Nothing. Anything. Bud and Georgie Booth up ahead of him, backs to him, walking briskly beside the concrete highway, rolled towels and swim trunks sticking up, bobbing with each stride, hands jammed into the pockets of

140

their jeans, heads down as if they bucked a headwind, shoulders slumped, talking, muttering, mumbling, what their fathers will say, do, for being so late at Prader's, ground them. It starts to come to Horse. What is so damn funny. This day, early evening, early in June, 1944.

He will bite his tongue, leap the drainage ditch, run off into the pines that are darker each minute, before he will let them hear his laughter, let it out. His face is grim, body tense. Inside him, the laughter shakes so hard he wonders how it is a person keeps from falling apart. As it comes to him, the answer. At least a little.

Everything. And nothing. Everything because no one thing (nothing) more than another. And all of it everywhere at once, all at the same time.

Now. In the instant he feels it, feels more than thinks. *Now.* The same as a moment before, so still the same. Now. *Now.* Always, everything, everywhere. Now.

Now, Bud and Georgie Booth walk ahead of him on the road's shoulder, slouched, hands in pockets, rolled towels and trunks bobbing in stride. Now talking (mutter-mumble) about their fathers' grounding them. Now worried the war will not last, wait for them. Now the dance at Prader's (behind them, back over Horse's shoulder now) pavilion they do not want to miss out on. Now walking still up ahead of Horse, talking still now. Horse closes his eyes to slits, darkening the darkening world. Thinks: now the Booth cousins walking ahead of him, talking, their fathers in town, waiting to ground them for the night (the week?) now, and the town there now, Wautoma, now, tonight, tomorrow, yesterday. Last year, the same the year before that, Horse (now) working for their great-grandfather, picking melons and cucumbers in acres that stretch out in sandy loam for summers beyond conception (now), right alongside Georgie and Bud (now walking ahead, talking fathers and Prader's dance and grounded for who knows how long) and Jamaicans as black as tar because the war (now) keeps Mexicans away somehow, picking until their hands swell up red and sore and ache comes into the base of the spine so bad there's no joking in it now, sweat soaking the headband through, filling Horse's eyes so he has to slit them, squint (now) to see the pale green vines in the row between his legs, feet burning through the soles of his sneakers ("Get yourself some shoes you can work in," says Great-grandfather Booth, *old*), and how the migrant Jamaicans sweat even harder than he does, but still talk and sing like they were English instead of black as tar, stinking worse. Now.

Now beyond laughing at it. In it, Georgie and Bud up ahead (no cars coming), the sky darker still melting into the pines across the ditch. Last night, tonight, tomorrow. Day. Night. Now. A great peace comes into Horse Batterman.

Their great-grandfather has his crops in the ground already. Come August he will harvest. He cannot get German war prisoners to pick for him. There are jobs for Georgie and Bud and Horse, but they will not (Horse knows) work the fields this year. Horse will not give up swimming at Prader's each afternoon (he still does not know when he will remove the adhesive tape from his back, does not know when he will know when it is time, right). Georgie and Budd will enlist in something (Marines, paratroopers) before August, they say. Afraid it will not wait. A great peace fills all the uncertain corners in him.

Now they walk the highway to town (no cars coming). Horse sees it all. The sky will darken until only the white t-shirts of the Booth cousins bob before his eyes up ahead. The sky and the tips of the pine trees to his right across the ditch will join in a deeper darkness. A car will come, stop or not stop for them (he is inspired to want to laugh, imagining how they will curse the car if it passes, throw a finger after its amber tail lights), they will ride the rest of the way to town, or walk it. Their folks will ground them for the night (or not), they will miss the dance at Prader's. Or not miss it. Horse's peace is rich.

Bud and Georgie Booth walk ahead, muttering, mumbling (their fathers will or will not ground them), the concrete highway stretches ahead, behind, unbroken, clear of cars in either

142

direction, a bridge or ribbon or dingy grey cord linking town and Prader's, and Horse treads it with the easy arrogance of a highwire artist, his need to laugh at the simplicity and perfection of it all settled now into a cool surety as soothing as the dark green depths of Silver Lake.

What he knows without knowing he knows. It is that all of it (*everything!*) is no more than Horse (he) *is*. The unbroken pavement connects town to Prader's pavilion, and Horse stands (strides now) between them. At the center.

The worn soles of his ragged sneakers make a plopping-shuffling sound in the sand of the low shoulder of the road. They scratch and scuff on patches of small gravel washed free by the spring thaw, early summer rains. On his left slides the dingy (ever darker, starker as the light gives way to dusk) strip of concrete highway, clean of cars now. Behind him, over his shoulder, a mile back, the lights are on at Prader's pavilion, preparations readying for tonight's dance. But, still (now), as Horse walks the highway to town, there at Prader's it is still midafternoon, the sun (now, dusk thickening to darkness among the pines across the drainage ditch) hits the surface of the lake, comes back to the eye (of Horse, atop the slide tower, the center) like the honed blades of knives floating on the even ripples.

And the pavilion lights are on now, a mile behind on the highway, and (now, as Horse walks to town) the dirt access road begins to fill with cars coming in from Wautoma, Redgranite, Berlin, Waupaca, Wild Rose, Omro, even Oshkosh. Older people entering the barroom, others taking the heavy wooden chairs, settling in to watch the dancing on the pavilion floor, the Oshkosh danceband tuning, setting up to play, Horse, his friends, the girls from town, lakers, paying Prader his four-bits to go in under the pavilion roof to dance on the whispering surface of the floor, coated with sand from the feet of the kids passing through all day from the beach.

Now, Bud and Georgie are indistinct in the lowering dark, their t-shirts white blots in the darkness that shift and flash in his eyes. Horse sees the glow of lights from Wautoma. They are over halfway home. A bend, then a rise in the road, and they will make out the lights of the A&w stand. His mother will talk to herself, ask who does he think he is, home no more than a place to eat, sleep, hang his cap when the mood strikes him. His father will say: leave him be, the war's getting him soon enough, isn't it?

Time: now, always, yesterday or tomorrow, so no reason to rush or wish.

Place: Prader's recedes to a soft glow that barely clears the line of the horizon behind him. Now the last rise, the A&w rootbeer stand will come into sight, the edge of town. The highway pavement slides past to his left with each step, the black stands of pines across the ditch to his right. Horse, there, here, now.

He is not thinking of what he thinks about (no need to). It is a moment he will not bother (not care) to recall (the deepness and calm of his great peace!) before he hears the pickup's horn (before he thinks that he is hearing it), the Booth boys calling to him.

"You coming or not?"

"Shake it, man!"

The farmer blows his horn again. Horse can barely discern the bulk of the pickup, the movement of Georgie and Bud as they vault up into the truck bed. Horse laughs, breaks into a trot, run, slams into the truck bed beside them.

"Slow ass," Georgie says.

"You like walking your stumps off?"

"Blow it out your other end," says Horse, and they have passed the A&w stand before he can stop laughing.

"I think you got a screw loose," Bud says.

"I was just thinking," Horse says.

"Tell me and we'll all laugh," Georgie says.

"Big deal," Bud says.

"Seriously," Horse says. "I was just thinking I'd know exactly when I should take that tape off."

"Big, big deal," Bud says.

144

"So, when? Maybe we should organize a street dance in town for it or something," Georgie says.

"When I know it," Horse says. "See? That's what I was thinking."

"I told you he had a screw loose someplace."

"Seriously. I figured out I'll know it's the right time to take it off when it's the right time. Get it?" Horse asks.

"What a jerk," Bud says. Horse punches him, hard, in the muscle of his arm, and the Booth cousins are on him, trying for holds to pin him. "Not in your lifetime, not on your best day you ever dreamed of," Horse says through his laughter, wrestling them off easily. He could throw the Booth boys forever, he feels, and would, but gets to laughing so hard he goes weak, and they pin him.

"Uncle," Georgie says, grinding Horse's neck in a squeezelock.

"Pretty please with sugar on it," Bud says, forcing Horse's arms up behind his back. Horse is laughing too hard to speak.

"Pretty please with sugar and whipped cream."

"Uncle," Horse cries at last through his laughter. "Uncle. Anything you say," and they let him up.

Batterman may have been the only man to serve involuntarily in Korea who did not indulge in bitching. He once reported all the bitching he overheard (this was among the men down in the troop deck of the ship carrying them all over to the Pusan staging area from the collection point at Eta Jima, Japan) to his immediate superior, the ship's troop commander. It was after officers' call, which was more like a stateside garrison coffee call, because there was never anything to add to anyone's orders at the regularly scheduled assemblies in the forward wardroom.

The troop commander had already been on line in Korea, along about the time General Dean was getting himself captured up at Taejon. The troop commander seemed to like to call all his officers to the wardroom to have coffee—and served by the Filipino and Negro stewards and mess boys, to rehearse general and standing special orders for the nth time, and then to lean intently against a bulkhead with his coffee mug in his hand, smoking and looking at the assembled officers. As if he wanted to look hard at men he knew he would fail to keep track of once they debarked.

His tour on line had been a long while before, up at Taejon, when it looked like everyone who was not killed or captured (like General Dean) by the North Koreans was going to keep on running until they fell into the Sea of Japan. The ship's troop commander had simply not gotten over Taejon (where they finally held, shortly after Dean was taken).

This was much later, after MacArthur flanked the enemy at Inchon, after they drove the North Koreans back up against the Yalu. This was shortly after the Chinese Volunteer Army came into it, and they were running back toward Seoul again (from places like the Choisin Reservoir). It was the time when they were funneling replacements in frantically, through Pusan from Japan, and the ship's troop commander, who had not gotten over Taejon (was feeling Taejon all over again in the advance of the Chinese Volunteers) seemed to like to get a very firm grip on the faces, the presence, of the officers he shuttled into Pusan. There was no good reason for holding to the official schedule of officers' calls.

"Sir?" Batterman said, coming up next to the troop commander's post against the bulkhead.

"What is it, mister?" The officers were uncomfortable under the commander's gaze, and no one ever asked even a fake question about the orders, never tried to talk to the commander. They sat at the wardroom tables, holding their mugs in both hands, as if the ship were rolling (the Sea of Japan was not rough this trip), smoking cigarettes they ashed frequently, declining refills on their coffee when the stewards and mess boys came around with the steaming, polished metal pitchers.

The assembled officers sat around until it was polite to leave. There was very little conversation of any sort. The officers calls were a bore and a bother, but they rattled the men more than they should have, because the troop commander stared at them from his bulkhead, and never spoke after the formalities were over, and because the assembled officers all knew about the commander's experience with Dean's command at Taejon, and so they were forced to think about where they were going. Which naturally made a good many of them wonder about coming back in one piece. Or coming back at all.

"I was wondering if it'd be all right to talk to you about a matter," Batterman said. "Not about standing orders, sir. Something else," he added. Now the troop commander was giving his full attention, looking him in the eye, but he did not seem to have heard.

"Batterman, is it?" the troop commander said. He had read the stenciled name tape sewed on over Batterman's left breast pocket. Fatigues were optional aboard ship, though the commander always wore heavily starched CKC's.

"Yes sir. Lieutenant Batterman. I was wondering if I could discuss a matter—" he started to say, feeling silly. If the commander could read his name tape he could also check his collar tab for the silver bar.

"You'd better get those off your combat fatigues, mister," the troop commander said.

"Sir?" Batterman was lost for a moment. He had something he thought he should discuss with his immediate superior. Batterman understood, accepted, approved, the principle of chain-of-command. He wondered if he had done something wrong. The officers crowded at the ward room tables were listening, watching, pretending to drink coffee, smoke cigarettes.

"As good as wearing a target," the commander said. "Haven't you ever been told to strip off those tags, mister? Word to the wise, you'll take off those bars as well. You ever noticed how the sun can pick up a piece of bright metal? Even in winter," he said.

"Yes sir," Batterman said. "I planned on getting that all squared away once we debark. What I wanted to discuss—"

147

the troop commander did not seem to hear anything he said.

"Where are they getting them?" the commander said. He did not seem to be speaking to Batterman, to anyone in particular. "Ninety-day wonder?" he said. Batterman did not understand that he was talking to him this time.

"Sir?"

"Look alive, mister. Keep in mind when and where you are. It might do you some real good some day. I said, are you a ninety-day wonder? How did you come by those bars, mister?"

"No sir. I mean I was ROTC. In college. University of Wisconsin. I'm reserve active. For the duration, I guess."

"You guess," the commander said. "OCS, battlefield commissions, ROTC. Listen to him." He stood away from the bulkhead now, staring past Batterman at the assembled officers in the wardroom, none of whom looked up from his coffee-and. Batterman wondered for a moment if he should consider himself dismissed. It was embarrassing to stand in front of a man who did not seem to truly see or hear him.

"Yes sir," Batterman said. He said it to get the commander's attention, to free himself of the sense he had of the men in the wardroom waiting for something to happen, hoping it would not involve them, waiting for it to be over so they could leave their empty mugs and dirty ashtrays for the stewards and messboys, clear out to their respective troop decks.

"You were saying, mister," the troop commander said. "You had something to say?"

"Yes sir," he said again. Now he had his attention. He could feel the men at the tables relax, exhale, loosen their grips on their mugs, light fresh cigarettes. "I wanted to discuss the matter of the men in the troop hold I've been assigned, sir. The enlisted men."

"What of it?"

"Well. Well, sir, it's sort of vague when you go to put a finger on it."

"I'll be the judge of that. Spit it out, mister."

"Yes sir. It's about the EM I'm responsible for, sir. On my

148

troop deck, they're doing a lot of grousing, sir. I thought I should at least bring it up to you."

"Grousing?" the troop commander said, as if he has never heard the word used. "Bitching," he said, and, "What of it?"

"Just that they're doing a lot of it, sir," Batterman said.

"About what?"

"Just about everything, sir. You name it. The ship, the chow, the noncommissioned officers, the way it's all being handled." Batterman tried hard to think of all the things the men were bitching about. "It's hard to put your finger on it when you go to detail it, sir," he said.

"Anybody saying as how he plans on not debarking when we hit Pusan?"

"Sir?"

"I said have you heard any EM state an intention to decline getting off this can once we're tied up at the dock at Pusan?"

"No sir," Batterman said. "What I meant was there's just a lot of pretty rough talk about most everything. I didn't mean to imply any special disobedience, disrespect, anything like that."

"Hang loose, mister," the ship's commander said to him. He leaned back again into the bulkhead, looked down into his mug to see if there was any coffee left in it, looked up, shot his eyes about the wardroom, as if searching for a mess boy with refills, or as if checking to see if he had the attention of the assembled officers. As if what he had to say now was by way of an addition to standing orders.

"You just hang loose," he said to Batterman. "A good soldier's no soldier at all if he isn't bitching about the chow or the logistics some way, mister," he said. "You just concentrate on keeping your keester close to the ground once we turn you loose. You keep your mind on your business. Less likely the gooks'll chew your keester up for you that way," he said to Batterman.

Batterman stood looking at the troop commander, feeling stupid, sure he looked stupid in front of the other officers in transport (who would never have approached the troop com-

149

mander), sure he had come off stupid before a superior officer, feeling stupid because he had not said what he wanted. He was not even certain now what, in the first place, he *had* wanted to say.

"That's all, mister," the troop commander said, for which Batterman was grateful, because it allowed him to turn and walk away, leave the wardroom for his troop deck, or go topside for air, the ship's store, anywhere. None of the other officers in transport to Korea ever said anything about the incident to Batterman. They were grateful because his leaving the wardroom was an excuse for them to mash their cigarettes, slide their mugs to the centers of the tables, rise and follow him out. They were released from another boring, irritating officers' call, and besides, none of them knew Batterman from Adam, and none of them expected to ever see him again once they all debarked at the Pusan staging area.

Batterman went back to his troop deck. He was a good officer, regularly presenting himself among the enlisted men in his charge, making a point of conversing with the senior noncoms, standing by at musters for chow and cleaning details, there to take reports from the NCO-in-charge at reveille and lights out, noting violations in safety and security SOP to pass on to the noncoms.

He put himself among these men, whom he did not know (and never expected to see again once they debarked at Pusan), and he listened to their bitching, and then he put it out of his mind, because he had been told to. That was good enough for Batterman.

The EM bitched about the chow because it was not as good as the chow at Eta Jima, and because the ship's cooks who cooked it were not good cooks, and because the EM were put on KP rosters to help serve it and clean up afterwards, and because they were forced to line up in narrow gangways and on ladders between decks before they could eat. And they bitched because they were going to Korea surface transport (some small whole-units were flown in from Japan), and they bitched because the ship was an old ship, and it stank of machine oil and the odor of all the men crammed aboard her, and because even a gentle sea seemed always about to crush the hull of the ship because the ship's screws made the bulkheads and decks vibrate, and they were afraid they would sink, drown, before they ever got to Korea.

They bitched because they had been drafted in the first place, and bitched about men they knew in their hometowns who should have been drafted ahead of them, but who had still not been drafted. The RA's bitched because they had been lied to by the recruiting sergeants, not received options they had enlisted for. Career noncoms bitched because they had not received rank they felt they rated, or bitched because they had not demanded special options when they reenlisted. The noncoms bitched because the men under them were poorly trained and slow to move when commanded. And they bitched because the officers failed to keep out of their way, and because all but a few of the officers in transport as replacements were National Guard or ROTC (like Batterman) or ninety-day wonders from Fort Benning. All the enlisted men, from grade E-7 down to the E-2s, bitched about the Truman Year of extended service laid on them by presidential order because of Korea.

They had been bitching since before Batterman had joined the consignment at Eta Jima, and they bitched all the way across the Sea of Japan to Pusan, Korea. But shortly after the ship's troop commander told him to forget it, Batterman stopped listening to it. He was the kind of officer who was perfectly able and willing to follow any order given him. Batterman still heard the grumbling whenever he went among them (as a good officer should). He simply no longer listened to it.

And Lieutenant Batterman, USAR, was not bitching, had nothing he felt like bitching about. Batterman was not worried.

Once he understood there was no need for him to listen to the EM placed in his charge enroute to Korea, and so no need to spend more than a perfunctory amount of his time with them, he kept to himself, because he enjoyed that. He attended the twice-daily officers' call, but he drank his coffee and smoked his cigarettes, asking no questions of the special and standing orders presented or elaborated, and initiated little conversation with the other assembled officers. He made a point of being at the head of the line when the ship's store opened to sell PX material, and he showed up for chow in the officers' galley, and he made his routine checks of the men in his assigned troop deck. He had it all down, understood, under control, the business of being an officer enroute to a combat zone, and because the slight pitch and roll of the ship did not bother him, and because the vibration of the turbines did not bother him, he enjoyed it. He had figured he would enjoy it, and he did.

What he enjoyed most was getting off by himself on the ship. He did not go off alone to *think*. He went off, sometimes to sit on some of the lashed cargo fore or aft on the top deck (officers were issued a red ID tag permitting this), sometimes to lean over the rail at the fantail, watching the wake of the ship below, the gulls that dipped and swooped close to the water, ready for the garbage jettisoned from time to time off the galley deck, sometimes to sit at the joint of deck and housing bulkhead, shaded from the sun, shielded from the wind that whipped the ship's rigging, the fine spray that came up over the bow. He enjoyed most getting off someplace alone like this, to watch the light swell of the glistening, oily-looking surface of the Sea of Japan, the streaked clouds in the distance, the churning wake, the hovering gulls. Anything, nothing, everything.

Batterman would think of things, but he was not *thinking*. Sometimes he watched whatever there was to watch. Sometimes he narrowed his eyes to the point where things blurred, saw things, but could not have said what they were. Sometimes he closed his eyes just to see what would come to his mind. What he enjoyed most was the sense he had of how much he was enjoying doing what he was doing, being where he was, who.

Batterman was not bitching. What was to worry? He was enjoying it, and sometimes, for reasons he did not understand or question, he came close to laughing. He did not laugh. Anyone seeing him off by himself would not realize that he often all but laughed.

Several members of the ship's crew took note of Lieutenant Batterman. Deckhands going fore and aft to check the tarpaulins lashed on the cargo got used to seeing him at the rail or seated in the shade of a housing bulkhead. EM's using the fantail to clean mops by dragging them at the ends of lines in the ship's wake had to ask him to give them room to work. Nobody ever saw him laughing.

And he did not laugh, and did not smile, but came close to it. It was like there was another Batterman, a *real* one, smaller (yet just as big and strong, stronger) than the Lieutenant Batterman leaning with his forearms on the rail, sitting, looking off at the sea, sky, gulls, everything and nothing. For all the world as if there were not crewmen walking past him to check deck cargo, or EM on fatigue detail, needing to get where he was, on the ship's fantail, with their dirty mops and coils of sealine for trailing the mops clean in the wake. The ship's crewmen and the detailed EM took note of him. A big, strong looking, handsome (Indian-looking almost, he was so dark and ruddy at the same time) first lieutenant, staring off at nothing and anything for all the world like there was no ship, no war just up ahead on the Korean peninsula (with all holy hell breaking loose, waves of Chinese Volunteers pouring over the Yalu up north, about to push the combined Eighth Army and the ROK's into the drink!).

Batterman did not worry, did not fear, because there was nothing he regretted. There was no past he could or would have pinned with the blame for this present, this now. And he understood how it might have looked to somebody else. How it *did* look to certain other people. Which was what made the little (the *real*) Batterman inside Lieutenant Batterman, USAR (Infantry Unassigned) laugh and laugh and laugh, until Lieutenant Batterman wondered at himself, how he was always able to keep that laughing (*real*) Batterman from breaking out to the outside.

153

Being when and where and who he was, *thinking*, for just an instant, of the way things turned out, and so, how foolish it made *thinking* much of anything about it at all. The way, for instance, it turned out about his missing the war (World War II, what people were already calling *the big one*). An example of how it turned out to make foolish the worry over thinking one way or another about anything.

He thought how Bud and Georgie Booth could not stand to have it happen without them. They begged (Batterman was not in on all of that, but had an idea of the show they made for their parents for consent to enlist) until they got consent, and went off to Milwaukee on a Greyhound to join the Marine Corps. In time for Iwo. Where Bud was KIA and Georgie so severely wounded he was over a year in a California naval hospital, where he met some woman, married her (ready-made with three kids, a war widow herself, lived to this day, never returned even to show his wife and ready-made kids to his parents, grandparents, great-grandfather (old Ward Booth still alive and kicking) in Wisconsin.

Which was to say next to nothing until any number of other things were added. Like, the notice of Bud Booth KIA published in the Waushara *Argus*, the black border on the front page, that summer of 1945, while Batterman was doing two-a-day drills at Camp Randall, the coaches already looking ahead to the asset he would be in the backfield, his sophomore year. Somebody (maybe Bud's mother?) sent him the front page of the *Argus*, to say: here's your best friend dead, another shot to pieces, on Iwo Jima and you practicing football.

Which made no sense at all unless he recalled a certain feeling in the air when the word came out he had been accepted in the ASTP program at the University, everyone knowing full well it was the football team wanted Horse Batterman, not the Army Air Corps.

Batterman-within-Batterman laughed and laughed, laughed, laughed.

154

He had been glad to be up early at Camp Randall for fresh-man football drills, not there in Wautoma on V-J Day, when the town closed down, turned the fire siren on for ten solid minutes, and the editor of the *Argus* put a display of the pic-tures of the dead (Bud Booth in dress blues, white hat, grin-ning—doomed in the instant the photographer's shutter snapped) in his window, and they erected the new Honor Roll in the park next to the mill pond, across the street from the Park Theater, where only Spanish movies were billed sum-mers, for the Mexican pickle pickers who had begun to come back, replacing the British-speaking Jamaicans and labor-service German POWs used in the pinch of the wartime man-power shortage.

Laughed. Because with V-J Day the vets came back, and it was Jug Girard who did the running for the University of Wisconsin Badgers in the Big Nine games at Camp Randall, and Batterman was seldom called upon even to block for the Jugger. There were plenty of vets, better by far than any eigh-teen-year-old from a Class C high school. And who, it turned out, was really not all that big or fast when put up against the teams fielded in the Big Nine starting in '46, all of them rich with returned vets. The Badgers, even with Jug Girard back from service, were no match for Michigan, Minnesota, or Ohio State.

"You got a bad break, one way of looking at it, kiddo," old Prader said to him during the summer of his junior year, when it was clear Horse Batterman would be lucky to earn a varsity letter in football. "The way it panned out," Prader said. He had given Horse a summer job at the pavilion each year since he left for college. The athletic department at the university could have fixed him up with something that paid, construction or truck driving, in Madison or Milwaukee, but Horse always elected to go home and work for Prader. Prader himself told him he could make better money working for old Ward Booth, supervising crews of pickers. Horse, not bothering to explain (not having explained it to himself), said no, he preferred working at the pavilion as long as he was welcome. And besides, his parents liked having him home. A miracle his father had said, how the war had not gotten him.

"That's what I meant by what I said, sort of," Prader told Horse. "If the war'd gone on another two-three years, you could have played football, made a break of some kind for yourself."

"I don't see it that way, Mr. Prader," Horse said. "You could look at it the other way around, too. Some people around here do. I had the football thing lined up, so I didn't run off to enlist like some did. That way, the war didn't turn out for me the way it did for some. The wrong kind of break, I mean."

"I don't get you," Prader said.

"I had in mind guys like Bud and Georgie—Booth," he added when Prader did not seem to recognize the first name.

"Booth? Yeah, sure. You get that silliness out of your head, boy. Sure, they're just kids, they didn't know what they were asking for. Still, everybody takes their own chances. Make your bed, you lie in it, good or bad," Prader said, and, "Which is it now got himself killed over there?"

"Bud," Horse said. "Georgie's still out in that hospital the last I heard." It was funny how he could say their names, *Bud*, *Georgie*, and not feel anything strange about it, not feel the one dead, the other supposed to be wounded so badly at Iwo Jima he had to be doped up twenty-four hours a day to live with it. Horse did not go to see their parents.

But he could say their names, hear them mentioned, think of them, and it was no different than it had ever been. As if they had not hopped a Greyhound bus for Milwaukee, enlisted, been killed, wounded. Sometimes it felt (when he said their names, heard them, thought of them) so much the same he believed he could look up toward the beach, pick them out among the swimmers out on the slide.

"You get that kind of thinking right out of your head," Prader said. "That's a waste of time. Listen," he said, "this ain't the first war I seen come through this country. There's a plenty men did like your pals, the drop of a hat went off to join the damn war. I'm talking 1917 now. You know Spaulding?"

"I'm not sure I know who you mean," Horse said.

"Spaulding. He's got the big old place just across from Moose Inn on the lake road there, down 21."

"I know who you mean, yeah."

"Yeah," Prader said, "he always used to bring his old mother up here for a drink in the afternoons, sit out there in the shade and watch you kids swimming and what not."

"I know who you mean," Horse said, not sure he knew, but wanting to be helpful, let Prader say what he wanted to say.

"Yeah, his old man," Prader said, "big lawyer, banker from Chicago, built one of the first places on the lake, damn near old enough to be *my* old man, dropped everything at the drop of a hat, went off and got himself killed. I think it left the two of them, his wife and boy I mean, cracked a little. Anyway, he went off over there and got killed. Me?"

"That's when you built the pavilion, isn't it? I remember you saying," Horse said.

"Damn right," Prader said. "Opportunity, I'm talking about," he said. "I seen the war coming as good as the next man. '17 I'm talking now. I got my hands on some money, how I won't go into just here, and I built me this place. I could make out what was going to happen with property around the lake, what with the good road over to Oshkosh, up from Chicago, Milwaukee, you name it. I could see what it'd mean for a resort area. Let me tell you," he said to Horse.

"They sure come," Horse said, "from first of June, even earlier, all the way through Labor Day."

"That's what I could see coming," Prader said. "It's not so sweet as it used to be. There's too many for them to choose from. Even on Silver Lake, you got your Moose, your Silvercryst."

They did not talk for a few moments. Prader stood behind the bar, leaning on his forearm, fingers interlaced, as if he held a small, rare insect in the cage of his hands. Batterman sat

157

across the bar from him on a stool, one leg over the other. Batterman looked out through the screened windows at the sparkling lake beyond the stand of pines above the beach. He was thinking how it did not *feel* as though Bud Booth was dead on the island of Iwo Jima. Nothing felt any different than it ever had. It made him want to laugh.

"Get that foolishness out of your head," Prader said to him. "That one I was telling you, Spaulding's old man, the big banker or what-all from Chicago, tried what he could do to stop me building this place. But I built it anyway. Until he went over there and got himself killed. Like your pals," he said.

"I don't let it bother me, Mr. Prader," Horse said.

"I know what you're talking about though. You forget it. Let that sort of people think or say all they want. You make your opportunities, you take what you can." They were silent for a moment again, and then Prader said, "You don't think you'll play much this year coming, huh?"

"No," Horse said. "I'm lucky if I even letter."

"It's a shame."

"I don't really feel that way about it. They got way too many really good guys came back from service. I'm just a shrimp up next to some of them, I swear," he said, and they laughed together, at the idea of Horse Batterman a shrimp beside any normal sort of man.

"Hell with them all!" Prader said in his laughter. "Anytime you need a job, you got it here with me, buster!"

"I'll keep that in mind," Horse said, and they laughed together again.

Lieutenant Batterman leaned over the ship's rail at the fantail, staring down at the tangled wake, or sat in the shade on the steel deck, his back against the housing, and the little-Batterman-inside-Batterman laughed and laughed and laughed.

Because he remembered anything, everything, but did not have to remember, made no point of it, did, and because it was all the same, all the time, always, all, because Bud and Georgie

158

had gone off with parents' consent, hopped the Greyhound in front of the drugstore on Main in Wautoma (where it had always stopped, still did, even now, in '51), carried off to Iwo Jima, to a naval hospital in southern California, to a grave on Iwo, to the arms of a war widow with three children, yet for Batterman-inside-Batterman were still in Wautoma (picking melons for their great-grandfather, swimming off the slide raft, thumbing rides back to town from the pavilion, hopping a Greyhound in front of the drugstore on Main), were still *here*, inside there with the Batterman within Lieutenant Batterman, who stood, lost in thought (not-*thinking*) at the ship's fantail, or in the shade of the deck housing.

Because there was no need to worry or think, nothing to sweat, because things happened or did not, and that was something happening too. Like Jug Girard returning to do all the ball carrying for the Badgers in the Big Nine. Batterman watched it all in a prime seat on the end of the bench, below the stands, on the field at Camp Randall. He did not letter. The last home game of his senior year, they lined up all the uniformed seniors on the field at half time for applause from the crowd, and there was tremendous applause. They played Purdue that day, and they always beat Purdue.

Somebody said later that the Jugger was weeping. The great Jug Girard wept as the band played *On Wisconsin* three times through without a pause, and thirty thousand fans in the stands at Camp Randall stood up, singing, screaming, waving Bucky Badger pennants all through it. Batterman heard somebody say even Jug Girard was weeping (because, he wondered, Wisconsin had not had enough to take Minnesota, Michigan, or Ohio State because Jug did not make All-American because there were men like Blanchard and Davis and Bob Chappius and the Elliot brothers at Michigan?), which may have been true. It was true that the men on either side of Batterman had wept, or nearly so. They sucked at the emotions rising in their throats, blinked their eyes at the welling tears. Batterman did not weep. He all but laughed. It was all the same to him. Any way it happened.

159

Lieutenant Batterman had nothing to bitch about. The ship rolled gently across the Sea of Japan to Pusan, the Chinese Volunteers poured across the Yalu, crossed the 38th Parallel, and it looked like they were going to meet. The ship's troop commander lived in dread of it (though he would return with the ship to Japan, for another load of replacements). The officers and men on their way to meet the advancing Chinese bitched (Lieutenant Batterman understood) about everything except the Chinese, which was why they bitched, haunted by the future as the troop commander was haunted by his past. Batterman did not sweat it.

There was no need to keep peeking around the corner for a glimpse of the road ahead. It was going where it was going, would go there, sooner or later. No need to keep looking over your shoulder to see where you'd been. That never changed, and a man (Lieutenant Batterman knew without knowing he knew it) kept all that stored up inside him all the time he kept on walking down the road, toward the next corner.

That was all inside there (not left behind, like the lights of Prader's pavilion glowing up from behind the big oaks surrounding Prader's pavilion house), inside with the *real* Batterman. That's what made him want to laugh sometimes.

Like the war ending in August '45, while he was up at Camp Randall, doing two-a-day freshman football drills, cutting as many classes as he dared for football, but keeping up the show of attendance for his ASTP meetings. *Take down your service star, Mother*, they sang as they marched to and from meetings in their suntan uniforms, *your boy's in the ASTP*.

The war was over (they blew the fire siren in Wautoma for ten minutes by the clock, his mother wrote him, and there was a picture of Bud Booth in his dress blues in the window of the Waushara *Argus*). His ASTP class was disbanded. A few men left school, unable to afford tuition, room, and board from their own pockets. Batterman hoped for a football scholarship, but that money was being held now for returning servicemen, vets like Jug Girard, who were proven quality (granted new eligibility in patriotic gratitude). They could not gamble on unknowns from Class C upstate high schools. But they could use a little influence with the army reserve unit based in Madison, and with the campus ROTC. They found room for Batterman in the ROTC.

Batterman showed up for weekly drill meetings and he put in his summer training at Camp McCoy, and when Korea broke out they activated him.

"I always used to fret your mother so," his father said the last summer Batterman was home, a college graduate with no apparent prospects, still doing schoolboy's work for Prader, "saying how sure I always was the war'd take you away from us."

"A shame, in a way," Prader said. "The war gets over and you end up picking up splinters off the bench. That could have been a fine opportunity for you, boy."

Lieutenant Batterman was too tired to bitch, laughing away inside, the way he did, crossing the Sea of Japan to Pusan, to meet (or not meet) the Chinese Volunteers on their way south, pushing the Eighth Army ahead of them, already at the gates of Seoul.

What was around the corner was around the corner. And would wait for him. What was past was not past. It was right there with him, running toward that bend in the road just ahead. It always worked out in the end.

They anchored the ship in Pusan harbor because there were no open berths. The retreat going full blast up north took a lot of logistics. Batterman borrowed a pair of binoculars from a captain standing next to him at the deck muster. He could make out the heavy Patton tanks they were hoisting out of cargo holds onto the docks with cranes. The replacements had to go over the side of the ship on nets, to the boats waiting below. It was awkward going over the side in full gear (steel pot and liner, pack, cartridge belt, weapon slung, only one hand free, duffel in the other). Batterman was posted by a ship's officer to straddle the rail, control the count of men going over the side to fill the boats that pulled up, one after the other, for a load of men off the nets.

161

The water was not rough, but the small, light loading boats, piloted by bored sailors who wore their life jackets, casually, open, tossed and bumped against the hull of the troopship. The men clinging at the bottom of the nets (the nets were long enough to trail into the opaque surface of the harbor) had to time it right to let loose of the nets, leap out for the swaying, pitching boats, avoid falling into the aisle of dark water that opened and closed like an eyelid between the boats and the ship.

"Sit tight here until you see a new troop deck come forward on the deck to go over. You can recognize the new color tags. Yours are red, the next deck's green, I think. Or yellow. Whatever," the ship's officer said.

"I got you."

"Just see you don't let more over into the nets until they get some empty boats under to catch them. We don't want to be fishing anybody out. That water's cold," he said to Batterman.

"I'll do my best."

"Just pay attention is all."

He was paying attention. The man falling was no fault of Batterman's.

He had to make a rough count of the men in the nets, descending, clumsy, awkward in full gear, estimate the space left in the waiting stand of boats. It was guesswork, but it went fine through two sets of boats, pulling up alongside like a row of taxis at a curb, idling, the bored sailor with open life jacket leaning on the tiller in each boat. The boats filled with the green uniforms, the clusters of steel pots like brown mushroom caps, the oily black slit of water that opened in the swell to eight, ten feet at a time, closed in a wink that left only a thin liquid line visible to Batterman on his perch on the rail.

He glanced up from time to time, took in the sweep of Pusan harbor, the crowded docks, the landing boats that circled as they waited their turn to approach the troopship, the neat wave of boats that receded toward the docks, their white wakes evaporating into the gentle black swell of the sea as the tide worked. Above him, the winter cloud cover hung low, as if it were just above the tips of the ship's rigging. Gulls hovered and swooped in the whipping, cold wind, screeching, waiting for something to be thrown on the water for them.

But he *was* paying attention. If he had not, the memory of the fallen man would have bothered him, he knew. But he was doing exactly as ordered by the ship's officer, had done it with no hitches through two sets of landing boats, pulling up, loading, pulling away. Batterman halted the flow of men going over into the nets each time, held them at the rail until the new boats were ready for them below. He knew he was doing it right. The ship's officer was there, observing, until halfway through the second set of boats. He did not come back until after the man fell.

The man's falling had nothing to do with Batterman's responsibility. He fell because it was sticky going, trying to get over the rail, catch a decent footing in the net with full gear on, only one hand free. He fell because he was afraid he would fall.

"I don't think I can make that, sir," somebody behind him said. He turned. It was the man who was going to fall.

"Relax," Lieutenant Batterman said. "We're none of us are going anywhere until they get those boats lined up." The third set of loading boats cut in from their holding pattern, slowing to a crawl as the first in line came alongside.

"Ain't no way I can go down that thing," the man who would fall said. "No sir. I couldn't even climb the tower on the confidence course in basic. They had me on KP until my breath smelled like the grease trap, but I couldn't do it, Lieutenant," he said. Batterman turned farther on his perch to see the man. He was a private, but there was no name tag where there should have been one. He could see the stitching holes in the private's field jacket where there had been a name tape. There were plenty of noncoms among the men who had done time on line in Korea earlier, like the ship's troop commander, and they had made the men tear off their name tapes, wrap their dogtags with adhesive to prevent noise.

"Couldn't climb the confidence course, no way I can do it with all that water under me," he heard the man who was

163

going to fall say. He meant to turn again, at least say something reassuring, but the helmsman in the lead boat below hand-signaled to send the men over into the nets. Batterman turned back to the men, waved them over.

"Hit it," Lieutenant Batterman said. The men went over the rail, steel pots, entrenching tools, slung weapons clanking, their duffels making soft popping sounds as they hit the rail, the hull, with each further step down in the nets. For only a second (no more) Batterman lost sight of the man who was about to fall. He lost him in the scramble of green combat fatigue uniforms going over the rail, the clatter and rattle of their gear. But he heard him speak a last time in the instant before he fell.

"Man, I *told* you I was subject to fall," Batterman distinctly heard him say. Then he saw him, falling. It was like having had a dream in which somebody is going to fall, and he knew it was a dream, so did not worry, then was shocked awake by a noise or a shout, and seeing somebody, real now, falling.

The tangle of men had somehow cleared, one bunch already over, descending slowly in the nets, the next not yet up on the rail, still getting a last firm grip on their duffels, tightening chin straps, reslinging weapons. Batterman had a clear view of the falling man from his perch. He fell like a mannequin, head first, steel pot squarely on his head, rifle slung, duffel still held in one hand, the other held out, away from his body, as if it were the one sound wing of a wingshot bird. He fell without a sound, as if he were a stuffed fatigue-colored sack dropped to measure the distance to the bottom of some deep well, and no one was to make noise, everyone to count the seconds silently to measure the depth, waiting for the splash at the bottom.

There was not much of a splash when he hit. Batterman watched from his perch, holding the cold rail between his legs tightly with both hands, squeezing the rail with his legs the way he had been taught to ride a bareback horse (old Ward Booth always kept a couple of riding hacks for his great and great-great grandchildren). Batterman stiffened, afraid the fall-

164

ing man would land on the closest bobbing boat, the force of his fall plowing him right through the light bottom of the wooden boat, or, worse, smack the boat's gunwales, splatter like a bad melon tossed into the weeds alongside the patch. Batterman held himself tight, waiting for it.

But the waiting boat slid sideways, away from the troop-ship, opening wide the eye of oily black harbor water, and the falling man slipped into it with no more break in the surface than a feeding bass makes going after a skating waterbug. The black eye of water opened, the falling man knifed into the surface, the surface closed as easily as an eye within an eye, and the waiting boat (the helmsman, bare hands tucked in armpits under the open life jacket, against the cold, did not see it) slid back against the ship's hull, bumped and bobbed there. Then everybody began to shout.

The men in the nets froze where they were, screamed up at Batterman to do something, cursed the helmsmen in the land-ing boats, who did not seem to know anything had happened. The men on deck jammed the rail to see what it was, jostling Batterman on his perch.

The boat moved away from the ship in the next swell. Batterman was trying to think how much of his gear to doff before it would be safe to jump for the man when he rose, tried to keep his eyes on the place where the black eye of water would open, wondered if anyone would hear him if he yelled for a rope or a preserver to throw over the side.

But the fallen man never came to the surface. Either he came up under the hull of the ship or one of the boats, drowned there and sank in his full gear, or never rose at all, went straight to the bottom of the harbor with all that metal hooked and slung on him. The eye of water opened and closed, opened and closed, opened and closed again, and all they ever found was the man's duffel, floating out on the other side of the landing boats. Batterman remembered he could get the man's name, stenciled, off the duffel, but he never got to see the rescued duffel.

They took him off his rail perch, put another lieutenant

there in his place. They questioned him, and the ship's officer chewed his ass good, probably because he was angry with himself for not being on hand when it happened. Then they sent him over the side with the last of the troop replacement. Batterman was the last replacement officer off the ship.

"Suppose you give it to us one more time," the ship's officer in charge of boats said.

"All I can tell you is what I already have, sir," Batterman said. "I didn't take him seriously enough, I guess. I lost sight of him for just a second. The next I knew he was halfway down upside down in the air toward the water. He never said another word that I heard. I don't think they even saw him fall, down in the boats. There's nothing more I can tell you, sir," he said.

"You're a cool enough customer, I'll say that for you," the ship's officer who had put Batterman on his perch said. Batterman could see him making what points he could with his superior, the officer in charge of all boats.

"Kept your mind on your job, this kind of thing tends not to happen," the ship's troop commander said. He was called in to the discussion because he was responsible for the men shipped in for replacements. His presence upset Batterman the most. He felt he had been given orders by the troop commander, at officers' call, followed them, but appeared not to have followed them. Lieutenant Batterman knew he had done nothing wrong, only that he appeared to have dogged off his duty.

"I can only say what I've said, sir," Batterman said.

"Cool as hell," the ship's officer said. Batterman did not understand what he meant, what he was harping at.

"Get him over the side," the ship's officer in charge of boats said. "We can't solve anything in this. I'll brief the old man. Get him on his way," he said to his subordinate, and to the ship's troop commander, "Okay by you?"

"I've got nothing to contribute," he said. Batterman looked at him; his eyes were as distant and vacant as if it were another officers' call, and he were watching everyone in the light of his time on line in Korea, in the days back up at Taejon, when the

166

gooks had nearly pushed them off the peninsula, when General Dean had been captured trying to stop gook tanks with a bazooka.

The ship's officer who had set him on the perch escorted him to the rail, and Batterman went over in the net, down to a single waiting landing boat. It was nearly dark. The ship's officer said it again.

"You're just cool as a cucumber, aren't you," he said to Batterman. Batterman could not remember what the officer's rank was, what the Navy called it, but he wore captain's bars on his collar tab, so he held back what he felt like saying.

"I wish you'd come on out and say what it is bothers you about me, sir," he said. He had his duffel in one hand, his carbine in the other, ready to sling arms, go over the side to the boat below. He did not want to spend more time with the ship's officer. It would be tricky enough going down the net without trying it in bad light.

"You," the ship's officer said. "Man drowns in front of your very eyes, you don't blink twice from where I'm watching you. That man's still on the bottom of this harbor this minute if he hasn't gone out to sea with the tide already, that is. You don't so much as blink at it from what I see. I call that one cool cucumber."

"You think I could have done anything about it?" Batterman said. "He never even came back up. What'd you expect me to do, skin dive for him with my steel pot on? I told you he fell when I was busy doing what you told me to do. You heard it all."

"Sure," the ship's officer said. "It don't hardly break your heart though, does it."

"You think that'd bring him up on the surface so you could rescue him?" Batterman said. He slung his carbine, reached for the rail with his free hand. "You think maybe if you'd been standing by here *you* might have stopped him falling?"

"Get your ass off this vessel," the ship's officer said.

"Yes sir." Batterman went over the side, down the net, into the waiting boat. The boat's helmsman smoked a cigar that

167

glowed in the deepening dark like a lighthouse beacon (like the fireflies in the woods around Wautoma, Silver Lake). It was very tricky going, in the net with the light failing, but he took it slow and easy, and knew (without knowing it) that he would not fall. Because he was not afraid of falling.

"Are you it?" the helmsman said around the cigar in his teeth, barely loud enough to be heard over the drone of the boat's engine, the whine of the wind, colder now with the light fading, the thick, heavy slap of the water against the thin, wooden gunwales of the loading boat.

"Me myself and I," Batterman shouted back to him from the other end of the boat. Then the engines revved, and the ship's lights diminished, the lights on the docks came up clearer over the bow, where Batterman sat, facing into the sharp wind, and then he was going through the Pusan repo depot with the last EM from his shipment. The culls, the eight-balls, left-footers, professional privates, not a good soldier or a combat veteran among them.

Which was what sent them all into the hands of the advancing Chinese Volunteers so quickly.

The way it happened, Batterman and three dozen of his culls were trucked into the line to replace casualties suffered by the 24th Division. They were given a hot meal (standing up, the steaming mess kits and cups in their hands, huddled next to the field ovens under a kitchen fly-tent to protect them from the ever-colder wind that blew out of the north), processed by a battalion adjutant, slipped into the bunkers that made up the most recent line of defense. The headlong retreat from the Yalu was over. The 24th figured to hold, southeast of Seoul.

It was comfortable in the company's headquarters bunker, dug in snugly into the front wall of the trench. There were field stoves in all the bunkers, and the bottoms of the trenches were well drained, lined with duck boards against the water that gathered when a cold rain fell, or the light snow that fell most nights and melted in the afternoons. It was dry and well lighted in the company HQ bunker. Batterman had been thinking about trenchfoot. He had been warned, in Japan, during the orientation briefing at Eta Jima, that trenchfoot took more men than the gooks did. Batterman was glad to be there, somewhere, finally, after the Pusan snafu (the fallen man), the long, deadly cold hours in trucks with his three dozen culls and left-footers from the troopship.

The company commander had paperwork on them, and was not so glad.

"Is there anything special about you that's not in here where I can read it, Batterman?" the CO said.

"No sir. I'm not exactly sure what you mean. I'm reserve active, if that's it."

"I could figure that from your serial number," the CO said. He looked younger than Batterman, and wore no insignia of rank. He had not been with the 24th for very long. He had not been with them long enough to have seen the snowy wastes of the Yalu River basin, but he had joined the division before they were pushed back across the 38th parallel, and so the papers on the three dozen new culls worried him. And Lieutenant Batterman worried him because the lieutenant had come in with the left-footers. The CO worried that the new officer was part and parcel of the duds who had been sent him by the battalion adjutant.

"What I can't figure is how you tie in with these new bodies," he said, waving the paper work on the new men at Batterman. The CO sat at a field table, next to the HQ radioman's table. He wore an OG shirt with the sleeves turned back. It was nicely warm in the bunker.

"No way at all, sir," Batterman said. "I was held up back on the boat, getting off at Pusan. They threw me in with them because we were all that was left when they filled the organization tables they had open at the time. I know what you mean about them, sir," he said, "I could see that just from looking. Half of them are stockade rejects, I'd bet on it."

"Would you now," the CO said.

"I can promise you I'm not one of them," Batterman said. He thought about telling the CO of the fallen man, explain it, tell him he was a graduate of the University of Wisconsin, but did not. "It's just an oddity in the way it happened to turn out, sir," he said. He had to keep from smiling, because the CO would not have liked it.

"We'll have to see about that," the CO said. The radio operator was reading a comic book, his earphones lying in his lap. There was another EM, a company runner or from the defense platoon maybe, hunkering near the field stove, but not listening to them. His eyes were vacant, as if he were concentrating on the unbroken whispering noise of the oil-burning field stove. His fatigues were filthy. Maybe he was a recon scout.

"I need me an exec, Batterman," the CO said, "but you're not it until I see what's up with you. Clear?"

"Yes sir."

"Meantime, you stay with those warm bodies you brought with you. You tag after this man,"—he flicked his tired looking eyes at the EM squatting by the stove—"He'll square you away for today. We'll talk tomorrow."

"Yes sir," he said, and the EM in filthy combat fatigues got up with a grunt, lead the way out through the trenches to the sector where Batterman and his culls were to occupy the parapets until the group was broken up and parceled out among the short-handed platoons in the company.

"This is your arc, all the way from where we cut in this trench to over there yonder where it cuts back in. Your maps and all is in the bunkers," the guide said.

"Wait a sec," Batterman said when the EM turned to go. He must have been a recon scout, he decided later, when there was so much time to decide things. The guide walked in a permanent crouch, even when they walked on the duckboards in the trenches, their heads a good foot or more below the parapets. He was so dirty that Batterman could not tell if it was plain dirt on the man's face, or dirt wiped there to keep the skin of his face from glowing while he was out on night patrols.

"You mean we're all that's holding this stretch of the perimeter?" he asked the EM.

"Heavy Weapons platoon is just off behind you, lieutenant," the EM said. "You got us and the Headquarter Defense Platoon, excepting it's not but two squads left of it for now, on your left flank."

"Who's on our right?"

"A whole battalion-ass size bunch of ROKs," the EM said. "Anyways, they was the last time I seen. I got to *chogee*," he said, turned left, trotting in his old man's crouch, his soiled uniform blending in with the walls of the trench, the rattling of his boots on the springy duckboards diminishing.

"Hey!" Batterman called after him. The three dozen culls had clustered about him, holding their weapons as if they were objects they held in check for the rightful owners to claim. The recon scout stopped, turned back to Batterman. Batterman had to think of something to say. He did not have a question in mind, but knew there were things he should ask.

"Are the ROKs any good?" he asked.

"One cut above piss poor," the scout said. "Better'n niggers. A nigger'll run in a minute when the shit hits the fan," he said.

"But what are we supposed to *do*?" Lieutenant Batterman said. "What the hell if it starts in before morning? I don't even know the situation."

"You'll darn sure *know* if they come on us, lieutenant," the scout said. "They's wire and trip flares and all, out front of you. You'll all *know*, do they come. You got walkie-talkie to the old man in your bunker. Ask him if you ain't sure."

"What would you advise?" Batterman said.

"If it was me, with these," the scout said, looking at the culls gathering close to the lieutenant, "I'd keep people on them firing steps, and pray God nobody's ass sucks blue pond water come time for using your weapons, lieutenant." They looked at each other, the scout and Batterman, without speaking, and then Batterman turned his eyes away to look at his men, three dozen no-goodniks. AWOL types, left-footers, stockade rejects, huddling in their battle jackets, faces lost in shadows under the rims of their steel pots, weapons clutched or slung awkwardly.

171

"Hey," Batterman said again when he turned back toward the end of the trench. The recon scout had disappeared, gone without the trace of a noise from the springy duckboards flooring the trench.

So Lieutenant Batterman was left on his own with a platoon-size sector of his company's perimeter to defend until the next morning or until the CO called them out of the line.

There were barely enough noncoms among his men to set up two shifts, but he organized the two shifts, working two hours on, two off, to man the firing steps. The off-shift was sent into the bunkers to keep warm, clean weapons, open ammunition boxes, eat their cold C-rations. Batterman stayed off the walkie-talkie. The scout, he figured, would have as good advice as the CO. He checked the parapet regularly through the day, the late afternoon, stopping in each of the bunkers long enough to warm up at the stoves, to let his men know he was watching them. His senior noncom was a staff sergeant with some National Guard time.

"Sir," he came out of his bunker to ask Batterman, "are we here permanent or what?"

"You know as much about it as I do."

"Yes sir. They told us at orientation back in Japan no full units, not even squads, was to go straight into line duty. We was told we'd always be in reserve, back, unless it was all hell broke loose or something."

"Maybe that's what it is," Batterman said. "If they put us here it must mean we're needed here."

"Yes sir. But you seen for yourself, sir, there's nothing doing out in front of the perimeter, sir."

"Let's all keep figuring it stays that way, okay? Now I want you out on the firing steps when I'm in the bunkers. I want these men to know somebody's after them, all the time. Okay?"

"Yes sir," the NG staff sergeant said, "but I don't like it any better than they do."

"I said let's not talk about it any longer, huh?"

"Yes sir."

172

"All these creeps need is to hear us talking like that to spook shit out of them. Let's not press it, okay, sergeant?"

"Yes sir. Only they said at orientation no units even squad size ever was to go straight on line."

"Like you said," Batterman said, "there's nothing happening out front. We got nothing to sweat."

It seemed that way, all day, up until dusk. Batterman checked, swept the sector with the mounted periscope, and there was nothing out front. The ground sloped, very gently, away from the parapet. The concertina wire was laid thickly at the bottom of the dry gully that defined the ridge they held. He could make out the wire, black against the pale sand and washed gravel. The slope of the facing ridge was steeper, with heavier brush, but nothing big enough to cover anything bigger than a foxhole or a sniper post. If they came, the gooks would come from behind the opposite ridge, which meant three hundred yards of open range for them to cross—under fire all the way . . . if his culls did not panic, suffer buck fever when they saw real Chinese coming for them. If the ROKs on his right flank could be counted on to hold tight. If Heavy Weapons, behind him, had their grid coordinated correct for that three hundred yards. How far to the right, Lieutenant Batterman wondered, could the weapons from HQ bunkers give flanking fire?"

"You keep them on their toes when you see me gone off in the bunkers," he told his NG staff sergeant. "I want them on the firing steps, and I want them ready." The NG sergeant nodded without speaking, which was not a good sign.

Batterman was not worried. He would keep after them all, and it would be all right in the end. Why shouldn't it?

The first attack went fine. They had all the warning in the world. Batterman was watching through the mounted periscope, noticing how the facing slope grew fuzzier as dusk seeped into the blank winter sky. The concertina wire in the bottom of the gully blurred into a blackness, and the spotty vegetation on both slopes seemed to melt, flow together, like a spreading stain.

173

Batterman heard the first bugle call as clearly as if it were a farm bell sounding to bring in pickers for weigh-in. It made him think of cavalry movies at the Park Theater in Wautoma. It was one long call on a bugle with a tone like a child's tin toy. He stepped down off the observation step, and then there were a dozen bugles, and smaller, higher-pitched little horns answering the bugle, all of it so clear in the clear winter air, so many of them it made it seem like they came from all over the two facing slopes, from deep down in the dry gully.

"Lock and load, pass it on!" he shouted both ways in the trench, then ran for the bunkers to bring up the shift warming at the field stoves. The mortars started in before he reached the first bunker. Incoming, the Chinese made a drawn out sucking sound, like the sound of tearing paper. When they hit, it felt like the trench floor vibrated under his feet. When they hit the concussion was the worst of it, like somebody had smacked him square on top of his steel pot (the way it felt when someone smacked you on top of your football helmet). It did not hurt, but it stopped you for an instant, until you could realize you were not hurt, and then you could go on to do what you were bent on doing.

"On the steps, lock and load, wait for the word!" he shouted in the bunker entrances, sorted the noncoms out from the men who piled out, got the grenade boxes and metal ammo cans started toward the firing steps.

Heavy Weapons, outgoing, was answering with their .60 and .80 mortars before he had all his men in place. Outgoing made the short crumping sound when it left the tubes in the placements to the rear of his trench, like a man getting the wind knocked out of him.

And there was artillery, from way back. It made no noise passing overhead, but they could all see the light where they hit, beyond the opposite ridge, where the Chinese were pointing for their assault.

The closest mortars, three or four of them just before the assault, just before the flares went up and the horns and bugles stopped (and the Chinese switched to shrill police whistles to signal back and forth as they came down the opposite slope toward the concertina wire), hit close enough to shower the trenches with fine dirt, small pebbles that fell like hail.

It did not shake his culls and left-footers. They stood on the firing steps, and nobody fired prematurely.

The three or four close mortar rounds hit close enough to make Batterman wonder if they were going to march the shells, a step at a time, right into the trench, when the flares went up. The mortars quit coming in from behind the facing ridge. All they heard for an instant, in the silence when the bugles and horns stopped, was the crump of the mortars coming out from Heavy Weapons behind them. The flares went up at the same time on both flanks. They must have coordinated on the walkie-talkie between HQ and the ROKs.

The flares went up like Fourth of July fireworks, starting with a pop and a bang louder than an M-1 made, only softer, scattering a trail of sparks that hung in the air, drifted down slowly as they burned out. Then they went off again, directly over the wire strung in the gully. For a second there was an uncertain, guttering light that threw fluid shadows on the slopes above the wire. It popped and crackled with a blue light, and then it began to burn bright, and there were more flares, a dozen or more in all, and they all seemed to start burning dully at once, and the light went from blue to yellow to white, clearer and sharper than daylight, all the while the advancing Chinese blew their shrill police whistles.

It was something to fright a man in the deepest parts of him, Batterman thought (later, when there was a year and a half of nothing to do but think, decide, wait for whatever came to happen, however it would happen in the end). It was something to fright a man, turn him, send him running, but his three dozen losers stayed on their firing steps, blinking at the light that glowed brighter and brighter overhead (their faces seemed to quiver, twitch in tics, as if in response to the police whistles blasting at their ears). They stayed.

They hung onto their rifles with both hands (to a man they had removed their trigger-finger mittens, hands bared to handle their weapons, lock and load fresh clips when it came time). They stayed on the firing steps, looking out at the dry gully, the opposite slope, the ridge over which the Chinese would have to come. Their faces (in the hot-white light of the flares overhead, the shrill whistles that seemed to be blowing everywhere) were like the faces of men looking into photographers' popping flashbulbs, men shy of cameras, intimidated by loud voices and sudden noises.

But they stayed fast, and the noncoms did fine, working under Batterman's NG staff sergeant at getting grenades laid out on shelves, metal ammo cans sprung open, the fresh clips unwrapped. Batterman watched them closely, afraid they would spook and run, stiffen up, freeze to their weapons in supreme buck fever, but they did not. *We can hack this*, he decided about them, and *Why not?* He made sure they would hold, and then he looked out again with the mounted periscope.

It was like focusing a biology lab microscope. First there was nothing. Not knowing if you are even looking correctly, not sure you know how to look, what you are supposed to see. He saw the burning light of the flares, patch of black vegetation on the facing slope, the black, stacked coils of concertina wire. Then you see a blur that might be something, but you do not know if it is really something, or only the trick of your eye, but you try to make it be something. Something fluid, shapeless, like a wiggling form of life on the slide, too low in the order of life to have a finite shape. Something moved, grey-white within the grey-white of the broken rock, the dry sand, of the opposite slope.

Then you see it. It is a blur, then it fuzzes even more for an instant, and then it leaps out in your eye, the clean, hard walls of a leaf cell, the tight form of a staph germ, the thrashing tail of human sperm. Then he saw them, flooding the face of the opposite slope, hell bent for the wire in the dry gully.

It was like kicking over a rotted log, the sudden, shocking mess of grubs exposed to harsh light. The Chinese ran for the wire, their grey padded coats, pile caps, black weapons in their hands, and Batterman stood up to give the command to fire on

176

them, and they started firing on his flanks, HQ and the ROKs, before he could say the words. And his culls and left-footers took that for the word, braced themselves on the parapet, opened up with the M-1s. Batterman was the last man in the trench to fire.

They never got close enough to have faces. They never got over the concertina wire. The noncoms had laid out loose grenades at each firing step, open boxes ready at the bunker entrances, but the Chinese never got within throwing range.

Batterman had worried about not having any machine guns, not even any BARs, among the weapons the culls carried over with them from Japan. But the ROKs had machine guns, on his right flank, and HQ had them on his left, light, air-cooled thirties traversing to left and right, all but covering the sector in front of Batterman's trench. He could follow (once he settled down, handled his own short panic) the tracers loaded in the belts, streaking out to the opposite slope like wires hot with electric current, scattering, feeling the waves of assaulting Chinese, who walked, trotted, ran full tilt into it like it really wasn't there.

Now and again a tracer bounced off the slope, shot up into the flare-lit air above the facing ridge, burned out like a shooting star.

It was the automatic weapons on his flanks (that, and the outgoing mortars from Heavy Weapons—they tracked the Chinese all the way into the far edge of the gully, never stopped dropping in, small mushroom explosions that tore gaps in the advancing lines of assault, the gaps filling in again, solid with the padded grey of the Chinese winter uniforms) that stopped them.

They never got over the concertina wire. The wire held the ones who got through the mortars and automatic weapons. They apparently had no satchel charges, no sappers to breach the wire, because the ones who made it to the gully were hung up on the wire. Batterman and his culls shot them up there like tin ducks in a carnival gallery, like pumpkins set on fence posts, like empty bottles lined up in the Waushara County

177

dump. You picked one out, struggling in the stacked wire, and you set him over the front sight blade, and then you squeezed off the trigger. He fell, or went limp, like a shredded rag caught on a clothesline. Or he kept wiggling, so you gave it a little Kentucky windage in sighting him, squeezed another one off.

It only took Batterman a few seconds to get himself in hand. The flares were up, burning, and the outgoing from Heavy Weapons crumped behind his trench, and his flanks opened up, silencing the shrill signal whistles, and he registered his noncoms and his culls, firing, standing fast, and the next thing he knew he was squeezing the trigger of his carbine, but nothing was happening, and he realized he had opened fire with the carbine on fully automatic, had fired off a full banana clip.

He laughed at himself, set a fresh clip, put the weapon on semi-automatic fire. He fired with his men, squeezing them off one at a time, nailing the ones who hung for him in the wire, cool, as cool as if he were putting bulls-eyes on the machine Prader had in the pavilion, a BB rifle, targets that flopped over if you could hit them dead center.

Batterman's trench was the last unit on the line to cease firing. The Chinese quit coming. They disappeared from the facing slope, the last wiggler in the wire fell or hung limp, the outgoing mortars quit, the automatic weapons on the flanks stopped. Batterman's culls blazed away until he left his firing step and got the word going down the line to cut it off. They stopped, and he thought he heard a last, fading whistle from the Chinese-held ridge.

"Keep them at the parapet," Batterman told his NG staff sergeant. "I want to check with the CO and see what the hell's for now."

"Did you see that, Lieutenant?" the sergeant said. "Did you see them bastards come at us? Man, them rounds coming in just like pulling targets on the KD range. I could hear them snapping when they passed over," he said.

"I can't say I noticed," Batterman said, and, "I must have

178

been too busy keeping my hole tight." They laughed. The men stood or hunkered, still holding their hot weapons, picking at the empty clips and cartridge casings that had piled up at their feet as they fired, souvenirs, smiling, looking at each other, at Batterman, like shit-eating cats. "Damn fine," Batterman said to the sergeant. "You pass on I said they were great."

The CO did not think it was so great. "Piss poor, Batterman," he said on the walkie-talkie.

"Sir?"

"What are they teaching you in the ROTC at college these days, lieutenant?"

"Reserves," Batterman said. "I'm reserve active, sir."

"I give a goddamn," the CO said. "Doo-doo's in the fan, I'm calling my guts out on the walkie-talkie for you, all I get's a dead key. Where the hell were you, Batterman?"

"With my men. On line, sir. I figured I better had be there every second. I haven't got a one even saw a shot fired before now. Any more than I did, sir," he said.

"You expect me to send a runner off line to get commo with you?" the CO said.

"No sir."

"Ever think it might work to leave one man in the bunker to pick up the horn if I need commo?"

"I didn't know what to expect, sir. You put me in here with these men. You know what they look like. The best NCO I have is National Guard. I figured I'd better have every one out in the line."

"Don't figure," the CO said. "Figure shit," he said. "Figure yourself a body acts like he can operate a butterfly switch on a field phone, then damn well put him on it. Understand?"

"Yes sir."

"Do I need to babysit you, lieutenant? Do I need to run commo checks on your position on the hour?"

"No sir. I've got what you said," Batterman said.

"We'll see," the company commander said.

"We stopped them, sir," Batterman said.

"Heavy Weapons stopped them. That and our automatic

weapons. And what the ROKs heaved at them. You and your duds played pussy with small arms."

"I don't have a single BAR, much less a machinegun, sir."

"Neither here nor there, lieutenant," the CO said. "You keep that horn open, and you keep half your strength on line. At all times. I'll be in touch. You better sure as hell be listening when I knock, Batterman."

"Yes sir," he said.

"You're lucky I don't send you out on recon. Freeze your butt some, you might stay with it."

"Yes sir."

It would have been better had he been sent out on the slope on recon, he thought (later, with so much time for thought—even though thought, he also thought, made no difference, never did, could not possibly). He never knew if there was any recon at all. If there was (the filthy EM who walked in a fixed crouch), then the Chinese took the recon patrol on their way in to take the perimeter.

In the frozen half-light of early dawn, Batterman tried to get a fix on the other prisoners sitting, standing near him, looking for the CO, the recon scout, his NG sergeant, but the light was so bad, the gooks were at him, taking everything he carried in his pockets, cuffing and slapping him around a little for the hell of it. Everyone looked the same, the grim, chattering little Chinese volunteers in their padded coats, pile caps, tennis shoes, jabbing him in the back, the ribs, with the blunt barrels of their burp guns, the other prisoners, stunned, sleepy-looking, trying to duck the cuffs and slaps, turning their pockets out, as if they were looking for a familiar face, but everybody looked the same to everybody.

The CO should have run an hourly commo check. Maybe he did. Batterman put a man on the walkie-talkie, told the NG sergeant to check on the man to see he stayed awake (Batterman turned into his bunker to sleep at 0230, waking the sergeant—the sergeant was to keep his shift awake and alert on the firing steps, check the commo man in Batterman's bunker to see he stayed awake at the switch—maybe he did). The man

180

detailed for commo was not in the bunker with him when Batterman woke up in his sleeping bag. He could not find his NG sergeant when he looked for him among the gathered prisoners. There was not much time. The Chinese took him away, put him with half a dozen other officers he had never seen before.

The ROKs on his right flank must have bugged out. There were no ROK prisoners anywhere. Unless the Chinese shot them all, somewhere out of Batterman's hearing.

"You're on," Batterman had told his sergeant when he woke him. He stood by while the sergeant got himself out of his sleeping bag. It was not really warm in the bunkers during the dead of night, the cold setting in close to the bone. It reminded Batterman of getting out early, before dawn, in a Fish Lake duckblind with his father. He smiled at the way things went.

"I'm awake, lieutenant," the sergeant said.

"I know you are. I want you on your feet so I know you're listening to me." He did not want to risk another excuse for the CO to jump him.

"It feels like I just now got to sleep."

"It always does. Now get this. Get your shift up. Relieve my men. Keep moving. Don't let them fall asleep on their feet out there on the line. I mean it."

"Anything going out there, you think?" the sergeant asked him.

"Not a thing. Scan it every so often with the periscope anyway. You can wake me at 0500."

"Yes sir."

"And for God's sakes keep him awake," Batterman said, unrolling his sleeping bag. The EM on the walkie-talkie sat like an Indian in a blanket, hands tucked up in his armpits, inside his field jacket.

"You heard what the lieutenant said," the NG sergeant said to him.

"I'm cold as hell," the man said.

"I'll talk to the old man about getting us some parkas in the

181

morning," Batterman said. He took his boots off, got into his sleeping bag.

"They should of issued us parkas back in Japan," the sergeant said.

"They should have two of them damn stoves for each bunker," the commo man said. "They should issue us hand warmers. You could keep one for each hand, right in your pockets."

"Crap," the sergeant said, "they aren't even supposed to put nothing bigger than a squad on line when you first come in. We should be in reserve."

"Piss on this shit," the commo man said.

"Knock it off," Batterman said. "Bitching won't change a thing." The commo man lowered his head, as if concealing his face from the light of the Coleman lantern would conserve his body heat against the bitter air that seeped in from the trench at the bunker entrance. The sergeant left the bunker to wake his shift, relieve Batterman's. Batterman zipped himself into his sleeping bag, where the Chinese found him just before dawn broke, when they overran the entire perimeter.

It was a short but perfect sleep there in his sleeping bag. The issue bags were good ones, lined, and beneath the bag, to insulate him from the cold of the bunker's packed dirt floor, was an inflatable rubber mattress. A man slept snug there, sound, zipped in all the way, no more than the tip of his nose showing, enough to remind him that it was cold, that he was warm in this cold, that his sleep would be snug, deep, total.

He did not dream. He went to sleep too quickly to have the certain stream of thought that leads into dreaming that is clear and sharp. He was surprised at how suddenly tired he felt, how weak, helpless after the firefight. He was too tired even to think back on the firefight, to wonder that it had happened, that he and his men had done so well, it had gone so easily.

He felt only the rightness of everything, focused on the comfort of his body in the sleeping bag, how it all answered perfectly to the aching of his body.

He *wanted* to think of something, the firefight, anything,

but could not. The soft warmth of the sleeping bag, the sucking noise of the field stove, the hissing glare of the Coleman lantern that forced his eyes to close. Thought evaporated before it could form, flow. He felt only so very, very well. Everything had a way of working out so well. His last waking sensation was the silly smile that broke, without effort, on his face.

They kicked him awake. They jolted him awake with the soles of their tennis shoes, yammering sixty-to-the-minute in Chinese. He popped awake, zipped in his sleeping bag. There were two of them kicking away (their speech sounding like the shrieks of caged monkeys) to wake him. One stood calmly, burp gun slung from his shoulder (but trained on his head). His kicks hurt. The other was too excited to do much damage. He waved his burp gun in the air, hopped about like his feet hurt, kicked off balance.

It was like waking from a dream that is very bad, frightening, when the fears of the dream stick with you for the first few moments awake, until you can remember the dream, and that it was only a dream, and so you can laugh at the fear, and the feeling runs out of you. They kept kicking at him, one hurting him, one only an annoyance, and Batterman tried to recall the dream that had carried over from sleep into this, but there was no dream, and so, for a few moments (until the calm man's aimed kicks began to really hurt), it was the worst sort of not knowing, not knowing what anything is, how it got to be this way, how it could have happened. When there was nothing he could think of that would make any sense of anything.

Then the worst passed, because the kicks hurt enough, made him angry. He wanted to get out of the sleeping bag, clean their clocks for them, wipe the dirt floor of the bunker with their yammering-sixty-to-the-minute Chinese faces, but the calm one had his weapon's muzzle only a foot from Batterman's head, and the wild one danced around, waving his weapon in the air like he wanted an opportunity to make some noise with it.

183

So he unzipped himself, catching their kicks all the while. He was lucky, they let him put on his boots. They kept up their screeching, kicking. Batterman all but laughed. It was the sort of stunt a Bud Booth (or his cousin) would pull. He would have gotten his boots laced, closing his ears to the shouting, dodging the kicks as best he could by swiveling on his fanny from side to side, protecting his spine, taking the blows in the ribs. Then he would have gotten up to clean Bud Booth's clock but good. But Bud Booth had been killed (half a dozen years ago) and there was an automatic weapon pointed at his face, so he wasn't doing anything more than they meant him to.

There was nothing funny about it, but he half-felt like laughing (the way things had of turning out!), going out of the bunker, up, out of the trench, hands on his head, trying to stay far enough ahead of the running kicks the two screamers aimed at him from behind.

A gang of them, half a dozen or more, jumped him as he got up on the crown of the parapet. They threw some punches (like monkeys, all of them, yelling), stuck some rifle butts into his ribs, but he kept his balance while they stripped his pockets clean. He kept his mind at the right distance from it all, looking for somebody (his NG sergeant, the commo man, the CO, the recon scout, the ROKs, his culls), which was maybe why, looking, everybody looked alike. Still trying to see how it had come to happen after the easy firefight, keeping on balance. He did not want them to have a chance at stomping him to see if he would break. Ignoring it, looking. He was lucky, they did not take his boots or his field jacket.

"Motherfuckers took my boots, man," a Negro lieutenant said to him when he joined the cluster of officers they had weeded out, down the slope toward the wire (they had cut a path in the wire in the night, wide enough for vehicles to pass, but the dead from the firefight were still there, sprawled, hanging).

"You better shut your nigger face," a major, the ranking prisoner, told him. "I'm senior here, and I still command," the major said.

184

"You'll be all right," Batterman said. "Maybe they'll give you some shoes."

"Motherfuck you, Jack," the Negro said. "Motherfucking mothers stole my damn boots, man!"

"That's one won't make it," another man said to Batterman. He could not tell the man's rank, because the Chinese had taken his field jacket and his fatigue shirt away. The man wore long-handled underwear, but he looked naked to the cold, dressed in white from the waist up, his dogtags hanging free on his chest.

"He's shook is all," Batterman said. "I'm shook. How in hell did they get on top of us? They just hauled me out of my fart-sack."

"I'll lay odds he won't make it a week. Less, if they march us any distance to speak of," the officer said. His bare hands, his neck, were red with cold, but he did not shiver or hug himself, as if he did not feel the cold.

"They walk us very far, his feet have had it," Batterman said.

"I'm not talking about his feet. I tell you I can tell if a man's going to hold up or if he won't. I spent near two years at this before," he said, and when Batterman did not understand, said, "Nineteen months, some odd days, European Theater. The big one," he said.

"You were a prisoner?" Batterman said. He still could not recognize anyone among the captured officers gathered on the slope they had defended the previous evening. He wanted to keep the officer talking, because there was no one else he knew to be seen.

"When you were still shitting yellow," the officer said. "They took me just outside Anzio, and they let us all go, GI's, British, Russians, you name it, outside Salzburg, Austria, the day before we would of been liberated anyway. I can tell a man's got the mark on him, I tell you."

"You won't have any picnic if you don't get something on," Batterman said. "If you can't scrounge something better, you can have my shirt. I'll be okay with just my jacket."

185

"Shoes or not, mox nix," the officer said. Batterman realized that the officer with no shirt or jacket could not really talk to him, not listen. Batterman kept looking for someone familiar. The officer kept talking about what he knew of being a prisoner of war.

"Maybe we won't have to hoof it," Batterman said to keep him talking. He would let the man talk, keep looking himself for a familiar face.

"I've studied psi warfare some, too," the officer said. "You tell by the way a man lets go, gives in to it. Gets the big shits. Like him," he said, waving his cold reddened hand at the Negro lieutenant, who continued to curse about the boots the Chinese had taken from him.

"They let me keep mine," Batterman said.

"You can tell how it's hitting them right between the eyes," the officer said. "They get on some kick or another, that's all you hear from them. I know. I've studied it. I've seen a man, camp in Austria, cozy as you please, curl up and die. You can tell the ones," the officer said.

Batterman had no chance to think of it just then. They all watched what happened to the Negro.

The major told him to shut his nigger mouth again, and the Negro had stepped away from the rough circle of prisoners. He stepped up to one of the Chinese who watched them, weapons slung, grinning, pointing, talking, as if the captured officers were an exhibit. The Negro cursed the Chinese, held up first one, then the other sock-clad foot as evidence. The Chinese listened for a minute, then slapped the Negro's face with his open hand.

"Serve you right, goddamn jungle bunny," the major said.

"See?" the officer without shirt or jacket said through his teeth to Batterman.

The Negro cursed the Chinese, never missed a beat. The Chinese laughed, then hit him full in the face with his fist, laughed harder. Two, three, four more came to join the fun, looked down at the Negro where he had fallen. They set up their chattering, pointing at the Negro, who rose slowly. He got to his feet, spat blood to clean his mouth, set in with his cursing again.

"See what I'm telling you?" the officer said.

"That man is disobeying direct orders I gave. You all witness," the major said. He had turned his back on the Negro.

"I ain't playing *no* fucking games 'till I see my fucking boots, Jack," the Negro said. They dropped him with the butts of their weapons, and they kept on hitting him, laughing and jabbering. They did not stop hitting the Negro with their weapons until he lay still on the ground. The Chinese stood back, quiet now, watched to see if he was going to get up and ask for more. Batterman noticed it was snowing lightly now. He noticed the tiny specks of snow catching, gathering in the Negro's short hair. The Negro lieutenant began to move a little, sat up, lifted his bleeding face. He could not speak. The Chinese only watched him struggle to his feet, did not have another go at him.

"Do I know what I'm talking about or don't I," the officer without shirt or jacket said to Batterman.

"I specifically ordered that man to shut his trap," the major said to the other captured officers.

"I been down that road once before," the officer said. "European Theater, '43 to April '45. I've studied up on the matter."

"Command authority goes on no matter what," the major was saying, "and so long as I'm senior I'll by Christ command. Break command responsibility, everything goes to hell in a handbasket."

"Are you going to tell me I don't know what to look for?" the officer was saying to Batterman. It began to snow harder. Batterman's ears were cold. He put his hands over his ears to warm them, then took them away, afraid they would stop talking. The snow was suddenly very thick.

"Boots, no boots, mox nix," said the officer who had been captured in Italy.

"Make no mistake," the major said. "I will press charges against any officer or enlisted man defying my authority. All in due time," he said.

"That man will fold and die like a foundered horse. I've seen it happen."

"They'll try to break our chain of command. My job—*our* job is to maintain it. Tighten it. All down the line."

It was snowing so hard, suddenly, the wind bringing it over the ridge line in great, thick billows, that Batterman could barely make out the faces that were not familiar to him.

"Any man willfully disobeys me, shows disrespect, his ass is grass and I am a lawnmower," the major said.

"See?" the veteran POW of the European Theater said to Batterman. "See? What did I tell you. It sticks out on a man like a sore thumb." The Negro was on his feet. He staggered, eyes rolling, as if he were drunk, his hair crusted woolly white with snow. He bled from his nose and mouth and one ear. He moved his torn lips, as if still trying to curse over his stolen boots, but no words came out. The snow was heavier, faster, the wind much colder. Batterman tried to squint through the snow, to see faces, but the snow made him want to blink, shut his eyes tight, lower his chin to his chest to escape it. The skin of his face hurt with the sudden cold, his ears tingled close to numbness.

"I'll organize a makeshift staff here in a minute," the major was saying. "I'll want every officer reporting directly to me until I set up staff."

"It's panic," the officer with no shirt, no field jacket said. "Hysteria. Shock. You get it or you don't. You get it, you come through it or you don't. Our colored friend, for example, will *not* recover."

Batterman turned, wiped his eyes with his fingers. Where had the Negro lieutenant disappeared to? The snow, gathering in his hair, his shoulders, felt very heavy. His ears and cheeks and the tip of his nose had gone numb. His toes felt numb in his boots. His arms and legs ached, and his breathing seemed rougher, his chest heaving. He could not concentrate long enough to isolate the features of any individual face among the prisoners.

Later (when there was time in which there was nothing to do but consider how it was that things happened to work out the way they did), Batterman figured he had come close to folding, to giving in to what he did not even realize was happening to him. The senior officer continued to insist on the necessity of good order and discipline, the officer with no shirt or jacket harped away on the accuracy of his prediction about the Negro (the Negro disappeared, left behind to freeze on the slope, probably, when they were marched away), and Batterman tried, hopelessly, to find a face he knew behind the swirling snow. He came close to giving in, running off up or down the slope in search of somebody he knew (the Chinese would have cheerfully, carelessly, shot him), or letting his aching, shaking legs give way, sink to the cold, wet snow (an inch, inch-and-a-half deep already), sit until they shot him or clubbed him to death, or only left him (like the Negro lieutenant) to freeze solid. Batterman came very close to it. So close. He laughed over it later, the way a man will when he has miraculously escaped a great danger, or when he realizes, later, that his terrible fear was pointless because there was nothing, after all, to fear.

The Chinese Volunteers provided a small miracle. They moved the captured officers out, marched them away. It was a good time to move prisoners back. The snowstorm would prevent a counterattack (if the 24th had not fled, what was left of it, all the way to Seoul before it reformed its perimeter), and there would be no air strikes, no strafing, no napalm. It prevented Batterman letting it happen to him.

There were suddenly many Chinese about them, much shouting, a little jabbing with the butts of their weapons, some cuffing and pushing, but only enough to get them moving. They marched down the slope they had so easily defended the evening before, through the wide gaps cut in the concertina wire. There was a quiet moment, when they were shielded from the wind and snow in the depths of the gully. The Chinese killed in the evening assault still lay among the wire, their bodies covered, thickly dusted with fresh snow now. Up the facing slope, over the opposite ridge, through the empty emplacements that were their forward positions until that morning, through the base camp where they had mustered for their assaults. Then they hit a washboard road they were free to use since there were no aircraft. After that it was only another long, forward march on a rough-road (no worse than Fort Benning training hikes). The cold was no worse than summer heat would have been, and it was a thing, hard marching, that Batterman was in shape to handle and there was time to come to know that there had been nothing to fear, after all.

It was just a washboard road (like the logging roads cut into the woods around Silver Lake by the Christmas tree cutters who had worked over the pines in recent years) that they had hit at an angle shortly after leaving the Chinese base camp. It was a road, and roads all stretched back to someplace, went somewhere. Either direction, Batterman understood, you had to get there.

And all the while you hoofed, where you came from was still back there behind you, and where you were going waited on you to get there. This road had been under artillery fire, and it had been bombed, so they left it often to cut around the craters (if they were too deep, or there were too many craters lined up in a row), or they slogged down into the shallower craters, back up out of them (the Chinese escorting them seemed to get very excited when they were slipping up and down through the snow and slush-filled bomb craters, yelling threats, encouragement, as if they were balky, clumsy pack mules, the Chinese nervous teamsters), and always, eventually, they hit the traces of the road again.

It was a winding road. It turned sharply to fit the topography of the broken, eroded ridgelines, but a road (Batterman knew, began to sense he knew) can twist and turn all it wants. Still, it is a kind of string, a chain, between back there, behind, and ahead, up front, and you always know where you are when you know (even if you do not bother to stop and con-

190

sider that you know what it is you know) you are on the road. Things are where (and what) they are because you are where (and what) you are. You know because you are walking on the road, either direction, and so what is behind is behind because you go away from it, and what is ahead is where (or what) it is because you are going toward it. A man was a fool to be afraid!

"What's so goddamn funny?" the major said to Batterman. He was very close to him, speaking almost in a whisper. They were not allowed to talk on the march.

"Sir?"

"Keep your trap shut. March discipline. There's nothing to laugh at. Put your mind on some way of getting to hell out of this. That's a direct order," the major said, moving away to march at the edge of the road before Batterman could answer him.

The officer without shirt or jacket winked at Batterman, then also moved away, farther up in the line of march. His face and hands had gone stark white with cold, snow plastered in his hair, on the flannel of his underwear top. He did not look as if he felt the cold or snow at all. He was more active than the other prisoners, moving back and forth along their line of march, as if checking each man for signs that meant what he thought only he knew. The major paid no attention to him, as though he saw there was no disciplining him. The Chinese escorting them did not seem to care that he so often broke march ranks to move up or down the line.

Batterman made only a minor effort to figure a way out of it, escape. It was too much effort, unnecessary. He had nothing to worry about. He ran through escape and evasion training, Fort Benning, but that was so past. Escape as quickly as possible, they taught. Since your guards will be more experienced later, it will be more difficult to escape, evasion will be more risky because you will be deeper in enemy territory. That was behind him, back on the road (whichever road, always a road, *one* road). Ahead would (of course) wait a prison compound, camp, lock-up of some sort. Experienced guards. Whatever, it was because Batterman was. On his road. Always.

Everything. All. Now. The Booth cousins, up ahead of him, swim trunks rolled in their towels, rolls stuck in the hip pockets of their jeans, hoofing it for Wautoma, Prader's pavilion lights coming up behind them (on the highways Redgranite, Omro, Oshkosh, Milwaukee, Chicago, on and on), and the Booth boys, one dead on Iwo Jima, the other shot up so bad he lies months in a Navy hospital in California, drugged against pain, up at last, married a war widow complete with ready-made family, settled in California (forever), and forever, both of them, simply behind him (*now*) on the road, and the Booths, each in a row of melons or cucumbers on either side of him (the sandy aisle between rows of plants like a dry road, like the snow-covered, crater-filled road he marched now), heads coming up rhythmically as they picked the heavy cantaloupes or long green cucumbers for the trailing sacks. Now old Prader (on his road), chin resting on the heel of his hands, at the bar, pronouncing the war a shame, because Jug Girard returned from service (the big one) to carry the ball for the Badgers on Camp Randall Saturday afternoons, that was an opportunity Batterman had missed. He did *not* miss his, the first one, built his pavilion over the opposition of a Chicago lawyer-banker named Spaulding, Spaulding fool enough to ship to France in order to die fighting the Huns in order to allow (young) Prader to build his pavilion in order to allow old Prader to pronounce war a missed opportunity for Batterman. Jug Girard returning from the big war (second one) to carry the ball for the Badgers at Camp Randall in order to beat Purdue and Northwestern, but lose to Michigan, Minnesota, Ohio State, in order to weep (they said) as the band played *On Wisconsin*, fans on their feet with banners and horns for the Jugger (weeping). Batterman taping adhesive tape letters to his back to form a silly name given him by childhood friends (for size, strength), his mother retaping them when the tape wore off because the war was going to get him soon (his father said), getting the Booth cousins instead, but ending in time to send Jug Girard to take Batterman's place, sending him to the bench to watch the big games from among the water buckets and sponges and quartered oranges and rolls of tape for wrapping ankles and shiver pads, but now *his* war, to grab him up, take him away from Wautoma (where he waited for something to happen, now, here on this road).

Not concentric circles, nor a mighty circle turning in on itself in a spiral, and not blocks of varied size stacked in neat or broken piles, nor swatches of crazy quilt pieced in here and there. A road. Or a string of beads in sure order of position. Or a chain of links linked to all other chains everywhere.

Now. Dusk began to fall, the early dusk of hard winter on the Korean peninsula. The wind sharpened, found the gaps at the cuffs of his field jacket, at his open collar. His boots were wet through, but marching kept his feet warm, the blood moving. He did not fear trenchfoot. He kept his chin down to protect his throat, his eyes on the ground (the road hidden beneath the snow, but there), let the snow cake on his head, protect him from the wind. No one spoke. Even the Chinese were too cold, miserable in the weather, to shout when someone wandered off the road for a few steps, tumbled full-face into a crater.

One foot in front of the other. Sooner or later they would have to stop, be given something to eat (he scooped clean snow up, let it melt on his tongue). Now, or in an hour, or by morning, or the morning after, sometime, they would reach where they were going, and they would stop, eat, rest. Move on or not. Stay or not. No difference. Whatever, when, it was all coming because Batterman moved toward it on the road, and he knew this (too cold now to think what he knew, knew he knew) because everything else up to now was just over his shoulder. Behind him, on the road.

One foot in front of the other. Shank's mare. No worry, no hurry. Now or later. No difference. Lieutenant Batterman thought of old (*old!*) Ward Booth, biggest raiser of melons and cucumbers in Waushara County. He could not remember how old the old man really was. The best he could remember, Ward Booth's mother had lived to nearly a hundred.

193

It grew darker, and colder, and the snow did not let up, but it did not bother Batterman.

They lost only one man on the long forced march. They lost the officer without field jacket or fatigue shirt. The Chinese Volunteers killed him. The cold got to the officer at last. He stepped into a crater, fell, could not get up. The march stopped. The Chinese stood at the edge of the shallow crater, called to him in Chinese, but he could only look back at them.

"I'll get him," Batterman said. "I can carry him if need be."

"Stand fast," the major said, and "Shut your trap unless you're looking for it too." Batterman stepped toward the crater, but a Chinese stopped him, shoved him back. He could see the officer's face. He did not look worried. His face was dead-white, painted-looking with frostbite, but his eyes were calm, certain. He seemed to know how everything was going to go.

The Chinese yelled at him a moment more, then shot him where he lay in the crater.

County statute said that Batterman's Redgranite Bowl-A-Go-Go had to close shop at one on weekdays, two-thirty on Saturdays, but nobody made an issue of it. The township's sole constable ran a check on El Gato to clear the Mexican pickers out. Let them run late and it would only start trouble. Either they got as drunk as they needed to start feeling mean, or they were ruined for field work the next day, which brought the growers in complaining. Emil Bender's tavern will close, sometimes, as early as nine or ten, when the last bachelor farmer decides he needs to get on home to be up early to rouse his pickers for the field.

But nobody troubles if Batterman keeps the doors open, the Seeburg on, the girls going in the cage, past the statute closing time. Business is business. If the trade warrants it, he stays open. If not, not.

This night, it worked out about right. It was hot and heavy, his waitresses and his bartender humping all they were worth, until just before one. The girls kept at it in the cage, and everybody seemed to want all they could get, cage and bar both. Batterman was busy at Mickey's side most of the night.

"Where do they all come from?" the kid said at one point. He was washing glassware in the sink, lick-and-a-promise, to keep up with the orders Batterman filled for Velma and Marge. The waitresses were too busy, too good at what they did, to waste time talking about it.

"All over," Batterman said.

"I never saw so many people in one place to get a lousy drink," Mickey said.

"You'll get over it," Batterman told him. "Hump those glasses, boy, I've got orders longer than your arm to fill here."

At the last break from the cage his girls took, he went out back to see how they were holding up. They sat side by side on the stoop, obviously very tired.

"How are we doing?" Batterman asked. "Can I get you something to wet your whistle?" Marilyn did not care for anything. Fluid in her stomach tended to make her feel sick when she was in the cage.

"I don't suppose anybody dast ask for a real drink, huh?" Bobi said.

"Not while you're working," he said. "You know that. Beer bloats you, anyway. Look at me and be warned."

"So make it something mixed," she said.

"You know we don't do that on the job," Batterman said.

"Pardon my dumb face for ever asking, but," she said, and turned away from him to make a show of lighting a cigarette.

"Those won't help you any either," Batterman said. "Take it from me. When I was your age I could have jiggled twenty-four hours straight up there if I'd had to. Not now."

"Too bad it didn't stunt your growth any," Bobi Peplinski said. For a second, Batterman would have liked to have cracked her one across the mouth, but Marilyn smiled at him, and he smiled at her, and left them. What would that have proved?

But the trade seemed to have some idea about statute closing time. Quarter to one, they began to flow out in groups of three and four, and by one there were less than a dozen left at the tables and booths, calling for more. Batterman had already sent Mickey back to the back to tell Bobi and Marilyn they were through for the night.

"What's the verdict?" Marge Doerflinger asked him.

"Give them one more round," he said, "but tell them that's last call for alcohol."

"Praise Dee Lawd," Marge said.

"I think my feet are broke," Velma said. They went to take the last round of orders.

"They're already on their way," Mickey said when he came back to the bar.

"Peplinski call me a choice term or two?" Batterman asked.

"How'd you know?"

"Wise," Batterman said. "Comes with old age." Mickey seemed unsure if he should laugh or not. "That's supposed to be a joke, son," Batterman said, but then it was too late for them to laugh. "Wrap up here," he said. "Don't break yourself, it's been a long night. I'll come in early if I have to."

Mickey began straightening up the back bar, washing dirty glassware. Marge and Velma served the last round to the dozen or so customers left. The jukebox was silent for the first time in hours, Batterman was about to pitch in with Mickey, get them ready to close quickly, when Romy Lewinski came in.

It was an unusual time for Romy to come in. Once a week, once every ten days or two weeks, he stopped in, but he came earlier, around ten usually, eleven at the latest. He came in when he had obviously taken the night off at the Silver Lake Pavilion, dressed for a night out. And he was alone. Usually he came in with the woman. He got a shorty beer out for Romy, set it in front of him.

"Still no class," Romy said.

"What's that?"

"Napkin," Romy said. "When you going to realize class is a napkin *and* a coaster with your drink, Batterman? I got to teach you everything?"

196

"With a shorty beer? Besides, this one is on me."

"It's your stock," Romy said. "Piss it away how you want."

"I only do that for special occasions. What brings you out at this hour all by your lonesome?"

"What," Romy said, "I need a permit to come here for a beer?"

"I just meant I'm surprised to see you. You know. *Alone*. Don't tell me you shut down the pavilion on time for a change? Come over to see me on the spur of the moment, sort of?"

"Not on your life."

"That's what I meant." He waited for Lewinski to say what brought him out, alone and at the wrong time of night, but he was not saying, or was not saying just then. He had long since given up trying to figure Romy Lewinski. He answered you, or he did not.

Sometimes he answered you later. Some questions he had never answered, probably never would. It made no difference to Batterman. He trusted Romy Lewinski's judgment in business matters beyond that of any other man he had ever met. And he had learned, some months after the night he came into Prader's bar, to like him. Batterman pretty well liked everybody he knew.

Romy slugged at his shorty bottle of beer, swiveled his stool to see the room. "Good night?" he said.

"Average to good. They started clearing out about a quarter to. Sometimes you luck out," Batterman said.

"Luck," Romy said. "Horse manure. You keep them broads up there—" he wiggled the bottle at the empty, unlighted go-go cage—"you could hold them until the damn sun comes up, but," he said. Batterman had to laugh. "So," Romy said, "it's your business. See how you do looking for luck to make it go."

"I'm sorry, Romy. It struck me funny."

"What's funny's all what people think." He looked away, scanned the room again. A table of four got up, left.

"You're right, Romy. Even when I think it's funny I always

know you're right when it comes to business." Romy swiveled back around, looked at him. "I'm serious," Batterman said. "I mean that. One thing I know, I can count on you to know what's what when it comes to business. I really do mean that, Romy," he said. For a second Romy Lewinski continued to look straight at him, and Batterman was not sure what he was thinking, if he was perhaps insulted or embarrassed. Like always, he was simply figuring it all out before he responded.

"That's nice of you to say, Batterman."

"I meant it."

"I figure you do. Thanks, hey," Romy said.

"You're welcome."

"Okay."

Then there was nothing they could talk about for several minutes, and Batterman kept half-busy behind the bar. He emptied the rinse tank and refilled it for Mickey, stacked glasses on the towels spread on the shelves where they would dry for tomorrow, opened his till and removed the few checks he had cashed, all but a hundred dollars or so in bills, banded it for the safe. Redgranite's only bank did not have a night deposit drop. There was nothing else to do until they were ready to lock up. Romy would talk when he was ready. Or he would not talk to him.

"Some place," Romy said. "Come in for a beer the bartender turns his back on you to count the take." Batterman closed the till, joined him. "Catch one on me, but," Romy said.

"Thanks. Nine times in a row I would. Sometimes I don't feel like a drink."

"House can't even drink with you, some friendly place. What is it with you? First time I seen you turn one down. First time I seen you, hey, you were tossing them off like mad, you and some hick farmer buddies. I couldn't hardly get a drink for myself as I remember, you were too busy with the dice cup. You want I should shake you liar's dice before you'll take a drink or a snit of beer with me, hey?"

Batterman poured himself a shot of brandy, offered one to

Romy, who covered the top of his beer bottle with his hand. "When the hell was this you're talking about?" Batterman said. Romy laid a bill on the bar, but Batterman did not take it.

"First time I ever seen you," he said. "First night I walked in the damn pavilion bar. You don't remember—you got as good a memory as my old babushka granny!"

"Can't say as how I do," Batterman said. He tossed off his brandy, rolled it in his mouth to let the kick out of it, let the flavor through, swallowed. He tried to remember, exactly the way it was, the first time he laid eyes on Romy Lewinski. For a moment, nothing came. For a moment he was just there, where he was, standing behind the bar in his own place, and it was closing time and Romy Lewinski, owner of the Silver Lake Pavilion (smartest businessman he ever met) sat on a stool on the other side of the bar, slow-nursing a shorty bottle of beer. That was all there was, all there could be.

"Sitting on your fat duff, shaking dice off a couple of farmers," Romy said.

Batterman remembered. It came very suddenly. All of it. How it felt leaning against the back bar in the pavilion barroom, the sound the leather dice cup made when it was rapped on the bar, the dice spilling along the bar, the smooth, warm neck of a liquor bottle as he took it off the shelf to pour for the men who rolled with him, the quiet warm night, late, the height of summer (his last as part-owner-manager of Prader's) the slick, black glimpses of the surface of Silver Lake that seemed to flick through the stand of pines above the beach, the screen door slapping open and shut again, the big man who came in, his ruddy face wet with sweat, as if he had run to the pavilion from a long way away, Batterman leaning against the backbar, waiting for his turn with the dice cup, comfortable, easy, not caring (no need to care) if he won or lost the roll (he got a drink either way), certainly about to stand up straight and give the big man a drink or information, whatever, but not yet standing up (why rush?), knowing that his wife and children were already (probably) asleep in the pavilion house, that his wife would stir, wake, speak to him when he entered the bed

199

beside her, when his friends had driven off, when this big man with a flushed, sweating face had what he wanted, had gone off wherever it was he had to go.

"What the hell are you grinning?" Romy said.

"Nothing. I think I recall what you were referring to is all."

"Am I buying you a drink or ain't I?" he said, nudging the bill closer to him. Batterman took the bill, but did not make change. Another table, three people left, and then two men, and there were only three customers left in the Redgranite Bowl-A-Go-Go, two men at a far table, one alone in a booth opposite the bar. Velma and Marge were finished, had gone to the ladies' bathroom, would be leaving in a minute.

"Go home, Mickey," Batterman said. Mickey had nothing left to do but try to look like he had something to do. "We'll see you tomorrow," he said.

"Keep his mitts out of the till?" Romy said as Mickey shut the front door behind him on his way out.

"Mickey? He's too young to even think seriously about it."

"Dreamer," Romy said.

"You're a cynic, Romy"

"That's why I'm where I'm at," he said. "I wouldn't give you two cents on any one of them I got. Take your eyes off them a minute, they any one of them rob you blind. I wouldn't take no chances," Romy said.

"Like with little Miss Peplinski?" Batterman said.

"You let her any place near your cash register, you need your head examined," Romy said.

"I don't. Maybe someday you'll let me in on her story."

"I said she could shake her ass okay for what you want," Romy said, looking at the empty cage. "I never said you could trust her farther than you can spit." Batterman laughed. "Maybe someday I'll tell you her story, but," he said. Batterman laughed again, but Romy Lewinski did not join him.

"Forget I asked," Batterman said.

"I already did."

"So what gets you out over here?" Batterman said. "They could cart away the pavilion while you're gone, couldn't they?"

200

"They're too scared of me. I dare any of them to pull something funny on me," Romy said.

"I was only kidding. Seriously, I usually see you early. Where's the woman?" Romy did not answer, because Marge and Velma came out of the bathroom, said goodnight, left. The table of three got up to go, and the lone drinker in the booth got up, followed them out. The lone drinker could not walk a straight line, hit himself with the door, getting it open, but managed to get outside.

"If I was smart I'd take his car keys away from him," Batterman said.

"It's no skin off you," Romy said. Now they were alone in the bar, and Batterman felt quickly, pleasantly tired. He had a good sense of all the things he could do. Did not have to do, any of them, if he did not want to. He could choose what to do, or do nothing at all, and it was all the same with him, no matter what. He could stay late in his bar, drink with Romy Lewinski, talk. He could stay in his bar, drink, sit like a deaf-mute with Romy Lewinski, never say another word before daybreak. He could sit, not drink, talk, or talk and drink. Romy Lewinski might get up and leave with no more warning than he gave when he came in, and Batterman could go home to his sleeping wife and children. Or Romy might leave, but still he, Batterman, sole owner of the Redgranite Bowl-A-Go-Go, might stay on, drink alone, or not drink, only stay, stand as he stood now, arms folded, until whenever he felt like doing something else. It was a very pleasant feeling, knowing all he knew he wanted or needed to know, at ease with that, but unconcerned for any of it.

"You consider me as a friend of yours?" Romy Lewinski said. "You consider you're my friend, Batterman?"

"What?"

"What, hell. You heard me. Am I a friend, as far as you're concerned, or ain't I? Forget it if I'm boring you or pissing you off."

"Okay, you're a friend," he said. "If it'll tell me why you're out here by your lonesome at this time," Batterman said.

"Forget it."

"I was joking. Seriously. Yes, I'm your friend, Romy," he said.

"I said forget it, okay?"

So he would sit there, and they would not, apparently, talk. He did not feel like drinking, so he would not drink. Romy Lewinski played with his beer bottle, peeled the label off, made a pile of the bits of paper on the bar. Batterman was so comfortable. He could have closed his eyes, slept standing up, like a tired, contented plowhorse. That would have annoyed Romy Lewinski, so he did not close his eyes, but it was as fine, as relaxing, as if he had. They would stay in the bar, and they would not talk, would not drink. And it was all the same to Batterman. He was ready to wait for the sun to rise, the traffic to pick up out on Redgranite's main drag, Mickey to show up (ready to give the place a heavy cleaning for the coming Saturday night). Still, they would be there, not talking or drinking, and it was just fine with Batterman.

"Broad ticks me off sometimes," Romy said.

"What'd she do?"

"Nothing. Nothing I can put a finger on," Romy Lewinski said. "That's what the whole trouble is. I get pissed sometimes for no damn good reason. I just get fed up with it all every so often," Romy said. "I tell you because I consider you a friend, see?"

"I see," Batterman said. Now he took the brandy bottle off the backbar shelf, poured himself one. He looked at Romy's empty on the bar, at Romy, but Romy shook his head no.

"The whole mess of it ticks me off sometimes, know what I mean, but?" Romy said.

"Sort of. Not really, I guess. You're the last person to be bitching, Romy. You got it made in the shade."

"Lot you know," Romy said.

"You're coining it there with the pavilion. Every time, over to Wautoma to see my folks, I barely recognize the place, you've added on so much. You take in more from the golf course than old Prader ever dreamed of from the pavilion as a whole. You should complain," Batterman said.

"I'm not talking money," Romy said. "I'm not talking about the woman, I'm not talking any of that."

"Half the people in Waushara County wish they had your problems, Romy."

"Lot they know."

"On the other hand," he said, "the other half hate your guts, too." He smiled, but Romy did not think anything was funny. He could not think of anything that Romy Lewinski had ever thought was funny. It made him want to laugh, hard, and he had to keep himself from laughing.

"They can lump it if they want," Romy said. "That's not it either, what I'm talking about. The thing is, I'm smarter than them," he said. "You got to be a man with a plan, see? I'm one. That's why I got all I got, see? These farmers can lump it. I bring more money in this county than any goddamn pickle farmers. I know just where I'm going at, see, which is why I get there, every time I make up my mind to something. They can all lump it, but."

"Granted," Batterman said. "So what are you bitching about? You're the richest man I know, Romy. And you'll be richer. Like you said, I *know* you. It's not your woman, it's not business. Are you talking about your family?" he said. Romy picked up his empty bottle, held it with both hands, as if it would give if he squeezed hard enough.

"I'm not talking my wife or my kids either. I can't say what it is, exactly," he said.

"I forget," Batterman said, "were you in service?"

"I was 4-F."

"That's right," Batterman said, "I remember you telling me that once. Anyway, what I was going to say probably won't make much sense to you. You ever heard tell a good soldier's no soldier at all unless he's bitching?"

"No," Romy said. "What the hell are you talking to me? I try to talk to him as a friend, he tells me goddamn war stories," he said, as though there were still other people in the room, listening, interested. "I should eat my damn problems," Romy Lewinski said, "all the good it does me talking. I should have stayed at my place, soaked my head up good in the hooch for a change," he said.

"You're no boozer, Romy," Batterman told him, "no more than I am. We're both too smart for that. You're *way* too smart for that, and I'm too smart for that myself."

"Big lot you know about me," he said.

"I never said I did. That much I do know. Nobody knows what you know about business for instance, about any special one thing, and boozes it besides. That I know."

"Sure thing," Romy said.

"I'm serious. An old line officer told me that, bitching, when I was on ship for Korea. You're one of those people likes to bitch once in a while, Romy. It's how you keep your peace of mind."

"Goddamn war stories," Romy said. "You were off screwing off in Korea, I was already running my own business."

"I don't doubt it. But it's true about you, Romy. If it isn't then I don't know the first thing about anything at all. Truer words were never spoken. It doesn't matter who said it, for that matter."

Romy Lewinski looked at him for a moment, and then he said, "Explain me something sometime, Batterman. Tell me once how the crap it is you're like you are, huh? I'm serious. I'm speaking as a friend now, not just smarting off, see? Explain once how you go around like you never had a worry in the world, but. I seen you with your ass whipped, trying to make the pavilion pay, and I seen you luck out with this dump. You wouldn't have did half so good if I didn't put you on first to getting the broads here." He looked at the empty go-go cage, back at Batterman. "You could lose your ass twice over in this tomorrow, still you'd be standing there like the world was standing in line three deep just to kiss your fan and beg your damn pardon for it."

He could not recall Romy Lewinski in the few years he had

204

known him (since the night he popped in through the screen door, into the pavilion barroom, when Batterman rolled dice for drinks with his last customers of the evening, came in like a man who had been running toward the pavilion, running hard from a long way off) ever saying so many words without a break for air. He was more interested in that, at first, than in what Romy had said, what he would say in reply to him.

"Explain me that one time," Romy said.

"I'm thinking."

"So what are you grinning again?"

"I'm sorry. I didn't mean to."

"Ask a serious question, get laughed in your face for it," Romy said.

"I'm really sorry. Come on, Romy," Batterman said. "It's late. I want to get home."

"Are you throwing me out? Am I some drunk you got to bump out the door? Some place. Some real friend," Romy said. He got off his stool, started for the door.

"Don't be stupid, man," Batterman said. He came out from behind the bar. "You know better. I know you know better. You just feel like bitching to somebody tonight, Romy," he said. "You'll feel fine in the morning. Wait and see. I promise you you won't have a worry in the world when you get up. You'll coin it this weekend like never before, you'll feel like a new man. Good night, Romy."

"What do you know so much?" Romy said. "You could fall flat on your ass tomorrow, you wouldn't know from it, but," Romy Lewinski said.

"Get a good night's sleep," Batterman said. "Come back tomorrow night, bring the gal, we'll all have one on me," he said.

"The trouble is with you," Romy said before he went out the door. "You don't even know enough to know what the hell I'm talking. I'm planning years ahead, sometimes," he said. "That's why you don't even recognize half the pavilion no more. I'm planning stuff years ahead sometimes, you're still standing around with your finger up your nose, but, waiting

205

for the world to line up and ask your damn permission. If it wasn't for me, Batterman, you'd gone broke twice over waiting for the pavilion to pay you a living by accident or something. You'd be out picking pickles with all the spics for some farmer if it wasn't for me, hey. What is it with you."

Batterman laughed. He had not realized how angry Romy really was. He laughed because he was surprised at that, and because Batterman could do nothing, say nothing, that would help. He only made it worse. "It's cucumbers they pick, Romy," he said. "You've been up here long enough to know that. They make them into pickles here in Redgranite."

Romy slammed the door hard on his way out.

It was hard not to laugh out loud, walking home, down Redgranite's main drag, the side streets very dark, nobody else in sight. It was pleasantly cool, even a little chill. Batterman breathed deeply, noisily, enjoyed the feel of movement in his legs, arms, after the long night on his feet behind the bar. It reminded him of how he had loved sports, football, as a kid. His summer shoes, crepe soles, made a comfortable padding sound on the sidewalk. He swung his arms as he walked, took long strides. He remembered how he had loved the feel of warming up before a practice or a game, the tight, ready feeling of movement, the feel of his cleated shoes tearing the turf, the sense of still being alone in the middle of so many other men, in front of spectators.

The incorporated township of Redgranite, Wisconsin, lay sleeping along its elm-shaded side streets, its main drag closed down for the night. Another one. Like yesterday. Another coming up with the sun in the morning. He felt good. Tired. *Good*.

It was hard not to laugh out loud, thinking of Romy Lewinski. He had heard his car pull out, fast, headed back toward Wautoma, the pavilion, as he locked up his bar for the night.

Lewinski. He was right. If it had not been for him, Batterman might be picking crops for somebody. He held back a laugh at that. Batterman, past forty, fat as a house these days,

206

bent over in a row of cucumbers or melons, filling baskets alongside the Mexican migrants. Maybe he would have ended up picking crops for old (*old!*) Ward Booth. Batterman laughed. He swung his arms harder, quickened his breathing, stepped out smoothly. He remembered how he had enjoyed marching in the army, the long training endurance marches at the Infantry School, Fort Benning. The forced marches he had gone through as a prisoner of the Chinese Volunteer Army. He laughed again, looked around, wondering if anyone else was awake in the town to hear him, see.

Nobody. Nothing. Emil Bender's Tap was shut up tight. El Gato had been cleared out on time, the migrants' pick-ups and jalopies gone back to their camps beside the fields they would pick in the morning. There was no breeze. The moon was bright, casting sharp angles of light and dark into the empty main street (Highway 21).

At the far end of town, the loading docks of the Chicago Pickle Company's cannery were on, like a lighthouse beacon, and the sound of machinery (forklifts, loading belts, pressure tanks releasing) came through the still air, as subtle as if it were a distant wind passing through distant pine trees, carrying sounds all the way to him from Omro, Oshkosh.

What was funny was Romy Lewinski being right about it, and all that upset on top of it. It was enough to make a man laugh out loud. Romy was right. That was the way things had turned out (like always), but Romy could not begin to understand that. Batterman did, but also knew he could not explain it, not to Romy, not even to himself. So Romy got mad, came out on the town to tell somebody about it, knew nobody but Batterman to tell, but Batterman could not talk about it, could only make Romy Lewinski madder. What could you do but laugh it off?

It worked out that Batterman stood behind the pavilion bar, manager-part-owner (with Prader's estate) of the Silver Lake Pavilion, Wautoma, Waushara County, Wisconsin (*that* point in space, time), so that he could be there, having a few slow drinks with a few last customers on a very quiet summer night,

207

rolling liar's dice for the drinks. Things just fine if he did not
trouble himself with remembering that he was going broke,
faster and faster, in the business, losing what little he had sunk
in it, losing what was left of the value of Prader's estate. All
this so he could be there, then and there, when a man from
Milwaukee, Roman Lewinski, came through the door, a big,
flushed, sweaty man, looking like he had run all the way from
a long way away just to catch him before the night was over,
buy the pavilion, lock, stock, barrel, save Batterman's invest-
ment, save Prader's estate, give Batterman the shove he needed
in the direction of Redgranite (just down the highway in the
direction of Oshkosh), the new business where he was coining
it (following the advice of Romy Lewinski to the letter), where
he had just locked up after a good Friday night's traffic, where
he walked home (now to his wife and kids in the new brick
ranch-style he had had built on the east edge of the township).
What else was there to do, if you couldn't explain it, but laugh
it off?

He was here (now) because Romy Lewinski had walked
into the pavilion that night to save him. He was there, that
night, because Prader had needed someone to take it over after
he suffered two heart attacks (later a third, killing him), and
Prader picked him because he knew him as well as he knew
anybody, because Batterman was doing nothing (had married,
tried a job in Milwaukee, had children, came home to
Wautoma, tried working for his father, retirement age himself
by then), and because Batterman had a stake to invest, a stake
that began with eighteen months accrued pay and allowances,
collected when he was exchanged, as a prisoner of war, at
Panmunjun, Korea, not all that much, but enough to buy in a
small piece of the pavilion, the piece growing as part of his
salary for running it, both before and after old Prader died of
his third coronary.

Romy did not understand how it worked, how it always
worked out, one way or another. Batterman could not explain.
What can you do (besides go along with it) but laugh?

Batterman had a stake (small, but enough) from his own

208

little war, because the war had come along just in time to catch him up, transport him across the Pacific Ocean to Japan, across the Sea of Japan to the Korean peninsula (he remembered a man who fell overboard in Pusan harbor), where some Chinese Volunteer woke him up with kicks and cuffs, marched him north through the snow. He remembered a man shot by the Chinese because he was too cold to keep marching. The man had thought he understood it all.

Batterman passed the cannery on his left, nobody on the loading dock at the moment, but the hammer and clatter of machinery poured out into the night, the high odor of pickling vats in the air, the glare of carbide lamps throwing back the summer darkness, cutting across the clean cut shadows laid across the town's main drag by the bright moon.

Romy Lewinski was right. His problem was he would never know it. So it made him mad. Romy (now) would be nearly to Silver Lake (behind Batterman, just over his shoulder, on the highway). Batterman's crepe soles made a pleasant padding sound on the sidewalk, crackled on the road shoulder as he left the sidewalk (the sidewalk ended, not extended yet to where the new streets had been laid, where Batterman's new brick ranch-style lay, down, off to his right, lost in the deep shadows of pines the contractor left standing when he built).

Behind him, Romy (barreling for all his Oldsmobile was worth) Lewinski took the highway back to Silver Lake, the pavilion. Further, the town of Wautoma (Batterman's aged parents) lay, waiting for anybody heading there. Batterman turned off on his street, a block and a half away from home now. He looked back at the highway. Omro, Oshkosh, Milwaukee, Chicago. Iwo Jima, Japan, Pusan, Republic of Korea, the defense perimeter outside Seoul, a ridgeline, a snow-filled mule track of a road (over twenty years ago). Farther, everything, the stadium at Camp Randall, the great Jug Girard, the Booth cousins on Iwo Jima, the Booth cousins walking ahead of him on the road, toward Wautoma. Batterman laughed.

That was the other direction on the highway. That was the thing, what Romy did not know he knew (Batterman could

209

not tell him, was not certain *what* he knew himself). Somehow it was like a huge circle (but *not* a circle). It *was*, and there was Batterman, at the center. Always.

He laughed, hard, then stopped himself. It might disturb his sleeping wife, children (*now*, standing before his home, where he had come, there because it was always there, waiting to be there whenever he reached it). Batterman stood before his home, folded his arms. Simply stood there for a moment.

He did not look up at the summer night's sky. Did not examine his house, sliced into light and dark stripes by the shafts of moonlight piercing the pine trees on his lot. He thought of nothing.

Above him, the moon cast a hard light. There were many stars visible. Above, beyond the stars, deep space stretched out forever. Batterman did not look up, thought of nothing. Simply stood, arms folded, as the center.

Then he shrugged, reached his hand into his pocket for his house key, entered his house, chuckled softly to himself as he checked his sleeping children in their rooms, joined his wife in their bed. She stirred, but did not wake at his soft laughter.

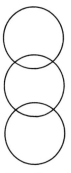

Polack Joke

Beasts of England, beasts of Ireland,
Beasts of every land and clime,
Hearken to my joyful tidings
Of the golden future time.

Orwell, *Animal Farm*

Until he made his move in life, Roman John Lewinski was the best bartender on the whole south side of the city of Milwaukee.

The south side is defined by the industrial valley running from Lake Michigan west for over sixty blocks. You cross the valley on viaducts, at Sixth Street, or Sixteenth, or Thirty-Fifth, to reach the south side. You smell the smells on the viaducts over the valley, the slaughterhouses and meat-packing plants, the tallow and hide yards, the smell of the yeast being cooked at Red Star for all the breweries, the diesel exhaust from the Milwaukee Road switch engines. When you are over the viaduct, on the south side, the smells are less sharp and heavy, but they never go away entirely. On the south side they get mixed with the hot metal smells of the foundries and machine shops. And you hear the industrial racket, in summer when the smells are strongest, from the open factory windows.

Romy Lewinski was born on Rosedale Avenue, in earshot of the bells of Saint Casimer's basilica, where he was baptized and confirmed, where he served at the altar, where he attended mass every Sunday until a couple of years after the birth of his last child. He did not lose his faith, nor was he indifferent. It just got to be too much to get out of bed for an early mass after a Saturday night working his bar. He would have liked to make drunkard's mass at noon, but he had to be open by ten o'clock for his regulars who made it up for eight o'clock mass and were thirsty and eager to get Sunday started.

He attended Saint Casimer's parochial school. He met his wife, Francine, there, in the third grade. He was married at Saint Casimer's basilica. The sermons at Saint Casimer's were preached in Polish, but that is all but passed, since the six o'clock communicants are mostly women old enough to be Romy's grandmother, and there is only one priest left who knows Polish well enough to deliver a sermon to the half-deaf and dropsical old ladies. There is still another priest, a sub-curate, who is Polish, but he cannot speak the language.

Romy's mother knew enough English to use it outside the house, when she rode the bus across the Sixth Street viaduct to shop downtown at Gimbels and the Boston Store. She spoke Polish to her children when they were small, but used English more and more as they grew and were taught by nuns at Saint Casimer's who did not speak Polish well or at all. Romy's older sister became a nun. She spoke perfect Polish, but she was sent to Racine to teach, so never uses it. Romy never spoke the language. He understood his mother perfectly as a boy, but never tried to speak it beyond the swear words he used on the street. His father spoke it with his mother, and with his male friends.

Romy's father worked for the Milwaukee Road in the valley. He started as a gandy and ended a brakeman. He was never dissatisfied or disappointed, because in those days no Pole ever got out of the yard or the roundhouse into the office. No Pole was ever a conductor on passenger runs, nor even a dispatcher's clerk, much less, say, a trainmaster. Which is why Romy never applied for work with the railroad.

His father worked hard, and reasonably regularly, even during the worst days of the Depression, and had never laid a hand on his wife or his children unless he was drunk, which was not often. He did his drinking at the Polonia Lodge, where he played on the same dartball team with the same men for thirty-eight years. When Romy was fifteen, as big as his father, he did not hate him when he had to carry him up to their flat, too drunk to climb the stairs. When his father took a swing at him one night, Romy just grabbed his arms and held him still

214

until he stopped cursing and struggling. Romy's mother saw that, and never got over her awe of her son.

The only thing special about Romy as a boy was that he went to work earlier and worked harder than anyone else his age. He cut lawns and ran errands and gathered pop bottles for the deposit. At every home game during the season he was outside Borchert Field to watch cars for the fans who came to see the Brewers play. Once Joe Hauser hit one over the right field wall. It bounced once on Burleigh Street and rolled to Romy's feet. He sold it to another kid. The day he turned twelve he got his permit at the Industrial Commission office on the other side of the valley. He carried a double Milwaukee *Journal* route in the afternoons, and got up at four-thirty to deliver a triple *Sentinel* route. When he got back from delivering, he ate breakfast with his father, who would be up for the first shift down in the valley. When he had collected his routes the night before, Romy used the time to sort his money, making neat dollar piles of the change, arranging the singles with Washington facing the same way all through the stack. His father sat across from him, watching, sucking at his teeth while his coffee cooled in the mug.

"So what you gonna do with all your money, you?" his father asked. "What?" he said when Romy did not answer.

"I don't know yet. I gotta think."

"Put it up the dresser drawer with all the other, hey?"

"Probably. Until I decide," Romy said. He knew his father was kidding him, but he did not like to talk about his money. The money was not the thing. The thing was he had not decided what to do with himself yet, and money was something to use once he had.

"Give your old man a loan," his father said, and laughed. "Loan me five until I get paid, you," he said.

"I would if you needed it," Romy said. His father laughed and blew on his coffee. When it got late and his coffee was still too hot, he poured it out in his saucer and blew on it. "I mean it," Romy said, "but you're just making fun."

"Some Jew I got for a kid," his father said.

215

"Leave him alone, you," Romy's mother said to his father.

He did not decide until he was seventeen. Before that he put in one summer puddling molten iron for dry sand castings at a small foundry, and another scraping hides and stacking them on wooden pallets in the valley. The foundry and the tannery paid good, but already they were starting to hire niggers from across the viaduct, from over around Walnut and Third Street. They hired the niggers because they would not get enough of the south side Poles during the busy season, and because Poles wanted too much money, or wanted unions, like on the railroad, and the niggers did not ask for any of this. The summer before his last year in high school at Don Bosco, Romy found the job that kept him from having to work on the Milwaukee Road, or in a factory, or with niggers.

He passed all his high school courses at Don Bosco, but could have done better. He was too busy working part-time jobs and concentrating on what to do that would keep him from the kind of life it looked like a southside Polack would have. The priest who coached football at Don Bosco was looking for boys Romy's size. The priest was anxious to make a real challenge to the north side teams in the Catholic Conference, Messmer and Saint John's, and Marquette, but Romy could not make the practice sessions the priest planned for the coming summer on the sand at South Shore Beach. "I got work, Father," Romy said. It was hard for him to say no.

The summer before what would have been his last year of high school, looking for work, he met Mary Janka.

Romy came into the Pressed Steel Tavern just after the second shift had gone on across the street. It was a hot day in the middle of June, but the venetian blinds were drawn, and it was nicely moist and cool inside the tavern. At first he could see nothing in the dimness after the hot light of the sun. Then he saw a man and a woman at one end of the bar, talking softly with their heads close together. He thought at first there was no bartender. She seemed to pop up from nowhere behind the bar.

"So what's?" Mary Janka said. There she was across the bar

from him, wiping a place clean and laying out a paper napkin. She was a little woman, barely five feet, if that, and very fat, but in a hard way, the kind of fat meaning tough and able to last a long time. She was a very ugly little woman. She wore thick glasses with steel frames, and she took them off often to look close at things, and to massage the dents the glasses made on each side of the bridge of her nose. She had one wild eye, which made it look like she was keeping tabs on you, no matter where she stood. When she spoke she never opened her mouth very much, not even enough to show her teeth. Her hair was black, but the obvious black, against the sallow skin of her face, that meant dyed. She wore a short-sleeved house-coat that needed mending in the seams under her arms. Her bare arms were short and fat, and with deep dimples in her elbows, and she wore a large man's wristwatch.

Later, when she came out from behind the bar to show Romy where things were kept in the basement, he saw her floppy carpet slippers, stockings cut off at the ankles. Her stovepipe legs were pale and blue-veined. It was impossible to say how old she was, and Romy never learned until she died and he got a look into the strongbox where she kept her papers that she was already in her late sixties the day he met her.

"So what you want, you?" she said.

"I didn't want no drink, Mrs.," he said. "I was just wondering if I could talk to you for a minute once."

"I ain't no Mrs.," Mary Janka said. But she listened to him tell her what he could do. He had been thinking of maybe linking up several taverns. He would come in once a week and do a really good clean-up, restock, all that. It was one of his schemes for keeping out of factories and the valley for this summer. She had a way of looking at him, while he talked, her thick glasses enlarging her eyes, that one cocked eye, that made him feel it would be impossible to lie to her, or ever to lie to himself while she watched him.

"Speak Polish?" she said when he finished.

"Some," Romy said. "I understand most everything. I don't speak it so much at home or nothing, but I understand good enough." He waited for her to say something in Polish for a test, but she did not.

"How old you?" she said.

"Twenty-two," he said quickly, finding suddenly that he could lie with no trouble at all if it made the difference in getting the job.

"Why you don't go across the street for a job, some-wheres?" Mary Janka said. "How's come a big guy, you, doing work like boys or old men?" She stared hard at him, and it was her, fat, ugly little Mary Janka, putting that wild eye on him. He knew the answer to that question, asked by his father and others. He held his shoulders straight and looked back at her as he spoke.

"I ain't being no dumb Polack all my life," he said. His voice boomed in the tavern. The man with the woman at the other end of the bar stopped whispering to listen to him. "I don't got to work on no damn railroad or in no foundry if I don't want. I don't got to be nothing but some dumb Polack!" He could not tell if she liked his answer. He was busy under-standing something about himself for the first time.

"So maybe you'll run for alderman, be a big shot," Mary Janka said.

"I said why," he told her.

"You drink, you?" she asked.

"No. I like my bottle of beer once in a while is all. I ain't no drunk Polack neither."

"Who you calling drunk Polack, Polack yourself, you!" yelled the man with the woman at the end of the bar. He swept his hand across the bar and knocked their glasses over, one rolling off and breaking behind the bar. The woman tried to shut him up, but he swung his hand again, knocking the other glass off the bar. This one did not break. Romy had not noticed how drunk the man was until then. The woman with him was not so steady herself either. "I get as drunk as I damn want, you Polack!" the man yelled. He was not even looking at Romy anymore. Romy figured the job was as good as lost with this.

218

"Throw him out once," Mary Janka said.

"What?"

"You want my job, let's see you do," she said. "See if you can throw him out once already." The man and woman were cursing each other in Polish. "Go on," Mary said. "He breaks my glass, I can't do nothing. See if you can toss him out."

So Romy went up to the man and took hold of him. He held him with one arm while he picked up the man's change and put it in his pocket for him. The woman started in cursing Romy, words in Polish he never heard a woman speak before. Romy bear-hugged the man and lifted him off the stool, carried him to the door, where he set him down to open the door. The woman came after him and began to beat on his back with her fists. He nudged the man out the open door, then held it for the woman to follow. She spat at him, but nothing came out of her mouth. Then she went out. "What did I ever do you?" the man said. Romy closed the door.

"That's good. You done good," Mary Janka said. Romy trembled a little.

"There goes your business with them," he said. Mary Janka laughed at him.

"I lose nothing," she said. "He comes back here next time because he don't get hurt when you throw him out, and he finds his money okay in his pocket. She comes back with him."

"I guess you know your business best," Romy said.

"You for goddamn sure I do, Polack," Mary Janka said. "Now come on. I gonna show you where all everything's at if you work for me." He followed her, seeing the slippers she wore, the cut-off stockings, the blue veins in her stumpy legs. "You ain't getting rich, this job," she said, "but maybe you learn what's it all about, huh?"

"Bartender," his father said, "big shot, you." He and Romy were not talking much since September, when Romy quit high school rather than admit to Mary Janka that he was only eighteen. "Clean up, mop and bucket," his father said. "I'll see can

219

I keep something open maybe for you by the roundhouse, huh, big shot?"

"Okay, Pa, okay," he said, "laugh now if you want. Wait and see someday is all I say." But his father never got to see. At exactly three-thirteen on the morning of New Year's Day, 1939, his father was hit by the Milwaukee Road 400, out of Chicago for Saint Paul. He was on his way home, drunk, from the celebration at the Polonia Lodge, taking the shortcut across the tracks, as he had a thousand times before when it was late and cold.

"Maybe now you going someplace else for a job, huh?" Mary Janka said. She looked toward the front window. The blinds were down, but they could hear the clank and hiss of the big overhead hydraulic presses, pushing tubes through dies, at the Pressed Steel Tank Company.

"I never said nothing about going no place else," Romy said.

"Your pa's gone, you got sisters to help your ma take care of, huh?"

"The one's a nun, I told you," he said. "You'd of seen her if you came to the funeral"

"I told you I got to keep my business open too," Mary Janka said. "You see my flowers? Okay. Still, a little sister you got, and your ma too."

"She'll get married probably," Romy said. "My ma's got the pension and that social security now, too. I help out some with my pay here too. Why you asking me this? I ain't going nowhere's else, okay?"

"What you looking for from me here?" she said. "Tell me once."

"I want to learn business. So's I can have a business. Myself," he said. They looked at each other for what seemed a long time to Romy.

"Okay, Polack," Mary Janka said.

Romy learned business, and business got better all the while the country tooled up for the coming world war. He learned how to estimate traffic for every hour of the day, every day of

220

the week, and from that how to estimate his orders from the beer and liquor jobbers. He learned to play one jobber off against another for discounts and specials, and when it was smart to stop playing them off. He learned a primitive but efficient cost control and accounting. He came to understand the legalities administered by the city's alcohol and tobacco commission. He learned to sense the delicate balance between investing in overhead, like newer and more fixtures, and the probable return they might mean. Thus he understood why Mary Janka allowed no dartball board on her walls. Dartball games went on forever and tended to cut rather than increase volume across the bar, whereas pinball worked just the other way. He learned the value of having dice cups available, but agreed with Mary in rejecting the offer in a share in a city-wide book run by a Greek named only Nick, who came by early one afternoon with his proposition.

There was nothing wrong, of course, with operating a punchboard. He saw that a jukebox was a good deal two ways, from the house's percentage of the coin box and for the effect polka music had on customers' drinking, and that the no-dancing rule must be strictly enforced if you wanted to keep your furniture from being kicked apart.

He learned the more subtle things a barkeep needs to know to keep trade up. He got so he could pour a shot to the fill-line, and then just a hair above. Not more than a hair above, but above it. He accepted the wisdom of giving away the last shot in a fifth. He absorbed the timing needed to know when the house should buy a round. Not too soon, never too late, when the customer was too drunk to appreciate and remember the fact.

He was sensitive to the feel of an individual customer, to know when one on the house would produce three or four coming back, and when it would not. He caught on to which customers needed an ear to talk to if they were to be expected back, and to those who needed leaving alone, and when in a man's drinking this should be switched around. He developed a memory for names and faces.

He knew distinctions, like between the Catholic charity collectors from the south side, who were given a little money, or space for their tin-can banks and posters, and those who were refused, or were allowed to post an announcement in the front window only in return for complimentary tickets, which were in turn distributed to those customers who cared about the concerts in Koscziousko Park or the boxing cards at the municipal auditorium. He studied the difference between a straight payment to the ward alderman, a definite mistake, and a seemingly anonymous contribution to the Ward Democratic Committee, which was solid insurance in a town where licenses were gold. He appreciated why it was Mary Janka took the beat cops into the kitchen when they came in to mooch a drink and a sandwich, instead of having them stand out at the bar. And he never forgot how to throw a mean drunk out without hurting or humiliating him so badly he never came back.

What he learned, basically, was to use his head for something besides a hat block. He learned how to use himself. And to look to the future with more than vague hopes. A little math on a piece of butcher's paper told him Mary Janka must have a fortune, and it was going to get better, barring disaster.

And it was more. He liked the work. For one thing, it was cool inside, the venetian blinds down. He remembered his two summers in the sweltering valley. Cleaning up before opening each morning, the clean odors of soapsuds and ammonia felt good in his nose against the memory of the acrid burn of molten iron in the foundry casting pit and the meaty, salt-rot stench of cowhides at the tannery. He liked the wet, thick feel of the mophead in his hands as he wrung it out over the bucket. He liked the glazed smoothness of the bartop under a rag, and the way the backbar mirror came clean of film when he wiped it with a wad of newspaper.

More. It was the order of things. He dusted and lined up the bottles on the backbar shelves in perfect rows. He liked it that each bottle was corked with a pouring spout that had a tag giving the price per shot. He liked opening the cooler doors and seeing what needed restocking, writing a list of what to bring up the narrow stairs from the dark, almost chilly basement. The grips of a wooden beercase were solid in his palms. He took three bottles at a time from a case, the glass necks wedged between his spread fingers, thrusting his arm shoulder-deep into the cooler compartments to get the new stock at the back.

The basement was especially good. The floor was bare, packed dirt, giving off the rich smell of a garden plot. He tipped a beer barrel on its side and rolled it to the pipes leading to the three taps at the bar upstairs. It took a carefully measured swing of the bungstarter to tap a barrel. There was a brief, cold spray in his face, a yeasty smell of beer. He knelt at the pile of empties at the foot of the chute, imagining himself dropping them one-by-one the previous evening into the mouth of the chute behind the bar upstairs. They rattled slightly as they rolled down the spiral chute, slow enough to prevent breakage, clattering safely onto the heap in the basement, rolling. Romy sorted them by brand and put them in the waiting, empty cases, stacked the cases at the foot of the double cellar doors at the far end of the basement, ready for the Schlitz and Pabst and Gettleman brewery drivers.

His last morning job was outside, in the alley where the trash bins were. He smashed the empty liquor bottles, holding them lightly in two fingers by the necks, shattering them against the inside of the concrete bin wall. Mary Janka believed strongly in observing the law prohibiting the reuse of liquor bottles, and Romy admired her for it. It was part of the order to things he liked so well.

Inside again, there were usually a few minutes before Mary arrived. Romy liked to stand in the middle of the barroom and look things over. It was nice. Wherever the sunlight coming in at the edges of the blinds touched, the floor and the fixtures, the bottles and glassware shone clean. There was a light sweat on his face, and his muscles felt just exactly enough exercised. It was easy to pretend, to feel like it was all his. That was good, the best feeling Romy had ever known.

Mary Janka took to spending more of her time sitting in the kitchen, less of it keeping an eye on him. Sometimes she studied the papers in her strongbox, wearing her green eyeshade against the glare of the naked overhead bulb. Often she just sat there, seeming to pay no attention as Romy handled the traffic in the tavern. Every once in a while she generated a really good idea, like the check cashing.

Romy cut a hole in the kitchen wall and put in the shelf and the wooden-dowl grill, where she could sit on a barstool in the kitchen on paydays, wearing her eyeshade, to cash checks as the shifts came off across the street. It was nice, she said, for her feet. She suffered badly from swelling feet and ankles.

If the amount of a man's paycheck ended in, say, eighty-seven cents, she might take a quarter for cashing it. If it came out to, say, twenty-four cents, she took a dime. A man never saw his whole dollars tapped, and there was always some little change pushed back to him too. It was worth it to the men, who could not be bothered to run to the nearest bank. Some said they wished for the old days when your pay came in cash in a plain envelope. But with Romy popping the caps off cold bottles of beer, the atmosphere of the Pressed Steel Tavern was too much to pass up. Besides, there was a lot of overtime on government contracts now.

They invested in some Goodwill tables and chairs for wives to come in on paydays to watch over those fresh-cashed checks. The wives always had a couple too, sitting at the tables, talking Polish, one eye peeled to watch for their husbands at the bar. The tables for wives was Romy's idea, as was the .32 which he carried loaded when he escorted Mary Janka back and forth to the bank. The lead-filled walnut police billy, kept behind the bar, was Mary's idea from before Romy knew her.

It was a good life.

There were two near-disasters. The first began in 1940, when after the law was passed Romy had to register for the draft. It came to a head in 1942, when he was ordered to report for his physical. He was twenty-two, and had gotten a bartender's license without saying anything to Mary about it, but if he was drafted he not only was out of the Pressed Steel Tavern for God knew how long, but she might get asking questions and learn he had lied to her about his age in the first place. But now he had the habit of using his head.

He debated taking the .32 and shooting the trigger-fingers off both his hands. He debated going in across the street and sticking an arm into the blades of a floor fan. He never considered getting on with the railroad or in a factory, where there were deferments if you knew who to talk to, which by this time, from working the bar, Romy did. He told his mother about it, and she said she would pray for him.

If everybody gets at least one good break, for no good reason, then this was Romy's. He reported for his physical, wondering up to the last if he had it in him to try to play crazy or queer. A doctor named Adamek rejected him temporarily for fallen arches that Romy could not see even when the doctor pointed to them. He reported every six months for a new physical, but the 4-F classification held throughout the war. He had a fair amount in War Bonds by V-J Day, too. That money came from the cigarettes he and Mary black-marketed out of the Pressed Steel Tavern during rationing. They knew better than to get into tires or gasoline, which were too big and dangerous.

Romy's mother believed her prayers for her son to the Infant of Prague had been answered.

The only family Mary Janka had left in the world were wiped out in a village east of Lublin. This she did not find out until 1946, when the second near-disaster had passed. Romy got married.

There was nothing so special about it. They met when Romy took a rare afternoon off. He took his mother to watch the Pulaski Day Parade on National Avenue. This was 1945. Germany was defeated, but the bomb had not yet fallen on Hiroshima. Truman was president, but Roosevelt's picture was still over Mary's bar, still draped with the black crepe she had insisted on. The Pulaski parade had been routinely canceled because of the war since the last one in '41, but the end was in sight, and Alderman Leon Dumbrowski, thirty-two years incumbent, had only to ask the mayor for the forthcoming official sanction.

Romy's mother had aged greatly since her husband's death. Watching the uniformed marching bands from Don Bosco and South Division high schools, the costumed Polonia chapters, the priests followed by gowned altar boys carrying icons and banners, Alderman Dumbrowski in an open car, wearing his marshal's sash and holding a gilded baton, the queen beside him, a pretty blond high school girl, she seemed to perk up a little. She stood close to Romy, almost leaning on him. She held one of the little paper Polish flags on a stick, passed out by National Avenue merchants.

"Isn't she pretty, Romy," his mother said, waving her flag at the passing queen, who smiled and waved at the crowd lining the curb. "She's a real pretty girl," she said.

"Yeah, she's that," Romy said. But he was looking at his younger sister in the crowd across the street. She was married, as he had predicted to Mary Janka, to a sailor stationed at Great Lakes. Romy seldom saw her. He noticed the girl with her. They both wore saddle shoes, their long hair Marcelled, like a couple of high school kids. Romy would not have waved, but then his sister saw him and their mother, and she waved, and he waved back, and then the two of them ran across the street when there was a space between the American Legion drill team and the VFW color guard.

His sister introduced him, and then he remembered Francine Litwiak from Saint Casimer's. He remembered only how her hair had looked from where he sat, her pigtails. She looked very young still. He realized seeing her how much older he felt now. Right away, she seemed to like him and be interested in him. He never asked, so never learned if his mother and sister had something to do with it. It figured. She was just too naturally interested in him for somebody meeting like that. She seemed, as time passed, just to be waiting to be asked to get married. It was strange. But Romy did not question his luck.

They never had dates, what you could call dates. Except for

226

one Sunday out at the state fair amusement park and a couple of August afternoons at South Shore Beach, they courted at the Pressed Steel Tavern. She was still working first shift at Allis Chalmers Manufacturing, a Rosie-the-Riveter, putting screws into switch plates with an electric screwdriver, so it was a sacrifice for her to come at eight on a Saturday night and stay till closing at three-thirty. Romy tended the crowded bar, and she sat at the extreme end, near the window, almost invisible, nursing a Rhine wine and seltzer or sometimes a blackberry brandy. Even if he was too busy to stop and talk, Romy made a point of catching her eye from time to time, and they smiled at each other. The customers knew enough to leave her entirely alone. Nobody tried to buy her a drink, nobody jostled her, and they even did their best to watch their language at that end of the room. She did not understand Polish well, so there was little chance of her getting her ears burned, anyhow.

Mary Janka stayed in the kitchen when Francine was there. If she wanted Romy for something, she never hollered out, the usual way, but just waited at the kitchen table until he looked in to see if she wanted anything.

"She don't leave you alone," Mary Janka said to him one night. "That one," she said unnecessarily, indicating the bar-room with her eyes.

"I get my work done," Romy said. "We're serious," he said. He waited for her to go on, to see if this was going to be trouble, but Mary let it drop. Romy was serious, but he had not made his final decision about Francine Litwiak yet.

After closing, the two of them walked Mary Janka to her corner and waited with her until her streetcar came. He knew where Mary lived, but had never been there, never been invited. Then he walked Francine home. It was walking her home like that, the streets empty, buildings dark, the breeze from Lake Michigan very chilly for deep summer, that Romy made up his mind he wanted to be married.

He had done some thinking about women before, but it had never been just exactly right before to think seriously, plan, figure on something lifelong with a woman. Walking her to her house, feeling pleasantly tired from the long day and night's work, knowing there was a week's pay in his pocket, money saved, feeling and knowing a sense of the permanent future lying out just in front of him, waiting for him to walk into it and take hold, it seemed right, now, to have a wife. He had too much good sense to question his luck, the forces that made things happen, that made this fairly good looking Francine Litwiak come along, with his grade school memory of her, at just this right time. If he had asked himself, he would have said he loved her.

"Tell me something once, Francie," he said. "What do you think about yourself? I mean, you know, if you're being honest and all, how would you say about yourself?"

"I don't get what you mean," she said.

"I mean, if you was asked. What kind of person you are when you think about yourself, and you're being perfectly honest and all."

"I'm nobody special," she said. "How come you're asking me this stuff? I'm just an average person, I think. I'm like everybody else. I don't know what you mean, still."

"I'm special," Romy said.

"And I bet you're real modest," she said, to make a joke of it.

"No," he said. "In a certain way I have to say I'm special. When I think about myself, like I said to you, being honest, serious, I have to think I'm a certain kind of special person, get me?" She continued to listen, so he did his best to get it out straight. "I mean, I can be some jerk in a lot of things, but I have to think I'm special and not a jerk when I'm really right down honest, figuring myself out, see?"

"I think so," Francine Litwiak said, and said just the right thing. "I think like that probably everyone thinks the same way."

"I just wondered if you thought so too," Romy said. When he kissed her goodnight on her front steps on South Thirty-Fifth Street, Romy had made up his mind. And she naturally and easily said yes, like she had been waiting for him ever since the Pulaski parade.

She did not come in on the night he told Mary Janka. Romy made an excuse so she would not come in, and when he eased the last customer out the door, he was afraid Mary Janka would start off with some crack about his woman not showing her face around for a change, something. He was afraid that getting married would lose him his place here. He did not care why Mary Janka did not like Francine, did not like any women for all he could tell, but he did not know what he would do if it came to choosing between a wife and the Pressed Steel Tavern. What he knew he could not explain to Mary Janka was how they went together. He needed the Pressed Steel Tavern, and for that to be just exactly right, he needed a wife now too. That was all he knew.

"I wanted to talk to you once for a sec if you could," he said, standing before her in the kitchen.

"What should I care a damn," she said. She spoke with her chin almost touching her chest, the words barely audible. Looking down at the top of her head, he saw how thin her hair had gotten. She had neglected to touch up her dye-job, the roots along her part a stark gray. The backs of her hands on the table were liver-spotted, the veins raised and purple. He wondered exactly how old she was.

"What's that?" he said. "I was wanting to talk to you about something important. I'm getting married I think." She did not answer, and then he realized from the gentle movement of her shoulders that she was weeping silently. He was horrified. Something ugly, embarrassing, was happening, and he was afraid of everything. He did not know what to do. But it was not at all what he thought it was, about him getting married.

"What the hell I care what you damn do!" she shouted, and she lifted her head. Her cheeks and chin were wet with her tears, her eyes swimming behind the thick lenses of her glasses. "Do what you want!" she said. Then she picked up the paper that had been under her hands and held it out to him. It was a letter, an official letterhead of some kind. He took it to read and saw it was in Polish, typed.

"I don't read no Polish hardly," he said.

She sniffed loudly, and coughed, and began to try to wipe her face with the frayed sleeves of her housecoat until Romy gave her the handkerchief from his hip pocket. "Means," she said, her voice rough and old from crying, "means, I got nothing no more. You can't read? Means I had a sister once, two uncles I had too. Now I got nothing!" It was an official letter from a refugee identification committee in Lublin, Poland, replying to one of the many queries Romy was hearing about for the first time. What was left of her family had disappeared, must be presumed dead, it said.

"I'm real sorry for you," he said.

"You don't know nothing," she said. "Jesus, do what you want, what should I care!" He tried to think what he should do, and finally he just left her there in the kitchen with her letter. He opened up at the regular time next morning, and when she came in her hair was touched up jet black again. They never spoke of her family again, and Romy went ahead and married Francine Litwiak.

"Where are you going to live now, Romy?" Mary asked him.

"After? I don't know, we're looking yet," he said. He had made a point of not talking about the coming wedding.

"You can stop if you want," she said. "You can have the upstairs."

"Eddie's there," Romy said. Eddie Czerwinski worked second shift across the street. His wife had only recently been laid off at Nordberg Manufacturing out on South Howell Avenue. Eddie was no big drinker, but since he and his wife were home together a lot now, they had some knock-down-drag-outs in the upstairs flat. Sometimes the bar would quiet, everyone holding their breath to catch some of the argument going on overhead.

Mary said, "Eddie can go in a week if I say so. He makes

230

trouble, all that noise ain't good for business. You can't find no better place for you. Sixty dollars a month," she said.

"Eddie pays you seventy I thought."

"Are you Eddie?" she said. "Take it, Romy. If you want I'll buy paint, wallpaper, you fix it up some before you move in if you want." Slowly, it got through to him that she wanted to make up for what she had said the night he saw her official letter.

"I can't thank you enough," he said.

"Good!" Mary Janka said. It was the last thing he remembered her saying with any force to it.

He and Francine were married in Saint Casimer's basilica. Mary Janka did not come. She kept the bar open. Romy had thought of having the reception at the Pressed Steel Tavern, but it was too small, really. It was held at the Polonia Lodge. Romy gave in to his mother and hired a polka band, but he held out for no beer. Mixed drinks, set-ups, only, which did not work well. Men got drunk sooner on whiskey than they would have on beer, so there were more and earlier fistfights than usual for a Polish wedding reception.

At one point, Romy sat down and put his head in his hands and nearly cried. Francine told him not to take it so hard, it was a lovely reception. He had hired three off-duty cops, and they did pretty well hustling the fighters outside for fresh air. Mary Janka gave them a check for a thousand dollars.

She spent fewer and fewer hours in the tavern. When there, she never left the kitchen except to go to the Ladies'. Romy handled it, stock, money, the traffic. Sometimes, working hard on a busy night, he would make a point of taking the trouble to look in on her in the kitchen. If she looked up, he spoke to her, anything, how good business was lately, had she noticed the Transport Company was ripping up streetcar tracks all over the south side, replacing them with trackless trolley lines and diesel buses.

Most of the time her head was down, or she stared off at nothing in the kitchen corner. Often she talked to herself in a voice too soft for Romy to catch any of the Polish. She was still a fat woman, but she seemed to get littler, somehow, littler and littler all the time.

Romy's mother died in 1949, of cancer. She died in Mount Sinai Hospital, her life sustained for several days after her collapse with blood transfusions and intravenous feeding, an oxygen tent, and at the last, injections of adrenalin and a respirator. Romy and his wife, his younger sister and her ex-sailor husband were there, and in the final hours, his sister the nun, who came up from Racine on the North Shore Line, accompanied by another nun. They all prayed, and the hospital's Catholic chaplain blessed them all after he gave their mother Extreme Unction.

The nuns passed their rosaries steadily through their fingers, and Romy's married sister cried hard. Francine stood behind Romy, afraid to look at the dying woman. Romy was struck most by his sense of helplessness. He clenched and unclenched his large hands, swallowed dryly often, mostly wondering if what he felt at his mother's dying was something that he could relieve by weeping or shouting or hitting something with his fist. He knew he would never do any of these things.

He tried very hard for a while to replace the sight of the thin, jaundiced old lady in the bed with images of his mother as he remembered her from his childhood, but it did not work. Nothing happened inside him. The only life he knew and understood now was the Pressed Steel Tavern, and his mother had no part in that. It scared him a little to catch himself thinking there was something right about her dying, now, even like this.

"It's terrible," said Francine back at their apartment.

"It's just as well it's over is all," Romy said, changing into some work clothes to go down and relieve Mary Janka at the bar. The state she was in these days, she could be giving the place away.

Miss Mary Janka died a week later. This was the year of the last Pulaski Day Parade. Polonia committees tried to get it

232

going again in '50 and '51, and again in '54, after Korea, but there was no real interest left. The National Avenue Merchants Association turned thumbs down on the request for money, and the band directors at both South Division and Don Bosco high schools reported they could never round up their students during vacations anymore.

She died alone, in bed in her flat over on Kinnikinnic Boulevard, perhaps without waking up. When she failed to show up by noon that day, Romy telephoned. When there was no answer, he called the Fire Department Rescue Squad right away, and met them at her address. They were reluctant, but he finally persuaded them to force her door.

After he had seen to the removal of her body to the Gomulka Brothers Funeral Home, Inc., Romy cleaned out her flat. He boxed the few clothes and called Goodwill to take them, and what little furniture there was. The framed picture of the Sacred Heart, last year's dried palm frond stuck up behind it, he gave to the neighbor lady who peeked in as he worked. The old *babushka* seemed the only person around who even knew Mary Janka had existed.

"I seen, when the firemen came. Something's wrong I says to myself, mister," she said.

"Did you know her very good?"

"Oh no. We never talked or nothing. I just seen her go and come all the time."

Nobody knew her. There were some old customers at the tavern, men who had been coming in since the day it opened after Repeal, but they knew nothing, how she came to open the bar, where her money came from, nothing. Later, when it was too late, Romy thought to ask Alderman Leon Dumbrowski, who would have known the details of her license application, but Alderman Dumbrowski fell and broke his hip outside City Hall downtown just two weeks after Mary died. Hospitalized a month, he caught pneumonia and went quickly. He was succeeded by his son, Richard, at the next election, but Richard was only a few years older than Romy, so knew nothing.

233

There was a box, private things, which Romy took home with him. He learned the date of her birth from her citizenship papers and her baptismal certificate, an ornate document, hand lettered and illuminated, in indecipherable ecclesiastical Polish and Latin. There were neatly bundled packets of letters from Poland, in a handwriting that hurt his eyes to look at it.

Mary Alicia Czernocki Janka had emigrated to the United States of America in 1894, at the age of twenty-three. He would never have guessed she was that old. For her funeral, he had seen to it her dye-job was touched up just right for the viewing of the casket. There were also a few photographs, some of them antiques, printed on stiff cardboard backs, men and women who somehow looked like they had never really been alive. One man wore a uniform with wide epaulets and high collar, the horns of his moustache turned up in waxed spikes.

"Will you look at that," Romy said to his wife. "You think he was some kind of general or something?" His wife could not say. There were some modern snapshots, curled and yellowing. There was a woman who looked rich, wearing a fur coat and a big hat. And there were some little girls, wearing costumes like at Polonia ceremonies, long ribbons in their hair, sashes, laced bodices, full, decorated skirts, but none of them faintly resembled Mary Janka to Romy. "She must have been related to the high classes," he said. "Maybe she wasn't some old Polack dame, huh?"

He closed the Pressed Steel Tavern the day of her funeral. Nobody except Romy rode out to the cemetery, but several regular customers showed for the solemn high mass at Saint Casimer's, and a few even came the night before to see the body and sign the ledger in the lobby of Gomulka Brothers Funeral Home, Inc.

The very day she died, Romy opened the strongbox in the tavern kitchen. He got right on the telephone to get Maynard Petrulak as his lawyer. Petrulak being a good Democrat, he in turn got Judge Howard Gorski to name Romy executor. Romy was not all that surprised to learn she had left him the tavern, lock, stock, and all.

234

What surprised him a little was her turning out worth a hundred and eleven thousand some odd dollars above and beyond the tavern, once the estate was shaken down. Romy got no money. She left a sum for perpetual masses for herself at Saint Casimer's, five thousand to the Milwaukee County Democratic Council, and the balance was split down the middle between the Polska-Amerikanski Refugee Relief Committee and the Little Sisters of the Poor.

"It's like those hermits you read about," Francine said. "Some old guy lives in a dump, and when he dies he's a millionaire in his will."

"No it isn't," Romy said. "She worked like hell and saved her money is all. Petrulak says she was buying up mortgages there before the war. She knew business is all." He meant to say more, but could not think straight about it.

On the one hand it was very different from his mother's death. Mary Janka was not wasted with a disease. He had no trouble picturing her. She was never tender with him, as his mother had been, but she left him a business, and he almost never thought of his mother anymore.

And more. Without Mary Janka, even if he had his own place, bought it himself, everything he knew and was would have been different, getting to be what at last he was. What bothered him, too much to be talking to Francine about it, was that he felt no sorrow at her death. Not really. It felt *right* for her to be dead too, like his mother. As it had been right for him to marry when he did.

Romy opened the bolt and raised the door blinds, ready for his first day in business for himself. "At least it wasn't like with your Ma," Francine said.

"It wasn't hardly the same kind of thing," he said just to get her off it. He would have liked to talk about certain things with his wife, about now, being a businessman, the future, how he had worked all these years. But she was eight months pregnant, for one thing. She could not sit still or concentrate very long on any one thing, it seemed. He looked out and saw Stashu Grabczyk coming down the street, his shoulders hunched,

235

hands jammed in his pockets. He would be Romy's first customer of his very own.

"Ho, Stashu," Romy called to him.

"How's the big business all open for business," Stashu Grabczyk said. He looked only fairly rough from the drinking he had done the night before.

"You ain't kidding, Polack," Romy said. He escorted him to the bar and poured the first one in a water glass so Stashu would not spill any with his shakes. "First one on the house from me, Stashu," Romy said.

So Romy Lewinski ran his Pressed Steel Tavern for ten years, until he made his really big move in life.

He worked hard, and he ran it well, and he made money, like most everybody else then. He had three children, a son and two daughters, just like his own father, and things did not change much otherwise. He quit going to church, which Francine did not like very much, but she and the children went, and his children attended Saint Casimer's school as he had. He added neon lights in the big front window, and a big deluxe Seeburg juke. He got in a console-type cigarette machine that hummed like it was an Xray. Selling cigarettes over the bar was time and trouble, and there was no money in cigarettes anyway. He bought a pinball machine and a medium-sized mini-bowl. He added a television set in 1957, the year the Braves won their first pennant and the world series to boot, but the television sat on a shelf high in the corner nearest the kitchen door, and he regulated when it was on and off, and how loud it played.

He still sold hot sandwiches and *Kielbasa*, but his wife could not handle the kids and the kitchen too, so he got one of those portable electric ovens, and the sandwiches came in cellophane packets now, right from the refrigerator into the oven and out on a plate when the buzzer went off, still in the sealed wrapper. There was some moaning and groaning when he quit selling *Kielbasa*, but nothing serious.

He had his stools recovered, got a new brace of sinks, and an all-new backbar display. Which is when he took down the

236

portrait of FDR and gave it to old Wadislaw Sarnacki, who said he wanted it because he had seen Roosevelt in person once in Chicago.

The closest thing to disasters he knew were the steel strikes, when traffic cut back two-thirds if they lasted long enough, and he had to make decisions about who not to let run a tab at the bar. But no strike ran long enough to ever really hurt.

He made money. He bought a fair amount of insurance on himself to protect his family. He did better than he had any right to expect on utilities stocks and a couple of mutual funds. He never gambled, what you could call gambling, so much as a dime. He bought a new car, a Plymouth, every other year. He lost some of his hair, and developed a pretty good paunch, but he felt great. Francine's hair turned prematurely grey. She asked him if he thought she should touch it up, and he said no, what for? His sister the nun was still teaching in Racine. His younger sister moved with her husband to California. They exchanged Christmas cards with notes every year.

And another guy came around wanting to let him in on another city-wide book, but this time the guy was a nigger with rings on the pinky fingers of both hands, dressed up to knock your eye out. Romy told him off before he had a chance to get comfortable.

"Would you believe it, Francie?" he said to his wife, who had seen the nigger. "Can you just imagine once what old Mary would have said if this guy'd walk in on her here?" Every so often, after closing, in the kitchen to fix a sandwich to take upstairs with him, Francine waiting up for him to talk, his kids dead to the world in their rooms, he would think of Mary Janka. It was a strange feeling, to suddenly think of her, think if Mary Janka came back as a ghost, would she haunt the kitchen? Would she like what he was?

Or strange, funny feeling, to suddenly think of her and wonder why it had been so long since he had thought of her. Funny, to think he could forget about Mary Janka for so long sometimes.

He had known all that he needed to know, to be what he

237

was, and wanted to be, for a long, long time. And it just went on, once he got there. It went on, and it seemed like it always would, barring disasters, and most of the time that was just fine with Romy.

Until one night, just before the Fourth of July, 1958, when Stanislaus Cecil Grabczyk caused a little trouble, and turned out to be, for all intents and purposes, Romy's last customer, as well as his first, at the Pressed Steel Tavern.

The last and biggest change in his life started one payday night just before closing time, when Stashu Grabczyk cold-cocked his wife, Cissy, right there in front of Romy in his bar.

Cissy Grabczyk flew off her stool and landed hard on the floor. She lay there on her back, rocking from side to side like she wanted to turn over on her stomach, holding her face with both hands, shouting curses in Polish at her husband and at the pain in her mouth, until Romy's wife came out of the kitchen and picked her up and took her to the Ladies' to quiet her down. Francine Lewinski still wore the green eyeshade she wore on paydays, when she cashed payroll checks for the shifts from the Pressed Steel Tank Company across the street. Romy had vaulted the bar and taken hold of Stashu in a bear hug to keep him from taking another poke at Cissy, or maybe kicking her in the ribs or the head and doing some real damage.

What surprised him, what got to Romy then, as his wife half-carried Cissy Grabczyk to the Ladies', was what he all of a sudden felt like doing to Stashu, helpless and cursing in his arms. What he almost did to him. At first he was just holding him still, but then he could tell he was hurting him, squeezing the little man hard, because Stashu was no longer mumbling in Polish, but yelling loud at the pressure Romy was putting on his spine. And he almost did not stop.

"Can you keep him quiet!" Francine called from the Ladies'. Cissy was still caterwauling too.

"I ain't hurting you," Romy said in Stashu's ear, lifting him by the elbows and sitting him back on his stool. "Shut up, you, you ain't hurt," he said.

"Not much he ain't from the sound of it," said one of his two other closing-time customers. They were young men, not even Pressed Steel Tank Company people. They sat at the other end of the bar, sipping tap beer and methodically eating hard-boiled eggs from the wire rack on the bar. Romy had kept count. Their hair was long, their t-shirt sleeves rolled up almost above their shoulders to show off their tattoos. Romy kept one hand on Stashu to keep him from taking a header off the stool.

"Out," Romy said.

"What?" one of them said.

"I said out. Take off. You heard me okay," he said. What got to him was that he knew he was wishing the two punks would make something out of it, invite him outside, come for him from their end of the bar. He was balancing Stashu Grabczyk on the stool with his fingertips now, figuring how he would take the two punks. The regulation police department walnut billy club, the core drilled out and filled with lead, was just under the bar on the same shelf with chore-balls and bar rags and scouring powder and the can of bartender's friend for sterilizing glassware. Romy could reach it by stepping up on the rail and leaning across the bar. Eighteen inches long, heavy as a plumber's wrench, he could kill the two punks with it. For that matter, the loaded .32 was in the bottom of the cash register drawer, but the punks could maybe reach him before he could get to it.

"What the hell kind of place is this, for Christ's sakes," one of the punks said, pushing back from the bar. They were not going to make anything out of it, and it bothered Romy, knowing he felt sorry nothing would happen now. The other punk got off his stool now too, looking very frightened. Romy heard the toilet in the Ladies' flush. Stashu was mumbling softly in Polish again.

"Buck twenty," Romy said.

"What?" He longed to let Stashu fall on his face, go after them.

"Buck twenty. You can't hear good or something? Six

239

eggs, twenty cents, and the beer. Buck twenty." He hoped they tried to leave without paying. But they dug for change, and between them, laid it out on the bar where Romy could see to count it.

"I paid already for my beers," one said.

"Who asked you," Romy said. "Now get. I catch you in here again, I kick your *dupa* up between your shoulders. Punks!" he screamed after them as they darted out the door.

"Will you knock it off, give quiet, you, so's I can get her shut up!" Francine yelled from the Ladies' again.

"You sit tight," he whispered to Stashu Grabczyk, straightening him on the stool, placing his hands on the bar for props. "You sit tight, you," Romy said very softly. He took Stashu's face in his two hands and leaned close to whisper. "You sit tight there and don't make no more trouble," knowing he meant to do nothing more, bothered that he should want to say it anyway, "or so help me God, I'll break your damn dirty neck for you, goddamn drunk Polack." His voice hissed over the edges of his teeth. Stashu muttered.

"What you say?"

"Polack your goddamn self, Lewinski," Stashu said.

"Yeah sure," Romy said. He smiled and felt how his neck and face were wet with sweat, even with the air conditioning, a new Trane climatrol unit, eighteen hundred bucks and some. "Sure, Polack myself," he said, and just for one second wanted to belt Stashu, push his face through the bar top, heave him out through the venetian blinds, even though he was positive he would do nothing, really. "What is wrong with me?" he said.

Romy was big enough to intimidate half the punks who came in feeling strong enough to tip the bar. With regular drunks like Stashu Grabczyk, he just stepped out from behind the bar and stared hard, hands on his hips to show he would not use them, but could and would if the drunk wanted. More often than not he only had to grab a man in a bear hug and hold him still. If it ever got really rough, there was the leaded billy on the shelf. And if some nigger or somebody ever tried

240

to stick him up, the pistol was in the cash register drawer. But it never really got rough in the Pressed Steel Tavern.

Except this payday night when Romy himself came close to hurting Stashu Grabczyk, a drunk, sure, but his most regular customer of any, not so bad a guy when he was half sober. And then Romy wanted to get really rough with the two punks, whom he had honestly nothing against. I must be going bats, he thought.

"You better get him in his car," Francine said, bringing Cissy Grabczyk out. Cissy was not hurt bad, but her denture was snapped in two.

"Damn drunk Polack bastard can just pay me for a new one," Cissy wept, drunk herself.

"I suppose I'm taking them home to bed," Romy said, pulling off the towel tucked into his belt he wore for an apron.

"Who else, me?" Francine said. "I still got checks to figure, you know."

"The hell with this whole mess anyway," Romy said, taking hold of Stashu, whose legs went rubbery on him when he tried to take a step.

"You love me, Lewinski, good Polack buddy," Stashu said.

"Yeah sure," Romy said.

"So go," Francine said.

He was irritated, when he returned, that his wife had not turned off the neon lights that framed the big window. To a passing squad car it looked like they were open after hours. Not that any police on Milwaukee's south side would turn him in for a license violation, but it made no sense to fool around with anything that even technically could lead to suspension or revocation. Half the police working the south side were men Romy knew from as far back as parochial school at Saint Casimer's. For the other half, Romy did not kick in heavy to Alderman Richard Dumbrowski's campaign kitties for nothing.

"You, Romy?" Francine called from the kitchen.

"No," he said, quickly angry. "I'm some nigger coming by saw your lights on for a signal you want held up!"

"Big deal," she said, "sue me." He might have answered

241

her back roughly, gone into the kitchen and slapped her a good one, but he was caught by the new impression the interior of the Pressed Steel Tavern made on him. He stood in the middle of the room, halfway between the bar and the row of tables.

There was still the cleaning up to do, either tonight or before opening in the morning, in time to catch the first shift coming off across the street, and the second going on. There would be forty, fifty men lined up two and three deep at the bar shouting for one more quickie before the last warning whistle blew. Romy shuddered involuntarily, as if he were cold, as if a sticky mist had closed against his skin.

The frame of neon tubing in the front window was still on, buzzing, ticking in short, random spasms. In the dull red glow, the specks of insect bodies, pasted to the tubing, seemed to quiver. The window needed washing, inside and out. He needed new lettering on the window. This was the original, gold leaf, and the backing was chipped badly. Paint next time. Who used gold leaf, except maybe banks and sheister lawyers anymore? The bar top was half done, the open 7-Up bottle and his rag at rest where he left them to jump and grab Stashu. The other half, in the indirect lighting from the backbar, showed the tacky rings of many glasses, dark cigarette scorches, and at the far end, a scattered mess of eggshell fragments. "Agh!" Romy said.

"So turn it off," Francine said from the kitchen. "The light you're so hot about, make it out." He turned it off, and turned off the backbar lights, and went to the big Seeburg juke and pulled the plug, and pulled the plugs of the pinball and mini-bowl. Now there was only the long path of light from the kitchen door. The floor was dotted with cigarette butts. He would clean up in the morning.

The hell with it, Romy thought. Take it easy, like he told customers who drank too much and got mad with everyone and everything. Take it easy. What's the use of business, of money, to go to pieces, go crazy?

"You fall asleep or die or something, hey?" Francine said from the kitchen.

"I'm thinking," Romy said. He was thinking, for the first time in a long time, of Mary Janka. "Baloney," he said to himself.

"Don't strain yourself to give anybody a hand," Francine said.

"Take a vacation," he said. "Let's go up to bed. Make us up some sandwiches, I'll get us a beer."

"Meanwhile what am I doing with this?" She came to the kitchen doorway, carrying three of the big canvas zippered bags from the bank for the night deposit drop. She had taken off the green eyeshade, but it was still like seeing Mary Janka's ghost for a second there in the doorway. "And since when you don't do the register on payday? What is it with you tonight, Romy?" It was not Mary Janka. It was his wife Francine.

"I forgot, okay?" he said, turning his back on her and going to the light switch.

"You're acting funny," she said.

"Funny hell," he said. "You forgot I'm a dumb Polack is all. I'm not so smart. Now I'm doing the register. So leave it alone, yeah?"

"Okay," is all she said. She stood in the doorway, watching him as he started in on the cash register.

"I got to get outta this," he said as he ripped the piles of tens and fives and ones from their compartments. He licked the ball of his thumb and counted, fast and accurate as a bank teller. "Tomorrow," he said, making notes on the pad he kept next to the register, "I'm doing something."

"What are you talking about, Romy?" Francine said. She moved closer, as if she was not sure who it was, to see him better.

"Doing something," he said. "I know a certain guy was telling me about a deal he knows. Up north," he said. "I just may do a real big deal here before you know it, Francie. What do you think of that, huh?"

"I guess maybe you'll tell me when you're ready to. I don't think you really feel like talking to me right this minute," she said. He had been thinking, his hands trembling as he added

243

columns on the pad, if she said something smartaleck, argued, even questioned, he would yank out the tray and kill her with the .32. Or himself. Or first her, then himself. Or her, then go upstairs and kill his three children, then himself. He would do something.

"Good," he said. She went back into the kitchen to get him one of the canvas bags for the surplus cash. He never kept more than a couple hundred dollars in the building because he had no safe.

"What'd you say?" she said, handing him the bag. Romy lit a cigarette.

"A safe. Next time I go in business I'm having my own safe, cemented, like to the floor, in a corner." She half-laughed, like he was making a joke. "Wait and see," he said. He checked his figures on the slip before wrapping the bills and putting them in the bag. "You wait and see."

"Okay," Francine said again.

"You know what the trouble with Mary Janka was?" he said. "She quit thinking. She stopped."

"That's the first time I thought of her, when you said her name now, in years," Francine said.

"That's the trouble with you," Romy said.

Labor Day was no time to be traveling. In the first place, he started late, what with showing Wisniewski around the place enough so he could handle it while Romy was gone. Francine went out of her way to keep from helping. "I told Wisniewski ask you if he has any special problems," he said.

"If I'm here," she said. "I'm probably taking the kids over to Ma's."

"So you'll be back, right?"

"We maybe'll stay overnight if it gets late," Francine said.

"Sure," Romy said. "You'll just hurt yourself giving me a little hand when I need it, won't you." He waited for her to pick it up. He felt like arguing, not looking forward to the drive, but she let it alone. "You kill me sometimes, Francie," he said.

244

"Don't try picking no fights with me," she said. "I told you what I think, so go do what you want."

"I will," Romy said.

"I bet you will."

"Enjoy yourself," he said. "Act like a jerk Polack, old *babushka*, all you want." She let that alone too, and a good thing for her she did.

In the second place, Romy Lewinski had not left Milwaukee County more than twice in the past ten years. The first time was the one time he got drunk since he went into business, when Jerry Grochowski, the second shift foreman across the street at Pressed Steel Tank Company, closed up the bar with him and they drove in Jerry's car all the way to Thiensville to what was supposed to be a whorehouse, but turned out to be just another after-hours gin mill.

The second time was this past July, when he went down to Wrigley Field in a chartered Greyhound with sixty of his customers to see the Braves-Cubs double header. After tickets, beer on the bus both ways, and dinner at Fossland's Restaurant at the state line on the way back, Romy cleared less than a hundred dollars. Which is why it was the last trip like that he ever organized.

The morning after he went to Thiensville with Jerry Grochowski, his wife asked him where he was so late. He told her they went out there to eat barbecue, but could not look her in the eye without feeling like hell, and every time one of his kids spoke to him he wanted to go lock himself in the john or someplace to be alone until he could get over his shame.

This time he left angry, and the traffic made it worse, everybody and his brother on the highway, refusing to dim their headlights, tail-gating him, blowing horns because he drove within the speed limit. It was pitch dark before he got there.

State Highway 21, going west out of Oshkosh, curved sharply to the right just ahead, and there it was right in front of him. The sign was as big as a city billboard, lighted with pale floods from the top, the paint peeling: *Batterman's Silver Lake*

Pavilion. There was a picture of a lake, some sail boats, and in one corner of the sign what looked like a champagne glass with bubbles rising out of it. The entrance road was unpaved, the gravel crackling under the tires as he left the highway. The Plymouth bounced in the pot holes. Behind him on the highway, the string of traffic, both ways, continued.

It was beautifully calm and cool when he got out of the car. A breeze came off Silver Lake, moving the pines that stood in an uneven row between the road and the lake. The air smelled especially good after the close, tobacco-smoked interior of the car. He could have sold this air by the bottle back in Milwaukee. Romy breathed in deeply, sucked up his stomach and tucked his shirt into his belt. The air was so good he walked around, looked around a little before going inside.

Wherever else the Labor Day crowd was going, it was not here. There were a few other cars, parked diagonally up against the pavilion porch, but the open-air pavilion itself was empty except for a couple of kids, wearing only bathing trunks, in the far corner, playing some kind of machine. The bar and grill was at that end, and he could see some people at the bar, but it was not well-lit, and no music played. Across the road, on the lake side, he could make out a long pier, and a little further out in the water, some kind of big raft with a structure on it, like an oil derrick. The lake must be good-sized, judging from the way dock lights looked here and there off in the distance. There was no bathhouse he could see, but off at one end of the beach was some playground equipment, merry-go-round, jungle gym. No wonder there's no crowd, Romy thought. First off you needed lights on the beach.

Up on the pavilion there was a row of heavy wooden chairs facing the lake, so big they left hardly enough room to walk the length of the porch without banging your shins. The chairs had wide arm rests, and Romy read some of the initials and swear words kids had cut into the wood with pocket knives. The only light was from a row of yellow bulbs at the edge of the pavilion roof, the kind supposed to repel bugs. No wonder,

246

he thought. You couldn't begin to move traffic on the porch until you got rid of those chairs.

He walked out on the pavilion floor, mud stained from the feet of swimmers just up from the beach. Sand scratched under the soles of his shoes. Ruin your floors for you, he thought. At the other end of the pavilion was something looked like a boarded-up stage. He watched the two kids play the machine for a minute.

It was an expensive machine. There was just the one machine, with a window where this bear ran back and forth. The players took what looked like a real rifle and stood back however far they wanted. The rifle hooked up to the machine by a length of black electrical cord. The bear ran back and forth in the window, and the machine hummed. The bear had a little glass hole in his side, and the players aimed for it with the rifle, which fired a beam of light. When the light hit the glass in the bear's side, it stopped, turned, reared up on its back legs, and roared, facing the players. There was another glass hole in its chest, and if you were fast enough, you shot it there, and it kept on roaring. If you missed, it went back down and starting running back and forth again. The electric rifle made a dull chinking sound when it fired. The cord was maybe thirty feet long, and the two kids started out shooting from way back, but they hit nothing until they got up pretty close.

"How much does it take?" Romy asked them.

"Dime," one of the kids said. They were horsing around now, bending over and shooting between their legs, but they hit nothing that way, close as they were.

Why only the one machine? Romy wondered. There was space for a whole wall of pinballs, and maybe a really good-sized, twenty-foot mini-bowl. There was no sign saying what you could win, like in Romy's place, not even free games. At the Pressed Steel Tavern, luck or one hell of a lot of skill got you a five dollar jackpot on the mini-bowl, and any number of combinations on the pinball were good for a free hooker and beer wash.

He went back out on the porch and entered the bar and grill. The screen door was a little warped, he noticed, and a lower panel needed new screen. The air still smelled good, even inside. If he tried using a screen door at the Pressed Steel Tavern, all he would smell would be the acid from the steel pickling vats in the factory yard across the street.

The first thing he noticed was the bartender did not even greet him. He did not even get off his duff to wipe the bar in front of the stool Romy took. No wonder, Romy thought.

What he noticed so far, he noticed only in passing, what almost anybody might see. Now he started looking, checking off the items that told the story of this business here at the Silver Lake Pavilion, which is to say they told him why there was almost no business to speak of on the Labor Day holiday, when by rights it should be choked with traffic coming off the highway for meals and coffee, from the lake cottages, wherever.

Item, he thought, the way he made notes on his cash register pad—item. The ashtrays all along the horseshoe-shaped bar were full. Which also explained the deep brown scars marring the bar its whole length. And the bar top was not clean. It was wiped at closing, maybe, but for sure nobody went after it with 7-Up or bartender's friend, something to cut the scum. Also there were empty glasses, the ice melted in the bottoms, or speckled white with dried beer foam, which had not been picked up when customers left. Same on one of the tables in the far corner, dirty dishes and silverware still lying out, balled napkins, cigarette butt in a saucer because nobody bothered to put an ashtray on the table. No wonder.

Item. The backbar was a holy mess, bottles not returned to their shelves, drawers left half-open, more dirty glassware. From his side of the bar, Romy could see the wash tank. Heaped with glassware, the water was left on to overflow into the drain in the rinse tank. The garbage pail needed emptying. There was a small safe, he noticed, set into the floor behind the bar, its round door hanging open on the hinges.

Item. Romy gave up. No wonder. The floor was unswept,

248

last week's date still on the wall calendar, a burned out bulb not replaced. No wonder. And the bartender was only now getting off his duff to serve Romy.

The bartender half-explained things. He was big, as big as Romy, but different in a way that half-explained things. He was soft. Romy stood six-two and a half, and he had the gut you naturally expect on a man just forty, with his natural weight and big bones. This bartender was an easy six-two or three, a good two-thirty or forty, but soft all over. His face was very smooth, puffy. His forearms were puffy, his fingers fat, his rear-end bulging his khaki trousers. He looked younger than Romy. His hair was long and thick where Romy's was thin and smudged with grey around the ears, and his face was tan where Romy's was pale and pitted from adolescent acne around the mouth.

He was the kind of man, if Romy sized him up physically, as if he were a stranger come into Pressed Steel Tavern, getting a little rough, Romy would have wondered just for a second if he should get the leaded billy out, but would have concluded right away he could handle him. He would handle him, Romy thought, if it came to doing a deal for this place.

The bartender got up to serve him. He had been on his fat duff, rolling the dice cup with three customers, men who did not look like money, and drinking shot for shot with them, win or lose. Romy had dice cups, three of them, but he kept them on the backbar until somebody called for them to play poker or horse or liar's dice for a round. Romy's rule was not to roll against customers, and if somebody got drunk enough to insist, then he rolled for a cigar or half-dollar for the Seeburg juke, never for drinks. He came over to Romy, and still he did not greet him. He just waited, eyebrows raised, like he was doing a big favor just being on hand. Romy wished somebody, even his wife, were with him to see this.

"Coffee black," Romy said.

"Kitchen's closed, my friend," he said. The customers were picking up their money to go.

"Shorty beer then."

"Glass?" he said, not even taking the trouble to wipe the beads off the bottle when he pulled it from the cooler. It would leave a wet circle on the bar top, which, Romy would bet, would not get wiped up before closing time.

"If it's okay by you," Romy said. The three customers left. The bartender gave them only a weak wave of the hand as they said so long. Not so much as thanks or no thanks or kiss my Polack foot! "How's business?" Romy said. He could not hear the bearshoot machine anymore.

"You're it," the bartender said.

"Labor Day, should be good." While he poured beer into his glass, the bartender reached the nearest bottle of rock and rye and poured himself a stiff hooker. He diluted it with a splash of sour mix, and hitched up his trousers to stand and talk to Romy. Romy noticed his beer glass had dried spots on it too.

"That's what I keep telling myself," the bartender said.

"You'd be Mr. Batterman," Romy said.

"I would," he said. He dusted the palm of his hand on his trouser leg before holding it out to Romy.

"Romy Lewinski," Romy said. "A friend of an acquaintance of yours gave me a sort of description of you in Milwaukee. I'm from Milwaukee. I got a place there, tavern, south side. I'm interested sort of in this place since they tell me you're looking to get out?"

"I didn't catch the name right I don't think," Batterman said.

"Lewinski. I'll write it out for you if we need it." He was indeed looking to get out from under, the way he squeezed Romy's hand and pumped his arm. "Let's talk about it a little," Romy said. "I mean, sort of talk around it and I can see maybe if I'm really interested in some kind of deal, okay?"

It was a bigger package than Romy had been led to believe by his contact in Milwaukee. There was the triangle of land lying between Silver Lake, State Highway 21, and Waushara County road DD. The long side of the triangle was all lake frontage that could be cleared in a day with a bulldozer and a gang of rakers and burners. In addition to the pavilion and the adjoining bar and grill, there was an eight-room house behind the pavilion. "You can't see it from the road even in broad daylight for the oaks and elm trees. That's the hardest part of it for me to give up. It's nicely shaded. It's a good house," Batterman said. Romy Lewinski had never lived in a whole house.

There were fifteen dilapidated weekend cabins on the property across the county road. Romy was already thinking about a septic tank system, a natural gas hookup for a trailer and camper park. Across the state highway was the biggest piece of land, mostly cleared pasture. Batterman let the Wautoma Senior High School use a corner of it for athletic practice. "They put up a chickenwire backstop every spring," he said. "People come out from town for the games and wander across the road for a drink. You could probably find yourself a farmer to graze stock on it if you looked around," he said. Romy already had a better idea. He found himself full of good ideas.

"What's your competition?" he said.

"I won't go so far as to tell you this is any great business," Batterman said. "It's been here nearly fifty years, one way and another. There's the Moose Inn two miles down on twenty-one. You had to pass it coming north. Silvercryst is nearly as big as I am, over on the lake road. There's a place down DD too, old Booth's, but that's largely groceries and outboard motor fuel for the summer people." There were deer to be hunted in Waushara County, but Batterman closed after Labor Day, to reopen in early May when families who summered on the Lake began arriving. "There's families been coming up here for generations from Chicago and Milwaukee," he said.

"Who's the law?"

"Sheriff. You never see him. Right now he knows his job, but you're liable to get some farmer. They can only do two terms. He'll come in to check for kids buying booze, but he gets his pinching speeders in Wautoma."

"So how big's the sweat transferring a license?" Romy said.

"No sweat at all. Why should there be?" If there was any one thing decided Romy that was it. He was used to a liquor

251

license being something handed down from father to son, something people chipped in together for in order to grease an alderman or an alcohol commission member, something that meant the difference between forty years on the railroad or in the foundry and forty years to build, make something. Here, you filed, and you got it. Oh Mary, you see! he thought.

"It's big and it's old," Batterman was saying, "but there's not a stick of rotten wood in it. Furthermore I'll tell you you get a whale of a lot of good will with it. There isn't a kid in this town, including me, who didn't grow up swimming out here every summer."

Romy asked, and it turned out the oil derrick thing he saw out in the water was a fifty-foot water slide. That was what drew the kids to the beach. "There's not another like it in the state of Wisconsin," Batterman said, "but insurance on it is murder."

They talked, and Batterman kept hitting the rye and sour mix steadily, and Romy held his glass of beer with both hands to keep from asking for pencil and paper to start his calculations. They spoke about money. Nothing exactly specific, but close enough that Romy knew he could handle it. He knew how long a rope he had with a couple of banks in the city of Milwaukee.

"You like to take a closer look around?" Batterman said. "I got one of those Coleman lanterns if you want to check the grounds out."

"No," Romy said. "I got to get back to my family. My kids wake up and I ain't there, they'll think I run off and died. You'll maybe be hearing from me after I study a few things out."

"I'd like like hell to count on that," Batterman said.

"I know you would," Romy said. "Let's just say for now I got a fair idea we can do some dealing, I think." Batterman shook hands with him like he was going down for the third time.

Driving out, not at all tired at the prospect of a hundred

and thirty odd miles, he got a glimpse through the trees of a lighted upstairs window in the house back of the pavilion.

A whole entire house, Romy was thinking. That should be enough to get any trouble with Francine out of the way. It could be a goddamn gold mine! he told himself. But it was more. He had done something, decided to do something about what had been bothering him so much since last payday night, when Stashu Grabczyk knocked his wife Cissy off a barstool in the Pressed Steel Tavern. He knew he did not understand it, and he did not care if he ever did. What it was, everything had been right in a certain way, all his life, and then it had not been right, not since that payday night, and now he was going to do something about it.

"You goddamn bet you, Polack!" he said aloud. It embarrassed him after he said it, as if the car radio, glowing in the middle of the Plymouth's dash, could hear him.

"If I could understand why, but, Romy," is all Francine said when he told her he was selling out to buy the Silver Lake Pavilion.

"What is it with you," he said. "You want to be some old *babushka* Polack dame all your life or something?" She never what he could call actually agreed, but she shut up, so he went ahead with it.

For the first year it seemed like he was throwing money hand over fist into a sinkhole. He had no right to expect a profit even the second year, so that was so much gravy. But for those two years, if he had not been so busy, the short, quiet moments of terrifying doubt might have panicked him. Batterman stayed on the first year to ease the transition, but sometimes he was as much hindrance as help, and sometimes he was no more help than some of the lazy college kids hired for the summer.

There was no trouble getting the license. At the county courthouse in Wautoma, Batterman hand-carried the papers around with Romy beside him. They made an unofficial call on the sheriff to let him know about Romy's first innovation, the rider on the license for an eighteen-year-old 3.2 beer bar. The carpenters were already at work, cutting a hole in the end of the pavilion wall adjacent to the bar and grill.

"I thought of that, you know," Batterman said, "but it's asking for headaches. You get a mob of stinko kids, they give you trouble, then roar all over the county drunk behind the wheel."

"I'll handle the trouble on my side," Romy said. "The law can take care of them on the highway."

Sheriff Schaeffer hardly looked like any kind of sheriff. He had a dinky little office in the jail, an ordinary table for a desk, and sat on a metal folding chair. He did not even wear a gun, though there were some shotguns in a locked wall rack. He wore civilian trousers, farmer shoes, and an old army shirt with a button over his small paunch popped off. From the looks of his shiny complexion, the watery film over his bright eyes, Romy would have given odds there was a quart stashed somewhere close by in the jailhouse.

"I hope you know what you're about, bringing on every kid in the county and then some," he said.

"I'll handle them," Romy said.

"You'll have to," Schaeffer said. "I've got one deputy and the two constables in town. I'd hate to see another yearly Lake Geneva riot up here."

"Don't you worry," Romy said.

"That's my business now, isn't it," the sheriff said. Batterman started talking about all the work they had out at the pavilion if they were going to get open by the end of May, what with all the changes Romy had in mind.

"Stop out and have a drink with us," Romy said. "When you're off duty sometimes, I mean."

"When I'm off duty I'm still in charge of this jail," Shaeffer said. "What was that name again?" he said, half-rising when they went to leave. Romy spelled it for him.

On the way back to the resort in Batterman's station wagon, Romy said, "Was he telling me to go to hell or something?"

"Search me," Batterman said. "These are small town people up here, Romy. It's bound to be a little different from what you're used to."

"Just as long as I got my license," Romy said. As they approached the access road, Batterman slowed to let him get a good look at the painter working from a scaffold on the billboard. Romy designed it himself. *Lewinski's Silver Lake Pavilion Resort*, smack dab in the middle.

The name would be set off with pictures of a girl waterskiing, a fish jumping out of the water for a casting plug, the legend, *Fine Food and Drinks* at the bottom, *Camp and Picnic Grounds* at the top, and some musical notes in the corners. "It's a little busy if you ask me," Batterman said. "But I suppose it'll show up good."

"I didn't ask you, but that's just exactly the idea," Romy said. He got the bulk of his changes done that first spring.

For a starter, he got rid of the water slide after he saw what premiums came to. Batterman mentioned calling some farmer with a tractor to drag it off the beach far enough into the water to float it out to its anchor. "Call somebody to haul it off or tear it down," he said.

"Are you serious?"

"It don't pay," Romy said. "A raft with a diving board's all you need for your beach. First off, your beach is just a draw. You get your kids in so's their parents eat and use the bar. Second, you throw a cyclone fence around the beach and get maybe a quarter for the bathhouse.

"What bathhouse?" Batterman said.

"The bathhouse I'll get built on the beach, if I can get you to do something for me when I need it. That's another thing. Get somebody can put cement blocks one on top the other in a straight line."

"That slide's been here thirty-five years," Batterman said. "I played on it as a kid. That's the one thing everybody knows this place for, man," he said.

"Man yourself," Romy said. "Not no more. By the way, you got a good color picture of it? Sitting out in the water and all?" Batterman thought he did; there were postcards for sale in Wautoma with the slide pictured. "Good deal," Romy said. "I got to get a blow-up like on glass or plastic, so I can put a light behind it. I want that thing for my backbar. That's class, that kind of picture in your bar."

"It's your say I guess," Batterman said. He looked at the large raft and tower, its oil-drum floats resting on the sand.

"Right," Romy said. "Also, is there anybody around here can do real masonry, I mean, make me some good looking stone walls?"

"I think so."

"Call him too, unless you got a lot of objections to that too. There's gonna be a low wall all around the pavilion so I can control traffic better."

"For what?"

"There you go again. For dances or what-all. You think I'm letting those kids use my floor for nothing? I can get six-bits a head, easy. What are you, dumb or something, Polack?" he said, forgetting in his enthusiasm where he was.

"What's that?"

"Nothing. An expression we got where I come from. Call that mason guy for me, huh?" Romy said.

"You got a lot of ideas," Batterman said.

"That's for fact. You know what I see when I see this place, the way I think about it? A first-class resort, for one, to begin with, and also I see a damn gold mine. If I can just last it out until she starts coming back at me. Wait and see." Batterman went off to telephone. Romy wished there were someone here to appreciate it. He imagined telling his wife of his detailed plans, or Mary Janka, but that was no good either.

"What say?" Batterman said, coming back from the office.

"Nothing," Romy said, "I was laughing to myself, something personal."

The stonemason did good work, but slower than somebody's grandmother. "He damn sure takes his sweet time," Romy said.

256

"He's touchy," Batterman said. "You have to handle these old cocks right."

The biggest Seeburg available, with a color wheel that revolved in front of a set of strong bulbs, sat across the room from the fireplace. There was another juke in the 3.2 bar, and still another out in the pavilion, along with the deluxe mini-bowl and the new pinball machines. "How you going to hear anything when you get all three going at once?" Batterman asked.

"If you mean me," Romy said, "I can stick cotton in my ears if I don't like it. The idea is to get play on them. What anybody else hears I could care less."

A color television was mounted over the bar, but it would be used only for things like the All-Star game and the Indy 500. He knew what a TV could do, running all the time, to volume at the bar.

He was lucky to get some advertising spots on the Brave's broadcasts in Milwaukee, because he waited until the first of May to start them. He liked to take time out to sit alone in the office he had roughed out off the kitchen to catch the ads. He was spellbound by the musical accompaniment, and by the beautiful voice of the announcer. *Lewinski's Silver Lake Pavilion Resort*. He could just imagine people in Milwaukee— Wisniewski, who was buying the Pressed Steel Tavern, his wife, his children, Stashu Grabczyk. He saw them hearing it. Oh, you should see, Mary, he thought. You should just see me once now!

It was shaping up, shaping up good, when he called a mass meeting of the staff Batterman had put together for him. Staff was no problem because Romy paid two-bits an hour better than Silvercryst, across the lake, better than any other resort as far away as the Chain O'Lakes up at Waupaca. There were five women to run the kitchen and wait tables, two assistant bartenders, one handyman-carpenter, four local boys to handle the boats and the beach, and one full-time clean up man for the pavilion, the grounds, and the bars. Romy stood next to Batterman, who introduced him. The pavilion stage had been spruced up with some drapes, a backdrop with the resort name in day-glow paint, and some music stands with silver gilt lettering.

"I just wanted to talk to you all once together at the same time," Romy said. "We open now soon, and I want you should all hear me once together and understand what's on my mind here." He tried to see their faces but the shade was too deep with the pavilion walled off. He had the feeling they were all grinning stupidly or making funny faces at him. "All's I want to say is, I got real big money tied up in this." He extended his hand, fingers spread, but no gesture he could have made would have caught how much he meant. "Which's everything I'm worth, what all I been working for all my life. I ain't going to sit and watch it go up the spout. I worked all my life for this, hard. Now I got it, I'm going to see it works. I'm paying good wages to do what I need you for. I'm no bad guy to work for. I'm saying . . ." He paused, wondering what else there was to say. More was needed, but he had nothing, no words. It reminded him of his mother's death, his decision to get married, picking over Mary Janka's private papers. He wished the overhead pavilion lights had been turned on, or that some music would play on one of the jukes.

"Stick it out, help me," he said, "they'll be the bonus after Labor Day Mr. Batterman here told you about when you hired." He turned away from his audience.

"Big damn deal," he heard from the floor, a man's voice.

"Who said that," he said, turning, but they were going out at the admissions gate.

"What?" Batterman said.

"Nothing," Romy said. "I thought I heard a question or something. I hope you know your business, hiring people," he said. "I don't want no problems I don't need."

His first problem came with the acreage on the other side of the state highway. It was early in the morning, before his carpenters or any of his regular staff arrived, before Batterman had come out of the house behind the pavilion, slow and

258

sleepy-eyed, to get started on another day's preparation for the opening. There was still dew on the grass, and the air off the lake was cool, smelling of the pine trees, but the sun was up and bright. Romy always got there early from the motel where he stayed until Batterman was ready to move to the house he was building in Redgranite.

Batterman, not having apparently yet learned that he knew from nothing about this business, had plans to buy into a small Redgranite bar. Romy waited for him, walking his grounds, finding the red boundary stakes, giving them a kick with the toe of his shoe. It was something to do while he waited for the rest of the world to get with it.

He reached the south end of his property and saw a pickup truck parked across 21, a gang of kids wrestling some heavy poles, a post-hole digger, some rolls of wire. He ran to them.

"What's going on?" he said.

"We got to dig out the holes before we can put the poles back in," one of them said. They all looked at him, then went on with their work, like he was some nosy hobo tramping by on the state highway.

"You put nothing in," Romy said. They seemed not to hear him at first. "I said you put nothing in this ground," he said again, louder. "Who in hell gives you the right to come screwing around here anyway, but?" They stopped, and they all looked at him again, and the same one who spoke before spoke again.

"Who'er you, anyway?"

"I'm Romy Lewin—" he started to say, but was suddenly too angry to do anything but shout. "I own this goddamn land! Now you get your crap in your truck and get to hell off my property!" They were shocked, frightened, boys of sixteen, seventeen. Romy was surprised at himself, but he felt no less angry.

"Batterman never said anything," the spokesman said, but none of them moved back to work.

"What Batterman says or don't say don't mean nothing," he said. "I own this land and you ain't putting nothing on it or in

259

it. I got special plans for this land, see," he started to explain. Now they began to load the wire back into their pickup. "I got a lot of plans for this here place," he said. The post-hole digger clanked on the truck bed. The spokesman got in the cab and started the engine, the others climbing up in the back. "I got to get seeding and landscaping here," Romy said before the driver popped the clutch and the truck lurched out onto the highway, headed back toward Wautoma. "A person could at least ask before they start doing stuff to people's property," he yelled after them, but his voice was lost in the truck's slipstream.

He nearly went for his Plymouth, to give chase, when one of the sullen boys in the back of the truck, far enough away to be anonymous now, raised his arm, middle finger extended, at Romy. He stood there a second, wondering if he was going to cry with rage. When he was able to recross the road, Batterman was out, yawning and stretching, wiping at the corners of his eyes with his knuckles.

"Tell whoever it is you know that there's no more baseball league or whatever going on over there no more," Romy said. He turned his head to the parched ground, rising slowly to crown in a clump of large oaks on top of the ridge. Batterman exhaled loudly, like he was disgusted with the sight of Romy.

"What the hell ideas do you have now for that?" he said.

"For right now, some rough landscaping, and getting it seeded so's next year I can get a golf course put in there. Nine holes."

"You're out of your mind," Batterman said.

"That's what you think. Go down once, in Milwaukee, any city course you pick, they line up for hours to get on."

"I never had occasion to check on it."

"Damn right you never," Romy said. "Look again over there, you don't see nothing but my golf course now that I told you, do you. I'll tell you, see that flat off on the right there? That's my clubhouse, only you can't see nothing there. I see it, in two years, with a big sign on both sides so you can read it both ways from the highway. Tell whoever it is I don't want

260

no baseball over there, like I said." Batterman turned away to hawk and spit in the grass, but Romy knew he would pass the word on playing sports on his property from now on.

"Now where in hell's my carpenters," Romy said, checking the position of the sun to estimate the time. "You could use some unions up here. You pay more, but your work gets done on time."

When the loan went through, the landscaping and the seeding were done. All summer the sprinkler network ran, and it seemed like that was that. But late in August, there was a rash of vandalism. Romy might wake up in the morning, and from his bedroom on the second floor of the pavilion house, he would see the vehicle tracks lacing the seeded fairways for as far as the eye could see in the early light. When he woke up and the sprinklers were not spouting their wide, glistening arcs, it meant someone had busted the pump mechanism or cut the lines with a saw again.

Sheriff Schaeffer as good as flat out refused to help. "What do you expect me to do," he said, "camp out there in the dark on a snipe hunt all night? I told you once I have only the one deputy. Summer people doing forty through town is all we have time or means for."

"You can't nose around and find out something?" Romy said. "I'll tell you for sure they're not hiding here in your jail keeping cool. It's some of those damn punk kids play baseball. The ones I run off, or their friends.

"You expect me to go on your word alone and run after some school kids, is that it?" Schaeffer said.

"In Milwaukee," Romy said, "a kid heaves a rock through your window, I'd tell the beat cop, inside a day he'd know from asking around who did it."

"Don't you tell me my job, mister," the sheriff said. "I was a city patrolman ten years, when you were wearing knickers. In Madison. You leave me to decide what my job is for myself. It sure as hell isn't being your private detective." He got up, like there was some immediate work for him in the jailhouse,

261

where there were maybe two or three Mexican migrants sobering up in the drunk cell, where his wife was an official deputy and got paid to run the jail kitchen to boot.

"You know what I got wrapped up, hanging out there on my neck?" Romy said. "All in all, I'm talking about half a million dollars now with the golf course."

"Do tell," the sheriff said.

"I'd sure like to know what I'm paying taxes for once around here."

"I reckon you pay them to sit out there at the lake and turn a nice little resort into an eyesore, which is one man's opinion," Schaeffer said. "And as I recall it you're the big shot told me how he'd handle his own troubles."

"Don't ever give me a chance to do you something, mister," Romy said as he left.

"I didn't hear a thing," the sheriff said. "Run for sheriff if you don't like the service. After all, it's a free country." All but laughing at Romy's back. Romy was making himself a solemn vow to get back at him, when the time got good and ready.

Anyway, the vandalism ended after Labor Day that first year, and in two years there was a clubhouse, and a parking lot jammed to the gills by seven every morning from late April to the end of September. With greens fees at two-fifty a head, discounts for summer and family rates, it was not so big a problem, the golf course, all in all. Though it gave Romy the shakes sometimes, like the time he spoke of it with the sheriff, just to think how deep he was in to a couple of Milwaukee banks. It used to make him wish he had not quit saying prayers before going to sleep each night. He could not remember how long it had been since he prayed.

He got his back against Schaeffer. He put just a little money where it did some good to elect Schaeffer's opponent. Schaeffer retired to a farm on the other side of Mount Morris, and the new sheriff gave Romy the kind of cooperation he had a right to expect for his money.

The big problem that first spring was Romy's wife. He

262

called her from his motel room. It was after ten, and he was tired from a big day at the pavilion, checking in stock for the opening. A day on his feet all day with a clipboard and a ballpoint pen, a day of large and medium-sized trucks backing up to the loading dock at the rear of the bar and grill, of counting cases and cartons and drums against the figures on bills of lading, of shouting orders to his staff, sending Batterman on one errand after another just to keep up with it. It was a warm night, and Romy lay on his bed with his shoes off, flexing and unflexing his toes to take the tingling out of his legs. He had a bottle of pop and his cigarettes on the nightstand beside him. His head ached, his eyes throbbed pleasantly.

"Hello?" Francine said. He closed his eyes and imagined their apartment, the sounds from the bar downstairs coming up faintly through the furnace registers.

"Hello yourself. What are you doing, Francie?"

"Romy," she said. "For God's sakes, what are you calling so late for? I just got everyone in bed asleep." The irritation in her voice made the throb behind his eyes worse. He sat up on the edge of the motel bed.

"I just got done working myself. I'm beat."

"So what are we talking for then?" He turned his face away from the receiver so she would not hear the sound of his loud, exhausted exhale.

"When are you coming up?" he said. "We'll be open for the first, like I planned. Everything's ready. Batterman moves the last of his furniture tomorrow. His wife's already gone with the kids. Close up there and come on up," Romy said.

"Don't talk silly," she said. "I can't come now, right away."

"Why not?"

"Look, Romy, I never said any certain date I'd come when you started all this. You started all this and never asked me what I wanted to do."

"What's keeping you?" he said. He was speaking louder now, as if she were in the room with him. He wanted to grab her by the shoulders and shake hell out of her.

"Plenty," Francine said. "For one, I'm not taking the kids out of school before it's over for summer." His youngest daughter was in her first year of all-day kindergarten.

"They got a school up here too, you know."

"I'm not is all," she said.

"So when's that? When's school out?"

"I don't know for sure. Sometime in the middle of June I think." They did not speak for perhaps fifteen seconds while Romy thought carefully of what and how to say it, determined not to lose his temper, yell at her.

"You come then when it's out. Right?"

"I got other stuff to take care of too, you know," Francine said.

"What more? Come on. I'm asking. What?"

"Romy," she said. Her voice was no longer angry or smart-aleck. She sounded like she wanted to weep, but would not let herself. It was the last moment, for Romy, of doubt so deep he wanted to fall on the floor and scream. It was the last, the worst, of moments like those he knew when he signed the papers to buy the resort, the papers selling the Pressed Steel Tavern to Bernie Wisniewski, the papers for his bank loans, when he had the sudden feeling he was in the dark with nothing beneath him to stand on, no light to reach for, no voice to call out for help. But this was the last such moment, as his wife talked.

"Why'd you do this, Romy? Move us away and yank the kids out of school and all? I don't understand you no more, Romy. Romy?" He took a swig of his lukewarm soda pop. "Are you still there?"

"I'm listening," he said, "but you're not saying nothing. You do what you got to do, like I told you. Sell what you want or give it to Goodwill, I give a damn. But I'm expecting you soon as school's over, see? I don't want no more excuses. You got enough money"

"I got money," she said. Now the old sound, smartaleck, sulky, was back in her voice.

"Okay. I mean it now."

264

"I wish you'd talk to me sometimes, Romy. I don't even know you anymore."

"Maybe you never did. You just get here, like I said." He would have liked to ask her about the children, about how Wisniewski was doing with the business, but it was not worth the effort. When he said goodbye she hung up without answering. He wondered a little, lying on his bed, if she would cry, or curse, or call her mother and give him hell to her. He fell asleep with his clothes on, without knowing it. He woke a little before five in the morning, feeling chilled and unrested, worried by a dream he could not remember exactly. And then it was opening day at Lewinski's Silver Lake Pavilion Resort at last, and he was too busy to worry much about anything.

It was slow at first, but he expected no better. There were banners announcing the opening, stretched over both ends of the access road, and the rock band he hired out of Fond Du Lac started playing in the picnic area at eleven o'clock, but business remained pretty slow all afternoon. At the same time, it was steady, a good sign. He thought what he should have done was hire a kid to wear something funny, a clown outfit or a cowboy suit, maybe two of them to stand at each end of the access road and wave to cars on the highways. But the music and the banners and the colored paper pennants flapping on the cables strung from the corners of the billboard brought in enough traffic to keep it from being embarrassing. Romy gave one of his college boys a roll of quarters and told him to keep the jukes going until he told him otherwise. The weather was good.

Batterman took a stool across from Romy at the bar. "Now," he said, "let me be the first to buy you a drink."

"Thanks but no thanks," Romy said.

"Come on."

"Nope. One thing you won't see is me drinking. I like a beer now and then, but I'm not what you call a drinker."

"In that case give me a beer. I'll be your first customer." Romy gave him a shorty. He did not want to offend him. The last of Batterman's furniture had gone early that morning on a farmer's truck to Redgranite. Romy would start sleeping in the pavilion house that night. On the other hand, he did not want Batterman getting the idea his job was to sit at the bar like an official greeter, swilling booze. He gave him a napkin and a glass, poured the glass half-full, tipping it as he poured to keep it from foaming too much, and shoved one of the heavy ashtrays to him. The noise the new heavy cooler door made closing was a good one, like the doors on a new car.

Batterman reached in his shirt pocket and took out a brand new dollar bill, not a single fold in it. "You can frame that right up over the register. Every new place needs a first dollar to start off right."

"That's nice of you," Romy said. He put the fresh bill on the cash register ledge, but later, when Batterman was out of the bar, he rang up the sale and slipped the bill in the proper compartment in the drawer. It was a new register, with a muffled ring, like chimes.

"Here's to you. Bumps," Batterman said, and drank. Romy saluted him with one finger touching his eyebrow. Behind him, he heard the old register in the 3.2 bar ring as the first of the young crowd came in. Turning, he counted three of them, two boys and a girl. That was two and a quarter for pavilion admissions right there alone. He was not worried. Next spring, he would do that, put a couple of kids out on the highway, dressed in clown outfits, to wave the traffic in.

Romy sized up his clientele. They were a world away from what he knew at the Pressed Steel Tavern. To begin with, they were better dressed, better looking, healthier looking, cleaner. The men were all clean-shaven, or if there was a moustache, it was trimmed up nice and clean. They dressed casually, but their clothes were good clothes, looking good on them even if they were wrinkled from a long haul on the highway. Many wore hats, or bright, often checked, caps. Near half of them wore Bermuda shorts.

Most of them wore sunglasses, the kind that concealed their eyes, reflecting what they saw, like dark green mirrors. They

266

were often fat, but they stood and walked with pot bellies and spare tires hanging and bulging free, almost as if they were proud of being overweight. They were soft, like Batterman, most of them, and many were balding, but in a way that did not make them look weak or old. They had big, soft looking hands, with solitary diamonds, and diamonds in their thick gold wedding bands, and Masonic symbols set off with diamonds in onyx, and not a one hand had dirty fingernails.

Most of them ordered at the bar and then went to wash their hands and comb their hair while the order was set up. They smiled when Romy greeted them, and answered softly, and when their teeth showed, they had good, white teeth.

If alone, they sat quietly. In groups, they spoke too low to be overheard. They did not spill their money out on the bar in a heap with cigarettes and matchbooks. They laid a bill out flat, and they stacked coins or arranged them in patterns, and their Ronsons and Zippos sat squarely on top their cigarette packs. They carefully pushed their empty glasses forward instead of yelling for the bartender or rapping on the bar. They toyed with their swizzle sticks, broke them in pieces and put them in the ashtrays, folded and refolded and neatly tore their napkins. They smiled when Romy picked up the ashtrays to empty them and give them a wipe. They drank Tom Collins and scotch highballs and sours and bottled beer. The biggest single thing Romy noticed was that he had not a single call, all day or all night, that opening day, for a boilermaker or a hooker with a beer wash.

The women, they were something too. First of all, they came with their husbands. And the husbands held the door open for them to enter, waited for them to mount stools before they sat. The women looked younger than their husbands. They wore good clothes, and bleached and tinted and streaked their hair. They plucked their eyebrows, shaved their legs and armpits, wore a little too much lipstick and face powder to suit Romy.

They wore shorts, midriffs bare, and the toenails sticking out of their open sandals were often painted flaming red and pink. And they wore sunglasses with colored flare-designed frames, sometimes set with fake stones. They drank and smoked as much as their men, but were never too loud. Their heads were bare. No hats, no curlers tied up in *babushkas*.

When couples came in who happened to know other couples already at the bar, Romy watched with his mouth open. The men shook hands, and the women kissed and hugged each other, and the women all kissed and hugged each other's husbands.

And not a soul got drunk that afternoon. Not a man or woman slurred words or walked crookedly or ran to the johns to vomit so long as the sun was up over the lake. And for the first time in a lifetime of tending bar, Romy received some tips, spare change left behind or nudged forward with the edge of the customer's hand.

A few of the kids in the 3.2 bar got a little loud, but Romy expected that too. Batterman was to keep an eye on them to see nothing rough started. They kept the juke going in there all day, and the volume per head across the bar figured out about two to one over the bar and grill, near as Romy could estimate.

These kinds were, first of all, enormous. They went barefooted, a good many, their shirts hanging open. The girls were just as bad, the way they dressed. But they were clean and healthy, skin glowing, hair long, some of them tanned already. They crowded the bar and talked loud and smoked a lot, or they bunched along the walls and in the corners in couples, talking with their heads close together, holding bottles of 3.2 beer and smouldering cigarettes that they dropped on the floor.

Romy could not figure out why he did not like the kids. He watched them closely, and he tried to remember himself as a kid, thought of his own children. The closest he came to doping it out was that he himself had never felt like those kids looked as if they must be feeling. He felt like he had been what he was all the forty years of his life. And that was okay. He could live without liking the kids who were a big chunk of his business.

Some of the kids drank too much, judging by the way they

whooped when they came out of the pavilion into the sun again, but nothing came of it during the day.

There was only one actual hassle the first afternoon. A man came in, letting the screen door slam hard behind him. "I'm looking for the owner," he said. Some of the customers turned to look at him. Romy signaled him from behind the bar and he came over. "Where the hell is Batterman?" he said. He looked around, stretched to look over Romy's shoulder.

"I'm the owner," Romy said. "It's me you want."

"I might have guessed," he said. "Would you mind telling me what's this hoo-ha about a quarter to dock my boat on the beach?"

"It's a charge," Romy said. He was a little man, and he was a good thirty years older than Romy. He wore an old hat with a fishing fly stuck in the crown, and sneakers without socks.

"Clearly," he said, "but what's the charge for? Can you explain that to me?"

"For docking on my beach," Romy said.

"You mean to stand there and have the gall to tell me I can't dock my boat to come up here for a beer without paying you a quarter?" Romy answered as softly as he could. Some customers were trying to listen.

"It's my pier and my beach," he said. "If you object, don't park your boat there no more." The man folded his arms across his chest and glared at him. His face twitched around his eyes, and his lips moved as if he practiced before he said it.

"I guess I hadn't heard the Jews had taken over here yet," he spat out, and he spun around and left, slamming the door even harder on his way out.

Romy could not tell if any customers heard, or if they heard, what they thought. It was the worst insult he had ever suffered. He had to go back to his office and stand behind the door for a few minutes to get over it. The only coherent thing he could think of was his father, kidding him, calling him a Jew boy for saving his paper route money, years ago. His fingers started to tremble, and he forced them into fists, closing his teeth together. He could remember his father joking about

269

it, and the roar gathering in his throat broke into what was almost a laugh. It was worse than if he had tied into the little old guy. It made him wait longer to get over it.

He ran out and found Batterman. "I heard it blow-by-blow," Batterman said.

"He ain't welcome here in future," Romy said.

"He's a laker, summer people. They tie up here all the time. I never charged a fee for it, but I guess I told you that when you decided on it, didn't I."

"I do," Romy said. "The lakers can go to Moose Inn and Silvercryst if they don't like it here."

"You're writing off a couple hundred people, more or less," Batterman said.

"I'll afford it. I can do without the summer people from the lake. This is no corner tavern I'm running for nobody here. And get one of those stopper things for the screen door. It sounds like a joint, slamming all the time."

"You're the man," Batterman said.

"I am."

When opening day was over, it was not like closing up the Pressed Steel Tavern. At the Pressed Steel, he eased the last customer out the door, agreeing with the last, repetitious point of some argument, laughing along with the punch lines of a final joke, saying goodbye and goodnight for the umpteenth time. Then, in the quiet, he checked out the register, cleaned up, and doused the lights after checking the locks on the door, front and back. He moved mechanically, tired but satisfied, his mind on no more than the warmth of the sheets of the bed, his wife stirring in her sleep, speaking. Sometimes he carried a bottle of beer upstairs, Francine waiting up with a sandwich and maybe a piece of pie. And he or she would suggest love making. And it was another day, like the ones before, the ones to follow, done with.

Here, it stayed with him, keeping him from the sleep he needed. There was no leisure in closing. It was after two-thirty before he had everything shut down tight, and Batterman,

270

yawning hard, left in his station wagon for Redgranite. He paid off the band, cleared both registers, then walked the beach to see the boats were secure, everything worth stealing stowed in the proper lockers. He stood over the staff to let them know right off he wanted things done right.

Then the lights. One master switch, and everything was dark. The insects were loud in the grass. He said goodnight to Batterman and went to the pavilion house, lighting his way with a flashlight. He set up a canvas cot in the big second-floor bedroom. He lay down, but could not sleep.

In the insect noise he still heard the deafening rock band from the pavilion, the vibrations of the barroom juke, the babble of voices, the thump of dancing feet. A car would pass on the highway, headlights sweeping the bedroom ceiling as it made the sharp curve. It reminded him of the two search lights he had brought over from Oshkosh to criss-cross the sky over Silver Lake, bouncing off the clouds, visible for miles.

He could not let it go long enough to fall asleep. It had been a good night, all doubts of success gone for good now. It was enormous, beautiful, and it was his! But he could not sigh with satisfaction and gratitude, roll over, and sleep. He kept thinking. *Now* what?

He met his peers, his competition on the lake that night, and disliked them both. Wally Weller ran the Moose Inn down on 21, and Wally Weller was an out-and-out drunk, the special kind of drunk who takes it on all day and all night, but never stops smiling or talking fast. The Moose Inn was just a bar, with stuffed animals hung all over the walls, and Wally Weller said, "Come down and see us for a drink now and again," and "My God, you're likely to run me off the road with all this!"

Silvercryst's owner was young, with very black hair and a black goatee and a black Kentucky colonel's tie. The staff at Silvercryst wore gay nineties hats, and somebody played a piano-bar, slides were flashed on a screen, and the summer people sang "On the Road to Mandalay" and "Danny Boy." Silvercryst's owner had rat eyes, and said, "This is quite an operation." Romy shook their hands and bought them a round when Batterman introduced them, and he knew he had no competition on Silver Lake.

He got out of bed and dressed, with a wild idea of calling Francine just to talk, argue, anything, but instead he walked the grounds. He circled the pavilion, tramped the beach, sand in his shoes, checked his lockers again, paced off his boundary lines. He was exhausted, but still not tired, not in the right way. The more he walked and looked and figured and planned, the more it excited him. He could not stop, rest. He ended by smoking cigarettes, sitting on the stone picnic area wall where it met the cyclone fence closing off the beach.

He watched the sun come up over the lake. There was already a fisherman out a quarter of a mile in a rowboat. He would have liked to call out and ask him if he was getting anything. Romy had never had a fishing rod in his hands in his life. But then the permanent clean-up man came in his car, and Romy went in the pavilion house to shave and put on a clean shirt. The second day was busier, but really no different from the first.

Business got better, gradually, all summer long. From ten in the morning on, the traffic was moving. There was always a gang of little kids on the merry-go-round, the teeter-totter, the junglegym. Romy had them fenced off and repainted, and after one of the kids took a header off the merry-go-round and split his noggin open four stitches worth, he hired a local girl with counselor experience to supervise. He also started charging a dime a head, to cover the cost of liability premiums and the girl's wages. All day long there was the squeak and squeal of the equipment turning, the shouts of the little kids.

The beach was packed, always a line of people, all ages, going through the bathhouse. He started renting umbrellas and innertubes by the hour. When he checked out the beach the greasy smell of lotions and oils drying in the sunlight hung over the sand like a fog. He started vending a line of salves and ointments at the bathhouse.

272

The beach crawled like a pit of snakes, backs, arms, legs. Kids churned the water, and out on the raft, sunbathers covered it from edge to edge. The rattle of the springboards was constant. He thought of raising the beach admission, but held off until the second summer. There was always a haze of charcoal smoke over the picnic area, the tables full.

The bar business was best of all. Morning, noon, night, the under-twenty-ones drank beer and played the jukes and danced on the pavilion floor. The volume in the bar and grill was almost as good. His bartenders were getting in overtime, and Romy was putting in one eighteen-hour day after another.

There was barely a moment for him to stop and smoke a cigarette, hear the shuffling feet of the dancers in the pavilion, the clanging of pinball and mini-bowl, distinguish the separate tunes going on the jukes, glance out and see one of his Lymancrafts go past out beyond the raft, towing a skier at seven-fifty an hour. He gave Batterman credit for never moaning about being on his feet all night, breaking up the occasional fistfights that started in and around the pavilion, checking ages in the 3.2 bar.

Parking space was hard to find. The trailer park across the county road was doing okay on its own, but next year he planned to cut it in half to make more parking. It would pay off, head for head.

The first thing his wife said when she got there, the last week of June was, "What am I gonna do with all this house Romy? I'll be cleaning all the time just to keep even."

"Hire somebody," he said. "The town's full of old farmer ladies begging for work."

"Get serious," Francine said. Her mother still worked a couple of days a week housecleaning for families on the upper east side of Milwaukee, despite the monthly check she got from Romy to supplement her deceased husband's social security.

He tried. He even bought another television for the house, with its own special antenna, but Francine still griped that

273

reception was lousy. His kids fell in love with the place, but Francine never learned to swim, and was so afraid of the water she made him buy life jackets to wear if they went near the beach. The jackets were bulky and uncomfortable, too much trouble, so the kids stayed close to the house most of the time. Romy only saw them when they came in the back entrance to the kitchen to ask for candy or pop. When he gave it to them he caught it from Francine if she found out. He tried to make the best of it.

The Fourth of July was good. Romy had two fireworks shows, one from out on the raft and the other from the middle of what was going to be his golf course. It was a big weekend, but Labor Day was better, almost too big. On Labor Day he found out just what he had let himself in for. He was glad his family was not there, gone on the Greyhound to visit Francine's mother.

It was threatened all evening. From behind the adult bar, Romy had a moment every so often to look out the windows at the kids milling on the asphalt road. He had the foresight to hire a second band to play from a platform in the picnic area, but the kids outside the pavilion did not seem to be dancing or listening. They just walked up and down the road, moved on and off the beach, converging on the pavilion admissions booth, where Romy had the foresight also to set up an emergency bar, selling 3.2 beer in paper cups. The emergency bar staff had no cash register and no time to sort money in a drawer. They wore carpenters' aprons, the pockets sagging with change, and used a burlap sack to stuff bills in when their apron pockets overflowed.

They were not dancing in the pavilion either. They milled, drinking and smoking, spilling beer on the floor, jostling. Before eight o'clock, Romy had started the 3.2 bar in the pavilion on paper cups too. Too many bottles were broken on the floor, and nobody could get through the crowd with a mop and dustpan to clean up. Romy did his best to keep an eye on things. He made a point of stepping outside, or into the pavilion bar. All he saw were heads, faces, a fog of cigarette smoke.

274

The pavilion smelled of spilled beer, sour in the close air, the unintelligible noise of voices lost in the blare of rock band and juke music. When the kids outside noticed him, they booed in chorus until he went back in the bar and grill. That was when he ordered no more bottles over the bar to under-twenty-ones. There were more boos when this was announced on the pavilion loudspeaker.

Fights broke out every ten or fifteen minutes, like clockwork, up to midnight. Batterman never got a chance to sit down. He circulated on the road outside and on the pavilion floor. There would be an especially loud shout, the sound of beer bottles shattering, the thud of feet on the resined floor, the scratch of sandals on the asphalt, and kids near the fight would start cheering. Batterman put his head down and charged, reached the fight, got between the kids squaring off, grabbed them by the neck and hustled them out of the light. By the time he got back to the crowds there was usually another fight, more cheering. Batterman's hair was hanging down in his eyes the last glimpse Romy had of him before the riot started. His shirt was hanging out, his shoulders slumped, his trousers spattered with somebody's beer down one leg.

"Hang in there tough," Romy said.

"Get off my back," Batterman said wearily.

"You're doing fine."

"All I want to know is if you figured on this when you were planning all those big ideas," Batterman said.

"All a part of the business," Romy said.

"Well you can count me out," he said, but went back out into the mob.

At midnight, Romy closed the 3.2 bar. It was a mistake. He stuck his head in and told the three bartenders to shut it off right then and there. They looked relieved, their faces damp and drawn, shirts soaked with sweat. They shouted the word to the six-deep crowd at the bar, all of them holding their hands up, waving money, fingers extended to show the number of beers they wanted. The word got around the crowd slowly. The bartenders stood up on chairs and waved their

275

arms to show it was all over. The booing got stronger and stronger. Either the six-deep crowd could not move back because of the press behind them, or else they refused to leave.

Romy went back to the office and called the emergency bar and the admission booth on the bitch-box system. "Close up," he said. "Wrap up your money and get back here to the office." He kept the switch open long enough to hear the booing spread out there. He turned it off, and now the booing was loud enough to fill the bar and grill. His customers there were looking a little uneasy. Romy doused the lights at the master switch, three times, quickly, to get the message across to the kids. It only brought the noise up louder and fiercer. "What the hell," he said to nobody in particular. For the first time in his life he was caught in something he could not handle.

He had not been thinking of where Batterman might be. Batterman just opened the door to the bar and grill and stood there, holding the door, blood running down over his face from his scalp. He had been hit with a bottle. "Hey, Romy," he said.

A woman at a table near Batterman screamed, and then there was a lot of cheering from the kids who had watched Batterman lurch all the way from near the admissions booth, where he had been hit from behind without provocation or warning. Batterman sank to his knees before Romy got to him, cursing the stinging pain of the cut in his scalp.

"Call the sheriff," Romy said to his nearest bartender.

The crowd had them for nearly twelve minutes, until Schaeffer and his deputy arrived in two cars. What Romy feared most was if they decided to set fire to his pavilion while they waited for the sheriff. He prayed, almost unconsciously, for the first time since he had quit going to mass at Saint Casimer's.

Inside the pavilion, they kicked in a lot of his pine panels, and they destroyed the juke and one pinball, and damaged the mini-bowl slightly. They did not storm the 3.2 bar. Romy's bartenders there, college boys, earned a twenty-dollar bonus each, standing behind the bar with an empty beer bottle in each hand for anyone thinking of coming over the bar for them. After this Labor Day, Romy stocked both bars with billy clubs and cans of tear gas spray.

For twelve minutes they waited in the bar and grill, the kids forming up on the porch and the road outside, chanting, *kill the pig!* and *open up the bar!* About the time they started throwing rocks and what few bottles they could find, they also started trying to tear down his beach fence, and they took a crack at his boat lockers too. They failed to get the fence, but sprung hell out of two sections of the cyclone mesh. The lockers and the bathhouse held by some miracle. For over two minutes, just before Schaeffer and his man arrived, Romy and his staff and his customers crouched behind the bar or crawled off into the kitchen and the johns to hide while the kids broke every window in the bar and grill. Most of the screens held, the glass falling just inside the sills. Nobody was hurt, but there was lot of swearing and screeching. One woman promised again and again that she would sue Romy for everything he was worth if she lived.

Romy scuttled into the office and listened on the bitch-box, afraid they would be tearing his emergency bar staff to pieces. All he heard was the crowd's chanting. The staff there got bonuses too. They sat on their money, joined by the rock band members from the pavilion stage, some of whom left their instruments behind when they fled. Romy had to replace a smashed amplifier. The band out in the picnic area got through it by stashing their equipment in the barbecue pits and joining the riot.

It was a good thing they came in two cars. Schaeffer's deputy led the way in the pursuit car, which was smart because it had both a fixed light on the roof and a siren, which reminded Romy of a Milwaukee fire engine. The light and the siren moved the crowd back for a second. They might have moved in on the pursuit car and tipped it over, but Schaeffer came up close behind his deputy, and that moved them a little more. Schaeffer's Dodge had no siren, but he had a portable light going up on the dashboard.

When the crowd started for the cars, Schaeffer did a very smart thing. He stopped, opened the door, and fired once in the air with his Savage pump. That drove the kids back toward the beach and the picnic area. It also cleared the pavilion. They streamed out, falling over each other, joining the mob on the road. Some girls were knocked down and skinned on the asphalt, but no bones were broken as far as Romy ever heard. Schaeffer and his deputy, a recently discharged Air Force military policeman, faced the crowd. Romy and two of his bartenders came out to join them. Batterman was back in the kitchen, holding a wet towel to his bleeding scalp. He wanted to come along and get a crack at the kids, but when he tried to get up he got dizzy again, and Romy told him to stay put.

The kids formed a solid arc from the picnic area to the admissions booth, blocking the road at both ends. They had stopped throwing rocks when Schaeffer fired his shotgun. Romy was smiling when he came out. He almost patted Schaeffer on the back.

"You goddamn Bohunk sonofabitch!" the sheriff said, speaking with his teeth clenched. "You'll handle it! What the hell did you ever come up here for anyway? Where do you people come from? Who the hell invited you? Goddamn you!" Romy could think of nothing to say, thought of nothing beyond remembering the vow he had made to do the sheriff something if he ever got the chance. "Get the horn, Vic," Schaeffer said, and his deputy got a battery powered bullhorn from the trunk of the pursuit car. The kids cheered when he brought it to his mouth and said, "Testing, testing," before he ordered them to disperse or face arrest. They booed.

"It happened too fast," Romy said.

"Get out of my way," Schaeffer said, stowing the bullhorn in his Dodge.

"Just tell us what to do," Romy said.

"Stay behind me. Hunky sonofabitch bohunk!" Here and there, a kid stood out from the mob and gave them the finger, swore at them, stuck out his tongue.

278

Polack, Romy thought, not Bohunk. A Polack isn't the same by a long shot. I'm a Polack. I got as much right here as anybody, he wanted to say.

"That does it," Schaeffer said when a stone hit the roof of his car. They made their sweep to the left to get them moving toward the county road. There was some more rock throwing until Schaeffer fired the Savage into the air again. They broke into a trot, Romy and his bartenders behind the two officers, and then the kids scattered, and it was all over. The deputy drew his pistol, but never fired it. He was the only casualty, hit in the mouth with a thrown shoe, bloodying his lip and loosening a tooth.

"Do the world a favor and go back wherever you people come from, will you?" Schaeffer said before he got in his Dodge and left.

Romy wanted to tell him to his face that he could count on losing the next election if Romy's money could do any good in the county, but all he said was, "What people's that? Go on, say. Names ain't hurting me none, let's hear you." Schaeffer gunned the engine and jerked away.

"I'm just a tavern owner, what should I know about something like this," Romy said later to Batterman.

"You're more than that now," Batterman said. "I'd close up for the year if I were you, Romy. Schaeffer could try and make it hot for you with the township council. They're a bunch of old retired farmers. You don't want a lot of new ordinances fouling you up."

"I figured on getting the deer season traffic."

"Suit yourself. Shut down and let it cool off. Next year they won't remember, and you'll know how to handle it next time."

"Next year," Romy said. "Swell chance. I'm a businessman. I bring money in here, even with what I buy direct out of Milwaukee I still bring in money." Batterman nodded, but he was concentrating on his wound, tenderly touching the edges of the cut with his fingertips. "Sure, thing," Romy said.

"Ah, what the hell. A man can't get a break. Hell with it."

"Why did you decide to come up here anyway, Romy, if you don't mind me asking you?"

"Tell me and we'll both know," Romy said.

He closed for the season. Francine stayed an extra week at her mother's. Both the *Journal* and *Sentinel* carried short items about the riot. She asked him about it when she returned, and he told her, only partly lying to make it seem a little less bad than it had been, and he knew she knew he was lying. That was no picnic to live with, but none of this was so much compared to the first winter he and his family spent in Waushara County.

The end of the season came down on Romy Lewinski like a ton of bricks. When he finished closing up the resort, he noticed it all around him.

He pushed his staff hard, and he pushed himself, keeping after them. The first day they did the beach, hauling the raft up on the sand, taking the pier out to keep it from breaking up in the winter ice, beaching the fishing boats, stacking them to form a square inside the picnic area. The Lymancrafts were stored in the bathhouse. While his boys worked, Romy stood by with a clipboard, making a rough inventory. The equipment lockers were carried in with the speedboats, and Romy had the hardware men come out from Wautoma to put some heavy-duty locks on. Wooden shutters were nailed over the bathhouse windows. The last thing was a general rake and pick-up of the beach. The trash barrels were emptied and put away for the winter beneath the pavilion loading dock.

The pavilion was boarded up the second day, and they started in on the bar and grill. That took two days, what with his inventory. The only problem was stock. "Why can't I just leave it in here till spring?" Romy said.

"You'll find beer all over the floor when you open up if you do," Batterman said. "It gets cold up here, Romy. You can't leave anything around that'll freeze. You have to get your beer in the house, down cellar, and we'll have to blow out your tap pipes if you don't want them bursting. Same with your machines." Romy said he would have to check with his wife.

"Not in my basement you don't," she said. "Where am I supposed to do laundry when you get all beer cases in there?"

"Take the laundry to the cleaners in town," he said.

"Get out," Francine said. "I still do my own laundry if you don't mind."

"Be a goddamn washerwoman all your damn life for all I care then," Romy said to her.

"We can sell it off easy," Batterman said. But it was not easy. Silvercryst had central heating, but the rat-eyed kid with the goatee swore he had no room. Wally Weller stayed open at the Moose Inn, but said he barely moved enough of his stock to have room to maneuver in his walk-in cooler. "I'll ask around in town," Batterman said. The best offer he got was from Tilly of Tilly's Bar, fifty cents on the dollar, take it or leave it. Romy had no choice.

"How exactly did he say it? His exact words," Romy asked Batterman.

"Half price, that's all."

"I'm asking you to be straight with me," Romy said. "We had our differences, but we had a pretty good summer, all in all, didn't we?"

"He called you a few choice names," Batterman said.

"Like what?"

"Holy balls, Romy, what are you after?"

"What he called me. I got to know."

"You mind telling me why?"

"So I know where exactly I stand. I got my reasons."

"Okay. A money grubbing Polack. Make you feel better?"

"In a certain way it does, yeah. What'd you say?"

"What?"

"What did you say back to Tilly? Or didn't you say nothing at all?"

"I said you knew your business. Okay? And Tilly said that's what comes of teaching a Polack to count over ten. Had enough?"

"Plenty. Thanks, too. You said just exactly what I'd of told

281

him. I'll get a chance to do something on old Tilly boy someday. Wait and see."

"You better just forget it, Romy," Batterman said.

"I will if I can," Romy said.

"Thanks to you I got another good enemy here," he said to
Francine that night.

"What? What are you talking about?"

"Never mind," Romy said. "Just thanks a lot is all."

"You must be getting crazy or something," Francine said.

"If I was I wouldn't bother telling you," he said.

"Good luck to you," Batterman said when he left for Redgranite for the last time, the closing finished. Romy had
wanted to invite Batterman and his wife for a big feed, maybe
drive over to Oshkosh and all, but the desire left him as he was
shaking hands. Then, with the last staff member paid off, with
the paperwork he needed moved into the pavilion house, with
the last padlock snapped in place, Romy noticed how everything around him was closed for the season.

"You want to go for a walk?" he asked his wife. She was
watching the one fuzzy channel that came in from Milwaukee.

"Walk where?"

"Just walk. Look at the trees changed color or something.
Just take a damn walk!" She might have come along, he
thought, if he had not raised his voice. But he was damned if
he felt like saying he was sorry.

"I'm watching television," Francine said. He asked his son.

"How far you going?"

"Who knows," Romy said. "Maybe all the way around the
lake if we feel like it. Come on, it's good for you. You sit
around the house too much. I was always outside, working,
when I was a kid your age."

"I don't feel like walking so very far," the boy said.

"What are you, some cream puff or something?"

"I said I'd go if we don't go too far," he said, going for his
jacket.

"The hell with it!" Romy said. "Stay and help your ma

282

watch the television so you don't strain nothing!" His son took off his jacket and went out of the room to put it away. "Some great fun family I got," Romy said. "Hell with it!"

He walked all the way around Silver Lake, starting out on County DD. He checked to see the chain blocking the entrance to his camping grounds was secure, then set off like a man hiking against a stopwatch. Everything was closed. The summer people had left with Labor Day. The cottage windows were shuttered, the grass a little long, their rock gardens gone to seed. Boats were belly up on sawhorses, piers pulled out of the water. There was no traffic on the county road. Half a mile down he passed Booth's. The grocery was closed, but there was some old coot, maybe old Ward Booth himself, sitting on a chair in the sun at the gas pump. Romy knew the old man did not see or hear so good, so he did not wave, and the old man never moved on his chair, like an old mud turtle getting the sun while it lasted before digging into the lake bottom to sleep out the winter. It was still warm enough in the sun, but he noticed the insect noise in the woods, a constant buzzing and drone all summer long that Francine said drove her bats, was gone now too. He followed the lake road where it forked away from DD.

Near half the summer people had special signs over their mailboxes, some of them very elaborate, special names for their properties. *Logan's Piney Slope*, burned into knotty pine boards, the ends cut zig-zag, like with a pinking shears. *Dun-Werk-In*. *The Millers*, with four smaller signs strung out like a ladder below it, *Bob, Phyllis, Jean, Andy*. Nice, Romy thought. *Strawberry Landing*, a large red berry on a black board, the property a small cottage set on top of a steep bank. One was cast iron, a silhouette of a family, a cabin, a dog, pine trees. Nice. One place had the mail box embedded in cement in a milk can. Another sat on a post made of welded chain links. It put Romy to dreaming of a new name for his resort, something fancy.

The mosquitoes were gone, for which he was grateful if

283

Francine would lay off spraying herself and the kids, all over the arms and legs and neck, three or four times a day until the whole house stank of repellent. He smelled it on Francine when he lay beside her in bed, trying to get his mind clear and get to sleep nights. Where the lake road was shaded by the canopy of overhanging trees, it was chilly.

The lake road ran into 21 at the opposite end of the lake from the resort. There were a couple of cars parked outside Wally Weller's Moose Inn, but there was no music, no sound of voices. He decided not to go in for a beer. He was in no mood to listen to the gabby alcoholic talk about how bad business was. He pushed on, brightened by the thought of the mound of paperwork he had to get through before next spring. An accounting to find out just how far in the red he was operating, to determine what was and what was not paying its way, a schedule of improvements to set up for next spring, the possibilities of increased advertising. He pushed on.

The only other human being he saw on his walk was an old man, a little dried-up looking old man, out raking leaves. He looked right at Romy, but bent again to his work in the very instant Romy waved. Maybe he had not seen the wave of the arm that Romy stopped short. Romy pretended to scratch the back of his neck. He was reminded of his own raking, around the pavilion house. Swell chance, he thought, of getting Francine or his son away from the TV to give him a hand with that. He walked fast, his mind running with the many things there were to be done.

But when he got there, walked in his own blacktopped access road, stood between the beach and the quiet hulk of the pavilion, he was not glad. The water looked green and cold, and the sun was behind a cloud, and there was no sound from the house. He did not feel like seeing his family. It came over him that while there was a lot of work to be done, there was a whole winter to do it in, and when the work was done there would be nothing else for him to do. He went in the house, walking like there was lead in the soles of his shoes.

284

Francine was still watching television. His son said, "You must of walked all the way around." He sat with them, as if he was going to watch television too. He heard one of his daughters open the refrigerator door out in the kitchen. He closed his eyes, and just for something to do, he systematically imagined, like painting a huge mural, the interior of the Pressed Steel Tavern. Every exact detail, right down to the .32 in the cash register drawer. The particular smell that came in the door with Stashu Grabczyk, first thing after opening every morning.

"So what'd you see walking all over the place?" Francine said when a commercial came on.

"What's it to you," Romy said.

It did not snow until the middle of October, but when it did it stopped everything for two days. There were no special plans made for it, like in Milwaukee where they called a snow emergency, and everyone had to keep his car off arterial streets for twenty-four hours. Waushara County had no extra crews lined up to put out on the roads with plows and salters and sanders. The state highway commission got 21 opened up late the first day, but when the second day passed and nobody came to plow out Romy's access road, he called the township office.

"When does a man get his drives cleared so he can get out to get some groceries he needs?" he said.

"The township doesn't plow your driveway for you, if that's what you mean," the clerk of council said.

"So who does then?"

"Nobody. Unless you do it yourself, I'd say."

"What am I paying taxes for?" Romy said. "Go ahead, raise my taxes and you can get somebody's farmer cousin a job, is that the way you do it?"

"I don't have to listen to this," the clerk said, and hung up on him. Romy threw the telephone on the floor, cursing loudly in Polish.

"Nice going," his wife said. "Cussing him out is going to get the snow plowed for sure, isn't it." Romy came very close to belting her one. He raised his open hand, but did not swing. "Go on," she said. "Just go ahead once." He saw his son and youngest daughter watching.

"I ain't giving you the satisfaction," he said. Luckily the phone was not broken, because Batterman called shortly to say he had forgotten to give Romy the name of the guy to call who came out with a tractor to take care of the snow. He asked, and Batterman told him business was so-so in Redgranite. Batterman did not ask how Romy was doing.

Another problem with the snow was getting to church. Saint Joseph's in Wautoma was only open through Labor Day, when there were enough Catholic summer people to justify the priest's coming over from Mount Morris. Since then, Francine had been driving over there with the kids each Sunday. "Did you put the chains on for me?" she said. He had, and there was a box of sand and a shovel with the handle sawed short to fit the Plymouth's trunk too. "It wouldn't break you to get up early for once and drive us," she said.

"Sunday's my day to sleep in, Francie," Romy said.

"You ain't doing nothing now, are you? You can sleep all you want seven days a week," she said.

"Will you get off me about mass? Go if you got to. If you're afraid to drive on the snow, then stay home."

"I'm not like some people," Francine said. "It's a mortal sin not to go."

"Then get a mortal sin. What are you, some religious fanatic? Don't talk that crap to me," he said.

"Don't swear about my religion."

"Oh, Francie, for the goddamn Christ's sakes—"

"I said don't you dare swear at my religion!" she yelled. He sat where he was and let her get it out. He knew it was more than going to church. She was so angry, near tears, her hands tearing at her apron.

"You don't go to mass and you don't confess! You'll go to Hell when you die! I don't let anybody swear at my religion! I'm a good Catholic, no matter what you are! You'll die and go

286

to Hell if you don't confess and go to mass! You don't take communion!" she screamed.

He let her get it out, watching her, because even hitting her would not have stopped her. For the first time he saw she had aged as much as he had over the past ten years or so. Her graying hair, the lines in her forehead and around her eyes, the skin of her long neck, the veins that stood out on her thin arms. He tried, but could not bring back the picture of her as she looked the day of the Pulaski parade, like some high school kid, crossing the street on the run with his sister. Her voice, wild, breaking short of sobs, was foreign to him. She could have been any half-drunk Polack dame come in off the street at the Pressed Steel Tavern to cause trouble.

"You all done now, Francie?" he said.

"Shut up!" she said. "Just don't you ever forget what I said."

"Not hardly." His kids heard it all too. She drove to Mount Morris over the bad roads, and did not speak a word to him for three days afterward. She did her best to stay at least a room away from him all day long, and when he listened hard he thought he could hear her crying softly, but he could not be certain.

On top of it, the county's school buses did not run for two days after the second storm, and Romy thought he would go mad with his children in the house all day and night. He had never been with them for longer than a few hours at a time before. They ran, they fell, they cried, they shouted from room to room, they fought and cried more. His son picked on the girls like some little Nazi, and when he tied them up with clothesline and pinched them, Romy picked him up and carried him upstairs and whipped him with a belt.

"Goddamn you," Francine said.

"Me? Me! You seen what he did! You approve that? What the hell kind of kid you raising, tell me once!"

"Did you hurt your arm on him?" she said, refusing to look at him as she held the boy across her knees, sitting on the edge of the bathtub, bathing the welts on his son's behind and the backs of his thighs.

That was the end, when she started sleeping downstairs. "It's cold up there all night long," she said. "The furnace is no good in this house. I feel like I'm freezing to death all night."

"Sure," Romy said. He knew that was the end with her, and with her went his children. It was not that he did not care. If he thought he could have sorted it all out, he would have tried. But there was nothing he felt he could say to her that would change what she felt and thought, and there was nothing, he was sure, she could say that he cared to listen to. It was the end with Francine and with his children, no matter how long it might take, and he understood now that there was just himself. And that would have to be enough. "Sure thing, Francie," Romy said.

After that he made an effort to keep out of her way. He woke early, alone in the big upstairs bedroom, and dressed in the silence of the house, looking out the window at the white expanse that rose slowly toward the ridge, where he could still make himself see the planned golf course and clubhouse. It was almost as if it warmed him while he dressed, shuddering involuntarily in the cold bedroom.

The elm trees that shaded the house in summer were bare, snow sticking to the windward sides of trunks and branches. Rarely, he might see a car on the highway.

He went quietly downstairs and made his own breakfast, then went to the office he had set up in the small sun parlor where Mrs. Batterman had kept fern plants. He planned and replanned everything for the coming spring, but there was really nothing for him to do. Sometimes he could shut out the noise of his family as they got up, dressed, breakfasted. He sat and dreamed of things to add to his resort. A pony ring, a curio-souvenir shop, a four-lane bowling alley, cages of live deer, bear, raccoons, a grocery. But it would not last. He got his coat and hat and gloves and went outside to walk his property. The wind blowing in off the frozen lake burned his face, made his fingers and toes feel like they had turned to stone.

288

Everything was white with the snow pack. Everything was shut and bare.

When the ice on Silver Lake was safe, there was a little activity. There were windbreaks put up by ice fishermen who sat on canvas stools, warmed by portable stoves, tending their set-lines.

But the fishermen used the public access road to get out on the lake, and there was no reason for them to approach the Silver Lake Pavilion, or, even if they noticed Romy standing on the ice in front of his beach, no reason for them to wave or yell a greeting. He did not shout or wave. The snow cover crunched beneath his boots, the ice squeaked and groaned and popped, and everywhere he looked was only the snow, white on white. If there was a sun out, glaring dully, like electric light, the snow was blue-black in the shadows.

During deer season he saw the bands of hunters, license numbers stitched to the backs of their red jackets and vests, going in and out of Tilly's Bar in Wautoma, their cars bunched outside Weller's Moose Inn on the state highway, and Romy looked forward to the next year, when he would stay open, and they would come to him. In his sun porch office, he made notes on hunting and fishing decorations appropriate for the walls of the bar and grill, come next winter.

Francine took the children to her mother's in Milwaukee for Thanksgiving. Romy pleaded paperwork to stay behind. Francine did not argue it. He regretted it, once they left. He sat alone in the house, and he smoked too many cigarettes. He remembered long, gray winter days at the Pressed Steel Tavern. The oil heat kept the barroom too warm for a coat. Men coming in for a quick one, bringing a shock of icy wind in the door with them, shivered and gladly took off their heavy wraps to soak in the heat of the room. They stamped their feet clean of snow, removed their rubbers and galoshes with a rippling, snapping sound, and the snow soon melted and evaporated on the rubber doormat put out for the purpose.

On a really cold day, after a night of ten or fifteen below, Stashu Grabczyk would call in sick to come and spend the late afternoon with him, drinking slowly, reading the early edition of the *Journal*, bitching about his job, his wife, money, the weather. Seldom was the juke played. Sometimes Stashu would bring his cribbage board and play Romy for drinks. Romy would draw a tap beer for himself, open a bag of Planters peanuts, and they talked about something in the newspaper, or Stashu told a new dirty joke, and maybe somebody else came in, and Stashu would greet him with a vulgar insult in Polish.

He got through Thanksgiving Day that way. When he ran out of the pictures he made of the Pressed Steel Tavern, he went on to imagine what he would have done if he had gone along to Milwaukee. He would have gone to the Polonia Lodge, talked with the old coots and their wives, bought all the drinks, eaten *kielbasa*. He imagined calling Stashu Grabczyk long distance, inviting him up for opening day next spring. Chartering a bus, inviting a whole gang, a barbecue out in his picnic area under the pines, a polka band. He had no idea what time the next day to expect his family back.

They did not come the next day, and imagination was no good anymore. For the first time in his life he sat for long periods and did nothing, thought nothing. He would be sitting, trying in vain to imagine something, remember something, and then, suddenly, as if a card had been flipped, a light flicked on, he realized he was sitting alone in his house, and he saw all the furniture in the room, the room itself. If he got up and went to the window, rubbed away the frost, there was the outdoors, the snow stretching forever, maybe a movement of the elm branches in the biting wind. When dark came he had to get out. He hiked down the road to Weller's Moose Inn.

There were three cars outside, and three other men besides Wally Weller inside, and about halfway through his visit, after half an hour or so, Romy figured out that this was a regular sort of group, formed to get them through the winter, and that he would never belong to it.

There was Wally Weller, drinking martinis-on-the-rocks behind the bar, speaking clearly, steady on his feet. There was the rat-eyed snot kid who owned Silvercryst, but who had shaved off his goatee like it was a summer uniform. There was a man called Major, who was a retired army major and lived all year round on the lake, and who spoke of nothing but the army and the two wars he had been in. And there was a man named Crowder who owned some rental cottages on the lake and lived in Wautoma. He gave Romy his real estate agent's card.

"There he is there he is there he is," Wally Weller said.

"The tycoon of Silver Lake," the rat-eyed kid said. While Weller got his beer, the rat-eyed told the others who Romy was, and then Crowder gave him his business card. He felt like asking Major would he like to take a picture, what was he staring at?

"Are you joining us?" Weller said. He noticed no money passed over the bar when the others had refills.

"Joining what?" Romy said.

"The Silver Lake Drinking Association," rat-eyed said.

"The Silver Lake Drinking Divorced Bachelors Club," Weller said.

"I bet you he's got a wife," Major said.

"All teetotalers have to go south until the snow melts," rat-eyed said.

"I think you guys got too good a start on me," Romy said.

"You disapprove?" Crowder said.

"Quartermaster's my guess," Major said. "Let's hear it, what'd you do in the service?"

"I was 4-F."

"I vote against him," Major said.

"Why doesn't a real rich cat like you winter in Miami?" rat-eyed said.

"Suck up suck up," Weller said, draining the ice in his glass.

"How'd you like to latch on to a nice piece of lake frontage I got my hands on near your place down there?" Crowder said.

"If you're married how come you're not home with your old lady on a night like this?" Major said.

"Come on, pour," rat-eyed said, holding his empty glass up to his eye like a telescope.

"I see your place is all boarded up," Romy said to rat-eyed, but Silvercryst's owner turned away to accept Crowder's challenge to arm wrestle.

"4-F, married, thumbs down," Major said. And nobody spoke to him again.

They seemed to go on like that, drinking and talking back and forth, not really to each other, and after Romy had gone to the john and come back out, it was like watching four crazies out on an evening pass. He stood behind the three seated men for a while, waiting to see if Weller would ask him if he wanted another beer, but it was like he was invisible. For a second he suspected they were having him on, and Romy stood there with a stiff grin on his face in case it turned out a joke, but they went on the same. Then he figured it was something deliberate, an insult, and he balled his fingers into fists and his face flushed, but they just kept on.

"—this first sergeant I had under me at Dix one time," Major said.

"—every five thousand my foot," Crowder said. "Your bus lines *reclaim* their *own* oil every twenty thousand."

"IhopebyGodtotellyouIswearbythesweetJesusIdo," Wally Weller said into his martini glass, nodding his head like a trick horse.

Romy shut the storm door hard on his way out, but standing outside he could still catch the unbroken rhythm of their voices. "For the Jesus Christ's sakes!" he said aloud, and then he was conscious of the cold.

He walked as fast as he could back to his place. Whenever he thought about it he shook his head, as if it was a dream, or a story a drunk told him. "Holy Jesus, give me a break," he said aloud. Not me, he thought, never happen! As he was falling asleep that night, he thought of a lot of people, of Francine, of Stashu Grabczyk, his parents, his sister the nun, old customers from the Pressed Steel Tavern. He saw their faces as if they were frozen in old, dim photographs, and he was telling them off, each one as he thought of the face, the name, reading them right off. Not on your goddamn life! he thought.

292

It was no big surprise to him, late the next day, when he got the call from Francine telling him she was not coming back up there, ever. "I could of told you that when you left," he said.

"It's your fault," Francine said. "You could of done something about it if you wanted to bad enough."

"That's what you think," Romy said.

By the time Batterman got around to dropping over that way from Redgranite again, he barely recognized the Silver Lake Pavilion. There was no special opening day in spring, because Romy stayed open all year around by then. The colored pennants were always strung over the entrance and exit roads, and red, gold, and green twists of foil bordering the billboard facing the state highway spun in the warm breeze, reflecting sunlight. At night, lit by floods concealed in the shrubs along the roadside ditches, they shone luminously. On the big weekends, Memorial Day, Fourth of July, Labor Day, searchlights swept the cloudbanks over the lake, visible as far away as Mount Morris. There was always music, a crazy mix from the jukes and the hired rock bands, day and night.

The traffic settled out. The swarms of little kids had the beach, the recreation area, the new pony ring, and the miniature pitch-and-putt golf game. Their parents had the bar and grill, the rental boats, the camping area, the barbecue pits, and the nine-hole golf course with its bar and locker rooms. The teenagers had the 3.2 bar, the pavilion dance floor, the beach, and anyplace else they wandered in pairs once the sun set.

The Labor Day riot of that first summer was never repeated. From four to ten special deputies were on duty nights, a deal done with the new sheriff. The summer cottage people on Silver Lake hated Romy, but they knew that with the taxes he paid he had the township council in his pocket. The lakers went to Silvercryst. The crowd was an old one there, the ones who did not like the noise and lights at Romy's. The word was out that Wally Weller would welcome a buyer to take the Moose Inn before he had to file bankruptcy.

293

The town of Wautoma did not hate Romy. Everyone knew what the resort meant for summer business in town. If people like Tilly of Tilly's Bar still bad-mouthed him, Romy was still waiting patiently for little old Tilly boy to give him the chance to do him a little something. Romy could afford to wait.

Most of the time Romy was too busy to think about it. He worked one eighteen-hour day after another from April to October. The rest of the year it was a one-man operation, getting set for the duck and deer hunters, and for the ice fishermen who rented windbreaks from Romy, and who bought bait and tackle from him, and who rented space on the ice from which Romy cleared the snow with his jeep. Romy did all his own plowing winters, just to kill time when the long, bitterly cold days began to get to him a little, year after year.

"You're coining it," Batterman said.

"You damn bet you," Romy said.

That first Christmas he drove to Milwaukee to see his family was the only rough one. He had a fierce gut ache just from nerves. His kids were no different that he could see, but they were wound up with presents and double-feature movies with their friends, begging Romy for money whenever Francine left the room. Which was often. She always needed something in the kitchen, the bathroom, running to take care of her mother, who seldom left her bedroom anymore. There was no point in talking much because Francine did not believe in divorce. She went to mass daily if she could get away from her mother and the kids long enough.

Romy spent most of his two-day visit in the flat, looking at television. He hated it when his mother-in-law did come out to sit for a while. Mrs. Litwiak had had a stroke, had to be propped up in a high-backed chair with pillows, her arms and legs horribly swollen with dropsy. When he met her eyes, she moved her mouth to speak, but said nothing. She stared at him, so he concentrated on the television like he did not notice, or looked out the windows at the slushy sidewalks below.

The closest he came to seeing anyone was the call he gave

294

Stashu Grabczyk the afternoon Francine had gone out shopping, leaving him alone with her mother sitting there.

"Who is this?" Cissy Grabczyk said.

"Romy. Lewinski. You forget my name already?"

"I figured it couldn't be nobody was around calling Stash. He's out by the county," she said.

"The which?"

"The county institution there, that clinic there, he's supposed to be learning to talk again. They cut his throat, Romy. He had the cancer."

"Jesus," Romy said.

"I figured it must be somebody wasn't around asking to talk to Stash. He's supposed to be learning to talk now from a hole they made in his neck. So how's it by you, Romy?" Cissy Grabczyk said.

"Okay, I guess," he said. She gave the hours he could visit Stashu at the county hospital, but he had no intention of going near the place.

Once the old lady spoke. He had to move closer to hear her, and it was a minute before he doped out she was talking in Polish and not having some kind of attack.

"What's wrong with you?" she said. "I don't know what's happening. Why is she living here and you away? Did you do something to her? Did you do something bad?"

"I don't know," he said. She kept asking, would not shut up until he yelled, again and again, "I don't know, see! I don't know nothing."

The rest of the year he sent a regular monthly check to his wife, and extra money for things like the kids' birthdays. On his Christmas visits he slept on a Murphy bed out in the living room. Which, if Francine thought she was doing him something, was no worry to Romy. Not since he met the woman at Batterman's place in Redgranite. Every so often he drove to Redgranite. They met at Batterman's little joint, and they stayed at the tourist cabins right there in town. Batterman seemed to get some kind of kick, seeing them leave for the motel. He always raised his glass and winked at Romy. The woman was divorced, and lived in Redgranite, and she did not ask for any more than the money Romy left for her in the room when he headed back home to his resort.

He was too busy to think much about anything, and most of the time things went well. One time he thought of Mary Janka; it was one night, working the bar, when somebody started in telling Polack jokes. Romy laughed right along with them. He could have cared less. Then he thought of Mary Janka, just her face, her name coming into his mind, nothing more. He just kept on laughing at the jokes.